We Are All Made of Glue

We Are All Made of Glue

MARINA LEWYCKA

FIG TREE
an imprint of
PENGUIN BOOKS

FIG TREE

Published by the Penguin Group
Penguin Books Ltd, 80 Strand, London WC2R ORL, England
Penguin Group (USA) Inc., 375 Hudson Street, New York, New York 10014, USA
Penguin Group (Canada), 90 Eglinton Avenue East, Suite 700, Toronto, Ontario, Canada M4P 2Y3
(a division of Pearson Penguin Canada Inc.)
Penguin Ireland, 25 St Stephen's Green, Dublin 2, Ireland (a division of Penguin Books Ltd)
Penguin Group (Australia), 250 Camberwell Road, Camberwell, Victoria 3124, Australia
(a division of Pearson Australia Group Pty Ltd)
Penguin Books India Pvt Ltd, 11 Community Centre, Panchsheel Park, New Delhi – 110 017, India
Penguin Group (NZ), 67 Apollo Drive, Rosedale, North Shore 0632, New Zealand
(a division of Pearson New Zealand Ltd)
Penguin Books (South Africa) (Pty) Ltd, 24 Sturdee Avenue,
Rosebank, Johannesburg 2196, South Africa

Penguin Books Ltd, Registered Offices: 80 Strand, London WC2R ORL, England

www.penguin.com

First published 2009
1

Copyright © Marina Lewycka, 2009

The moral right of the author has been asserted

'I Will Survive' words and music by Dino Fekaris and Freddie Perren © copyright 1978
Perren-Vibes Music Company / PolyGram International Publishing Incorporated, USA.
Universal Music Publishing Limited. Used by permission of Music Sales Limited.
All rights reserved. International copyright secured.

Set in 12/14.75 pt Monotype Dante
Typeset by Rowland Phototypesetting Ltd, Bury St Edmunds, Suffolk
Printed in Great Britain by Clays Ltd, St Ives plc

A CIP catalogue record for this book is available from the British Library

HARDBACK
ISBN: 978–1–905–49022–6

TRADE PAPERBACK
ISBN: 978–1–905–49023–3

www.greenpenguin.co.uk

To my father, Petro Lewyckyj
Poet, engineer, eccentric
October 1912 – November 2008

I

Adhesives in the Modern World

I

The gluey smell

The first time I met Wonder Boy, he pissed on me. I suppose he was trying to warn me off, which was quite prescient when you consider how things turned out.

One afternoon in late October, somewhere between Stoke Newington and Highbury, I'd ventured into an unfamiliar street, and come upon the entrance of a cobbled lane that led in between two high garden walls. After about fifty metres the lane opened out into a grassy circle and I found myself standing in front of a big double-fronted house, half derelict and smothered in ivy, so completely tucked away behind the gardens of the neighbouring houses that you'd never have guessed it was there, crouched behind a straggly privet hedge and a thicket of self-seeded ash and maple saplings. I assumed it was uninhabited – who could live in a place like this? Something was carved on the gatepost. I pulled the ivy aside and read: Canaan House. Canaan – even the name exuded a musty whiff of holiness.

A cloud shifted and a low shaft of sunshine made the windows light up momentarily like a magic show. Then the sun slipped away and the flat dusky light exposed the crumbling stucco, the bare wood where the paint had peeled away, rag-patched windows, sagging gutters, and a spiny monkey puzzle tree that had been planted far too close to the house. Behind me, the gate closed with a clack.

Suddenly a long wailing sob, like the sound of a child

3

crying, uncoiled in the silence. It seemed to be coming from the thicket. I shivered and drew back towards the gate, half expecting Christopher Lee to appear with blood on his fangs. But it was only a cat, a great white bruiser of a tomcat, with three black socks and an ugly face, who emerged from the bushes, tail held high, and came towards me with a purposeful glint in his eye.

'Hello, cat. Do you live here?'

He sidled up, as though to rub himself against my legs, but just as I reached down to stroke him, his tail went up, his whole body quivered, and a strong squirt of eau-de-tomcat suffused the air. I aimed a kick, but he'd already melted into the shadows. As I picked my way back through the brambles I could smell it on my jeans – it had a pungent, faintly gluey smell.

Our second encounter was about a week later, and this time I met his owner, too. One evening at about eleven o'clock, I heard a noise in the street, a scraping and scuffling followed by a smash of glass. I looked out of the window. Someone was pulling stuff out of the skip in front of my house.

At first I thought it was just a boy, a slight sparrowy figure wearing a cap pulled down low over his face; then he moved into the light and I saw it was an old woman, scrawny as an alley cat, tugging at some burgundy velour curtains to get at the box of my husband's old vinyls half buried under the other junk. I waved from the window. She waved back gaily and carried on tugging. Suddenly the box came free and she fell backwards on to the ground, scattering the records all over the road, smashing a few of them. I opened the door and rushed out to help her.

'Are you okay?'

Scrambling to her feet, she shook herself like a cat. Her face was half hidden under the peak of the cap – it was one of those big jaunty baker boy caps that Twiggy used to wear, with a diamanté brooch pinned on one side.

'I don't know what type of persons is throwing away such music. Great Russian composers.' A rich brown voice, crumbly like fruitcake. I couldn't place the accent. 'Must be some barbarian types living around here, isn't it?'

She stood chin out, feet apart, as if sizing me up for a fight.

'Look! Tchaikovsky. Shostakovich. Prokofiev. And they throw all in a bin!'

'Please take the records,' I said apologetically. 'I don't have a record player.'

I didn't want her to think I was a barbarian type.

'Thenk you. I adore especially the Prokofiev piano sonatas.'

Now I saw that behind the skip was an old-fashioned pram with big curly springs into which she'd already loaded some of my husband's books.

'You can have the books, too.'

'You heff read them all?' she asked, as though quizzing me for barbarian tendencies.

'All of them.'

'Good. Thenk you.'

'My name's Georgie. Georgie Sinclair.'

She tipped her head in a stiff nod but said nothing.

'I've not lived here long. We moved down from Leeds a year ago.'

She extended a gloved hand – the gloves were splitting apart on the thumbs – like a slightly dotty monarch acknowledging a subject.

'Mrs Naomi Shapiro.'

I helped her gather the scattered records and stow them on top of the books. Poor old thing, I was thinking, one of life's casualties, carting her worldly possessions around in a pram. She pushed it off down the road, swaying a little on her high heels as she went. Even in the cold outside air I could smell her, pungent and tangy like ripe cheese. After she'd gone a few yards I spotted the white tomcat, the same shaggy bruiser with three black socks, leeching out of the undergrowth of next door's garden and trailing her down the pavement, ducking for cover from time to time. Then I saw there was a whole cohort of shadowy cats slipping off walls and out of bushes, slinking along behind her. I stood and watched her go until she turned a corner and disappeared from sight, the Queen of the Cats. And I forgot about her instantly. I had other things to worry about.

From the pavement I could see the light still on in Ben's bedroom window and the computer monitor winking away as he surfed the worldwide waves. Ben, my baby boy, now sixteen, a paid-up citizen of the web-wide world. 'I'm a cyber-child, Mum. I grew up with hypertext,' he'd once told me, when I complained about the time he was spending online. The square of light blinked from blue to red to green. What seas was he travelling tonight? What sights did he see? Up so late. On his own. My heart pinched – my gentle, slightly-too-serious Ben. How is it that children of the same parents turn out so differently? His sister Stella, at twenty, had already grabbed life by the horns, wrestled it to the ground, and was training it to eat out of the palm of her hand (along with a changing ménage of hopeful young men) in a shared rented house near Durham University which, whenever I phoned, seemed always to have a party going on or a rock band practising in the background.

In the upstairs window the coloured square winked and disappeared. Bedtime. I went in and wrote my husband a curt note asking him to come and remove his junk, and I put it in an envelope with a second-class stamp. First thing next day, I telephoned the skip hire company.

So let me explain why I was putting my husband's stuff on a skip – then you can decide for yourself whose fault it was. We're in the kitchen one morning – the usual rush of Rip getting off to work and Ben getting off to school. Rip's fiddling with his BlackBerry. I'm making coffee and frothing milk and burning toast. The air is full of smoke and steam and early-morning bustle. The news is on the radio. Ben is thumping around upstairs.

Me: I've bought a new toothbrush holder for the bathroom. Do you think you might find a moment to fix it on the wall?
    Him: (Silence.)
    Me: It's really nice. White porcelain. Sort of Scandinavian style.
    Him: What?
    Me: The toothbrush holder.
    Him: What the fuck are you talking about, Georgie?
    Me: The toothbrush holder. It needs fixing on to the wall. In the bathroom. (A helpless little simper in my voice.) I think it's a rawplug job.
    Him: (Deep manly sigh.) Some of us are trying to do something really worthwhile in the world, Georgie. You know, something that will contribute to human progress and shape the destiny of future generations. And you witter on about a toothbrush.

I can't explain what came over me next. My arm jerked and suddenly there were flecks of milky froth everywhere – on the walls, on him, all over his BlackBerry. A gob of froth had caught in the blond hairs of his left eyebrow and hung there, quivering goopily with his rage.

Him: (Furious.) What's got into you, Georgie?

Me: (A shriek.) You don't care, do you? All you care about is your bloody world-changing destiny-shaping bloody work!

Him: (Shaking his head in disbelief.) As it happens, I do care very much. I care about what happens in the world. Though I can't say I care deeply about a toothbrush.

Me: (Watching, fascinated, as the gob of froth works itself loose and starts to slide.) A toothbrush *holder*.

Him: What the fuck's a toothbrush *holder*?

Me: It's . . . ah! (There she goes . . . Splat!)

Him: (Self-righteously rubbing his eye.) I don't see why I should put up with this.

Me: (Flushed with achievement.) No one's asking you to put up with it. Why don't you just go? And take your bloody BlackBerry with you. (Not that there was the slightest chance that he'd have left *that* behind.)

Him: (Hoity-toity.) Your outbursts of hysteria are not very attractive, Georgie.

Me: (Lippy.) No, and you're not attractive either, you big self-inflated fart.

But he was attractive. That's the trouble – he was. And now I've well and truly blown it, I thought, as I pictured Mrs Shapiro pootling away up the street with his precious collection of great Russian composers tucked away in her pram.

2
Pheromones

I was sitting at my desk, staring at the rain and trying to finish off the November edition of *Adhesives in the Modern World*, when the skip lorry arrived. Adhesives can sometimes, I admit, be quite boring, so it was nice to be distracted. I watched it reversing and clanking into position, lowering the chain loops to winch up the overflowing skip, dangling it in the air with the damp spare mattress, the dishevelled papers, limply flapping magazines, the bin bags of clothes and the boxes that contained all the soggy detritus of his Really Important Work, and crashing it down on the back of the truck with a satisfying thud. When it was ready I went out and paid the skip man, and I must confess I did feel a pang of extreme apprehension as it trundled out of view. I knew Rip would be furious.

When he'd got back from work that day – the day of the toothbrush holder – I'd calmed down but he was still in a rage. He started piling up his stuff in his car.

Me: (Nervous.) What are you doing?

Him: (Stony-faced.) I'm leaving. I'm going to stay with Pete.

Me: (Clinging. Pathetic. Despicable. Self-hating.) Don't go, Rip. I'm sorry. It's only a toothbrush holder. I'll put it up myself. Tell you what (little giggle), I'll learn to do rawplugs.

Him: (Clenched jaw.) But it's not just that, is it?

Me: What d'you mean? (A terrible truth dawns on me.) Are you . . .?

Him: (Sigh of boredom.) There's no one else, if that's what you're thinking. Just . . .

Me: (Relief.) Just . . . me?

Him: (Looking at his watch.) I'd better get going. I told Pete I'd be there at seven.

Me: (Feeling like a despicable worm too low even to crawl out of its miserable hole, but putting on a show of non-chalance.) Fine. If that's what you feel. Fine by me. Give my regards to Pete.

Pete was Australian, Rip's squash partner, and a senior colleague on the Progress Project. We called him Pectoral Pete, because he always wore tight white T-shirts and big white trainers and made loud jokes about lesbians. In spite of that, I quite liked him. He and his wife Ottoline lived in a tall-windowed house overlooking a square in Islington, with a top-floor flat that they sometimes rented out. I went and stood outside one evening, looking up into the lighted windows. They couldn't see me standing down there in the dark with tears pouring down my face.

It lasted for a few weeks, the crying phase. Then rage took over.

'I'll come back for the rest of my things,' Rip had said as he left.

But he didn't. The shoes in the hall – I gave them a kick each time I went past – the old clothes in the wardrobe – they still carried a faint whiff of him – the back copies of *The Economist* and the *New Statesman* stacked up against the wall, the filing cabinets bulging with progress. Even his used under-pants he'd left in the laundry basket. What was I supposed to do – take them out and wash them?

I didn't want him cluttering up my new independent life with his old discarded stuff. I'll be fine, I told myself. I'll get over it. I'll meet someone else. And just to convince myself that I really meant it, I hired a skip. Perhaps I should have taken it all to Oxfam, but I didn't have a car and it just seemed too complicated. And besides, if I had done, this story might never have been written, because it was the skip that brought Mrs Shapiro into my life.

About an hour after the skip had gone, the doorbell rang. So soon! I stood frozen, paralysed by the enormity of what I'd done. I listened as the bell rang again, a long, persistent, I-know-you're-in-there ring. No, best not to answer it. But what if he looked in through the window and saw me standing there? Maybe I should take my shoes off and silently sneak up to the bedroom. But what if he looked in through the letter box and saw me creeping up the stairs? What if he saw my silhouette in the window? I tiptoed into the corridor, lay down on the floor out of the sight line of any of the windows, and held my breath.

The doorbell rang again and again and again. Obviously he wasn't fooled. Then the letter box clattered. Then silence. As I lay stretched out on the floor watching the light fade on the ceiling, I could feel my heartbeat slowing down and my breathing getting calmer. After a while, a song drifted into my head.

'You thought I'd lay down and die. Oh no, not I! I will survive!' Gloria Gaynor. It was one of Mum's favourites. How did it go? 'At first I was afraid, I was petrified.' I started to sing. 'I didn't know if I could something something without you by my side ... something change the locks ... I will survive!' I'd forgotten most of the other words, but I still knew the chorus, 'I will survive! I will survive!' I belted it out over and over again.

That's how Ben found me when he got back from school, lying flat on my back in the corridor, singing at the top of my voice. He must have let himself in so quietly that I didn't hear the door; then I looked up and saw his face looking down at me.

'Are you all right, Mum?' His eyes squinted with concern.

'Course I am, love. Just . . . enjoying a musical interlude.'

I clambered up from the floor and looked out of the window. The street was empty. It was raining again. There were no signs the skip had ever been there apart from a few shards of black vinyl on the road. Then I noticed a leaflet on the doormat. Ben picked it up curiously. *The Watchtower. Watch and pray for ye know not when the time is.*

'What's this about?'

'It's the Jehovah's Witness magazine. It's about the end of the world, when Jesus returns, and all the true believers get whisked up to heaven.'

'Hm.' He flicked through it, and to my surprise he stuck it in his pocket and clomped upstairs to his room.

What a shame. I could have done with a comforting heart-to-heart with some nice Jehovah's Witnesses.

The doorbell rang again as Ben and I were about to sit down for tea. Ben answered it.

'Hi, Dad.'

'Hi, Ben. Is your mother in?'

Nowhere to hide this time. I had to face him across the table. Pectoral Pete was with him. They were both wearing their jogging gear. They must have run all the way over from Islington. I could smell the sweat on them. The whole kitchen reeked of pheromones, and I felt a mortifying stab of lust – my traitor hormones letting me down just when I thought I was beginning to get things under control.

Him: (Lounging in his chair and stretching his legs out as if he owned the place.) Hi, Georgie. I got your message. I've come to rescue my stuff.

Me: (Oh, help! What have I done?) It's too late. They took the skip away this morning.

Him: (Eyes round and blinky. Mouth open in a little round O that makes him look like a hooked trout.) You're kidding. (Yes, definitely more trouty than destiny-shaping. Ha ha!)

Me: Why would I be kidding? (His hair seems to have receded a bit, too. Good. He's not as gorgeous as he thinks he is.)

Him: (Disbelieving.) They took the records? My great Russian composers?

Me: (A sly smirk.) Mmhm.

Him: (Even more disbelieving.) My first-fifteen rugby boots?

Me: All the junk. (How can a man who discards his loyal and devoted wife without a frisson of sentiment get all dewy-eyed about a pair of mouldy old football boots?)

Him: (World-weary sigh.) Why are you being so childish, Georgie?

Childish? Me? I picked up a plate of pasta. I could feel that twitching in my arm again. Pete was grinning with embarrassment, trying to bury his face in the *Guardian*. Then I caught the frightened look in Ben's eyes – poor Ben, he didn't need to see his parents behaving like this. I put the pasta down, bolted out of the room and ran up the stairs; I threw myself on to my bed, blinking the tears out of my eyes. I will survive. I will grow strong. I will change the locks. Look at Gloria Gaynor – she turned her heartbreak into a song that sold millions. As I sat there listening to the voices down below, and wishing

I'd kept my cool, an appealing thought floated into my head. I can't sing, but I can write.

In fact I was already halfway there. I had a working title and a terrific nom de plume. My mind lingered on a seductive image of myself as a published author, trendy in crumpled linen with a stylish leather bag full of proofs slung casually over my shoulder, jetting around the world with an entourage of poet toyboys. Rip would be revealed to the world as a self-obsessed workaholic, pitifully underendowed, with an insatiable Viagra habit and dandruff. His wife would be beautiful and long-suffering, with a fabulous bum.

'*Forget! Survive!*' Gloria Gaynor's voice seemed to chide in my head. '*You'll waste too many nights thinking how he did you wrong. Change the locks! Grow strong!*'

And to be fair, she had a point. My previous attempts at fiction, twelve and a half full exercise books, were stowed away in a drawer, along with a file of hoity-toity rejection slips.

Dear Ms Firestorm,

Thank you for sending *The Splattered Heart* for our consideration. Your book has some colourful characters and displays an impressive array of adjectives, but I regret to say I was unable to summon sufficient enthusiasm . . .

That sort of thing is bad for morale, and my morale was already low. But it was no use – a seed of optimism had lodged itself in my heart, and the opening lines were already sprouting in my head. There was one empty exercise book left.

The Splattered Heart
Chapter I

It was past midnight when Rick rolled exhaustedly on to his broad, ~~muscular~~ slightly podgy back and casually ran his ~~powerful~~ fingers with their chewed-down fingernails through his thick curly, ~~naturally blond~~ discreetly highlighted hair.

Okay, I know it's not your Jane Austen. Maybe Ms Insufficient Enthusiasm had a point about the adjectives. I sat staring at the page. Had I developed writer's block already? Downstairs I heard voices in the hall and the click of the latch. Then my bedroom door opened a crack.

'Are you all right, Mum? Aren't you having any dinner?'

3
Shelf life

After Rip moved into Pectoral Pete's top-floor flat we agreed that Ben should spend half a week with each of us. One day I noticed him with his watch and his pencil ticking off the days on the calendar. Sunday, Monday, Tuesday: Dad. Wednesday, Thursday, Friday: Mum. Saturday – that's the tricky one – one week with Dad, one week with Mum. We broke him in half and divided him between us. I could see the frown of concentration on his face as he tried to work out which week we were in. He was determined to be fair to both of us.

As the rage against Rip congealed in my heart, I was sometimes taken over by a numbness so intense it felt like pain. On the days when Ben wasn't here I found it almost unbearable to be in the house alone. The silence had an intrusive jangling quality, like a persistent tinnitus. When I walked from room to room I could hear my footsteps on the laminate floor. When I ate, I could hear the scraping of my knife and fork on the plate in the echoing kitchen. At first I tried having the radio on or playing music, but that made it worse: I knew the silence was there even though I couldn't hear it.

When the silence got too much I'd take a walk, just to get out of the house. Wearing my comfy trodden-down trainers and an ancient brown duffel coat with a wide flapping hood and sleeves like bat's wings, I flitted about at dusk, peeping through lighted windows into other people's lives, catching them eating an evening meal, or sitting on a sofa watching

TV, and tried to remember what it felt like to be still stuck together. Maybe I should have been prettying myself up and keeping my eye open for another man, but the wing-sleeves of the coat enfolded me like arms, and at that time, it was the only comfort I had. The look was not so much Bat Woman as batty-woman, but it didn't matter because I never met anyone I knew, and anyway, the coat made me invisible.

One afternoon I went as far as Islington, thinking I'd get a few things I needed from Sainsbury's and catch the bus back. It was about four o'clock, and the sticker lady was doing her end-of-day reductions. A crowd was milling around her like a piranha tank at feeding time. Mum had always been a great advocate of sell-by-date shopping, and I remembered with a twist of nostalgia how, when I was little, she used to send me scampering along the aisles looking out for the bright red REDUCED stickers that pouted like scarlet kisses on the cling film. She didn't think much of Listernia and Saminella, and even an unpleasant experience with some mature crabstix didn't dampen her enthusiasm. She would pat her elasticated middle. 'Waste not, want not.' Mum always looked after her pennies as if they came from heaven. Funny how long after you leave home you still carry a bit of your parents around inside you. Now, without the certainty of Rip's salary landing in our joint bank account with a generous kerchung! each month, I understood that sharp edge of insecurity that Mum must have felt all her life. Or maybe I was just so dejected at the time that I felt a queasy kinship with the curled-at-the-corners pastries, the sad rejected chicken wings. Anyway, I pushed forward to join the crush.

The sticker lady was working incredibly slowly, spewing out labels that kept jamming the machine. No sooner had she stuck a new label on something than a hand reached out of the throng and grabbed it from her. The reduced items weren't even reaching the shelf. I noticed it always seemed to be the same hand – a bony, gnarled, jewel-encrusted hand, darting out and snatching. Turning to follow it with my eyes, I spotted an old woman diving in low beneath the shoulders of two fat ladies. Her hair was tucked up into a jaunty Scotch plaid cap with a heart-and-arrow diamanté brooch pinned on one side, and a straggle of black curls escaping under the brim. She was reaching and grabbing like a virago. It was Mrs Shapiro.

'Hello!' I called.

She looked up and stared at me for a moment. Then she recognised me.

'Georgine!' she cried. She pronounced it with hard 'G's and an 'eh' sound at the end. Gheorghineh! 'Good afternoon, my darlink!'

'Good to see you, Mrs Shapiro.'

I leaned and gave her a peck on each cheek. In the enclosed space of the groceries aisle, her smell was ripe and farty like old cheese, with a faint hint of Chanel No. 5. I could see the looks on the faces of the other shoppers as they backed away and let her through. They thought she was just a bag lady, a batty-woman. They didn't know she collected books and listened to the great Russian composers.

'Plenty good bargains today, darlink!' Her voice was breathless with excitement. 'One minute full price, next minute half price – same thing, no difference. Always tastes better when you pay less, isn't it?'

'You should meet my mum. She always likes a bargain. She says it's because of the war.'

I guessed she was a bit older than Mum – in her late seventies, maybe. More wrinkled, but more energetic. She was of the age when she should have been wearing those extra-wide-fitting bootees held on with Velcro, but in fact she was tottering about daintily on peep-toe high-heeled shoes like a lady of style, the grubby toes of her grey-white cotton ankle socks poking out in front.

'Not only the war, darlink. I heff learnt in my life to make the ends meet. A hard life is a good teacher, isn't it?'

Her cheeks were flushed, her eyes focused and alert, her brow slightly furrowed with the effort of mental arithmetic as the new labels were stuck on top of the old.

'Come on, Georgine – you must grebbit!'

I squeezed in beside one of the big ladies and grabbed at a passing chicken korma, reduced from £2.99 to £1.49. Mum would have been proud of me.

'You heff to be quick! You like sossedge? Here!'

Mrs Shapiro snatched a pack of sausages reduced to 59p out of the hand of a bewildered pensioner, and tossed it into my basket.

'Oh . . . thanks.'

They looked unappetisingly pink. Seizing me by the wrist, she pulled me towards her and whispered in my ear, 'Is okay. Jewish. No sossedge.' The pensioner was staring at the sausages in my basket.

'You Jewish also, Georgine?' She must have noticed me eyeing the sausages with distaste.

'No. Not Jewish. Yorkshire.'

'Ach, so. Never mind. Can't help it.'

'Have you been playing the records, Mrs Shapiro? Are they all right? Not too scratched?'

'Great records. Glinka. Rimsky-Korsakov. Mussorgsky. Such a music. Take you straight up into heaven.' Her bony hands spread theatrically in the air, the rings glittering, the varnished fingernails bright like little bunches of cherries. Close up I saw that the red highlights in her cheeks, which I'd mistaken for a flush of excitement, were actually two circles of rouge, one with a clear thumbprint in the middle.

'Shostakovich. Prokofiev. Myaskovsky. My Arti has played with them all.'

'Who's Arti?' I asked, but she was distracted by a 79p quiche Lorraine.

I didn't like to admit that classical music wasn't my thing – I always thought of it as Rip's look-at-me-I'm-doing-the-hoovering music. I'm a Bruce Springsteen and Joan Armatrading fan myself.

'I don't think I have much of an ear for music.'

Rip used to tease me that I was tone deaf and even my singing-in-the-bath efforts were painful to the cultivated ear.

'Not all great art is for the messes, darlink. But you would like to learn, would you?' She batted her azure eyelids. 'I will play for you. You like the fish?'

As she said the word, I noticed a fishy undernote welling up through the cheese-and-Chanel. It was coming from her trolley. I saw that among her bargain produce were several packs of fish, all REDUCED. I hesitated. This fish definitely smelled off. Even Mum would have given it a miss.

'You come in my house, I will cook them for you.'

Poor old thing, she must be lonely, I thought.

'I'd love to, but . . .' But what?

I was trying to muster an excuse when she let out a blood-curdling shriek.

'No no! You teef!'

There was a sudden angry scuffle in the aisle and a clang of shopping trolleys being barged. The pensioner from whose hand she'd grabbed the sausages had sneakily tried to pinch them back out of my basket. Mrs Shapiro snatched them from him and brandished them in the air.

'Teef! You pay for you own sossedge full price if you want it!'

Defeated and humiliated the pensioner slunk away. She turned towards me, flushed with triumph.

'I am liffing not far from you. Big house. Big garden. Too many trees. Totley Place. Kennen House. You come on Saturday seven o'clock.'

'Have you got a Nectar Card?' asked the girl at the checkout, swiping my bargains over the bar-code reader (where did that vile-looking cheese sauce come from?).

I shook my head, and muttered something Rip-like about the surveillance society. Behind me, Mrs Shapiro had got into an argument with someone else in the queue and I was planning a quick getaway.

'Bravo, darlink! These surveyors are getting everywhere,' she cried, barging her way towards the exit, bashing the legs of the man in the next queue with her trolley. He was a big man with a stubble of close-cropped blond hair, built like a rugby player. He turned round and gave her an unsmiling stare.

'Sorry, sorry, darlink.' The crimson lipstick flashed. The blue eyelids fluttered. The man shook his head, as though saddened by the presence of lunatics.

He made his way through the checkout and out into the car park. I watched him load his purchases into a massive black tinted-windowed four-by-four parked in a disabled bay in front of Mrs Shapiro's pram. Immediately behind him, a blue Robin Reliant had pulled in tight, sideways on. It had a disabled badge in the window. He put the four-by-four – it looked like one of those American military Humvee things – into reverse and started to back up, but the Robin Reliant was blocking him in. On the other side, Mrs Shapiro was loading her purchases into her pram. He edged forward and stuck his head out of the window.

'Can you just shift your pram, lady, so I can pull round?'

'One moment, please!' Mrs Shapiro cried. 'I need a new reduction!' She'd found a bruise on a not-reduced apple, and was heading off back into the shop to negotiate a discount.

While I was waiting, the owner of the Robin Reliant returned. He was a little shrivelled man, propping himself up with a stick. He got into the Reliant, took a meat pie out of a paper bag, and started to eat. The man in the Humvee beeped his horn loud and long, but the meat-pie man carried on eating. The Humvee started to reverse, slowly slowly, until its rear bumper touched the door panel of the Reliant. Tunk! There was a distinct jolt as it made contact. By now a few people had gathered on the pavement to watch. I spotted the two fat ladies from the sticker scrum, eating biscuits out of a bag. The *Big Issue* seller had come round from the front of the store, and a girl who'd been handing out leaflets when I arrived. They were all yelling at him to stop. The meat-pie man was taking his time, savouring every bite.

Suddenly the Humvee driver slammed into forward, swung the wheel round as far as it would go, and started inching his chrome bumper towards where I was standing by Mrs Shapiro's pram. There was something about the fixed set of his jaw and the way his eyes stared straight ahead, refusing to look at me, that made me livid. I positioned myself defiantly in front of the pram, gripping the handle tight, with my own shopping bags wedged between my feet. I hadn't picked this fight, but I was prepared for martyrdom. The driver beeped his horn and carried on inching. He was going to barge the pram right out of the way with his bully bull bars!

Then Mrs Shapiro emerged beaming from the supermarket, brandishing the apple, which now had a REDUCED sticker on it.

'They give me five pence off!'

She pulled a packet of cigarettes and a box of matches out from under the hood of the pram, offered me one – which I declined – and lit up.

'Thenk you, Georgine, for waiting.' She nodded in the direction of the *Big Issue* salesman and the leaflet girl, and whispered loud enough for them to hear, 'Looks like gypsies, isn't it? They want to steal my shoppings?'

'No, they're . . .'

'Just shift your bloody pram, you old bat!' snarled the Humvee driver out of his window.

'Don't you dare talk to her like that, you big bully!' I hissed back.

'What he is saying, Georgine?'

'I think he wants you to move the pram, Mrs Shapiro, so that he can get his car out. But just take your time.'

She fluttered her azure eyelids at him.

'Sorry, sorry, darlink.'

Swaying a little on her heels, she manoeuvred the pram out of the way and tottered off down the road towards Chapel Market, still puffing away.

4

Bonding dissimilar materials

When I got home, I put the kettle on for a cup of tea and phoned Mum to tell her about my pram adventure. I knew she'd be as intrigued by Mrs Shapiro as I was. (Dad, on the other hand, would approve of my befriending a vulnerable old lady.) Mum had turned seventy-three in October and time was weighing down on her. Her eyesight was beginning to deteriorate ('immaculate degeneration') and the doctor had told her she shouldn't drive any more. Dad had been struck down with the 'waterworks mither'. Her son, my brother Keir, five years divorced, with two sons he hardly ever saw, was posted in Iraq. And now I was splitting up with my husband. Just at the time when she should have been sailing into a rosy sunset, everything on her horizon seemed stormy and unsettled.

To cheer her up, I launched into a description of my bargains.

'Chicken korma, Mum. Reduced from £2.99 to £1.49.'

'Oh, lovely. What's a chicken corner?'

Mum isn't stupid, but she's partially deaf – my nana had measles during her pregnancy. Dad and I tease her because she refuses to wear a hearing aid. ('People'll say I'm an alien if I start going around wi' bits of wire coming out of my head.' Actually, where I come from, in Kippax, they might.)

'Chicken korma. It's Indian. Sort of spicy and creamy.'

'Oah, I don't know if your dad'd fancy that.' Her voice sounded flat and defeated.

I tried another tack.

'Have you read any good books recently, Mum?'

In the right mood, this is her favourite topic, a guilty pleasure we share. When I was sixteen, Dad had given me a copy of *The Ragged Trousered Philanthropists*, which I'd pretended to enjoy but had secretly found depressing and tedious, and Mum had introduced me to Georgette Heyer and Catherine Cookson, whom I pretended to despise, but secretly devoured.

'Always look out for the underdog,' Dad had said.

'There's nowt to beat a happy ending,' said Mum.

'I just finished *Turquoise Temptation*,' she sighed down the phone. 'But it were rubbish. Too much heavy breathing and ripped-up underwear.' A pause. 'Have you seen owt of Euridopeas?'

I knew she secretly hoped we would get together again. I didn't tell her he'd been round to pick up his stuff.

When Rip and I first fell in love, I sometimes used to imagine us as romantic characters in a great tempestuous love story set against the turbulent background of the miners' strike, transgressing boundaries of wealth and class to be together. I was his door into an exotic world where noble savages discussed socialism while soaping each other's backs in t' pit baths. He was my door into Pemberley Hall and Mansfield Park. We were so full of illusions about each other, maybe it was bound to end in a splattering.

After Mum had rung off, I made myself a cup of tea and picked up my pen.

25

The Splattered Heart
Chapter 2

It was a sunny October day, and ~~Rip~~ck's mind was on carnal things as his ~~mini~~ Porsche ~~nosed its way~~ roared up over the ~~Roaches~~ hills still brilliant with dazzling autumn colour. After a few miles ~~after Leek~~ ... (Should I change the location as well as the names? I tried to cast my mind back to my journalism course with frisky Mrs Featherstone, but I couldn't for the life of me remember what she'd said about libel.) ... *the road turned sharply to the right, and Gina saw the entrance to a driveway, with a cattle grid and two stone gateposts, and there at the bottom of the valley, a good mile away, was ~~Holtham House~~ Holty Towers, sailing like a stone galleon in a shimmering red-green-and-gold sea.* (Pause for admiration; that was good – the galleon bit.) *Despite herself, Gina ~~was impressed by~~ found herself inexorably drawn towards the ~~house~~ stately pile and she could not help noticing ~~that these people obviously had a bob or two~~ the stunning period features. So this is how the other half live, she thought. ~~Actually, she found it quite appealing.~~ How disgusting.*

In fact Rip was always much less troubled by the differences between our two families than I was.

Me: (Whisper.) You never told me they were so posh.

Him: (Murmur.) But when you have money, you realise how little it really matters.

Me: (Loud whisper.) Yes, but it matters if you haven't got enough.

Him: (Quietly confident.) Inequality only matters if it makes people *feel* unequal.

Me: Yes, but . . . (But that's a load of crap.)

Him: You don't feel unequal, do you, Georgie?

Me: No, but . . . (Of course I bloody do. I don't know what to do with all the knives and forks. I feel as though they look down their hoity-toity noses at me. But I can't admit it, can I, without seeming like a complete loser? So I'd better keep my mouth shut.)

Him: Mmm. (Kisses me tenderly on the lips, then we end up in bed. Which is always nice.)

5

Fish

It was already dark on Saturday evening when I made my way up the lane to Canaan House for my dinner date. As I moved out of range of the spooky sodium glow from the street lamp on Totley Place, the shadows closed in on me, and I must admit I felt a tremor of apprehension. What was I letting myself in for?

The night was cold and starry. The moonlight etched silvery outlines of trees and the gables of Canaan House on to the darkness. But even in that ashy light there was something cheerfully eccentric about its hodgepodge of styles: Victorian bay windows, a Romanesque entrance porch with twirly columns supporting chubby rounded arches, exuberant Tudor chimneys, and a mad Dracula turret with pointed Gothic windows stuck on one side. I wouldn't go so far as to say I was *inexorably drawn*, but I did quicken my step. The garden path was almost overgrown with brambles but a narrow trail led towards the porch. I pulled my duffel coat around me and looked for signs of light up ahead. Had she forgotten I was coming?

The house itself was dark but I had a sense of eyes watching me. I stopped and listened. I could hear nothing but a faint rustling of leaves that could have been the wind. There was a smell of earth, mouldering vegetation and a musky foxy stink. I took a couple of steps closer to the house, and as I approached the porch a cat burst out of the undergrowth on to the path in front of me. And another. And another. I couldn't count how many cats there were in that soft seething throng, rubbing up against me, purring and mewing, their eyes glinting gold and green, as if I'd stepped into a teeming shoal of furry fishes.

The front door had a frosted glass panel through which I could now see a faint sliver of light far away inside. There was a bell to one side. I pressed it and heard it ringing some-where in the depths of the house. The sliver of light widened into a crack and then into a rectangle as a door opened. I heard shuffling footsteps, a safety chain being unlocked, then Mrs Shapiro opened the door.

'Georgine! Darlink! Come in!'

It's hard to describe the stench that hit me as I stepped over the threshold. I almost gagged and I had to struggle to keep the look of disgust off my face. It was a smell of damp and cat pee and shit and rot and food mould and house filth and sink gunge and, cutting through all that, a rank, nauseating, fishy stink. This last smell, I realised with a sinking feeling, was dinner.

The cats had slunk in beside me – there were only four of them after all – and dashed up ahead into the back of the house. Mrs Shapiro clapped her hands as though to chase them away and smiled indulgently.

'Little pisskes!'

She was wearing a long-sleeved dress in carmine velvet, shaped at the waist and daringly cut away at the front and back to reveal her wrinkled shoulders and the loose skin of her chest. A double string of pearls gleamed around her throat. Her dramatic black curls were piled on top of her head with a collection of tortoiseshell combs, and she'd painted on a dash of matching carmine lipstick – not all of it on her lips. I was wearing jeans and a baggy pullover under my brown

duffel coat. She stepped back on her high heels and eyed me
critically.

'Why you wearing this old shmata, Georgine? Is not flettering for a young woman. You will never get a man this way.'

'I . . . er . . . I don't need . . .' I stopped. Maybe a man is what
I needed after all.

'Come. I will find you something better.'

She led me into the wide tiled entrance hall, from the
centre of which a polished mahogany staircase curved away
to the next floor. Underneath the staircase were piles of black
bin bags, bursting with – I don't know, really, what they
contained, but I could see clothes and books and electrical
items and crockery and bedding spilling out where the bags
had split. To one side was parked the old high-sprung pram,
now apparently full of bundled rags, on which a couple of
stripy felines were dozing. She shooed them away and started
to root among the bundles. After a few moments she began
to tug at a piece of dark green stuff which, when she pulled it
out, turned out to be a dress in some heavy silky fabric with
long scalloped sleeves.

'Here,' she held it up to my chin, 'this I think is more
flettering for you.' I looked at the label – it was a size 12 – my
size – and a Karen Millen. In fact it was a gorgeous dress.
Where on earth had she got this from?

'It's lovely, but . . .' Actually, when I thought about it,
I could guess where she'd got it from – she must have pulled it
out of a skip. '. . . but I can't possibly take it.'

Who would put a dress like this in a skip? Then I thought of
Rip's clothes, which I'd put in the skip, and in a flash I understood – another heart had been splattered somewhere.

'Is too big for me,' she said. 'Will look better on you. Take
it, please.'

'Thank you, Mrs Shapiro, but . . .' I brushed away the cat

hairs that were clinging to the silky fabric. As I shook it out, I could smell the faint sweat and expensive perfume of its previous owner, and I wondered what had driven her lover to get rid of the dress.

'Try it! Try it! No need to be emberressed, darlink.'

Did she expect me to put it on straightaway? Obviously she did. She stood over me as I stripped down to my knickers in the cold foul-smelling hall and slipped the dress, still slightly warm from the sleeping cats, over my head. It slid down over my shoulders and hips as though it was made for me. Why was I doing this? I asked myself. Why didn't I just put on my own clothes and firmly but politely say goodnight? I thought of escaping, I really did. Then I thought of the trouble she must have gone to, to prepare the meal, and how let-down she would feel. And I remembered my empty house and the bright pink sausages in the fridge and *Casualty* on TV. And by then it was too late.

'Wait, I will zip it!' I could feel her hands, bony like claws, on my skin as she wrenched the zip up behind me. 'Beautiful, darlink. You already looking much better. You are a nice-looking woman, Georgine. Nice skin. Nice eyes. Good figure. But look at your hair. Looks like a sheep's popo. When you last been at the hairdresser?'

'I can't remember. I . . .' I remembered the way Rip used to look at me, the way he would run his fingers through my hair when he kissed me.

'You want I will put some lipstick on you?'

'No, really, Mrs Shapiro.'

She hesitated, looking me up and down.

'Okay. For tonight is okay. Come, please.'

I followed her through a door into a long gloomy room where an oval-shaped mahogany table had been spread with a white cloth and two places set at one end with cutlery, napkins and glasses. In the centre of the tablecloth, the large white tomcat was curled up asleep.

'Raus, Wonder Boy! Raus!' (She pronounced it Vunder Boy.) She clapped her hands.

The cat stretched one muscular black-socked leg behind its ear and began licking its private parts. Then it scratched about, sending bits of fluff flying everywhere. Then it rose to its feet, stretched itself a couple of times, jumped down from the table, and sauntered around the room.

'This is Wonder Boy. Looks like he has made a little wish in the corner.' There was a wet patch on the wall by the door, more or less at the height of Wonder Boy's tail, that reminded me of our first meeting. She reached out and scratched him behind the ears, and he let out a purr like a motorbike starting up. 'He is my darlink. Soon you will meet Violetta and the Stinker. The pram babies you have already met. Mussorgsky is somewhere hiding. He is a little bit jealous of the Wonder Boy. Borodin you will not see. He comes only to take the food. Seven altogether. My little femily.'

I handed her the bottle of wine I'd brought. White Rioja. Nice with fish. We both struggled with the corkscrew, but she got it open and poured us each a glass.

'To bargains!' she said. We clinked.

'Can I help you with anything?' I was nervous about what could be happening in the kitchen, but she gestured me severely to a chair.

'You are my invited guest. Please, Georgine, tek a seat.'

Close up I could see that the tablecloth was not white at all but a sort of mottled greyish yellow, bristling with cat hairs of many colours. The napkins weren't white either, they had pink and red blotches that could have been wine or beetroot or tomato soup. While Mrs Shapiro busied herself in the kitchen, I discreetly tried to clean away the gunge that was encrusted between the prongs of my fork, and to study the room I was in. The only light came from a single long-life bulb screwed into a brass chandelier whose other five bulbs were defunct. On the wall opposite the door was a marble fireplace, and above it a large gilt-framed mirror so spotted and clouded that, when I stood up to take a peep at myself in the green dress, I seemed faded and grey, sadder and older than my mental image of myself, my eyes hollow and too dark, my hair wind-snaggled and too curly, the dress so different to anything I'd worn for ages that I hardly recognised myself. I turned away quickly as if I'd seen a ghost. On the facing wall were two tall windows that seemed to be boarded up behind the curtains, and between them hung a photograph in black and white, an old-fashioned studio portrait of a young man in evening dress with sharp clean features, fair curly hair swept back from a high forehead, and in his left hand, held up against his cheek, the neck of a violin. He had startlingly pale eyes staring out of the picture that caught and held my gaze as though he was present in the room. Strangely, although the photograph was in black and white, it seemed more vivid and alive than my own image in the mirror.

As I studied the photograph I became aware of a smell – a faintly fishy aroma that seemed to have wafted into the room. I looked round and saw that Mrs Shapiro was standing in the doorway carrying a large silver tray on which were two steaming bowls.

'*Soupe de poisson. Cuisine française*,' she beamed, placing one bowl in front of me and seating herself opposite me with the other. I looked into the bowl. It was a thin scummy-looking liquid in which some greyish gobs of matter were floating part-submerged.

'Please start. Don't wait.'

I dipped my spoon in. Probably it won't kill me, I told

myself. I've eaten worse than this in Kippax. Across the table, Mrs Shapiro was slurping away with gay abandon, pausing only to dab her lips with her napkin. Ah – that's what those red blotches were. I found that if I held my breath as I swallowed I could manage the liquid. The grey gobs I tried to mash up in the bottom of the bowl so it wasn't obvious how much I'd left.

'Lovely,' I said, trying to find a clean corner of napkin to pat my mouth.

The second course was in some ways better and in some ways worse. It was better because there were boiled potatoes and leeks in a white sauce which, although lumpy, looked reasonably edible; it was worse because the fish, a whole curled-at-the-corners fillet of something hard, brown and yellow, smelled so sickening that I knew I would never be able to bring myself to swallow it. Even Mum never served anything as bad as this.

As I was poking away at the potatoes and leeks I felt a sudden warm pressure in my groin. I looked across the table at Mrs Shapiro. She smiled. The pressure turned into pounding, rhythmic and insistent. What the hell was going on?

'Mrs Shapiro . . .'

She smiled again. I could feel a vibration accompanied by a strange rasping sound like a car engine trying to start on a cold day. Now through the silky stuff of the dress I felt a sharp prick of claws on my thighs. I slipped my hand down under the tablecloth and touched warm fur. Then I had an idea.

'Mrs Shapiro, that photo,' I pointed to the wall behind her, 'who's it of?'

As she turned her back for a moment, I slid the fillet off my plate on to the floor, and gave the cat a shove.

'That is my husband,' she turned towards me and clasped her hands together, 'Artem Shapiro. My beloved Arti.'

Beneath the table the purring had intensified, and turned into a satisfied chomping.

'Was he a musician?'

'One of the greatest, darlink. Before the war. Before the Nazis got him into the camp.'

'He was in a concentration camp?'

'Besides the Baltic Sea. Many Jews from all over Europe ended there. Even some we knew from Hamburg.'

'Your family was from Hamburg?'

'Left in 1938.'

'But Artem – he got away, too?'

'This story is too long, Georgine. Too long and too long ago.'

The young man in the picture held me with his pale intense eyes. I noticed how elegantly his fingers were clasped around the neck of the violin. In *The Splattered Heart* the heroine's lover would have hands like this, I thought. Ms Firestorm was already on the prowl, looking out for a great romance set against the turbulent background of World War Two.

'Please tell me, Mrs Shapiro. I love stories.'

'Yes, this is a loff story,' she sighed. 'But I do not know if it will heff a happy ending.'

The story she started to tell me that night did turn out to be a love story of sorts, and though she related it in her funny hobbled English, my imagination filled in the spaces between the words so vividly that afterwards I couldn't remember what she'd said and what I had imagined.

Artem Shapiro, her husband, she told me, was born in 1904 in the small town of Orsha in a country that sometimes belonged to Poland, sometimes to Russia, sometimes to Lithuania, and most of the time was just a place where people – Jewish people, anyway – got on quietly with their business, keeping their heads down during the years of wars and pogroms and the political machinations of the great powers.

'It is our way. We believed if we kept quiet we would survive.'

His father was a violin maker, quite a successful one, and he thought the boy would learn the trade, too, but one day Artem picked up the instrument and began to play, and that was how it started. Every day for an hour or two after working with his father, he would sit outside in the backyard and play the popular tunes he heard on the street. Then he tried to improvise his own tunes. The neighbours would drop whatever they were doing, and hang over the fence to listen. It was not long before he began to show real promise as a violinist.

'Darlink, everybody who was listening was astonished. They could not believe that such a young boy would be playing like this.'

When Artem was in his teens, the family moved to Minsk, the capital of Byelorussia. His parents paid for him to have lessons with a violin teacher, and it was the teacher who suggested that the young man should go to St Petersburg, or Leningrad as it was by then, several hundred kilometres to the east, to study at the conservatoire.

'He was tooken to it like a duck into the water!' she said, gobbling up the vile brown-yellow fish with apparent enthusiasm as she talked.

After the revolution, Leningrad was a hub of political and cultural life; musicians, writers, artists, film-makers, philosophers were caught up in the ferment of political ideas. Many had revolutionary sympathies and were eager to put their art to the service of the people. One of these was Sergei Prokofiev, who met the talented young violinist from Orsha when he conducted the orchestra in which Artem was playing.

'Arti, too, wanted to bring the great music in front of the masses.'

He had learned his socialist sympathies from his father, who was a Jewish Bundist, she explained. Before I could ask what a Bundist was, she rattled on, 'So long as you were not saying something bad about the Bolsheviks, in that time you could play what music you liked.'

By the late 1930s Artem was playing lead violin with the People's Orchestra and had just started to perform as a soloist. But as Stalin's grip tightened musicians, too, were booted into line. Mrs Shapiro frowned and wolfed down her fish.

'Like poor Prokofiev. He had to repent, isn't it? When I listen to the seventh symphony I think always of how they made him change the ending.'

The false sense of security afforded by the Molotov–Ribbentrop pact meant that Russia did not anticipate the German invasion in the summer of 1941. So when Artem heard that his father was ill, he felt safe enough to set out to visit his family in Minsk in June that year. Byelorussia was at that time in the eastern part of the former Polish territories, which had recently been annexed by Russia, and rumours were flying about of what had happened to Jews in the German-occupied west. Artem hitched a ride on a goods train heading west at exactly the time when every Jew in Europe who could flee was heading east, just as the pact collapsed and the German armies swept eastwards through Poland into the Soviet Union.

'But he was reunited with his family?'

'Yes. His parents and two sisters still were there. But the Nazis were building a wall of barbed wires around the streets in Minsk where the Jews lived so no one would run away.'

'A ghetto?'

'Ghetto. Prison. Same thing. But ghetto is worse. Too many peoples crammed inside. No food. Potato peels and rats they were eating. And every day soldiers were shooting people in the streets. Other ones died from diseases. Some suicided themselves out of despair.'

Mrs Shapiro's voice had grown so quiet that I could hear a tap dripping in the kitchen, and the scuffle of a feline scratching itself under the table.

'But what happened to Artem's family?'

By the time Artem arrived in Minsk, the population was already swollen by the thousands of Jews who had fled eastwards, as well as by German Jews for whom there was no longer room in the German and Polish ghettoes or concentration camps. Despite starvation and the periodic typhus and cholera epidemics that raged through the ghetto, and daily summary executions, sometimes of hundreds of people at a time, they just weren't dying fast enough. Shooting them all would use up too much ammunition. Then a local Nazi commandant came up with a clever idea to kill Jews efficiently without wasting precious bullets.

One morning some forty Jews were picked up at random off the streets, herded to a woody spot on the outskirts of town, and forced to dig a pit. Then they were roughly roped together and pushed into the pit they had dug. Russian prisoners of war were ordered to bury them alive.

'But the Bolshie Russians refused to do it, so the Jews had to be shot in the end and the Russians also. So even more bullets was used up, isn't it?'

Artem's father was among the forty.

To save bullets and time, mobile gassing vans were set up to tour the district. But why waste all that human labour potential, when the munitions factories were struggling to find workers? It was decided that able-bodied Jews like Artem should be made to contribute to the war effort.

'So they put him in the camp.'

★

The camp to which Artem was dispatched was a labour camp, not an extermination camp, though it was no holiday camp either, buffeted by cold winds off the Baltic, squatting inside its cage of barbed wire under a perpetually pewter sky. In this miserable spot, a number of German companies, including some that are now household names, contracted to use the cheap labour facilities. Those inmates who could work could eat, the others died.

But the Lithuanian guards were lax and lazy, and couldn't always be bothered with the security procedures demanded by their new bosses. One early morning on his way to work Artem came upon a guard, still tipsy from the night before, pissing against a wall – he had chosen a private spot where the wall turned a corner behind the barracks. Artem knew immediately that this was his chance; live or die, he had to take it. Although he was weak from months of semi-starvation, surprise was on his side. He picked up a stone and bludgeoned the Lithuanian over the head; then he stole his uniform and papers.

'And he ran away on all his fastest legs into the forest, to join the partisans.'

She paused and reached for a cigarette. Beneath the table a fight had broken out over the remnants of my fish. There was a screeching and thrashing of tails.

'Raus, Wonder Boy! Raus, Stinker! Raus, Violetta!' She tried to kick them under the table but her feet got tangled in the tablecloth and she sat back with a sigh of resignation.

'What happened next?' I prompted.

Straightening herself out, she lit her cigarette.

'Ach, Georgine, I cannot tell this story while we are eating good food and thinking of these poor hungry peoples. Another time I will finish it. Better now I should play you some music. Great Russian composers. You would like?'

I nodded. Under the table, hostilities had been suspended

while the cats waited for their next course. Wonder Boy was licking his bottom again. Violetta was rubbing herself against my legs. Mrs Shapiro gathered the plates and tottered off into the kitchen, leaving her cigarette smouldering in a saucer. I was beginning to feel a bit strange. Between us, we'd almost polished off the bottle of wine. The dim long-life bulb cast fuzzy downward shadows on the table and walls that made everything seem faded and unreal – or maybe it was the images from the terrible story working on my imagination.

After a while I became aware of a sound in the next room, a low mournful sound, like a voice calling from the nether-world. For a moment I thought it was a cat, then I realised it was music – such soft, sad music – that had crept in quietly through the open door. At first it was a single violin, then it was joined by others, and then a tune emerged, throbbing with melancholy and repeating itself over and over, growing louder and higher. For some reason I found myself thinking of Rip – of Rip and me together, of Rip and me making love, our hands and bodies fumbling for each other in the dark, always finding each other, always coming together, each time the same yet each time different, repetitions and variations.

Now the tempo of the music changed; it became louder, more violent, with cymbals clashing and drums throbbing away like a headache, and the violins racing up and down, faster and faster, arguing with each other, contradicting each other, in a turmoil of sound. I thought of Rip again, and I remembered the terrible fury and churning of our last argu-ment. No, I realised, it wasn't just the music. A gut-churning feeling was building up in my stomach right now. Then Mrs Shapiro reappeared in the doorway with another tray.

'Now we heff a dessert.'

'Er . . .'

She placed the tray on the table. It looked like some sort of shop-bought pie, still in its foil dish. I could handle that – I'd grown up on this sort of food. There was a tub of REDUCED cream on which the sell-by date was clearly visible. I did a quick calculation. Only two days overdue. I'd eaten worse. '. . . just a little.'

I tasted the pie cautiously. It seemed perfectly all right. I had only a tiny drop of cream, which also seemed all right.

'You like it?' asked Mrs Shapiro.

'Yes, lovely. Delicious. What is it?'

'Prokofiev. *Symphonic Song*. Wait. It will get better.'

As I listened the tempo of the music changed again. It became graciously flowing and jubilant; the original melody had returned, but with more depths and heights of emotion, as though it was leaping over itself, over the contradictions and arguments, over the terrible drumbeat and stomach-churning turmoil, into a new world, a new happy world where everything was going to be all right again for ever and ever. Tears welled up in my eyes; heavy and warm, they rolled down my cheeks.

The music stopped and silence seeped into the room. Across the table from me, I saw that Mrs Shapiro was dabbing at her eyes with her napkin. Then she fumbled in her bag for her cigarettes and matches, lit up again, inhaled and then gave a long sigh.

'We heff been living here in this house playing music together. I was playing piano, he was playing violin. Such great music we made together. Now I am living here alone. Life goes on, isn't it?'

I could feel my tears welling up again. How much better it would be, I thought, to love and be loved like this until parted by death, and even after death, than to feel love shrivel and die while life goes on around you, dreary and loveless. Oh heck, there goes my splattered heart again.

41

'Why are you crying, Georgine? You have lost someone, too?'

'Yes. No. It's not the same. My husband . . . he walked out on me, that's all.'

'You are still young, you will find somebody else.'

I wiped my tears and smiled. 'If only it was so easy.'

'Darlink, I will help you.'

The next thing I can remember is throwing up on my own doorstep. I was still wearing the green dress, with my jeans underneath and my pullover and duffel coat on top. I felt terrible. My head was throbbing, and I was alternating violently, frighteningly, between burning hot and clammy cold. Above my head, stars were spinning in the blackness. I knelt on the stone steps and puked again. Then I felt a warm furry presence beside me. It was Violetta. She must have followed me home. 'Hello, cat.' I stretched out my hand to stroke her, and she arched her back and purred, rubbing herself against me. Then she started lapping up the sick off the doorstep.

6
Sticky brown stuff

On the Sunday morning after my dinner with Mrs Shapiro, I woke up at about ten o'clock. There was a horrible taste in my mouth and a bowl with some slimy stuff by the bed. I must have thrown up in the night, but I couldn't remember anything. My head was throbbing. A hard beam of sunlight was hammering between the curtains where they didn't quite meet, like a chisel splitting my brain. I got up and attempted to fiddle with the curtains, but as soon as I stood up dizziness brought me down again, and I flopped back on the bed. The ceiling seemed to be moving backwards and forwards above me, like in an earthquake. I pulled the covers over my head, but that brought on a panic of suffocation. What had I been dreaming about? I had an image of people roped together, pushed into a pit to be buried alive. Was that a nightmare? No, it was worse than a nightmare – it was something that had really happened.

I staggered into the bathroom and gulped cold water from the tap, then splashed some on to my face and returned to the bedroom. The light was too harsh. I rooted through my drawer for something to cover my eyes and found a pair of black knickers; I slipped them over my head like a hood. The waist elastic just reached the tip of my nose. I lay back down on the bed and let the darkness enfold me. That was better. If Rip had been there he'd have laughed at me. If Rip had been there he'd have made me a cup of tea and comforted me. I remembered that music, the bounding, soaring, happily-ever-after melody that had carried me along in its arms last night. Was that a dream? Yes, it was.

At our wedding, the organist had played the *Arrival of the Queen of Sheba* and Dad overcame his scruples about religion enough to walk me up the aisle on his arm. It was the first time Rip's parents and mine had met, and it was all excruciatingly polite. Rip had discreetly removed the engraving of the Staffordshire coal mine which some ancestor had owned in 1882, and I'd persuaded Dad not to wear his National Union of Mineworkers tie. Mr Sinclair engaged Dad in conversation about rugby, drawing on his own school experiences but skirting around the fact that the sport had been named after his own school, and Dad did his best to keep the conversation up, skirting around the differences between rugby union and rugby league. Mrs Sinclair complimented Mum on her hat, and Mum asked her for the recipe for the chocolate peripherals; Mrs Sinclair skirted around the question without revealing that everything, including the profiteroles, had come from a catering firm in Leek. Mum didn't say anything about the olives on the canapés, but I could see her eyeing them with suspicion. It was 1985, remember, and olives hadn't yet reached Kippax. To be on the safe side, she slipped them under a cushion. Later, I saw Mrs Sinclair shaking hands with the vicar, with three olives adhering to her behind.

I poured myself a large glass of water, and went back to bed. I must have dozed off, for when I woke up later, in the afternoon, I felt much better. I went downstairs to rummage in the fridge for something to eat and ended up pouring myself a glass of wine instead. My stomach was still feeling delicate from its Saturday night trauma, and probably it would have been sensible to stick to tea and toast, but I needed something to cheer me up. An after-mood from the nightmare still clung to the edges of my mind. And I was missing Ben. Three more days until he'd be back with me. Carrying my glass of wine I went back upstairs, and I noticed that the door to his room was slightly open, so for no particular reason I went inside.

It smelled of Ben, or to be precise it smelled of Ben's socks; and here they were, in a waiting-to-be-washed heap near the door. Also in heaps on the floor were his school clothes, his not-school clothes, the books he was halfway through reading, the books he would never read, exercise books, notebooks, and loose papers that might have once been in books, a collapsed stack of DVDs, a mound of CDs and various bits of mysterious electronic gear. A triangle of dried-out pizza with two symmetrical bites, one on each side, was propped against a half-empty bottle of lime-green fluid on the mouse mat. On the walls were posters of the Arctic Monkeys and Amy Winehouse, and a *Lord of the Rings* poster featuring a close-up of Orc dentistry. My eyes roved around the busy cluttered space and I smiled to myself – dear Ben.

The desk was a tip of crumpled papers, broken pens, chewed-down pencils, bottle tops, gum, wrappers, flyers, tissues, all splattered with some kind of sticky brown stuff – it may have been congealed hot chocolate – that was also daubed on the keyboard of his computer, and even on the monitor, where a Windows logo was whirling mindlessly around. A small photograph was stuck to the bottom of the monitor with Blu-tack. I leaned forward to look, and my heart squeezed in my chest. It was Ben and Stella. They were sitting on a park bench surrounded by greenery, grinning their heads off.

I bent down to get a closer look at the photo – Ben's innocent open-mouthed grin; Stella's pretty smile, more posed and self-conscious – and my sleeve caught the glass of wine, which splashed everywhere, mingling with the brown stuff. I took a tissue from my pocket and started to mop, taking care not to disturb anything, because part of me was thinking that I didn't want Ben to know I'd been poking around in his room. As I wiped the mouse, the computer suddenly whirred into life and the screen came up – a black background with a single word flashing in red, animated with dancing flames: *Armageddon*. It looked like some stupid computer game.

After that fish dinner I avoided Mrs Shapiro for a couple of weeks, then I forgot about her. Life carried on with its limping rhythm: Ben, not-Ben, Ben, not-Ben. I was learning to walk with the limp and I slept better with the black knickers. Sometimes, to cheer myself up, I fantasised about revenge. In *The Splattered Heart*, feisty Gina, having discovered Rick's infidelities, was also planning something dramatically unpleasant involving extra-spicy Madras vegetable curry and/or a subtler approach based on fish soup diluted with pee.

I was sitting at my laptop one dull afternoon in November, trying to write about adhesives but sneaking back every few minutes to the exercise book which was open on my desk, when the phone rang.

'Mrs Georgina Sinclair?' An unfamiliar woman's voice, squeaky like a rusty gate.

'Yes. Sort of. Who's speaking?'

'I'm Margaret Goodknee from the Whittington Hospital.'

My hands went cold and my heart started to thump. 'What's happened?'

'We have a Mrs Naomi Shapiro in A&E.'

'Oh, dear.'

I must confess, all I felt was relief. Not Ben. Not Stella.

'On her admission form she's named you as her next of kin.'

2

Adventures with Polymers

7

Pick and mix

'Why me?' I wondered, half curious and half irritated, as I made my way down a long busy ward looking for Mrs Shapiro. 'Doesn't she have anyone closer?'

I found her at last, shrunk down into the hospital bed, with only her little face peeping out above the sheet, and her black curls straggling over the pillow. The silver line along the parting was several centimetres wide, but apart from that, without her weird make-up, she actually looked better than before.

'Mrs Shapiro? Naomi?'

Her face lit up with a smile of recognition, and she reached out her hand from under the covers to hold mine.

'Georgine? Thenk Gott you come. You heff to get me out of here.'

'I'll do my best, Mrs Shapiro. When you're better. What happened?'

'Slipped on the ice. Wrist brokken.'

She waved her left hand at me, which was plastered and strapped, the fingers protruding from the dressing like bent grey twigs with splashes of chipped nail varnish at the tips.

'You heff to get me out. Food is terrible. They mekking me eat sossedge.'

'Shall I tell them you want a kosher diet?'

'Kosher pick and mix. No hem, no sossedge. But bekkon I like.' She winked a mischievous eye. 'A little bit of something does you good, isn't it?'

The sister in charge was a small brisk unsmiling woman with scraped-back hair who sniffed at the idea of pick and mix, so I asked her to put Mrs Shapiro down for kosher. She scribbled it in the file, then she added, 'She doesn't seem to be registered with a GP. We need her NHS card or some form of ID to verify her entitlement.' She must have seen my jaw tighten. 'It's the rule now. Just a box I have to tick.'

When I came back to her bedside, Mrs Shapiro was sitting up looking chirpy and trying to get into conversation with the woman in the next bed, who was lying on her back, breathing through an oxygen mask.

'Mrs Shapiro,' I asked, 'are you registered with a doctor?'

'What for I need the doctor?' She was in a fighting mood. 'These young boys, what do they know? Only to ask schmutzig questions. When you last been on the toilet? Please stick out the tongue. What kind of a doctor says this? In Germany we had Doctor Schinkelman – this was a real doctor.' A faraway look had come into her eyes. 'Plenty medicine. Always red. Tasted of cherries. And plenty tablets for *Mutti*.'

'But do you have a medical card? Any form of ID?'

She sighed dramatically and passed her good hand across her brow.

'Seventy year I been living in this country, nobody ask me for no card.'

'I know,' I soothed. 'It's like Sainsbury's – the surveillance society. But you need something to show how long you've been living here. What about the bills on the house? Council tax? Gas?'

'All papers are in the bureau. Maybe they will find something.' She sat up and blinked rapidly. 'They are looking into my house?'

'I'm sure it's just a formality. I'll go and get them, if you prefer.'

She turned around, gesturing with her strapped-up hand.

'Key to my house is in the coat.'

In the bedside locker was a dark brown astrakhan coat with a turned collar and cuffs, elegantly fitted at the waist, and conspicuously moth-eaten, with bare patches down to the leather all along the back. She saw me examining it.

'You like this coat? You can heff it, Georgine.'

'It's very nice but . . .'

It smelled of old cheese.

'Please. Tek it. I heff another. What's the matter – you don't like it?'

'. . . I think it's a bit small for me.'

'Try. Try it.'

I made a show of taking off my duffel coat, and trying to squeeze myself into it. It had a heavy satin lining torn under the armpits, with a sheen of grease around the buttons and cuffs, but still it had a residual touch of luxury. Once, about fifty years ago, it had been a fabulous coat.

'It suits you good, darlink. Tek it. Is better than your coat.'

True, my brown Bat Woman duffel coat, even in its 1985 heyday, had been in a lower league.

'It's lovely. Thank you. But look, it doesn't fit.' I pretended to struggle with the buttons.

'You must be more elegant, Georgine. And look at your shoes. Why you don't wear mit heels?'

'I'm sure you're right, Mrs Shapiro. But I like to be comfortable.' I slipped my hands into the generously deep satin-lined pockets. 'Where's the key?'

'Always in the pocket. You must be more elegant if you will catch a man, Georgine.'

I rifled through the pockets. There was a disgusting snot-caked handkerchief with traces of dried blood, a box of matches, a cigarette butt, a sticky boiled sweet with bits of fluff stuck to it, half a crumbled biscuit that had covered everything in greyish crumbs, and a pound coin. No key.

'Should be in there. Maybe is fallen in the leaning.'

The key had slipped through a hole in the pocket, and was shaking around in the hem of the lining, along with a stub of black eyebrow pencil, two more cigarette butts, an apple core, and some loose change. I fished them all out through the hole and put them in the other pocket.

'Here it is. I'll have a look in your bureau and see if I can find something official to keep them happy.'

'You must look only in the bureau. Not everywhere poking, Georgine.' She was smoothing the bedclothes with a nervous movement. 'Darlink, I am worrying about the Wonder Boy. If you go to my house, you will please put some food for him? Other cats can catch, but this poor boy he is always hungry. And next time you come, Georgine, you bring some cigarettes mit you, okay?'

'I don't think smoking is allowed in hospital, Mrs Shapiro.'

'Nothing is allowed.' She breathed a dramatic sigh. 'Only sleeping and eating sossedge.'

In the next bed, the woman with the oxygen mask had started to make a horrible gurgling noise. A couple of nurses rushed up, and drew the curtain around the bed. The gurgling continued. There was a clatter of instruments, and low voices talking urgently.

'You heff to get me out, Georgine.' Mrs Shapiro gripped my wrist again. 'Place is full of krankies. Everybody dying.'

I stroked her hand until her grip relaxed. 'You'll be home soon. Would you like me to bring you anything?'

She gave me an appealing look.

'If you could bring the Wonder Boy . . .'

'I don't think they allow pets in here.' Especially not Wonder Boy, I was thinking, with his disgusting habits. 'What about your photo of Artem? Would you like to have it with you? I'm sure they'd allow that.'

She shook her head. 'Too many teefs in here. But Wonder Boy nobody will steal.'

Well, she was right about that. Rather than getting drawn into a plan to smuggle Wonder Boy into the hospital, I changed the subject, thinking maybe reminiscence would settle her, for old people often feel more at home in the past than in the present. And I was curious to know the end of the story she'd started to tell me that night over the fish dinner, twisted up in her convoluted English.

'You never finished telling me the story about Artem. How he got to England. How you met.'

Letting go of my wrist she sank back on to her pillow.

'It is a long *megillah*, Georgine.'

'You said he ran away to join the partisans in the forest.'

'Yes, in Naliboki. Almost six months he was living mit the Pobeda partisans.'

Shlomo Zorin and his Pobeda band of partisans had set up a family camp along the same lines as the Bielski camp in a clearing in the vast Naliboki forest in Byelorussia. Here they sheltered any Jews who made their way there, and even sent scouts back into the ghettoes to organise escapes. Artem Shapiro undertook several of these missions, using stolen papers; his bright blond hair, inherited from his grandfather, allowed him to pass himself off as a Christian.

'Such a beautiful blondi, he was. He could pass easy.' Mrs Shapiro's voice wavered. 'So one day he made his journey back to Minsk.'

Early in the autumn, while there was still plenty to eat in the woods and before the snows started, Artem set out to find his mother and sisters, thinking to lead them back to the forest with him. But the Minsk ghetto, when he arrived, seemed like a ghost town of living skeletons shuffling around the once-familiar streets with death in their eyes. He learned from a former neighbour that his mother was dead – she had died of starvation, or maybe of a broken heart, shortly after he had been taken away. One of his sisters had died of typhus. No one knew what had happened to the other sister. Someone told him that she'd been taken to Auschwitz; someone else told him that she'd used her mother's gold teeth to bribe a local brigand, and had got away, 'To Sweden. Or mebbe to England.'

After that visit to Minsk, something broke apart inside Artem's heart. All the music died. A terrible chorus of wailing filled his head night and day, so he could neither sleep nor work nor think. In a situation where morale is crucial, he felt himself becoming a drag on the Pobeda camp, undermining everyone's spirits with his own misery. One morning, after a night of wailing dreams, he smashed his violin against a tree. Then he said goodbye to Zorin and headed eastwards through the silent snow-laden forests towards his birthplace at Orsha. Maybe he was hoping to make contact with surviving members of his family, but when he arrived in the spring of 1942 the Orsha ghetto had already been liquidated. Thousands of Jews had been shot and the remainder had been herded on to freight trains.

'They put them on the trains but they been transported to nowhere. They been poisoned where they waited, in the wagons. The Russian prisoners dug up a mass grave and buried them.' She paused. Her breath came slow and rattly. 'Truly they wanted to kill us all.'

Artem did not return to Zorin. Such a fury possessed him that simply surviving in the forest was no longer enough. The chorus of wailing resolved itself into a single long howl –

the howl of a wounded animal ready to kill. He headed north to join up with a group of Russian partisans who were harrying the German army, which had by now encircled Leningrad. The first time he ambushed a German jeep with a tree felled across the road, he taunted them with savage delight: *'Ich bin der ewige Jude!'*

'Shut up that nonsense!' bawled Velikov, the commander of the unit. 'Just shoot!'

The partisans were trying to open up a supply route into the beleaguered city. It was a dangerous mission, for the German grip on Leningrad and the Finnish corridor was almost total, but by early 1943 Meretskov had brought the front forward from the east, and a few supplies started to get through. Artem was with a group of partisans who were driving a sleigh loaded with potatoes and beet across the frozen Lake Lagoda when they came under fire from a German patrol. The other three perished instantly, along with their stubby-legged Mongolian pony, but Artem was only wounded in the shoulder. He knew that running away over the ice in winter would be certain death; instead he crawled into the sleigh, hid under the wolfskins which covered the beets, and waited for his destiny to catch up with him. Either the Germans would take him, or the Russians would rescue him, or he would freeze to death. Everyone knows that hypothermia is a pleasant drowsy death. At least I won't die of hunger, he thought. He waited and listened, trying to staunch his wound with a cloth wrapped around a lump of ice. He could hear shooting and voices calling, but they seemed to be getting further away, not closer.

'Then started the snow to fall.'

He must have fainted or drifted off to sleep, for he lost track of how long he'd lain there, when he was jerked into sudden consciousness by a sharp jolt of the sleigh. He peeped from under the snow-heavy wolfskins, and saw that it had been harnessed to what he thought was another pony that was trotting over the ice into the whirling blizzard. Seated above and behind him, he could hear two men talking. He caught the sound of laughter and a whiff of cigarette smoke. Were they talking German or Russian? He couldn't tell.

'And all this time the pony was walking in the snow and the ice, and the snow was falling all the time, and the pony was walking on in the freezing snow and on and on over the ice and on and on . . .'

She stopped. I waited for her to continue. I thought she must be remembering and maybe she found the memories too painful to talk about. But after a while I heard a gentle snoring and I realised she'd fallen asleep.

'When do you think Mrs Shapiro might be able to come home?' I asked the sister at the desk on my way out.

'It's too early to say. We'll see how she gets on,' she replied without looking up.

'But it's only a broken wrist, isn't it?'

'I know, but we'll have to assess her home situation. We don't want her to go back and have another fall. At her age, she might be better off in residential care.'

'Why, how old is she?'

'She told us she was ninety-six.' She looked up. Our eyes met, and mine must have betrayed my astonishment. 'Isn't she your gran?'

'No, she's just a neighbour. I live a couple of streets away. I don't really know her that well.'

Could Mrs Shapiro really be ninety-six? But why would she lie about her age?

'Another reason it'd be useful to have some ID.'

8

Biopolymer

I spotted Wonder Boy lurking in the porch of Canaan House
as I walked up the path. He was ripping the guts out of a
bird he'd caught – it looked like a starling. It was still alive,
struggling between his paws. Feathers were everywhere. He
bolted off into the bushes as he saw me coming, the bird still
flapping in his jaws. This cat can well take care of himself, I
thought. Usually I'm fond of cats but there was something
horrible about Wonder Boy. I tried to imagine catching
him, stuffing him in a bag, and taking him on the bus to the
hospital. No way.

The key Mrs Shapiro had given me was only a Yale; in fact
any enterprising burglar could have just smashed the frosted
glass and put his hand through to turn the lock. I pushed
the door open against a heap of mail that had piled up on
the inside. As soon as I stepped into the hall the stink hit me, a
bitter must of cat pee, damp and rot. I put my handkerchief
up to my nose. Out of nowhere, Violetta materialised around
my ankles, mewing pitifully. Poor thing – she must have been
locked in the house for at least three days. I picked up the mail
and flicked through it in case there was anything that needed
attention, but it all seemed to be junk. There was even an
offer for a Sainsbury's Nectar Card.

I followed Violetta through to the kitchen. A chaos of dirty
plates, dead cups with remains of disgusting brown fluids,
empty tins and greasy ready-meals packaging was spread

across every grimy surface. In a cracked pot sink under the window, a stack of unwashed dishes and congealed food remnants was soaking in scummy water on to which a cold tap was drip-drip-dripping. The gas cooker was crusted with dark brown gunge, and so old that it had levers instead of knobs. There was an Aga, but it was unlit and seemed to be used for storing old newspapers. A dank mouldy chill pervaded everything. I shivered. Even in my warm duffel coat I was cold.

I hunted around and found a dozen cat-food tins in a cupboard. I spooned some out into a bowl for Violetta and she wolfed it down, almost choking in her desperation. Then I unlocked the back door – the key was on the inside – refilled the bowl, and put it out on the step. Wonder Boy appeared, hissed at Violetta, batted her out of the way, and polished it off. A few other scrawny moggies were hanging around too. I fed them all – there must have been a good half-dozen of them, miaowing and rubbing themselves against me. A couple of them sneaked indoors between my legs. I locked the kitchen door and returned to the house.

The bureau Mrs Shapiro had been talking about was in a downstairs room which could have been a study. The window had been boarded up behind drawn curtains, so the only light was from a lone surviving candle-bulb in the heavy gilt candelabra that cast a feeble glow over the old-fashioned floral wallpaper, floor-to-ceiling bookcases, Persian rugs, and a tiled fireplace above which an ornate ormolu mirror would have reflected the blocked-out view over the garden. Even in the gloomy light I could see it was a lovely room. The smell was different, too, musky and dusty, with only a faint trace of cat pee. There was a spoon-back armchair and two desks – a mahogany kneehole desk by the window, and a tall oak bureau-bookcase in an alcove beside the chimney breast.

I decided to start here. I have to confess that, even then, Ms Firestorm was looking over my shoulder and whispering in my ear, there must be a story here – maybe a better story than *The Splattered Heart*.

The bureau was full of papers, mostly bills in the name of Naomi Shapiro, and some, the older ones, in the name of Artem Shapiro, and bank statements from a joint-name account. The most recent of these, to my astonishment, showed a balance of just over £3,000. The oldest I could find dated back to 1948. There was, it seemed, a small monthly income from an annuity, as well as Mrs Shapiro's widow's pension going into the bank. I took a selection of statements at random; would these give the hospital the information they needed? In the same drawer, held together with a rubber band, was a bundle of receipts including one for £25, dated 26th October from Felicity NU2U Dress Agency, and one dated 16th October for £23 from P. Cochrane, Antique and Secondhand Emporium, New North Road. That explained the pram.

There must be something else, I thought, something personal to show a date or place of birth, of baptism or marriage, education or employment. You can't live a whole life that's only recorded through bills and receipts. The kneehole desk was crammed full of stationery, crumpled notepaper, dried-up pens and stubs of pencils, receipts, old tickets, train timetables years out of date, a library card, also out of date, and assorted out-of-date leaflets about pensions and benefits: the useless bits of officialdom we cart with us through life. One drawer housed a correspondence with the Council about the monkey puzzle tree, which Mrs Shapiro had wanted to cut down, although apparently it had a tree preservation order on it.

In the last drawer there was a thick brown envelope stuffed with official-looking papers. This was what I'd been searching for. An odd-looking passport, light blue with a black stripe on one corner. Artem Shapiro; date of birth 13th March 1904; place of birth Orsha; date of issue 4th March 1950, London. Ration book: Artem Shapiro 1947. Driving licence: Artem Shapiro 1948. Abbey National Life Insurance plan: Artem Shapiro 1958. Death certificate: Artem Shapiro 1960; cause of death: cancer of the lung. Knowing his story, I felt a special tug of intimacy as I turned the flimsy typewritten paper over in my hands. So that was how his journey ended: the ghetto, the barbed-wire camp, the silent forests, the ice-bound lake. I folded the death certificate and put it back, hoping he'd died in his sleep, cosseted with morphine.

But what about her? A Co-op savings book was the only document that had her name on it: Mrs N. Shapiro 13th July 1972. There has to be something else, I thought; and I remembered what she'd said – *you must look only in the bureau*. So if anything had been deliberately hidden, I wouldn't find it here.

In a frenzy of curiosity, I poked through the other rooms. The sideboard in the dining room where I'd eaten the death-defying fish dinner yielded nothing but plates and cutlery. The sitting room was dark, the windows boarded up, and the light switch didn't work. I'd need a torch to search in here. Under the staircase, behind the pram, a narrow door opened on to a stone stair leading down to the basement. A wave of trapped musty air rose up towards me. I felt with my hand along the wall for the light switch, and a fluorescent strip light juddered into life, flickering madly on and off, plunging the low-ceilinged room alternately into light and pitch darkness.

It seemed to be some kind of workshop. A glass-fronted cabinet was fixed to the wall with rows of tools neatly arranged, the blades now tarnished with rust. Below it was a workbench with a variety of clamps. Bits of strangely carved wood were hanging from hooks. I realised after a few moments that they were panels and necks of unfinished violins. There was a pot of dried-up glue, a small dried-up brush sticking out of it. The glue was clear and amber-coloured, still exuding a faint sickly whiff. Animal glue. Bio-polymer. Used for woodworking, veneers and inlays, until better modern synthetic glues came along.

My boss Nathan once told me that the Nazis had made glue from human bones. Lampshades from human skin; mattresses stuffed with human hair. Nothing wasted. I was beginning to feel dizzy. Maybe it was the strobe effect of the faulty fluorescent tube, or the memories trapped in the ghost-breathed air.

I made my way back up the stone stairs. As my fingers felt for the light switch I turned back towards the workshop, and that's when I saw a flash of colour on top of the tool cabinet – a couple of millimetres of blue just visible above the architrave. Curious, I went back down and pulled up a chair to have a look. It was an oblong tin, a bit rusty, with a picture of Harlech Castle surrounded by an improbably blue Welsh sky. I lifted it down and eased it open. It was the sort of tin that would once have held toffees or shortbread biscuits, but all it had in it now was a few photographs. I slipped it under my arm and went back up into the light.

From the hall, a wide staircase with a curved mahogany banister led up to the first floor. As I mounted the treads, still clutching the tin, a threadbare Axminster carpet secured by brass rods released clouds of dust under my feet. The same mahogany handrail galleried the first-floor landing, off which nine doors opened. One of them was slightly ajar. I pushed it further open. A scurry of movement. Two lean stray cats bolted out between my legs. The room was large and light, with a double window overlooking the front garden, and dominated by a massive art-deco walnut double bed on which a tattered-eared tomcat – he had the same moth-eaten look as

Mrs Shapiro's astrakhan coat – was curled up asleep. Raising his shaggy head he followed me with his eyes as I came in. The stench in here was terrible. Phew! I opened a window. 'Shoo! Shoo! Piss off!' I tried to chase him out but he just looked at me with contempt. Eventually he uncurled himself, jumped down from the bed flicking his tail grumpily from side to side, and sauntered towards the door.

This, I guessed, was Mrs Shapiro's bedroom, for her clothes were scattered everywhere – the Scotch plaid baker boy cap, the peep-toe high heels, and on the floor by the bed a pair of peach camiknickers trimmed with cream lace, a faint stain yellowing the silk. The walnut wardrobe, carved with art-deco sunbursts, was full of clothes on satin-padded hangers, reeking of moth-balls, stylish and expensive like costumes in a Humphrey Bogart movie. A matching sunburst dressing table stood in one corner, with a triple-hinged mirror facing the window through which I had a view of the garden. I rifled through layers of ancient decomposing make-up and musty, slightly stinky underwear. There was nothing of interest, so I sat down on the edge of the bed, opened the Harlech Castle tin, and spread out the six photographs.

Most were in black and white, but the top one was in sepia, creased and tattered at the edges. It was a family portrait from the turn of the century: the mother in a lace-collared dress cradling a baby, the father with a beard and a tall hat, and two children, a little girl wearing a flouncy dress and a strikingly blond toddler in white pantaloons and an embroidered shirt. There was writing on the back that didn't seem to make sense. Until I realised it was in Cyrillic script. All I could make out was the date: 1905. He must have carried it with him, hidden in a pocket or a lining, all that way.

Next, a wedding photograph caught my eye: a tall man, fair and handsome, grasping the hand of a pretty woman with ardent eyes and thick curly black hair pinned up beneath a crown of white blossom. They were gazing out of the photograph, wide-eyed, half smiling, as though taken by surprise at their own happiness. The man I recognised as Artem Shapiro. But who was the woman? An attractive heart-shaped face with wide-set dark eyes and a full, generous mouth. I studied it carefully, for people's faces do change as they age, but, really, there could be no doubt. The woman in the photo was not Naomi Shapiro.

I was still staring at the photo when suddenly I heard a sound outside in the garden – voices, and the clack of the gate. My heart thumped. Quickly I slipped the photos into my bag, closed the tin and shoved it on top of the wardrobe out of sight. In one of the panes of the triple mirror I could see a reflection of the window and, through it, the garden. A man and a woman were standing on the path; they were standing and gazing at the house. The woman was a stout redhead, wearing a vivid green jacket; the man was stocky and red-cheeked, wearing a blue parka, smoking a cigarette. The man stubbed his cigarette out on the path and spoke to the woman. I couldn't catch his words, but I saw her toothy laugh. By the time I came down to the door they'd gone.

9

Rubber

There was a different nurse on duty when I went back up to the hospital next time. She examined the papers I showed her without comment, ticked a box on Mrs Shapiro's notes, and passed them back to me.

'How's she doing?' I asked.

'Fine. She'll be ready to go as soon as we can get her home assessment done.' She flicked through the notes. 'I understand you have the key to her house. I'll get Mrs Goodknee to ring you for an appointment.'

Mrs Goodknee again. I imagined someone in a miniskirt with chubby dimpled knees.

Mrs Shapiro was sitting up in bed, her hair combed back tidily, the hospital nightgown, antiseptic green, buttoned up to her throat. She seemed well; the stay in hospital had fattened her up. Her cheeks were rosy and her eyes looked bluer – yes, her eyes were definitely blue.

'Hello. You look good, Mrs Shapiro. Are they feeding you well? Are they still making you eat sausages?'

'Not sossedge. Now is better. Now is chickens and fry pottetto. Did you bring the Wonder Boy?'

'I tried, but he ran away,' I lied.

I wanted to ask her about the photographs, but I held back because I didn't want to admit that I'd been rifling through her house and had discovered the hidden tin. I would have to find another way of worming the story out of her.

We sipped the thick, bitter tea that came around on the trolley and munched our way through the box of chocolates I'd brought in my role as next of kin.

'Mrs Shapiro, I'm worried that your house is ... well ... don't you think it's a bit big for you to manage? Wouldn't you be happier in a nice cosy flat? Or in a home where you'd have someone to look after you?'

She looked at me with wide-eyed horror, as though I'd put a curse on her.

'Why for you say this to me, Georgine?'

I couldn't find polite words to explain my concern about the smell and the gunge and the crumbling fabric of the house, so I just said, 'Mrs Shapiro, the nurse thinks you might be too old to live on your own.' I studied her face. 'She told me you're ninety-six.'

Her mouth twitched. She blinked. 'I am not going nowhere.'

'Mrs Shapiro, how old are you really?'

She ignored my question.

'What would heppen to my dear cats?' A stubborn look had come over her. 'How is the Wonder Boy? Next time you must bring him.'

I told her about Wonder Boy's starling – 'That notty boy!' – and Violetta's plaintive mewing – 'Ach! Always she is singing *La Traviata*!' – and the cat that sneaked upstairs to sleep on her bed. 'That is Mussorgsky. Maybe it is my fault, I allow it. Darlink, sometimes I am so lonely in the night.'

She glanced at me, and my face must have given something away, because she said, 'You also are lonely, Georgine, are you? I can see in your eyes.'

I nodded reluctantly. I was the one who was supposed to be asking the questions. But she squeezed my hand. 'So, tell me about your husband – the one who was running away.'

'Oh, it's a long story.'

'But not so long as mine, isn't it?' An impish smile. 'It was a story of loff at first sight?'

'Actually, it was, Mrs Shapiro. Our eyes met across a crowded room.'

In fact it was a courtroom in Leeds, where two miners from Castleford were on trial for a picket-line scuffle. Rip was defending; he was still doing his articles and volunteering at the Chapeltown Law Centre. I was a junior reporter on the *Evening Post*. After the verdict was announced – they were cleared – we went for a celebratory drink. Later Rip drove me home to my parents' bungalow in Kippax, and we made love in front of the fire. I remembered how I'd teased him about his name.

Me: (Twisting my fingers into his curls.) Knock, knock.

Him: (Fumbling with my bra, his mouth wet on my ear.) Who's there?

Me: (Pulling him down on top of me.) Euripides.

Him: (Hand up my skirt.) Euripides who?

Me: (Giggling between kisses.) You rippe dese knickers off . . .

So he did. It was strange, because we hardly knew each other, yet it was as if we'd known each other for ever.

'And your parents, what did they say? They were a little surprised, isn't it?'

'Fortunately we were dressed by the time they got back. Mum fell for him at once. He could really put on the charm. Dad thought he was a class enemy. You see Rip was from a moneyed family, and I thought he might patronise my parents. But he was nice . . . respectful.'

She flicked her head impatiently. 'So tell me more about Ioff.'

'Well . . .' the memories tightened in my throat, 'you could say it's a tempestuous story of forbidden love between an almost-aristocrat and a humble girl from a mining village.'

She nodded. 'This is a good beginning.'

They'd been out to the Miners' Welfare in Castleford – a retirement do for a fellow pit-deputy. There'd been a sing-along and speeches, and then more beer was drunk. Dad was glassy-eyed and unusually talkative. Mum, who'd drawn the driving straw, was also not stone-cold sober.

Dad: (Mutters to Mum.) What the heck's our Georgie brought home?

Mum: (Whispers to me.) You've landed a good fish here, Georgie.

Me: (Embarrassed, to Rip.) Meet my parents, Jean and Dennis Shutworth.

Rip: (All charm and golden curls.) Rip Sinclair. Delighted to meet you.

Dad was wearing his best three-piece suit, the waistcoat all buttoned up. The only concession he ever made to slackness was a slightly loosened tie. Mum, on the other hand, had long since surrendered to the lure of the elasticated waist-band, but she'd made a special effort for the occasion, with a Cupid's bow of cerise lipstick and a dab of Je Reviens behind her ears.

Mum: (Taking extra care with her vowels.) Rip. That's an unusual name.

Rip: (A dimply self-deprecating grin.) It's short for

Euripides. My parents had great hopes for me. (His smile makes my heart jump about all over the place. I'm in love.)

Dad: (Whispers to me.) Not your type, Georgie.

Me: (Whispers to Dad.) You've got it wrong. He's not like that. He's on our side.

Dad: (Jaw tight. Silence.)

Mum: (Getting in quick.) Would you care to join us for some tea?

'And so he drank the tea?' Mrs Shapiro stifled a yawn. 'Mit your parents? This is quite normal in Germany.'

'No. In Yorkshire, tea also means dinner.'

Mum had pulled the giant-sized pack of oven chips out of the freezer, shook the contents into a Pyrex dish, and slipped a dozen pre-cooked BBQ-flavour Chicken Drumstix under the grill, heated up a tin of Jackson's own-brand mushroom soup in the microwave and poured it over the drumsticks. My heart shrank into its boots. 'Chicken chez-sewer,' she said, sprinkling them liberally with salt, in case Mr Jackson had been stingy in that regard. Rip made a great show of pleasure, chomping noisily and wiping his mouth on a torn-off square of paper towel. Mum was completely charmed.

We'd all squeezed round the bench and table in the kitchen. Rip was wedged between Dad and the corner. I was sitting on the other side with Mum.

Dad: (Still suspicious.) So what do you do for a living?

Rip: (A strange look of panic has come over him.) I'm training to be a . . . (he catches my eye) . . . Johnny . . .

Me: (What's going on? Why has he turned suddenly weird?)

Mum: (From the cooker. Awed.) That sounds interesting.

Rip: . . . a solicitor. (Dad is chomping a drumstick. Rip is gesturing to me behind the table – a hand movement that looks a bit like wanking.)

Me: (Proud.) He was defending the miners in court today, Dad.

Dad: (Determined not to be impressed.) You mean Jack Fairboys and Robbie Middon?

Rip: (Giving me a kick under the table.) Yes, Jack and Rob. Rub. Rub . . . ber.

Dad: (Gives him a funny look.) They got off, din't they?

Rip: (Shifty.) Absolutely. Scot free.

Dad: (Concentrating on the ketchup bottle.) Lads being lads. Should never have gone to court.

Rip: (More covert under-the-table wanking.) No case to answer. On the floor. By the fire. Justice was done.

Me: (A light dawns.) Excuse me, Mum . . .

I squeezed out past her and into the sitting room. There it was on the floor by the fire, glistening and slippery. I picked it up and tossed it into the embers. There was a brief sizzle and a smell of burning rubber. In the kitchen I could hear Mum saying, 'I like a man with a good appetite. Euridopeas! Well I never!'

I looked across to see whether Mrs Shapiro had got the joke, but her eyes were closed, and I realised she'd drifted off to sleep long ago.

When I got home, at about three o'clock, there was a message on the answering machine from Mrs Goodknee. Would I be so kind as to ring her – a tinny, middle-aged voice. I rang, and got another answering machine. I left a message. Then I made myself a cup of tea, and took it up to my room. I'd taken the six photographs out of my bag and spread them across the floor in front of the window like playing cards.

Now, crouching down beside them, I frowned as I tried to puzzle out the story I was sure was there.

First, the Shapiro family in which Artem was the toddler, taken in 1905. Then the wedding photograph – a different woman. Artem Shapiro must have been married to someone else before Naomi. The same couple, Artem and the mystery woman, were pictured in another photograph standing in front of a fountain. There was snow on the ground. He was wearing a cap pulled down low over his eyes and smoking a cigarette, grinning broadly at the camera. She was wearing a tight-waisted coat and a beret cocked rakishly to one side, looking up at him. There was something scrawled on the back: *Stockholm Drott* ... I couldn't make out the rest of the word.

There was a group photo, a man and four women wearing formal clothes seated around a piano. *Wechsler family, London 1940* it said on the back. I looked closely, but the faces were too small to be distinct. In another of the photographs I recognised Canaan House with the monkey puzzle tree, quite a bit smaller than now, in the background. Two women were standing in front of the porch. The taller of the two looked like the brown-eyed woman in the wedding photograph. The other, curly-haired and elfin small, I didn't recognise. I turned the picture over. On the back was written *Highbury 1948*. I looked more closely – although the facial features were indistinct, there was something familiar about the defiant feet-apart pose of the smaller woman. I remembered the slight boyish figure in the light of the street lamp, pulling things out of the skip. Naomi. So they'd been together in Canaan House, they'd known each other.

I recognised the taller woman in another photo; this time she was alone, standing in an arched stone doorway, wearing a flowery dress, her dark eyes squinting into the sun, smiling.

On the back was written *Lydda 1950*. That's a pretty name, I thought, for a pretty woman. But who was she?

Downstairs, the front door slammed; the house shook. Ben coming home from school at half past four. I heard the thud of his school bag in the hall, the slap of his parka on the floor, and the thump-thump of his footsteps on the stairs. A few minutes later, I heard the Windows welcome chimes. He hadn't even said hello. I felt something in my chest fall away and flap against my heart. Sweeping the photos together into a pile, I went down to the kitchen, made two cups of tea and carried them upstairs. I knocked on the door of his room but he didn't answer, so I pushed it open with my foot. Ben was sitting at his desk staring at the computer monitor. I caught a quick glimpse of the screen – a flash of red writing on a black background. A single word, picked out in flickering white flames, leapt out at me: *Armageddon*. Then with a click of the mouse the screen changed to a Microsoft sky.

'Ben . . .'

'What?'

'What's the matter, love?'

'Nothing.'

I reached out and ruffled his hair. He flinched under my touch and I withdrew my hand quickly.

'It's okay to feel upset, Ben. It's a hard time for all of us.'

'I don't feel upset.'

He was still staring silently at the screen, his hands clenched into fists, resting on the front of the keyboard as if waiting for me to go away. The blue light of the monitor caught the curve of his cheek and his upper lip, lightly shadowed with dark, soft down.

'Is it school? How's the new class?'

'Okay. Fine. Cool.'

The move from Leeds to London had been hard on Ben. He'd resented being plucked out of his group of friends, some of whom he'd known since pre-school playgroup, and having to fight his way into the unwelcoming circles of his North London comprehensive. He never brought any friends home, but a few times he'd come back from school later than usual, and muttered something about having been with someone called Spike. Spike – what kind of a name was that? Although I burned with curiosity, I knew better than to press for details.

'What would you like for tea, love?'

'Anything. Spaghetti.'

'Okay. About half an hour?'

'I'll come down, Mum. All right?' he said without looking up, in a voice that meant 'leave me alone'.

I went into the kitchen and poured myself a glass of Rioja, feeling my failure sink inside me like a stone. Failed wife. Failed mother. Friendless – for my old Leeds friends were Rip's friends, too. I tried ringing Stella in Durham, but she was out, and the resident rock band was in session. Mum had enough troubles of her own – I'd ring her when I was feeling better. I downed the Rioja in a couple of gulps, and poured another. Maybe I should get a cat – or seven or eight.

No, I'd just have to pull myself together and make new friends here in London. In fact I'd made one already. (The Rioja slipped down, warmly reassuring.) Sure, her food hygiene left something to be desired, but we were mates. And I had online work colleagues, too, whom I'd known for years but never met. I'd drop in at the *Adhesives* office in Southwark one day and say hello. I was particularly curious to meet Nathan, the boss. He had a soft, confiding voice when we spoke on the phone, as though he was sharing a secret, not just passing on technical information. I'd no idea what he looked like, but I imagined someone hunkily intelligent, with horn-rimmed glasses and a sexy white lab coat. Penny told me he was single, so I was in with a chance, and he lived with his elderly father, which seemed gentle and caring.

Penny was the admin manager; I'd never met her either, but she liked to gossip on the phone in her booming voice, filling me in about all the other people I'd never met: Sheila the office junior; Paul and Vic, who took care of the technical side and, alternately, of Sheila; Mardy Mari, the cleaner from hell; Lucy from design, who was a Jehovah's Witness and got up Mari's nose. Then there were the other freelancers like me, whose intimate lives she dispensed without inhibition.

Rip's new Progress Project colleagues were frighteningly high-powered. I'd met some of them at a Christmas party last year. He'd introduced me to a couple called Tarquin and Jacquetta (Mum would think they were a kind of food bug) and Pectoral Pete and his wife Ottoline. He was bulging pectorally out of a loud check jacket. She was like a china doll – dainty and expressionless, with a perfect bow-shaped scarlet mouth and a voice that tinkled like cut glass. Rip had spent most of the evening out in the corridor tapping at his BlackBerry.

I poured myself another Rioja. My cheeks began to glow pleasantly. I went and fetched my exercise book.

The Splattered Heart
Chapter 3

'Darling, I have to attend to some really important work on my BlackBerry,' ~~said~~ remarked Rick one evening.

'Of course, beloved,' Gina ~~said~~ murmured softly. (Vary your vocabulary, Mrs Featherstone used to say.) 'Your work is really important and must always take precedence over everything else.'

'How lucky I am to have such an understanding wife,' ~~said~~

he uttered, and kissed her on her cheek before disappearing.
(I know this is a bit unbelievable, but it is fiction.)

An hour later Gina was surprised to hear a ringing sound
suspiciously like Rick's BlackBerry coming from the study.
But Rick was nowhere to be seen.

Suddenly I felt the pressure of a warm hand on my shoulder.

'When's dinner ready?'

Quickly, I closed my exercise book and pushed the almost-empty wine bottle aside.

'Sorry, Ben. Just catching up on a bit of work.'

He frowned. 'You should go easy on that stuff, Mum.'

'What, this?' I giggled. 'It's only a little Rioja.' Was he worried that I would turn into an unfit mother? I caught the anxious look in his eyes, and pulled myself together. Maybe he had a point.

We cooked dinner together. Pasta with anchovies, broccoli and Parmesan – a recipe Mrs Sinclair had taught me. Dad once boasted that he had never eaten broccoli in his life, and never intended to. Mum said that anchovies – anchoovies she called them – made her breath smell. Parmesan they did eat – they sprinkled it out of a cardboard container straight on to tinned spaghetti hoops. Mum said it gave them a touch of distinction.

Ben slurped his spaghetti noisily, pulling a goofy face to make me laugh, like when he was a little boy pretending to eat worms. From the next room, we could hear the television booming, the chimes of the evening news. I wasn't really paying attention; I was still thinking about Rip – his BlackBerry obsession, my toothbrush-holder obsession. How had we let our happiness be ruined by such trivial things?

'Why do they do that?' Ben asked suddenly. His face clouded over and he seemed to hunch himself lower over his plate.

'What?'

'Suicide bombers – why do they blow themselves up?'

He was listening to an item on the news.

'It's because . . . when people are desperate . . . it's the way they draw attention . . .'

The warm glow from the Rioja had worn off and a gnawing headache was burrowing into my skull. 'It's when you want to hurt someone so much you don't care if you hurt yourself, too.' Desperate. I remembered the frothed milk splattered all over the kitchen.

'But why do *that*? It's gross.' Ben was still staring into his plate, twirling the remaining strands of spaghetti around his fork. Then he said, without looking up, 'It's like . . . There was this kid at school who cut his arms with a razor.'

'Oh, Ben. Why . . .?' I felt a rush of anxiety – I knew the cruelty kids could unleash on each other.

'Dunno. Like you said. Drawing attention.'

My heart lurched. A buried image from my own schooldays had pushed its way up into my mind. Kippax. It must have been about 1974. A girl cut her arms in the toilets.

'Ben, if you're feeling . . .'

'It's all right, Mum. I'm all right. Don't stress.'

He smiled fleetingly, loaded his plate into the dishwasher, and slouched off upstairs.

10

Polymerisation

Next morning I found myself nursing a headache from last night's Rioja, worrying about Ben, and wrestling with a chain of polymers. Polymerisation is the key to the chemistry of adhesion – it's when a single molecule suddenly grabs on to two other similar molecules on each side, to make a long chain. A bit like line dancing. Not what you feel like first thing in the morning. Then the phone rang. It was Mrs Goodknee, trying in her squeaky voice to get me to hand over the key so she could do her home assessment. I insisted we meet at Canaan House and look around it together. We arranged to meet at noon.

I wanted to give Mrs Shapiro the best chance I could, so I went over there about an hour earlier to prepare for her visit. I'd filled a plastic bucket with cleaning stuff, air-freshener spray, and a pair of rubber gloves, and set off at a brisk pace. Instead of the batty-woman outfit I was wearing a smart grey jacket which I hoped would make an appropriately serious impression. The hard wintry air made my centrally-heated lungs gasp with the shock of the cold at every breath, and the brightness of the light stung my hungover eyes, but I forced myself to look up at the sky. The clouds had cleared and a shaft of low sunlight gilded the upstairs windows of the terrace of houses along my road. My heart lifted. Winter sunshine – it seemed like a gift, a promise of warmer days to come. I started to hum, '*Here comes the sun . . . na na nah na . . .*'

There was another clump of bird feathers on the path at Canaan House – a pigeon, this time. I kicked them out of the way. The cats must have been waiting for me because the moment I approached the house they all appeared, clamouring around me, miaowing with their pink hungry mouths. I fed them outside, taking care not to let them sneak indoors.

Then I got to work on the kitchen. I took off my smart jacket, pulled on the rubber gloves and cleared the festering detritus out of the sink. I filled up a couple of bin bags with packaging (mostly labelled REDUCED), and the oozing contents of the disgusting fridge. To think that I'd eaten food stored in this fridge, prepared on this table, cooked in these pans – I was lucky to be alive. Maybe it wasn't the fish that had nearly killed me that night but some lethal bug endemic to this kitchen, to which Mrs Shapiro had long since become immune. In the bottom of the fridge I found three black, wizened human fingers. It took me a moment to realise they were carrots.

I poured bleach into the sink and swept the floor in the kitchen and hall, removing a pile of cat poo mouldering beside the telephone table. Still fifteen minutes to go before midday. I went upstairs to Mrs Shapiro's room, opened the windows, sprayed the air-freshener around and picked up the clothes on the floor and shook the bed covers out of the window. As an afterthought, I pushed the Harlech Castle tin further back on top of the wardrobe where it would be completely out of sight. I'd worked up a bit of a sweat with all the exertion, and my cheeks glowed self-righteously.

I was admiring my handiwork when I heard a woman's voice in the garden. I froze and listened. She must have been standing directly below the open window. It was an ugly, metallic voice, like a rusty gate, and she was talking loudly, the way people do into their mobile phones.

'I'm just going in to have a look around.' (A pause, while

she listened to the voice at the other end.) 'I'll let you know.' (Pause.) 'It's an old biddy who lives here. She'll be going into a home.' (Pause.) 'I don't know yet. I'll get a good valuation.' (Pause.) 'Hendrix.' (Pause.) 'Cash. Five grand.' (Pause.) 'Damian.' (Pause.) 'I'll find out. And I'll ask about the tree. I'd better go now.' (Pause.) 'Bye-ee!'

A few moments later, I saw her walking back up the path smoking a cigarette. I recognised her at once as the redhead who'd been in the garden the other day – that toxic-green jacket. Its quilted texture reminded me of lizard skin. She stopped by the gate – she was waiting for me, thinking I'd be coming up the road. I didn't want her to see me emerging from the house so I grabbed my jacket, let myself out of the kitchen door, locked it behind me, and looked for another way out. A mossy path led down through the long back garden to a derelict mews block at the back. Beside it was a gate. It was bolted, but I managed to force it open and found myself on another cobbled alley that must once have been an access to the mews, now overgrown with brambles that led back on to Totley Place. As I turned into the lane I could see Mrs Goodknee waiting for me at the gate, flicking through a file.

'Hi. I'm Georgie Sinclair. Sorry I'm late.'

She must have been in her mid-forties, about the same age as me, perhaps even a bit younger, but she had a stiff over-groomed style that made her seem middle-aged. I couldn't see her knees, but I doubted they were dimpled and chubby. She handed me a business card. Ah.

'Margaret Goodney. I'm a senior social worker at the hospital. Thank you for coming. Have you got the key?' Her Essex vowels squeezed themselves into a bland corporate dialect.

She followed me up the path. Fortunately the cats had gone

off to do their own catty things. Only pretty, friendly Violetta appeared, rubbing herself against our legs.

'Hello, kitty kitty,' Mrs Goodney squeaked. 'Who's a pretty kitty, then?'

She took a spiral-bound notebook out of her shoulder bag and turned to a new page. *Canaan House, Totley Place*, she wrote at the top. Then she underlined it twice.

'A bit of a jungle, isn't it? That tree needs to be cut down.'

'It's got a preservation order on it.'

She made a note.

Seeing Mrs Shapiro's house through Mrs Goodney's social worker eyes made me realise how pathetic my clear-up efforts had been. Her nose wrinkled the moment we walked in through the door.

'Poo! It's like the black hole of Calcutta in here.'

The air-freshener had worn off already. Her heels click-clicked on the loose tiles in the hall. Her eyes darted around. She made a note on every room we walked into. Her note on the dining room read: *Good proportions. Original fireplace.* Her note on the kitchen read: *Total refurbishment.* She saw me craning to see what she'd written, and flicked the page.

'A house this size is a liability,' she said, not unkindly. 'She'd be much happier in a nice care home.' She made another note. 'Mm. No food in fridge. That's a sure sign of self-neglect.'

'I cleared the fridge.'

'What did you do that for?'

'It was going mouldy.'

'That's what I mean. We have to do what's best for her, don't we, Mrs . . .?'

'Sinclair. Call me Georgie. Doesn't she have any say in the matter?'

'Oh, yes, of course we have to get her consent. That's where you could be very helpful, Mrs Sinclair.'

I felt a flush spreading up my cheeks. Was she going to offer me five grand? But she just smiled her toothy smile.

As we stepped into the bedroom, she quivered and put her hand to her nose. Mussorgsky had managed to get in there ahead of us and had taken up his position on the bed. He raised his head and yowled as we came in. Violetta had sneaked in with us and was lurking in the doorway, giving Mussorgsky the eye.

'These cats – they'll have to go.'

'They're her friends. She gets lonely.'

'Yes, companionship – that's another of the advantages of residential care.'

She made a note in her book.

On the floor by the bed were Mrs Shapiro's peach silk camiknickers, pretty but whiffy, which I'd overlooked in my whirlwind clean-up. She bent down and picked them up, held them for a moment between finger and thumb, then let them fall.

'She fancies herself, doesn't she?'

I saw her wipe her fingers discreetly on a tissue. I can't explain why, but it was that contemptuous finger-wiping gesture that really made me hate her.

The bathroom came as a shock to both of us. The smell was definitely human, not cat pee. The toilet bowl, originally white porcelain patterned with blue irises, was now brown-stained, cracked and encrusted. The stain had seeped in a damp acrid circle into the rotting floorboards, which had partly collapsed under the toilet bowl, making it lean at an alarming angle. Hanging loose from the wall was a basin in the same iris design, with green-yellow drip-trails beneath the taps. A large enamel claw-foot bath stood under the window, with an old-fashioned shower head above it. The grime circles inside the bath grew in layers, like trunk rings in an ancient tree.

'It'll all have to come out,' she murmured, jotting in her notebook. 'What a shame.'

Downstairs in the hall, she stretched out her hand to shake mine.

'Thank you very much, Mrs ... Georgie. I'll go and write my report.'

'You're going to put her into a home, aren't you?' I blurted.

'Of course my recommendation is entirely confidential.' She pursed her lips. 'But I think residential care could be an appropriate option. We have to do what's best for her, not what suits us, don't we, Georgie?'

'What do you mean – what suits us?'

'It can be hard for a carer to let go, when the time comes. They like to think they're doing it all for the other person, when really they're just being selfish, trying to hang on to their caring role even when they're no longer needed, because they want to feel valued.'

She smiled a bland professional smile. I felt like strangling her with her repulsive reptilian outfit and stuffing her nasty cube-heel shoes into her squeaky creaky gob.

'So you think I'm just a selfish bitch with a cat-poo fetish?'

She glanced at me sharply, decided I must be joking, and her lips twitched in a thin smile.

'We wouldn't want to be held responsible if she had another accident, would we?'

She turned and click-clicked down the path.

As soon as I got home, I took out the card Mrs Goodney had given me, phoned the number, and asked for Damian Hendrix. There was a long pause.

'This is the hospital social work department,' a woman's voice told me. 'Are you sure you don't want the local authority Social Services?'

I looked up the local authority number in the phone book and tried again.

'Could I speak to Mr Damian Hendrix?'

'I'm sorry, we don't have anyone by that name here. What was it about?'

'It's about an old lady going into a home.'

'Hold on, I'll put you through to elderly.'

The line crackled.

'Elder-lee!' a cheerful voice chimed in my ear.

'I'm looking for Mr Damian Hendrix.'

'Mm-mm. No Hendrixes here. Are you sure you've got the right name?'

'I'm sure about the Damian. Have you got any Damians?'

'Mm-mm . . .' I heard the voice call to someone else in the room, 'Eileen, 'ave we got any Damians?'

'Only 'im in't store,' said Eileen.

'Only one who works in the resource centre,' said the cheery voice.

'No, it must be someone else. Thanks.'

I put the phone down.

Eileen – that voice – she must be from Yorkshire. I felt a little stab of homesickness, remembering how I'd felt when we moved down from Leeds to London, after Rip was offered the job on the Progress Project. We'd hovered for weeks like lost souls in the limbo of estate agent offices, looking for a place that might one day feel like home. We'd been dismayed at London prices, and at how poky the houses were – at least, the ones we could afford. The squat Edwardian semi we finally bought had seemed brighter than most. It had been all done out for a quick sale by the builder, painted in neutral shades to compliment (sic) the stunning period features, with laminate floors (authentic-oak-style), a granite worktop (Uba Tuba) and fitted well-known-brand kitchen appliances. It smelled of newness and fresh plaster. It had no character at all. I'd liked it at the time – it had seemed like a fresh canvas on to which we'd paint our new life. But that's not how it worked out. Maybe things had been going wrong for ages and, like damp seeping into a basement, I just hadn't noticed the warning signs.

Later that afternoon, as I was walking down the local parade of a dozen or so shops, I remembered the other reason we'd chosen our house. This little neighbourhood had seemed an intimate island of friendliness in the vast anonymous bustle of London. There was the Turkish bakery, strangely famous for its Danish pastries; the Song Bee, our favourite takeaway, recently opened by two young women specialising in Chinese and Malaysian cuisine; Peppe's Italian delicatessen; Acne Al, as Ben called the newsagent by the bus stop; and two estate agents, a local branch of Wolfe & Diabello on the corner where I was standing, and across the road Hendricks & Wilson.

Then it dawned on me. Hendricks! Should I barge in and make a scene? Instead, on impulse, I pushed open the door of Wolfe & Diabello. If Mrs Goodney was going to get her little Damian to do a valuation on Canaan House, at least I could get one, too, for comparison.

A small bosomy girl with sleek blonde hair and careful eyes was sitting at a desk by the window. Her name badge said Suzi Brentwood.

'My aunt's thinking of selling her house. Could you give us a preliminary valuation?'

'Of course.' She flashed her little pearly teeth at me. 'I'll make an appointment with one of the partners. Is next Friday all right? We're a bit busy. What's the address?'

Her eyebrows rose a fraction when I told her.

Black treacle

By the time Friday came round it was raining again, a miserable December drizzle that stained the streets and rooftops melancholia grey. I was starting to regret my appointment with the estate agent, and I thought of ringing up to cancel, but something about Canaan House had pricked my imagination. As Ms Firestorm would say, I was *inexorably drawn.*

I left home in a rush without an umbrella, and the hood of my duffel coat kept slipping back as I ran, so I arrived breathless and thoroughly bedraggled. As I turned the corner into Totley Place I saw a black sports car, a low-slung mean-looking machine, skulking with predatory menace on the road outside Canaan House. Skulking like a Wolfe, though I soon saw it was in fact a Jaguar. When I came close the driver's door opened, and a long lean form uncurled itself on to the pavement. Tall, dark, handsome. I stopped and caught my breath. There was something oddly familiar about him.

'Mrs Sinclair?'

I nodded. He raised a quizzical eyebrow and proffered his hand, which was warm and firm. My heart flipped like a hooked fish. I became aware of a pleasant sensation in my pelvic area.

'You must be Mr Wolfe,' I said, trying to shake the rain out of my wet-sheep hair.

'No, I'm Mark Diabello.' His smile made rugged creases in his craggily handsome cheeks. The cleft in his square, manly chin dimpled seductively. His dark and smouldering eyes seemed to gaze right into my soul – or perhaps right into my underwear. I noticed the pleasant pelvic glow once more. 'It means beautiful day, I've been told.'

His voice was like black treacle – sweet, with a hard mineral edge.

'Not like today then.' I batted my wet eyelashes. What was happening to me? This man was an estate agent, and definitely not my type. 'Er . . . unusual name. Italian?'

I was regretting that I'd worn my batty-woman clothes.

'Spanish. My father was an itinerant mandolin player.'

'Really?' He was still smiling, and I couldn't tell from his face whether he was joking, but the idea was, mmm, appealing. 'I've got the key,' I mumbled. 'Do you want to look around?'

The cheeks crinkled into a smile. The eyes smouldered. I gazed into them. My poor fish-heart tugged feebly at the line, but it was caught.

Wonder Boy, Violetta and their mates had congregated at the front door. I let them in and fed them in the kitchen because it was too wet outside. It was bitterly cold indoors, a dank pungent chill which hit you with the stink of stale cat food mingled with other odours which were quite a lot worse. Then I became aware of another, more pleasant smell, faint and spicy like expensive soap. That was *him*. Inexorably drawn, I followed along as he wandered around the house, murmuring to himself under his breath. He had a little instrument like a torch with a laser beam that bounced enticingly against the walls of the rooms, to measure the size. I watched, transfixed. Click. Flash. If I asked nicely, would he let me have a go with it? He wrote the details on the back of what looked like a crumpled till receipt.

He seemed completely unfazed by the smell. Even when he

stepped in a pile of fresh cat poo in the hall (how did that get there?) he just bent down and cleaned it off with an immaculate white cotton handkerchief from his breast pocket. I watched, awestruck, as he deposited it in the kitchen bin.

'I could live in a place like this,' he murmured huskily in his deep manly mineral-edged voice that spoke directly to my hormones, bypassing my brain completely. I realised now where we'd met before – in the pages of *The Splattered Heart*. He was just as I'd imagined the hero. Except that in my book the hero was a poet, not an estate agent.

'Character. That's what you so rarely get in the housing market nowadays.'

We were standing together in the entrance porch at the end of his tour. The rain had stopped and the weak wintry sun was putting in a brief appearance, so it was warmer out here than indoors, and much less smelly.

'Ornate plasterwork; period arches; decorative corbels. I mean, don't get me wrong, Mrs Sinclair, there's a lot needs doing. You'd have to do it sensitively, of course. Keep all those stunning period features. Get a couple of designers in to give you ideas. You could open up the attic, for instance. Make a fabulous penthouse suite.' A flame flickered in the depths of his eyes.

'Everybody seems to fall for this house.'

'It's the potential. You can see the potential. You'd have to cut that tree down, for starters.'

'It's got a preservation order on it.'

'Doesn't matter. You just pay the fine. The tree gets cut; the Council gets its cut. Everybody's smiling.'

I hadn't much liked the tree myself, but now it suddenly felt like an old friend.

'You can't do that!'

'So when's your aunty planning to put it on the market?'

'She just wanted an idea of its value, in case she decides to sell. What do you think?'

He looked at the notes he'd scribbled on the receipt, crinkling his eyes and furrowing his handsome brow in a way that was faintly reminiscent of Aristotle. Well okay, only very faintly.

'Half a million, maybe?'

I don't know exactly what I'd been expecting, but our own semi with its three poky bedrooms and narrow strip of garden had cost almost that. He saw the look on my face.

'The area brings it down. And we're looking at a cash buyer, of course, not a mortgage. I'll put it in writing for you.'

I gave him my address. We shook hands. He climbed into his hungry-looking car, and was gone in two puffs of hot air from the chunky twin exhausts.

I walked back slowly, still feeling slightly giddy from my encounter. As I came up the street, I could see that Ben was already home, the blue square of his monitor winking away through the window as he tried to navigate the lonely cyber-seas, teeming with who knows what pirates and sharks. My mother-heart tightened with a little squeeze of sadness: it wasn't good for him to spend his evenings up there on his own.

'Hey, Ben, shall we go to the pictures tonight? We could go and see Daniel Craig as James Bond.'

Sean Connery, Roger Moore, Pierce Brosnan. While my mother-heart ached for Ben, my woman-hormones were still tingling for Mark Diabello.

'Sounds like crap.'

'It probably is crap, but it might be entertaining.'

'I don't find crap entertaining, Mum? But we can go if you want to?' I noticed there was something different about his voice – a new rising inflection at the end of his sentences – questioning, or apologetic. I wondered whether he was like this when he stayed with Rip. Somehow I imagined that life in Islington would be an endless round of stimulating activities and highbrow conversations, and it was only with me that he spent his hours closeted with his computer. I would have rung Rip to ask him if we'd been on better terms, but we weren't, and I didn't.

Instead of going out, we ordered dinner from the Song Bee and ate it by the gas fire in front of the TV. It was a cop drama, I can't remember what. I'd just been thinking that the male lead looked a bit like Mr Diabello when suddenly Ben turned to me.

'Mum, do you believe in Jesus?'

His question hit me out of the blue. I drew a slow breath.

'I don't know. I'm not sure what I believe, Ben.' What was this all about? I wondered. 'I believe Jesus was a real person, if that's what you mean.'

'No, what I mean is, Mum, do you believe Jesus'll save you at the end of the world?'

'Ben, love, the world isn't going to end.'

I had a sudden memory of how I'd been at his age – I believed that nuclear war would wipe out the human race before I'd even had a chance to lose my virginity. We'd sat around on Saturdays in the Kardomah café in Leeds, my mates and I, fantasising about how we would spend our last four minutes after the final warning.

'It's like . . . I really love you, Mum. You and Dad. I don't want . . .' He was mumbling, as though his mouth was full of sand. 'All you have to do is accept Jesus into your life?' His eyes, when he looked up at me, were wide, the pupils dilated, as if fixed on some private nightmare.

'The signs are there, Mum? All the signs are in place?' That strange questioning inflection – it was as though someone else, an alien, had got inside him, and was speaking through his mouth, staring at me through his eyes.

'The world's been around for a long time, Ben. Don't worry.'

I pulled him into my arms and hugged him tight. He stiffened against me at first, but I held him close until I felt him relax, his head resting on my shoulder. Whatever it is, I thought, he'll grow out of it.

Next day I overcame my pride and phoned Rip.

'I'm worried about Ben. Can we talk?'

'I'm just in the middle of something. Can I ring you back in half an hour?'

But he didn't.

Ben didn't go round to Rip's until late on Saturday. He spent the day upstairs on his computer, and I spent the day working on *The Splattered Heart*. Outside, the rain lashed at the garden, and the wind made a spooky whistling noise through the ill-fitting secondary glazing, but inside we had the central heating on and Snow Patrol keeping up a soft background rumble. Each time I walked into Ben's room, he minimised the screen he was looking at. We took turns to bring one another cups of tea, and treated ourselves to Danish pastries from the Turkish bakery and dim sum for lunch from the Song Bee. I needed the extra sustenance; now we were getting down to the nitty-gritty: *The Splattered Heart, Chapter 4*.

It was hard to decide whether Rick should be a lust-crazed sex fiend or a minutely endowed, impotent Viagra case. I crossed out a whole page, and started to think about Rip. No, it wasn't sex that had gone wrong between us, but whatever had gone wrong had taken the shine out of the sex, too. Keep the romance in your marriage, Mum's magazines used to say, and they advised strategies like wearing sexy underwear, and greeting your hubby in your negligee when he got back from work. Actually, I tried that once, but he didn't notice.

He called round at six to pick Ben up in his Saab convertible and they went straight off to the cinema – they were going to see Daniel Craig as James Bond. After they'd gone, that horrible silence settled on the house, like a coffin lid closing.

12

Marine biological glues

It wasn't until Monday morning that I remembered I hadn't fed Mrs Shapiro's cats. I heard a familiar yowling sound in the garden, and when I looked out of the upstairs window, there was Wonder Boy lurking under the laurel bush. He was looking up at the window with a reproachful look on his face. All around him was a mass of grey and brown feathers, sodden in the rain. Seeing him here in my garden made me furious – I didn't want him killing my birds; in fact I didn't want him at all. I pulled on my brown duffel coat and my wellies and strode off round to Totley Place. He followed me, slinking along at a distance, ducking into a gateway or garden if I stopped and looked back. Then I noticed that the Stinker was following me, too; and another scrawny tabby. I was turning into the Queen of the Cats. The other cats were waiting for me in the porch when I arrived, a purry, enthusiastic reception committee. None of them looked particularly wet.

There were three weird things I noticed on that visit. The first was a pile of fresh cat poo, almost in the same place where Mr Diabello had stepped in it the other day. It had a distinctive curled macaroon shape, unlike all the other brown shrivelled-sausage deposits that I found around the house from time to time. I was sure that I'd got all the cats out of the house when we left. Who was the culprit – and how had he got in? I cleared it up and counted them as they milled around my legs – one, two, three, four, five, six, seven. When I left, I'd make sure to count them out.

As I straightened up, my eye fell on a picture on the wall directly above where the cat poo had been. It was a photograph, rather grainy and washed-out, of an arched stone doorway with a cross on top, Corinthian columns on each side, and above the door a carving of a man on horseback with a spear. Something about it was familiar. I must have looked at it dozens of times without really seeing it. What I saw now was that it was the same arched doorway as in one of the Harlech Castle tin photographs, the one with the dark-eyed woman: Lydda. The columns and the harshness of the light made me think of Greece.

The third thing I noticed, when I went through to the kitchen to feed the cats, was that the key to the back door, which should have been inside in the lock, was missing. Someone had taken it. I realised in a flash that it could only have been wicked, wolfy Mr Diabello.

I fed the cats quickly and rushed home in a rage, but just as I picked up the phone to vent my fury at Wolfe & Diabello, it rang in my hand. It was Penny, the admin manager from *Adhesives*, wanting to know whether I'd received the press release about the new research into marine biological glues. The truth was, it had come two days ago, and I hadn't even looked at it. I mumbled something vague and apologetic, but she saw right through me.

'What's going on, Georgie?' she boomed. 'Something's not right, darling, I can tell. Is it that husband of yours again?'

'No. It's another devious man.'

I explained about the missing key and the dodgy estate agent.

'Hm.' I could hear Penny breathing on the other end of

the phone. Nothing about her was quiet. 'Don't rush into any-thing, darling. You could be wrong about the key, then you've blown your chances with that sexy man.'

How did she know he was sexy? Was I that obvious?

'You should get a second opinion, darling. Two second opinions. One about the price of the house, and one about the social worker.'

The same thing had happened to her Aunty Floss, she said, who'd been put in a home by the Council and died six months later of unspecified complications.

'God bless. I'm sure she's up there in heaven, tippling sherry and looking down and cursing those bloody scumbags who got her house.'

'Do they allow tippling and cursing in heaven?' I giggled.

'Well, if they don't, darling, I'm not going there.'

The thought of all that tippling and cursing cheered me up, and I promised Penny I'd get on with the marine biological glues – yes, straightaway – but first I'd take her advice and try to get another social worker assessment.

Mrs Goodney, I knew, worked at the hospital, not the Council, so next day I telephoned the Council's social services department again. I explained to the cheery 'Elder-lee!' voice that an elderly neighbour had gone into hospital and needed an assessment before she could go home.

'Mm-mm. Can you hold the line a minute? (Eileen, what's 'er what does 'ome visits?)'

Eileen's voice, muffled by distance, said something that sounded like 'Bad Eel'.

'She's out on 'er coffee break,' I heard her say.

'You need to speak to Muz Bad Eel. I'm afraid she's in a meeting. Can I take your number and ask her to call you back?'

Bad Eel. I pictured someone slim and slippery, with scarlet lipstick and a small silver gun tucked inside a frilly garter.

I spent the whole morning at my desk, looking out of the window at the wind chasing stray leaves around the dank patch of lawn, and waiting for the Bad Eel to phone me back. I was supposed to be working on the press release Penny had sent about marine biological glues. Some company was developing a synthetic version of the glue that bivalves such as mussels and oysters use when they cling to the rocks. One of the strongest bonds in nature, apparently. They use fine thread-like tentacles called byssus, which are rich in phenolic hydroxyls. Phenolic hydroxyls: something about those words just turned my brain to glue.

I started thinking about bivalves living down there in the dappled light, how they filter the algae from the water, how they close themselves up against the sea. It must be wonderful to be a bivalve, to be able to shut yourself away in your own mother-of-pearl-lined world, hanging on to the rock while the waves and tides churn outside. Ms Firestorm showed up to help me out. *Cloistered in their shimmering watery depths, the loyal bivalves cling passionately together* ... Yes, we could learn a lot from bivalves. I realised I wasn't very interested in commercial applications, and when the other elusive marine creature still hadn't called by lunchtime, I wrapped up warm against the wind and set out for the hospital.

Mrs Shapiro was sitting in the day room when I arrived, wearing a pinafore-style hospital dressing gown tied at the back and a pair of woolly socks on her feet. I felt a pang of guilt. Probably it was my responsibility, as her next of kin, to bring in some suitable hospital gear for her. I'd have to remember for next time.

A tattered magazine was open on her knee, but she wasn't reading; she seemed to be engaged in a fractious and incoherent argument with another old lady sitting beside her.

'But 'er were on this ward when she shouldn't of been,' the old lady was saying vehemently, 'and new sister said it weren't 'er business anyway.'

'Well, if they was no longer there someone must heff tooken them.'

'No, because she weren't supposed to be. That's what I'm sayin' to yer.'

She looked up and saw me in the doorway.

'That's 'er there. Ask 'er.'

Mrs Shapiro turned, and stretched out her hands to me.

'Georgine, you got to get me out of here. All this people is mad.'

'She's talkin' tripe,' said the old lady, and heaving herself up out of the chair she minced off along the ward, muttering aloud.

'What's going on?' I asked.

'She is a bonker,' said Mrs Shapiro. 'Brain been amputated.'

The old lady stopped, turned, flicked two fingers at us, and carried on.

'How are you doing, Mrs Shapiro?' I pulled up a chair beside her. 'I thought you'd be going home by now.'

'I am not going nowhere,' said Mrs Shapiro. 'They say I must go into the oldie-house. I tell them I am not going nowhere.' She folded her arms determinedly across the front of the green dressing gown. The argument with the old lady was obviously just a warm-up for a much bigger argument to come.

There was a new sister on duty, a young girl who looked hardly older than Ben.

'What's happened with the home assessment?' I asked.

'The report's just come through. They're recommending residential care. I'm afraid she's not very happy about it.'

'I really don't see why she needs residential care. She was managing fine.'

'Yes, but you know, once they start falling, they can very easily lose their confidence. Especially at her age.'

She brushed a stray hair off her face and looked over her shoulder towards the nurses' station. I could see there were a dozen things she needed to be doing more urgently than talking to me.

'What if she refuses to go?'

'We can't discharge her into an unsafe situation.'

'So she just stays here?'

'She can't stay here. She's blocking an emergency bed that someone else could use.'

'So what are the options?'

'Look, I think you'd better talk to Mrs Goodney. The social work office is over by physio.'

I went back to sit with Mrs Shapiro. 'It's okay,' I said. 'I'll get them to do another assessment.'

'Thenk you, darlink,' she said, gripping my hands. 'Thenk you very much. And my dear cats, how are they?'

'They're fine. But Wonder Boy seems to be killing a lot of birds.'

'Ach, poor darlink, he is upset. You must bring him here. Next time. You promise, Georgine?'

I mumbled something evasive, but just then the tea lady appeared with the trolley.

'You heff no kräutertee?' said Mrs Shapiro grumpily. 'Okay, I tek this horse's piss. No milk. Three sugar.'

Cradling her cup in her hands, she settled back on the pillows.

'Now, Georgine, your running-away husband. You heffn't finished telling me.'

'I did tell you. It was so boring you fell asleep.'

She caught my eye and gave a little laugh.

'You told me about your parents. That was quite boring, isn't it? But what about the husband? He was a good man? You were happy in loff?'

'We were happy at first. But then ... I don't know ... He got absorbed in his work. I had babies. Two – a girl and a boy.'

And a miscarriage in between. Then I started writing a book.

After the miscarriage I'd given up my job and started freelancing. Rip had taken his articles but found the solicitor's work tedious and applied for a job in the northern office of a national charity. He was keen and committed, out and about all over the place, so one of us had to be home-based. The freelancing didn't fit easily around children so, inspired by my earlier introduction to Mum's preferred reading matter, I decided to try my hand at romantic fiction. I got a couple of short stories published in a women's magazine and after that encouraging start I plugged away at a romantic novel – it was about a plucky young heroine who is inexorably drawn to a grand but gloomy house inhabited by a handsome, moody, extremely rich poet (I know, but it *is* fiction) who falls in love with her but alas dies of a mysterious ailment on the eve of their wedding, which is terribly tragic, but then she falls in love with the local schoolteacher who lives in a cute rose-covered cottage and is penniless but has a good sense of humour and is great in bed.

I thought I'd got the genre spot-on, and it grieved me that no one wanted to publish it. I tried changing the font, changing the ink colour, I changed my nom de plume, but the rejection slips just kept coming.

'*Splettered Heart*. This is a good title for a book, Georgine. Povverful.'

'Thank you. Rip thought it was too melodramatic.'

'Ach! He is a man. What does he know?'

'He thought I should call it *The Shattered Heart* or *The Broken Heart*, but I thought that was a bit clichéd.'

'Exactly so. And it has been published?'

'No. Not yet.'

'But you must not give it up.'

'I'm completely rewriting it. A new version. But it's hard to find the time. I've got another job now, writing for online trade magazines.'

'Lane tred? What is this?'

'It's a group – *Adhesives in the Modern World*, *Ceramics in the Modern World*, *Prefabrication in the Modern World*, things like that. I work on all of them, but mainly *Adhesives*. I've been doing it for about nine years.'

'But this is fascinating!'

'Well, it's just for the building trade. It's not exactly world shattering.'

'Too much shattering is going on nowadays, Georgine. Building is much better.'

Nathan had conducted a cursory interview over the telephone, during the course of which he'd asked me, among other things, what my favourite pudding was (Bakewell), whether I'd ever been to Prague (no), and which team I supported (Kippax Killers, of course), and told me after five minutes that I was just the person he was looking for.

'Glue,' he'd said. 'Don't worry, it'll grow on you.'

Romantic it wasn't, but it paid the bills, and it meant I could be at home for the kids. Strangely enough, it did grow on me.

'So that's my story so far. Not very exciting, really.'

'Well, we will heff to see if we can make you a happy ending.' She raised her teacup. 'To happy endings!'

On my way home from the hospital, I dropped in at Canaan House to feed the cats and do a quick tidy-up in case the Bad Eel should deign to visit. The wind was still blustering, swirling up dead leaves and litter on the pavement. Wrapping my coat tight around me, I turned into Totley Place. At once I saw there was something unusual there – something brightly coloured at the entrance to the cobbled lane that led up to Canaan House. As I drew closer my heart began to beat with rage and trepidation. Yes, it really was what I'd suspected, half hidden there among the creepers – a large green-and-orange For Sale sign, with the name written in bold black letters: Wolfe & Diabello.

It was stuck into the ground beside the wall. I grabbed the post and heaved. It held firm, so I pushed and pulled it backwards and forwards, to loosen it up. Then I got round behind it, scrambling through a climbing dog rose that clung to the wall. Surely Mr Diabello hadn't done this, the thorns picking at his Italian-styled suit? It must have been some strong-arm minion in a white van, hammering the post into the ground with a mallet. I'd worked myself up into a frenzy, but still it wouldn't budge. If anyone had seen me, they'd have thought I'd gone mad. I grabbed the post in both hands, arched my back and bent my knees for one last heave. It slid out of the ground as smoothly as a knife out of butter. I slid with it, staggered, lost my balance, and fell back-wards into the rose bush. A thorn jagged my cheek. Wonder Boy appeared yowling out of the undergrowth. It started to rain.

★

I'd been all fired up to storm into the Wolfe & Diabello office and demand an explanation, but I called in at home to pick up my raincoat, and the phone was ringing as I opened the door. It was Rip.

'Hi, Georgie, I just wanted to have a quick word about Christmas.'

I steeled myself. 'Fire ahead.'

'I wondered if you'd made any plans?'

'Not really. Why? Have you?' I felt a quiver of dread – Christmas: the time when families are supposed to be together. Would I be able to survive a Christmas on my own?

'I was wondering about going up to Holtham with Ben and Stella . . .'

'Fine.' Actually I felt like drowning myself in a tub of lukewarm piss, but I managed to put on a brave show of nonchalance. 'Do that. Fine by me.'

'What about you?'

'I haven't really thought about it.'

After he'd put the phone down, I went up to my bedroom, flung myself down on the bed, and let the tears flood into my eyes. I sobbed and sobbed until my chest ached and my shoulders heaved and my nose ran with snot – I sobbed for my broken marriage and my broken family, all the hurts and humiliations I'd ever endured in life, my ailing parents, my absent brother, my too-far-away daughter, the general sorrows of humankind, starving babies in Africa, kids who self-mutilate, suicide bombers and their victims, they all came washing saltily in on the same vast relentless indivisible tide of human misery. I thought about the bivalves, the curved pearly walls inside their shells, the greenish light filtered through seawater; whatever the extraordinary glue was that enabled them to hold so tight while the storms swirled around them, that's what I needed now.

13

No job too small

By next day, the fight had gone out of me a bit, but I decided to walk across to Wolfe & Diabello anyway. I needed to clear my head, and I still had a couple of bones to pick with them. It was another raw, blustery December day, the sky teeming with grey scurrying clouds. I pulled my hood up, and put my head down into the wind, and maybe that's why I didn't see it until I almost stumbled over it – a post lying across the pavement. Attached to the post was a For Sale sign. Not Wolfe & Diabello, but Hendricks & Wilson. That was odd – it had been windy in the night, but not *that* windy. Even odder – as I turned the corner, there was another one, stuck into a hedge, a few hundred metres up the road. Then further along, I spotted another lying in a skip.

There was no one in the Wolfe & Diabello office when I went in. I opened and closed the door again, making it 'ping', but still nothing happened. The third time I did it, Suzi Brentwood emerged from a door at the back; I thought I spotted a shifty look flit across her face before her professional smile composed itself.

'Hello, Mrs . . . How may I help you?'

'My aunty is thinking of selling her house before Christmas,' I said very loudly.

As if by magic, the door at the back of the office opened, and Mr Diabello appeared.

He was wearing the same dark stylish suit, a clean freshly

folded handkerchief peeping out of the breast pocket.

'Hello, Mrs Sinclair. What can we do for you?'

'The For Sale sign in the garden at Canaan House – you put it there?'

He smiled, that irresistible cheek-creasing smile.

'We have to keep one step ahead of the competition.'

'What do you mean?'

'We heard on the grapevine that Hendricks had sent a valuer in.'

It must have been Damian, I thought. But how did he get in?

'No harm in that, Mrs Sinclair. It's a free market. Shop around. See who can offer you the best deal. But, you know, I felt after our chat the other day that you deserve a – how can I put it? – a more focused view of the service we offer here at Wolfe & Diabello.' His eyes smouldered with dark fire. His quizzical eyebrows quizzed.

Ms Firestorm popped up briefly to take a look, and she was well impressed. 'Deserve. Focused. Service.' She repeated the words slowly in her head. They sounded deeply sexy. But they still didn't make sense.

'You mean you just marched up and stuck a For Sale sign in someone's front garden without their permission?'

'It's a bit cut-throat around here,' he murmured apologetically. 'Hendricks & Wilson – I don't like to say this about another estate agent, but they aren't the most reputable in the business. Underhand tactics. Stealing our customers. You'll never believe this, but sometimes they even go round and pull our sale boards out. What valuation did he give you, by the way?'

I looked him in the eye.

'He said she should be able to get a million for her house. At least a million. Maybe more.'

He didn't bat an eyelid.

'I'm sure we could match that for you, Mrs Sinclair. And we could agree a special rate on the commission.' His handsome nostrils flared tantalisingly. A hint of a smile played at the corners of his sensual mouth. 'If your aunty decides to sell before Christmas.'

I could have swooned into his rugged manly arms at that point, but then I remembered my second issue.

'The key. You stole the key.'

'Pardon me?'

'The back-door key. To the kitchen. It was in the door.'

His eyes seemed to widen a fraction.

'I think you've made a mistake.'

'No, I haven't. You took it. It must have been you.'

His brooding brow furrowed.

'Mrs Sinclair, it wasn't me, I assure you. Have you considered the other possibility?'

'What other possibility?'

His mouth tightened. His head twitched.

'Them.' His head twitched again, a sort of reflex jerk to the left. 'Hendricks.'

'It couldn't have been them.'

Then I thought back. I was in the kitchen feeding the cats. Mr Diabello was wandering around scribbling on the back of his receipt. I was feeding the cats in the kitchen because it was raining. I didn't open the back door. Was it locked? Was the key in the lock? I couldn't remember. When was the last time I was sure I'd seen the key? Was it when I was showing Mrs Goodney around? I realised I was totally confused.

'I'll look into it.' Maybe I'd misjudged him after all. 'If I've made a mistake I apologise,' I said stiffly.

Anyway, all I need to do, I thought to myself, is change the lock. Where do you get a new lock? My mind went blank.

Then I remembered a commercial I'd seen on TV. B&Q. For some reason, the thought was pleasantly appealing. The nearest branch to me was in Tottenham.

It wasn't till next day, as I made my way in through the sliding glass doors past the displays of Christmas baubles and end-of-line kitchen units, that I realised what it was that drew me to B&Q: it was the men. Yes, although Rip was both handsome and brainy, he was definitely deficient in the DIY department. There's something deeply attractive about a man with a screwdriver in his hand, I was thinking. If you wanted to be Freudian about it, you could say it was a father-fixation, for Dad was always fixing things about the house, while Mum brought him cups of tea and Keir and I got under his feet. These B&Q types reminded me of the men in Kippax – not destiny-shaping men; not even craggily handsome splatter-your-heart-type men; but nice ordinary blokes wearing jeans and pullovers with comfortable shoes, their pockets bulging with tape measures and hand-drawn diagrams on bits of paper; sometimes a bit paunchy; even a tattoo here and there. Who cares? So long as they weren't always dashing off somewhere to change the world. Maybe if I hung around, one of them would come along to measure me up, would compliment my tasteful decor, be stunned by my period features.

I should come here more often, I resolved, as I made my way through the mysterious aisles. There, on my left, was a whole section of rawplugs. I glanced at them quickly – they seemed alien, frightening things, with their poky plastic shells, their complicated colours and numbers – the sheer *rawness* of them. But the worst thing is, that you have to make the hole in the wall with an electric drill, then you have to hammer the right-sized rawplug into the right-sized hole, and you can't just use any old screw – you have to know the right size and type. I held my breath and hurried past.

At last I found my way to the section that displayed locks – there were dozens of them. I picked up one or two at random, trying to remember what the one on Mrs Shapiro's door had looked like. It was definitely not a Yale type of lock; it was the other type – the type with a big key. Yes, a mortise. The trouble was, there were so many different models and sizes.

A man was browsing among the hinges and doorknobs at the end of the aisle – a small tubby Asian man. I caught his eye and smiled a sweet damsel-in-distress smile. He came over at once.

'You need help?'

His eyes sparkled darkly. With his neat moustache and beard, he looked like a well-groomed hamster.

'I'm looking for a lock. Mortise. With a big key. Only I've lost the key.'

'You know what type? Union? Chupp?'

I shook my head.

'You don't know this? You must know. Otherwise impossible to replace it.'

'It's for a back door.'

'What it looks like? Can you describe?'

'I can't remember exactly. I think it's a bit like this one. Or that one.'

I pointed randomly.

'In my country we have a saying, knowledge is the key. But you have no knowledge and no key.' He sighed, fished in his trouser pocket, and handed me a small dog-eared business card – the sort you can get printed at the railway station.

HANDIMAN
Mr Al Ali
Telefon 07711 733106
No job too small

14

Reindeer meat and dried fish

The phone was ringing when I got home. I could hear it through the door as I fumbled with my key, but by the time I picked it up, they'd rung off. There was a message on the answering machine.

'Hello Mrs Sinclair. This is Cindy Bad Eel from Social Services, returning your call.'

I rang back immediately, but I just got another answering machine. I left a message asking her to ring as soon as she got back.

Next day, she still hadn't rung, so I tried Social Services again.

'Elder-lee!'

'Could I speak to Mrs Bad Eel please.'

'It's Muz. Not Missis.'

'Well, can I speak to her anyway?'

'Hold on a minute.'

('Eileen, where's Muz Bad Eel?' 'She's just 'ere. 'Old on. Who is it?')

'May I ask who's speaking please?'

'It's Georgie Sinclair. I rang about the old lady going into a home.'

('It's that woman about t' old woman.' 'She says she'll ring back in a minute.')

'She's just in a meeting. She'll ring you as soon as she gets out.'

'No – please tell her it's urgent. I need to speak to her now.'

There was a lot of muttering and crackling in the background, then a new voice came on the line – a low, smooth, sultry voice with a slight drawl in the vowels.

'Hello-o. This is Cindy Bad Eel.'

'Oh, hello Mrs Bad Eel. Ms. I really need your help – I mean, a friend of mine needs your help.' I was gabbling, fearful that she would hang up. 'Mrs Naomi Shapiro. She's in hospital. She broke her wrist. Now they won't let her go home. They want to put her in a home.'

'Slo-ow down, please. Who am I speaking to?'

'My name is Georgie Sinclair. I left a message for you.'

'So you did, Ms Sinclair. Slow down. Take a deep breath. Now, count one, two, three, four. Hold. Breathe out. One, two, three, four. Rela-ax! That's better. Now – would you describe yourself as her carer – an informal carer?'

'Yes – yes, a carer. Informal. That's definitely what I am.'

Waves of calm engulfed me. I suddenly felt very caring.

'How old is the lady?'

I hesitated. 'I don't know exactly. She's quite elderly, but she was getting along fine.'

'But you say she had an accident?'

'The accident was in the street, not in her house. She slipped on the ice. It could have happened to anyone.'

'And you say she had a home circumstances assessment visit?'

'It was someone from the hospital. Mrs Goodney. The house was a bit untidy, but it wasn't *that* bad.'

There was a long silence. I started to anticipate her response, her stock of excuses for doing nothing. Her phone-answering track record had not been impressive. Then she spoke again, slowly.

'It isn't for us to judge another person's lifestyle choices. I will visit the house, but I need her permission. Which hospital is she in?'

As soon as I'd put the phone down, I ran into my bedroom and stuffed a few things into a carrier bag – Stella's old dressing gown, a spare pair of slippers, a hairbrush, a nightie – and set off for the hospital. I wanted to forewarn Mrs Shapiro, and make sure she said the right things. I didn't want her to blow this chance on another bout of cussedness.

The rain had stopped, but there were still puddles in the road as I raced to the bus stop, and big damp clouds were hanging just above the rooftops like billowing grey washing. I was the only person on the top deck of the Number 4 bus as it lurched and swayed along the now-familiar roads, brushing against the dripping trees, so close to the houses I could see right into people's bedrooms. I recalled my lonely afternoons wandering the streets peering enviously into other people's lives. What had all that been about? It seemed an age ago. Now Mrs Shapiro and Canaan House were keeping me so fully occupied I hardly had time to think of anything else.

In the bus shelter outside the entrance to the hospital there was the usual little knot of people huddled over their cigarettes. I'd passed them before without really noticing, but this time, a voice called out to me.

'Hey! Georgine!'

I had to look twice before I recognised Mrs Shapiro. She was enveloped in a pink candlewick dressing gown several sizes too big for her, and so long that it trailed on the ground. Below it, just peeping out in front, was a pair of outsize slippers – the sort that children wear, with animal faces on the front. I think they were *Lion Kings*. Ben once had a similar pair. Her companion was the bonker lady with whom she'd been arguing last time. Now they seemed to be getting on like a house on fire. They were sharing a cigarette, passing it between them, taking deep drags.

'Mrs Shapiro – I didn't recognise you. That's a nice dressing gown.'

'Belongs to old woman next to me. Dead, isn't it?' She grabbed the cigarette from the bonker lady, who'd had more than her fair share of puffs. 'Cigarettes was in the pocket.'

'Nice slippers, too.'

'Nurse give them to me.'

'She give me these,' said the bonker lady, lifting up the hem of her dressing gown to show off a pair of fluffy powder-blue wedgie-heeled mules. Her toes were protruding out of the ends, with the most horrible thick crusty yellow toenails I'd ever seen.

'Them should heff been for me,' said Mrs Shapiro sulkily.

We left the bonker lady to finish the cigarette and made our way back to the ward, where I handed over my carrier bag of things; she took only the hairbrush, and gave the rest back to me.

'I have better night cloth-es in my house. Real silk. Not like this shmata. You will bring one for me, next time, Georgine? And Wonder Boy. Why you didn't bring the Wonder Boy?'

'I don't think they'd let him in. He's not very . . .'

'They heff too many idiotic prejudices. But you are not prejudiced, are you, my Georgine?' she wheedled. 'You are so clever mit everything. I am sure you will find a way.'

'Well, of course, I'll try my best,' I lied.

The ward was busy with visitors, so I pulled two chairs up by the window in the day room. It was a square featureless room near the entrance to the ward, with green upholstered chairs dotted randomly around, a TV fixed too high on the wall, and a window that looked out on to a yard. It smelled of disinfectant and unhappiness.

'Mrs Shapiro, I've asked for another assessment from Social Services. Someone's going to come and visit you. She's called Ms Bad Eel.'

'This is good. Bed Eel is a good Jewish name.'

This surprised me, but what did I know? We didn't have any Jewish people in Kippax.

'Tell her I've got the key and I'll meet her there to show her around. She has my phone number but I'll write it down for you again.' I wrote my number on a scrap of paper, and she stuffed it into the pocket of the candlewick dressing gown. 'If anyone says anything to you about going into a residential home, just tell them you're having another assessment. That should keep them quiet.'

She leaned across and clasped my hand.

'Georgine, my darlink. How can I thenk you?'

'There is one problem. She's certain to ask how old you are.'

She looked at me – a clear, canny look. She knew I knew she wasn't ninety-six.

'What I should say?'

'Mrs Shapiro, I'll help you if I can. But you have to tell me the truth.'

She hesitated, then leaned up and whispered close to my ear, 'I am only eighty-one.'

I didn't say anything. I waited. After a moment she added, 'I told them I am more older.'

'Why did you tell them that?'

'Why? I don't know why.' She shook her head with a stubborn little flick. 'I heff never met anybody asking so much questions, Georgine.'

'I'm sorry – it's because I come from Yorkshire. Everybody's nosy up there.'

I tried to recall the picture of the two women in front of

the house. *Highbury 1948.* I did a quick calculation. She would have been about twenty-three when it was taken.

'So do you know your date of birth?' I probed. 'She's bound to ask you that.'

'Eight October nineteen hundert twenty-five.' A quick, precise answer. But was it the truth?

I wanted to question her more, but I didn't want to confess that I'd already searched beyond the bureau in the study and that I'd found the photos in the Harlech Castle tin hidden in the workshop. I had questions to ask about Lydda. Who was she? When did Artem marry her? What had happened to her? And I was aching to know who'd hidden the tin, and from whom.

We were the only ones in the day room, but the TV was blaring away in the corner. I looked for a remote control to turn the volume down, but I couldn't find it, so I switched it off and settled myself into an armchair in listening mode.

'You didn't finish telling me about Artem.'

'You heffn't told me about your running-away husband. Why he was running away?'

'It's your turn, Mrs Shapiro. I'll tell you my story next time.'

'Ach, so.' She laughed. 'Where heff I gotten to?'

'The pony ...'

'Yes, the pony that was trotting on the ice. But you see it was not a pony, it was a reindeer. The reindeer people took him away mit them.'

The Sámi men who had hitched up Artem's sleigh were from Lapland. Part traders and part bandits, they made forays down across the ice to exchange smoked fish, reindeer meat and furs for wheat or tobacco or vodka or whatever they could find. When they discovered him under the wolfskins, they debated whether to kill him; but as he opened his eyes, he smiled to find himself still alive, and started to sing a Russian peasant song.

'Ochi chornye, ochi strastnye ...' Mrs Shapiro's voice quavered. 'It is a beautiful song about the loff for a woman mit black and passionate eyes. He used to sing it often.'

The song saved his life. The faint croaky voice of the wounded soldier made the men laugh, so they took him with them to their settlement in a vast snowy wilderness beyond the Arctic Circle, where the white horizon merged into the long pale sky. He was treated first as a prisoner, then as a curiosity, and finally as a great source of entertainment.

He stayed with them for several months living on a bed of skins in the corner of a fishy, smoky, snow-covered hut, eating reindeer meat and drinking some horrible herbal concoction which they also poured on to his wound. When he had drunk a few cupfuls, he would start to sing – Jewish songs from his childhood in Orsha, partisan songs from the time in the woods, Russian folk songs, even a few arias. The men slapped their thighs and threw their heads back with laughter. The women giggled and retreated into their furs, watching him curiously with their strange cat-like eyes. At night he studied the mysterious coloured lights playing across the sky and tried to work out his position from the stars. When he was fully recovered, and smudgy light broke into the sky on the southern horizon for a few hours each day, the Sámi people offered to take him back to Russia. He explained with gestures that he wanted to go the other way, towards Sweden. So they took him to a place where he could see the next Sámi settlement over the Swedish border, gave him a small sleigh and a bag of dried fish, and sent him on his way.

'He was looking for his sister. But she was already gone. Maybe she never was there. In that time Sweden was full of

Jews who were running away from the Nazis. Everybody was looking for somebody or passing on the news of somebody.'

'So when did you meet him? Did you go to Sweden, Mrs Shapiro?'

She started to say something, then stopped. A sad-looking lady attached to a drip tube had just walked into the day room, trailing her bag of fluid behind her. We watched her for a few moments in silence, then Mrs Shapiro whispered, 'That is enough for today. Now is your turn, Georgine. This your husband – why he was running away? There was another woman?'

The drip lady was searching for the TV remote control. I hesitated. I didn't want to go into details about the rawplugs and the toothbrush holder, but I found myself saying, 'I don't think so. He said there was no one else. He was too obsessed with his work.'

Mrs Shapiro was looking at me quizzically. She obviously preferred the 'other woman' hypothesis.

'Why you think this?'

'He was always full of big ideas. He wanted to change the world. I think he was just bored with domesticity.'

There, I'd said it. Even putting it into words made me feel better. Mrs Shapiro wrinkled her nose.

'Ach, so. This is a typical story. He wants to change the world but he doesn't want to change the neppies, isn't it?'

'Sort of. The children were already out of nappies.' I wanted to explain that it was the same roving, inquisitive spirit that had brought him to me in the first place. 'When we met, I was different to the other people he knew. He used to call me his rambling Yorkshire rose.'

'Don't worry, my Georgine.' She grinned merrily. 'When I am mended we will go rembling again.'

The drip lady had slumped into an armchair and was

gazing mournfully at the fluid in her drip bag, which looked like watered-down tea. Mrs Shapiro threw her a contemptuous look.

'Too many krankies in here.' She sniffed. 'So this husband – when he is finished mit the rembling, you think he is coming back?'

'I don't think so. I threw all his stuff in the skip.'

'Bravo!' She clapped her hands. 'So what he said then?'

'He said . . .' (I put on a hoity-toity voice.) '. . . why are you being so childish, Georgie?'

She rocked back in her chair and shrieked with laughter.

'This running-away husband is quite a schmuck, isn't it?'

It was such a jolly, raucous laugh that I found myself laughing, too. Our laughter must have carried right down the ward, for a few minutes later the bonker lady came waltzing in to see what was going on, dancing around and lifting up the hem of her dressing gown to flaunt her new slippers. She winked at me, pulled a cigarette out of the pocket, and waved it under Mrs Shapiro's nose.

'Look what one of the porters give me. Mind, I 'ad to drop my knickers down for 'im in the lift. I says if yer give me the packet you can 'ave yer wicked way wiv me. 'E says no thanks, missis, I've seen better on the mortuary trolley.'

Mrs Shapiro let out another shriek, and that set the bonker lady off, cackling and waltzing around and flashing her appalling toenails, and that made me laugh some more, and even the sad drip lady managed a dribbly chuckle. We were all clutching our sides, screeching and hooting like a flock of mad geese, when the ward sister came along and ticked us off. On the bus on the way home I felt a strangely pleasant aching sensation in my chest. I realised I hadn't laughed as much as this since . . . since Rip had left.

15

The Bad Eel

The Bad Eel phoned me back a couple of days later. We made an appointment to meet at the house. As before, I went an hour earlier, with some cleaning things. The Phantom Pooer had been at work again; there were two fresh macaroon-shaped deposits in the hallway. I cleared them away and did a quick round with a duster and a brush, paying special attention to the bedroom and bathroom, though the latter was really a lost cause. I did what I could and sprayed the air-freshener around liberally. Although the weather was dry, I couldn't feed the cats by the back door because I didn't have the key, so I fed them in the kitchen, and counted them again. There were only five. Wonder Boy was in there, right at the front, batting the Stinker out of the way. Borodin crept in, his belly low to the ground, snatched his food and disappeared. One of the pram babies, I noticed, had a weepy eye. Mussorgsky and Violetta were missing. Violetta appeared at the front door a few moments later, her pretty tail swaying as she walked, and behind her was a person who could only have been the Bad Eel.

The first disappointment was that she didn't look at all like an eel. In fact she was uninhibitedly exuberantly plump, with curves that bulged in soft roly-poly layers beneath a tight stretchy blancmange-pink outfit which revealed each elastic-line of her startlingly skimpy underwear. She held her hand out to me. Each finger was like a meaty little chipolata sausage.

'Hello, Mrs Sinclair. I'm Cindy Baddiel.'

She stressed the second syllable. That was the next disappointment. She wasn't a *bad* eel at all. Her honey-gold hair fell in loose curls from two large butterfly clips above her ears. Her eyes were the colour of angelica; her skin was like peaches; she smelled of vanilla. Despite my disappointment, there was something very edible about her.

I must have been staring rudely. Violetta broke the silence between us with a chatty miaow. We both bent to stroke her at the same time, our heads touched together, and we laughed, and after that, everything was easy. She strolled around the house. ('Lo-ovely. Pe-erfect.') She greeted the Stinker like an old flame. ('Well, hello-o, boy.') She did flinch for a moment in the bathroom, but her only comment was, 'There's no accounting for cultural diversity.'

'One thing surprises me,' she remarked, as we were walking back down the stairs. 'She doesn't seem to be getting support from the Jewish community. Usually they're good at looking after their elderly.'

The same thought had once occurred to me, but I understood now that Mrs Shapiro was, like myself, someone who'd come unstuck.

'I suppose it's her personal choice.' She'd taken a little notebook out of her bag – it had a picture of a floppy-eared Labrador puppy sitting on a cushion – and a biro with a very chewed end, and was writing something down.

At the end, when we were standing in the hall, I asked her the question that had been pressing at the back of my mind since my meeting with Mrs Goodney.

'What would happen to her house, if she had to go into a home?'

'Oh, I don't think it'll come to that.'

'But if it did, would the Council take it from her?'

'Oh no, we don't do that! Where did you get that idea?' She shook her golden curls. 'If someone goes into a care home, we assess their financial situation. If they have assets of more than twenty-one thousand pounds, then they have to pay the full cost of their care.' She was still scribbling in her notebook as she talked. Her voice was so soothing that I found it hard to concentrate on what she was saying. 'Below that, the Council picks up the bill. It can be quite expensive – four or five hundred pounds a week – so we try to maintain people's independence in their own home. It's usually what they prefer, too – familiar surroundings – chosen lifestyle.' She gave me a peachy smile.

'Twenty-one thousand pounds? That's not much, is it? So would their house – this house for example – would that be classed as an asset?'

'If no one else is living there, and the person is in a home, it could be sold to cover the home fees.' She was still making notes, pausing ruminatively, looking around her and chewing on the end of her biro.

'But what if the person didn't want to sell?'

'Don't worry.' She took my hand and squeezed it between her little chipolatas. 'I can see no reason for her to go into residential care at this stage. I'm going to recommend a means-tested care package that'll support her continuing to live at home.'

I held back my impulse to say I was sure she didn't need a care package. There was something about her that made me want to take a big juicy bite, but I hugged her instead. It was irresistible, really, that soft pink bolster of flesh. Probably she was used to it, because she just stood there and smiled.

'You're very demonstrative, Mrs Sinclair,' was all she said.

Mrs Shapiro, on the other hand, was disappointed in Ms Baddiel.

'Not Jewish. Too fet.'

She shook her head with a grumpy face.

I'd rushed around to the hospital immediately to tell her the good news, and we were sitting in the day room again, in front of the window. The bonker lady kept wandering in and out, making smoking gestures at me, trying to catch my eye, but I ignored her.

'She said you can have a care package in your own home.'

'Vat is this peckedge? Vat is in it?'

She wrinkled up her nose, as though she could smell it already.

'Well, maybe a home help, to help you keep the place clean. Someone to help with your shopping and cooking.'

'I don't want it. These people are all teefs.'

I tried to persuade her, worried she'd lose her chance to get back home through her own stubbornness, but she looked at me with a little smile.

'You are a clever-knödel, Georgine. But I heff another news for you. I heff hed a visitor.'

She produced a card from the pocket of the candlewick dressing gown, a garish orange-and-green card, with a bold black inscription across the top in mock-Gothic letters: *Wolfe & Diabello*. Beneath, in smaller letters, a name: *Mr Nick Wolfe*.

'Quite a charming man, by the way. He has made me an offer to buy up my house.'

I gasped. My breath was really taken away. These people, they don't miss a trick.

'Mr Wolfe! How much did he offer you?'

She turned the card over. On the back, written in blue biro, was the figure: £2 million.

'Very nice-looking man, by the way. Would be a good husband for you, Georgine.'

I felt suddenly out of my depth. The social workers, the nurses, I could handle them; but men who flashed around those amounts of money scared the pants off me.

'It's a lot of money. What did you say?'

'I said I will think about it.'

She caught my eye and smiled impishly.

'What for I need two millions? I am too old. I already heff all what I need.'

The nurse – it was the brisk young woman I'd met on my first visit – was happy with the care package, and a date was set for Mrs Shapiro to return home. I promised I'd be there to meet her, and would drop in regularly until she was settled. There was one more thing I needed to sort out before she came home. I didn't want Damian or Mr Diabello – whichever one of them had the key – barging into the house while she was there on her own. I must get that Asian handyman to change the back-door lock. I rang the number on the card and made an appointment with him for the next day.

16

The handyman

Mr Ali arrived on a bicycle. I'd been expecting a man in a van, so I didn't notice him at first, wobbling quietly up the lane. He was smaller and tubbier than I recalled, and he was wearing a pink-and-mauve striped woolly hat pulled right down over his ears, which was sensible, because the morning was cold. It was hard to tell how old he was; his face looked young, but his beard and moustache were heavily flecked with grey. He didn't look at all like a handyman – for one thing he didn't seem to have any tools.

He jumped off his bike, removed the cycle clips from his ankles, straightened out his trouser bottoms – they were grey flannel, with neat creases down the fronts – and greeted me with a polite nod of the head. I noticed now that there was a small leather bag – it could have been a woman's handbag – on a long strap slung across his chest, with the head of a hammer poking out at one side.

'I have come to fixitup lock,' he announced.

He pushed his bicycle up the path, and propped it in the porch at the front door.

'Jews live here?'

There was something sharp in his voice that took me aback.

'Yes. How did you know?'

'Mezuzah.' He pointed out something that looked like a small tin roll pinned on to the door frame. It had been painted over, and I hadn't noticed it before.

'Strange thing for me,' he muttered. 'Never mind. Here in London is no broblem.'

He took his pink-and-mauve cap off – I saw now that his black hair was also threaded through with grey – and stuck it in his pocket, along with the cycle clips.

'You Jewish?'

I shook my head. 'Yorkshire. It's almost a religion.'

He gave me a funny look – I don't think he realised it was a joke. His dark eyes darted around, taking in the details.

'Every house speaks its history to one who knows how to listen.'

So, not your typical handyman, I thought.

'Where you have this broblem lock?'

There was something cutely hamster-like, I thought, about the way he sometimes confused his 'p's and 'b's, though I have no evidence that hamsters actually do this.

I led him through to the kitchen. The back door was heavy pine, painted to look like walnut, with two panels of blue engraved glass.

'For this one you have lost the key?'

'That's right.'

'Hm.' He stroked his beard. 'Locked up.'

'Yes – that's why I called you.'

'Hm. Only way to open must be with force. You want me to do this?'

'I ... I don't know. I thought maybe you could unscrew something.'

'This type of lock sits inside door frame, not screwed on outside.'

'Oh, I see.' Actually, now he pointed it out, it was totally obvious.

'But usually,' he said, stroking his beard again, 'usually

there exists more than one key for every door.' He turned the door handle up and down. 'You do not have another key? You have lost it, too?' He sounded reproachful, as though I'd been unreasonably careless.

'It's not my house. I'm just feeding the cats while the owner's in hospital.'

'The key that proves the ownership of the house.'

I was beginning to feel annoyed. I wanted a handyman, not a philosopher.

'I think it's been stolen. Really, if you can't help, Mr Ali, I don't want to waste any more of your time.'

'Certainly I can help. But better not to break down the door if we can open it by some other way. You have looked for another key?'

'Where should I look?'

I was thinking that a lad in a van might have been easier to deal with. He looked at me as though I was completely stupid.

'How can I know this? I am a handyman, not a detecteef.'

He scanned the room with his hamster eyes, then he started opening cupboard doors and pulling out drawers, rifling through the mouldy tea towels and crusty cutlery.

In the built-in pine cupboard at the side of the chimney breast was a jumble of crockery, pots, tins, jars, bowls, vases, candlesticks, and other stuff which could loosely be described as bric-a-brac. Mr Ali stood up on a chair and went through it all methodically, working from the top down, taking each item from the shelf, shaking it, and replacing it. Inside an ornate silver coffee pot on the middle shelf, he found a bundle of obsolete ten-shilling notes and a bunch of keys.

'Try.' He passed them to me. One of the keys fitted the back door.

'So now your broblem is fixit,' he beamed.

'Yes, thank you very much, Mr Ali.' I resisted a sudden urge to stroke his little hamster head. 'But I'd still like you to change the lock, if you can, so the person who took the other key can't use it.'

He rubbed his chin. 'I understand. In that case I must buy new lock.'

He replaced his cycle clips and wobbled off down the road.

As soon as he was out of sight, I took the opportunity to continue my investigation of the house. I wasn't sure what I was looking for, but I was driven by the conviction that there must be a stash of documents or letters somewhere that would provide the key to Mrs Shapiro's story, and the identity of the mystery woman with beautiful eyes. However, apart from Mrs Shapiro's bedroom, all the upstairs rooms were sparsely furnished, with nowhere much to hide anything, and I began to feel disheartened.

From an upstairs window, I watched the cold shadows sidle into the garden. A few cats were still prowling around; I caught sight of Wonder Boy in the bushes beside the mews block and Violetta sitting on the roof of a ruined outhouse. The bedroom I was in had a bleak institutional feel, compared with the stinky decadence of Mrs Shapiro's room. Mrs Sinclair's old burgundy-coloured curtains, which I'd put in the skip, had been spread as bedcovers on the two single beds. I checked the drawers, but they were empty, and there was nothing under the mattresses. I drew a blank. When I looked out of the window again, some minutes later, Wonder Boy was up on the outhouse roof, too; he appeared to be raping Violetta. I banged on the window and he slunk away.

Mr Ali was gone for ages, maybe an hour, and I was getting fed up of hanging around in the dank empty smelly house. Next time I need a handyman, I was thinking, I'll get someone out of Yellow Pages. I returned to Mrs Shapiro's bedroom and sat on the edge of the bed, staring at the garden path through the mirror, wishing he would hurry up. And that's when my eye fell on another drawer in the dressing table, a low, curved, concealed drawer without a handle, beneath the mirror. I hadn't noticed it before, and I realised it had been designed not to be noticed. I eased it open. It was full of jumbled jewellery – necklaces, earrings, brooches. A lot of it seemed rather grotty and broken, but there were one or two pieces that looked as though they might be valuable. Was it wise for her to keep it here in the house? As I lifted out a blue bead necklace I saw there was a photograph underneath the jewellery at the bottom of the drawer. I pulled it out to add to my collection, but it was only a landscape in black and white of a not very appealing hillside, barren and rocky, planted with terraces of shrubby trees. In the valley below was a scattering of flat rooftops. It looked like Greece. I turned it over. On the back was written *Kefar Daniyyel* and two lines of verse.

> *I send my love across the sea*
> *And pray that you will come to me*
>
> *Naomi*

Another name: Daniyyel. How did he come into the story? Had Naomi had a secret lover? There was a long person-shaped shadow in the foreground – it must be the photographer standing with his back to the sun. So who had taken the photo?

Then I heard the tink-tink of a bicycle bell outside, and a moment later Mr Ali reappeared.

'Very sorry for delay. I was looking everywhere for right size of the lock. Old-style lock not easy to find.'

It took him less than ten minutes to lever out the old lock and fit the new one. I took one of the new keys and put it back on the key ring in the coffee pot; the other I put in my pocket with a smile. In my imagination, I pictured Mrs Goodney and Damian tiptoeing round to the back of the house at dusk, fiddling and fiddling with the old key, trying to get it to fit. In the end they gave up and stomped away, tripping on brambles and ending up covered in cat poo. Serve them right.

I settled up with Mr Ali – he asked for ten pounds, plus the cost of the lock, but I persuaded him to take twenty – and thanked him profusely.

'Always better,' he said, packing his tools back into his shoulder bag, 'first to try the non-violent solution.'

17

The care package

It was quite late next evening – it must have been after ten
o'clock – when the telephone rang.

'Is that Mrs Sinclair?'

A grating voice, familiar, but I couldn't place it.

'Speaking.'

'This is Margaret Goodney from the social work department at the hospital.'

Surely she wasn't still at work.

'Oh, hello, Mrs Goodney. Is everything all right?'

I smirked to myself. Maybe she and Damian had already
tried their key and failed to get in.

'I think you know what I'm ringing about.'

'No. I don't know. Please tell me.'

In my mind's eye I could picture her at the other end of
the telephone, smoking a cigarette, wearing her lizard-green
quilted jacket, covered in cat poo.

'I know what you're up to.'

'Excuse me?'

'That ridiculous care package you and Mrs Whatsit've
cobbled together. You should keep your nose out of this.
Leave it to the professionals.'

'Ms Baddiel is a professional.'

'She's not a professional.' An ugly nasal sneer. 'She's a box-
ticker. Those local authority social workers don't know what
real social work is.'

Before I could muster a reply, she struck again.

'You won't get away with it, you know. If I have to, I'll call the police in.'

I was completely thrown.

'I'm sorry, I have no idea what you're talking about.'

'You persuaded her to name you as next of kin, didn't you? We've seen it all before, you know – someone befriends a vulnerable old person, then the next thing we know, they've altered the will and the new friend gets the lot.'

My adrenaline was up. I could feel my heart starting to race.

'Nobody has altered any will.'

'But that's what you're after, isn't it – the house?' she hissed.

I suppose I should have put the phone down, but I was too shocked.

'I'm not after anything.'

'Being all friendly, going round and cleaning up, feeding the cats.'

'It's called being a good neighbour. Looking out for the vulnerable in our society. Wouldn't you do the same?'

'Nobody does all that without expecting something in return.' Her malevolent rusty-gate voice made me wince. 'You're not family. In fact you hardly seem to know her. And all of a sudden you go barging into her life, taking over her affairs.'

'You're accusing me of . . .'

'I'm not accusing you of anything, Mrs Sinclair. I'm just saying that if you were to be found to be applying undue pressure or benefiting in an improper way from this relationship, then it would be a matter for the police.'

It took a moment for the sheer audacity of it to sink in.

'*I'm* the one who should be reporting *you*. You and Damian.

I know your little plan. Then you have the nerve to ring me up in the middle of the night and accuse me . . .'

'I'm not accusing you, Mrs Sinclair. Get this straight, will you? I'm just advising you of the consequences that could follow from certain actions.'

She put the phone down. In the silence that followed, I could hear the clock ticking, and the faint ker-chunga-chunga coming from Ben's room. I realised my hands were shaking.

Despite the veiled threat in Mrs Goodney's phone call, Mrs Shapiro was discharged before the end of the week and returned home by taxi to an ecstatic welcome from Violetta, a languid welcome from Mussorgsky, and a dead pigeon from Wonder Boy. The other four were all there too, rubbing against her legs, rolling on their backs and purring like trail bikes.

I'd cleaned up the mess in the hall, put a fan heater on to take the chill off the place, brought some shopping in, and put a vase of flowers on the hall table. I'd also replaced the key in the lock, so she'd be able to use the back door. She looked in good shape, and excited to be back. She took off her astrakhan coat and emptied out a carrier bag which contained the pink candlewick dressing gown and one high-heeled shoe. The other was lost. She was still wearing the *Lion King* slippers on her feet.

I made a pot of coffee and some sardines on toast – probably not a good idea I soon realised – and we sat at the table in the kitchen. The cats circled around, attracted by the smell of the sardines, and I wiped some bread in the oil and put it down for them. They gobbled it up in a flash, and carried on circling. Wonder Boy leapt up on to Mrs Shapiro's lap, and started kneading her thighs vigorously with his big bruiser paws; from time to time, he reached one out and snatched a piece of sardine-on-toast from her plate. Violetta sat on my knee, purring sweetly when I stroked her.

'You heff been a very good friend for me, Georgine. Without you I'm sure they would heff put me away into the oldie-house.'

We clinked our cups together.

'To friendship.'

But something still niggled at the back of my mind. Each time I looked at her I found myself wondering about the other woman in the photo, Lydda.

'Don't you have a family, Mrs Shapiro? Any sisters? Or brothers? Anyone who could look after you?'

'Why for I need someone to look after me? All was okay before this accident.'

'Any grown-up children? Or even cousins?' I persisted.

'I am not need nobody. I am okay.' She bit fiercely into a piece of toast.

'But even if you're all right now, you're not getting any younger and . . .'

'I think I will sue the Council.'

'. . . of course I'm happy to help, but . . .'

'They should be tekking care better of the pavements. They think we elect them only for giving our money away to immigrants? I am paying rets on this house sixty year. I think they must pay me a compensation.'

'Well, before we get on to that . . .'

'Yes, I will sue for the compensation. I will go to Citizen Advice this afternoon.'

'I don't think you should go out anywhere just yet, Mrs Shapiro. Wait till you're a bit better. And the lady is coming this afternoon, from the Council. Remember? Your care package?'

'Peckedge schmeckedge.'

'But I think you should . . .'

'I don't want no peckedge. Definitely no peckedge.'

Mrs Shapiro's care package was a thin dour Estonian woman called Elvina with blackheads and an economics degree. She did make some impact on the chaos in the kitchen, and the house looked generally cleaner but, as if in response, the Phantom Pooer redoubled his efforts, and now as often as not there were two little macaroon-shaped deposits each day, one in the hall, and one in the kitchen just behind the door. Elvina shouted at the cats in Estonian, and went for them with the broom. Mrs Shapiro called her a Nazi collaborator and sent her packing a week before Christmas, claiming she had stolen a silver coffee pot and some cat biscuits.

18
Sherry

A couple of days before Christmas, I set off for Canaan House to deliver my Christmas present – a little basket of scented soap and body lotion that I thought Mrs Shapiro would like. A nippy wind flicked my hair against my cheeks and made my batty-woman coat flap against my legs. There were no leaves left on the trees, but tattered shreds of plastic bags fluttered from the branches like pennants, and bits of wind-driven litter skittered along the street in front of me.

As I turned the corner, I saw a massive four-by-four, black with darkened windows, tractor-sized tyres, and doubtless a global-warming-sized engine, parked at the bottom of the lane. It looked vaguely familiar, but I couldn't place it. I quickened my step. Violetta was waiting for me in the porch, her fur fluffed out against the cold. I rang the bell.

There was a long silence, then footsteps, then Mrs Shapiro appeared at the door. She was wearing full make-up and a rather stylish striped jersey, with brown slacks, and a different pair of high-heeled shoes – these were snakeskin, with peep-toes and slingbacks, a couple of sizes too large. Her left wrist was still strapped, and in the other hand she was holding a cigarette.

'Georgine! My darlink!' She grabbed me in her arms, the cigarette waving dangerously close to my hair. 'Come in! Come in! I heff a visitor!'

I followed her through the chilly hall – yes, there was a little deposit in the usual place – to the kitchen, where the fan heater was on at full blast and a kettle was steaming away on the gas stove. There was the usual smell of cat piss and decay, and, above it, a new smell, musky and potent, of perfumed aftershave. A man was sitting at the kitchen table. He was turned away from me, but even from his back I could see he was a big man, broad, with close-cut blond hair, and muscles that pushed against the seams of his clothes. He rose to his feet and turned to greet me as I came in. He rose and rose – he must have been well over six feet tall, and heavily built, like a slightly-gone-to-seed rugby player – and then our eyes met. A flash of mutual recognition passed between us and in that moment we made an unspoken pact to forget that we had ever met before.

'Nicky,' said Mrs Shapiro, fluttering her derelict eyelashes at him, 'this is my dear friend Georgine.' She turned to me. 'This is my new friend Mr Nicky Wolfe.' She obviously didn't recognise him at all.

'Pleased to make your acquaintance.'

He gripped my hand – his palm was moist and meaty – and pumped it up and down.

'Hello, Mr Wolfe.'

I don't automatically think of sex when I meet a man, but I did with him; I thought it would be quick, painful and humiliating. I would be Violetta to his Wonder Boy. There was that look in his eyes.

'Call me Nick, please.'

'Hello, Nick. You must be from the estate agents.'

'Got it in one. How did you guess?'

'Mrs ...' I usually addressed her formally, but I had to impress on him that we were close. '... Naomi showed me your card. She said you'd made an offer for her house.'

'An offer I hope she won't be able to refuse.' He leered at her.

'Georgine, darlink. Will you heff a drink?'

Mrs Shapiro's cheeks were flushed beneath the two little circles of rouge.

'A cup of tea would be nice.'

The kettle was still hissing away, filling the kitchen with steam. Then I saw that on the table, amidst all the clutter, were a sherry bottle and two glasses, his full, hers empty.

'I heff only kräutertee. From herbs.'

'That's fine.'

'Why not heff a little aperitif?'

'It's a bit early for me, Naomi.' I loaded my voice with reproach. 'It's not yet ten o'clock.'

'Is it so early?' She looked around with wide scandalised eyes, and giggled. 'You are a very notty man, Mister Nick.'

He chuckled, a rapist's chuckle. 'Never too early for a bit of fun.'

I turned the gas off and poured the boiling water from the kettle over a tattered tea bag in a cracked and stained porcelain cup. It tasted like not-very-clean pond water. Actually, I could have murdered a glass of sherry.

'Happy Christmas – I mean, festive season – Naomi.' I passed her my little package.

'Thenk you, darlink.' She held it up to her nose and breathed in, closing her eyes with pleasure. 'But I must find something for you!'

Her eyes wandered around the kitchen, resting for a moment on a REDUCED packet of biscuits on the counter, a squashed box of Maltesers, a half-eaten packaged cake.

'Oh, no. Please. You're too kind; I don't need anything. What will you be doing for . . . for the festive season, Naomi? Will you be all right on your own?'

'Darlink, I will not be on my own. First Christmas we will celebrate, then Hanukkah. Turkey breast and latkes. Pick and mix non-stop festivity, isn't it, Wonder Boy?'

But Wonder Boy was nowhere to be seen.

'I'd better be going. I'll leave you two ladies to your fun.' Nick Wolfe towered over both of us. 'I've still got three valuations before I can knock off. An estate agent's work is never done.'

'Please, Nicky, you heffn't finish your drink.' Mrs Shapiro had gone all fluttery again.

He picked up the full glass and downed it in one go. I could see that with his body mass, it wouldn't make the slightest impact.

'But you must take your bottle.' She pushed it towards him.

'I wouldn't dream of it, Naomi. Please keep it as a small token of my regard.'

He sidestepped her with a rugby player's deftness and moved through the door out into the hall. Would he step in the cat poo? No, he didn't. Pity.

She saw him out to the front door. As I waited in the kitchen I became aware of a strange unsettling animal noise coming from the study. I went to investigate. There, in front of the fireplace, was Wonder Boy, his back arched, his muscular haunches pumping up and down, rasping and grunting on top of a small brown fluffy cat that lay motionless on the fender. Was it squashed dead, poor thing? I looked more closely . . . no, it wasn't a cat, it was one of the *Lion King* slippers.

'He is quite an adorrable man, isn't it?' Mrs Shapiro minced back into the kitchen with a radiant look on her face. 'Next time I will invite him, you also must come. You must put on a bit of mekkup, darlink. And better clothes. I heff a nice coat

I will give you. Why you always wearing this old brown shmata?'

'It's kind of you to think of me, Mrs Shapiro, but . . .'

'No need to be shy, Georgine. When you see a good man, you must grebbit.'

'. . . are you sure you wouldn't like a nice cup of herbal tea?'

'No, thenk you, darlink. I heff enjoyed my aperitif.'

A sound like a satisfied grunt came from the direction of the study.

Next morning – it was Christmas Eve – I was woken up at seven o'clock by the phone ringing. I guessed straightaway who it was.

'Georgine? Is this you? Come quick. Something is heppening to my votter.'

'Is it leaking? Is it a burst pipe?' I muttered groggily, wishing she could have waited an hour before ringing me.

'No, nothing. I turn on the tap and nothing happens.'

'Look,' I said, 'I'm not an expert on plumbing. But I know a handyman. Would you like me to give him a ring?'

There was a pause.

'How much he is charging?'

'I don't know. It depends what the problem is. He's very nice. His name's Mr Ali.'

There was another silence.

'Is he a Peki?'

'Yes. No. I don't know. Look, do you want me to ring him or not?'

'Is okay. I will ring my good friend Mister Nick.'

She put the phone down. I rang Wolfe & Diabello but only got an answering machine. A few minutes later Mrs Shapiro phoned back.

'Is not there. Only answering machine in the office. These

people are too lazy, isn't it? Sleeping all morning instead of working. What is the number of your Peki?'

When I went round to Totley Place at about ten o'clock I saw that Mr Ali's bicycle was already propped up in the porch and he was sitting in the kitchen drinking a cup of that vile pond water. He stood up when I came into the room and greeted me warmly.

'Fixit broblem, Mrs George.'

'What was it?'

'Something peculiar,' said Mrs Shapiro. 'Someone has turned off the votter tap outside. Mr Ali has found it underneath the back door. Such a clever-knödel!'

'Water was all off,' nodded Mr Ali, beaming. 'Now back on.'

'But why?'

'How can I know this?' He shrugged mildly. 'I am a handyman, not a pseecholog.'

'That *is* strange,' I said. My mind started to race. Who would do a thing like that?

Mr Ali finished his tea and stood up to go.

'Any more broblem, you telephone to me, Mrs Naomi.' (He pronounced it Nah-oh-me.)

'But wait, I must pay you. How much it is?' Mrs Shapiro fumbled in a brown leatherette shopping bag that was under the table.

'Is okay. You no pay this time. I did nothing. Only turn tap.'

'But I must give you something for coming to my house.'

'You have given me cuppa tea.'

He slung his bag of tools over his shoulder and I rose to show him out to the door.

'Thank you for your help,' I said, following him out into the hall.

Suddenly he stopped by the quaint little phone table with

its barley-twist legs. I thought at first he'd stepped in the cat poo, then I saw that his eyes were fixed on the framed photograph of the stone arch. He leaned forward for a closer look.

'It looks quite old, doesn't it?' I said chattily, though I had no idea of its age.

'Church of Saint George,' he said. 'In Lydda.'

'Lydda.' A place, not a person. 'You've been there?'

'One time, I went back. Looking for my family.' He said it so quietly it was almost a whisper. 'I was born nearby to that place.'

'In Greece?' I was surprised. He didn't look Greek.

He shook his head. 'Palestine.'

Before I could think what to say, he'd disappeared through the door. I heard the tink-tink of his bicycle bell as he pushed it down the path. Mrs Shapiro was beaming when I came back into the kitchen.

'Very good Peki,' she said.

I didn't tell her he was a Palestinian.

My mind was still whirling. This story was turning out to be much more complicated than I'd thought. Nothing was what it appeared to be. Lydda was a place not a person; Mr Ali was from Palestine not from Pakistan; and someone had turned Mrs Shapiro's water off. Why? A practical joke? Or harassment? The more I thought about it, the more I was sure it must have been Mr Wolfe. He must have noticed the stopcock when he was snooping around. He knew how vulnerable she was. He had sat there, on that chair in the kitchen, plying her with sherry and flattering her. That was the carrot. And at night-time, when she was on her own, he had applied a bit of stick.

The phone rang at that moment. Mrs Shapiro shuffled

out to the hall. I could see her through the open door, gesticulating as she talked.

'Nicky! You got my messedge at your office . . . thenk you for ringing . . . Is okay. Votter problem is solved, but you can come anyway. Georgine is here . . . Ach, so. Never mind. Any time you want to drink coffee mit me, you are very welcome. Yes, and happy Christmas to you, Nicky.' She fluttered her eyelids as she talked, as though he was there in the room. When she put the phone down, she turned to me.

'Very nice man. Would be a perfect husband for you, Georgine. Rich. Hendsome. What you say?'

I laughed. 'Not quite my type.'

'Ach, you young girls! Nowadays, you heff too much choices. In my days, if you seen a good man, you had to grebbit.'

'Is that what you did, Mrs Shapiro? Like the sausages at Sainsbury's?' I teased.

Her face clouded over. She started fishing around in the ashtray for a cigarette butt, frowning as she tried to work out which was the longest one.

'You know, in the wartime so many men were getting killed. If you seen one you liked, you must grebbit quick.'

3
Bonding

19

Christmas with all the trimmings

I went back to Kippax for Christmas, though I wasn't in a particularly celebratory mood. It was my first Christmas away from Ben and Stella, and there was a sore cavity in my heart as if from a couple of extracted teeth. I was worried about Mum and Dad, too, and the worst thing was, I could sense they were also worried about me. Dad was still quite poorly; the latest hernia operation had knocked him back, but he was determined not to let it show, and he prowled about the bungalow in his new Santa slippers pinning up the Christmas decorations. I caught him wincing once or twice when he thought no one was looking. The heating and the TV were both on full blast. Mum was wandering around the kitchen in a daze, wearing a pair of jokey reindeer antlers, wondering what she'd done with the bread sauce, and still insisting steadfastly that she had to do Christmas right, with all the trimmings.

When I lived at home, Mum and I always used to sneak off to the midnight service at St Mary's on Christmas Eve. Mum liked to join in the carols. Her voice, piercing and slightly off key, used to make me cringe with embarrassment. But as I got older, I cultivated a blank what-d'you-think-you're-looking-at stare for the people in the pews in front when they craned round to see who was making the racket. Dad stayed obdurately at home and played his old Woody Guthrie records. Keir, my younger brother, went out with his

143

mates to the pub. But this year, even the lure of loud singing couldn't persuade Mum to go out in the cold, and we all settled down on the sofa in front of the TV.

On Christmas Day, instead of the traditional turkey, we had a traditional-style turkey breast roast, which came with a sachet of bread sauce – which Mum had lost. Dad made the gravy out of granules mixed with warm water. He put a pinny on specially for the occasion.

'I bet you never thought I'd turn into a new man, Jean,' he said to Mum.

'No, I din't,' said Mum. 'Which are the new bits?'

She was busy defrosting the chipolatas in the microwave. They were from Netto's bargain range. They reminded me of the Bad Eel's fingers, pink and plump. When I bit into one, pink juice oozed out.

Mum had set a place for Keir at the dinner table – he got the Loch Lomond placemat, which had always been my favourite. I was stuck with Edinburgh Castle again.

'To absent friends!' She raised a glass of tepid Country Manor – her third. 'And death to Iraqis.' The reindeer antlers had slipped down her forehead and were pointing forward, as though she was getting ready to rut.

'Mum,' I whispered, 'Keir's supposed to be liberating them, not killing them.'

But it was too late. Dad leaned back in his chair and thumped his hands on the table.

'Got no business to be there at all.' His voice was loud enough to be heard next door. 'If they 'adn't shut all t' pits, they wouldn't be so mad for oil now, would they?'

The war had thrown into sharp relief the differences between them: Mum passionately loyal to her family, Dad stubbornly loyal to his principles.

'Don't start now, Dennis. It's Christmas.' Mum reached

out and laid her hand on his arm. She was wearing all her rings: gold, sapphire and diamond.

'Aye, but it in't Christmas for them, is it?' said Dad, always the internationalist.

The Christmas lights on the tree winked on and off, competing with the turned-down TV in the corner, where King's College choirboys were soundlessly singing their heads off.

'What d'you think of this turkey breast?' asked Mum, changing the subject. 'It were on special.'

But Dad wasn't to be deflected.

'I'd sooner 'ave 'ad Tony Blair trussed up and roasted. Wi' all 'is gizzards in.'

Mum leaned over to me and whispered loudly, 'I don't know what it is, but Christmas always gets 'im gooin'.'

As she said it, I had a sudden vivid image from another Christmas – it was long before the strike, I must have been about ten at the time, and Keir five. A group of carol singers had come to the door. They were kids from the local school. They rang on the doorbell, and when Dad answered it, they started to sing in their little squeaky voices:

> We three kings of Orient are,
> Bearing gifts we travel afar.

Dad stood patiently and waited for them to finish. When they got to the end of the second verse, they fell silent. Probably that was as much as they knew. Dad reached in his pocket and gave them some change. Then just as they were mumbling their thanks, he burst into song:

> The people's flag is deepest red,
> It shrouded oft our martyred dead . . .

His voice was deep and loud. Keir and I crept away and hid behind the sofa. The children stood there gawping. When he got on to the bit about the limbs growing stiff and cold, they suddenly turned and made a dash for it, and didn't look back until they'd got to the end of the street.

'What d'you do that for, Dennis?' Mum scolded.

'They should teach 'em in school,' said Dad mildly. 'Proper history, not fairy tales.'

When we went back to school after the Christmas holidays, the kids were there waiting for me.

'Your dad's potty,' they said.

'No 'e in't.' I stood and faced them out. 'It's because your singing were crap.'

I saw Dad wince now, as he shifted in his chair, and a stab of his pain got to me, too. Dear Dad – he'd never been afraid to jump in deep, and he'd always done what he thought was right, regardless of the consequences. I thought with a pang of sadness of Rip, Stella and Ben, spending their Christmas at Holtham without me. The food would be better, the gifts more extravagant, the decor subdued and tasteful. There would be no Santa slippers or reindeer antlers, no political arguments, no Highland-scene placemats or plastic tree with winking coloured lights. Stella would wallow in the jacuzzi and flirt shamelessly with her grandpa. Ben would come back with some hi-tech gizmo for his computer, which he would discreetly hide in his bedroom so as not to upset me.

'Never mind, duck,' said Mum, reading my face. 'There's nowt like being wi' yer own family at Christmas.'

We clinked our glasses together, Mum's filled with the last of the Country Manor, Dad's and mine with Old Peculier. The mystery of the bread sauce was solved when Dad poured it over the Christmas pudding.

★

That night I lay awake in my old bed, listening to the voices in the next room. Mum had left a thick Danielle Steel out for me, but I couldn't get into it, my mind was wandering into the past, retracing the journey I'd made away from my family.

It was books that had changed my life – had catapulted me out of the coal-smoke semis of Kippax into university and a wider world beyond. When the careers teacher at Garforth Comp had asked me what I wanted to do, I said I wanted to be a writer. 'Writing's a great hobby,' he'd sighed, like one who knew. 'But you'll need a day job, too.'

I took an English degree at Exeter, then a postgraduate course in journalism at the London College of Printing. I was the first in my family to go to university – I know it's a cliché now, but it wasn't a cliché for us. After a traineeship on the *Dulwich Post*, I came back up to Yorkshire for a junior reporter's job on the Bradford *Telegraph and Argus*, in order to be nearer to home. Then I got a lucky break on the *Evening Post* in Leeds. Somewhere along the line, it happened so gradually that I didn't notice, I stopped talking Yorkshire and thinking Kippax. Nowadays you might just notice the flatness in my vowels when I say 'bath'; and marrying Gavin Connolly is no longer the pinnacle of my ambition. They didn't resent it. Mum kept a scrapbook of news clippings with my byline, which she brought out on any excuse. They were proud of me, my mum and dad.

They'd made their own journeys, too. Dad had gone into the coal industry after the war, and when he'd had a pint or two he would wax lyrical over the post-war settlement, when the family, the community, the pit, the union, the government, the nation, the United Nations, had all flowed seamlessly one into the other. It had given him all he had, and he'd done his bit in return, studying at night school to get his deputy's ticket, reading his textbooks at the coal face by the light of his lamp, because it was his belief that he should use his abilities on behalf of those less able than himself. When Ledston Luck closed in 1986, along with 160 other pits that closed in the wake of the strike, men like my dad and my brother were thrown out of that embracing society into a different kind of world. 'Maggie's Britain', Dad called it, and he never said it without a sneer. It wasn't his country any more.

Keir – he was just twenty-one at the time – survived by finding himself a new family: the Royal Engineers filled the gap left by the pit and the NUM. There were postcards of Keir building bridges in exotic places surrounded by smiling dark-skinned children; Keir wearing civvies and drinking a beer against the backdrop of an awesome snow-capped mountain; Keir and his mates grinning under their helmets, posing beside a jeep in a desert somewhere. 'Look where 'e is now, our lad,' Mum would murmur, running her fingers over the glossy prints.

Dad was shifted to the Selby coalfield, and when that closed, too, he was still young enough to get the redundo, old enough to get a decent pension and free coal for life, and bolshie enough to take on the chairmanship of the local Labour Party. He dedicated his life to the overthrow of Maggie, and pursued it with the same dogged diligence as he'd once sniffed out the firedamp. He never quite forgave Keir for joining the army, nor me for marrying Rip, but he never gave up on us either, just as he never gave up on the Labour Party, even when Tony Blair turned out to be, as he called him, the mini-Maggie.

Mum, on the other hand, had blossomed during the eighties. She loved the shoulder pads and the jewellery. She loved gadding about on coaches during the strike, and shouting at the top of her voice. Afterwards, rather than accept defeat, she put her new-found organising skills to good use and enrolled in a night class in Castleford to learn book-keeping. Just as Dad was squaring up to retirement, Mum was opening the door on a new career, doing the books for Pete's Plaice, Annie's Antiques, Sparky Steve, All-night Abdul, Curl Up and Dye, and various other small businesses that came and went in the former pit villages. For the first time in her life she was financially independent. Then around the time Rip and I were splitting up, she started to lose the central vision in her left eye. It would be slow, the doctor said, but progressive.

Somewhere in the darkened house, a door clicked and a toilet flushed. It must be Dad, battling with his prostate as stubbornly as he'd once battled with global capitalism. Then there was a second flush and a sound of voices in the kitchen. The whistle of the kettle, the clink of cups. In the daytime, they'd put on a brave face for me, but at night all their worries crept back and beset them. They couldn't get to sleep, so they were having a cup of tea together. My mum and dad.

I lay there in the dark, listening to the murmur of their voices and thinking about Christmas. Really, when you consider, it's not a very nice story. Okay, a baby was born, and there were angels, and a star in the sky – that bit's not so bad – but what about poor Mary having to travel all that way on a donkey – in her condition? The three kings with their sinister gifts? Then the slaughter of the innocents? And that was just the beginning; after that, there were crucifixions, a resurrection – with Armageddon and the Second Coming still to look forward to.

My mind flashed to the conversation I'd had with Ben about Jesus and the end of the world, the look of fear in his eyes as he tried to rationalise the irrational. Yes, Christmas is a dangerous time, I thought. Sometimes it can be better just to stay at home until it all blows over.

20

The festive season

When I got back to London on the day after Boxing Day, Wonder Boy was waiting for me at the front door with a dead bird. I supposed it was his idea of a gift, so I let him into the kitchen and gave him a saucer of milk, even though I'd previously resolved not to encourage him. Well, it was Christmas. He thanked me by lifting his tail and spraying against the dishwasher. Thanks, Wonder Boy.

Ben wasn't going to be back for a few days. Even *Adhesives* was having a break – the next issue wasn't due out until early March. Nathan phoned me to wish me a happy New Year and share a joke with me.

'What beats glue when it comes to bonding?' he murmured in his conspiratorial voice.

'I don't know. Tell me.'

'Hybrid bond. Glue and a screw. Geddit?' I imagined him with his white coat casually unbuttoned, chuckling glueily at the end of the phone. After he'd hung up, the silence of the house closed in around me.

That first night at home, I tossed and turned in my half-empty double bed and wished I was back in my old room in Kippax with the TV on too loud and Mum and Dad making cups of tea in the middle of the night. Of course, I knew that if I'd been there I'd only be wishing I'd stayed here – it wasn't here, and it wasn't Kippax – the bug was inside me, gnawing away.

It's at moments like this that you seek consolation in literature. I made myself a cup of tea and reached for my exercise
book.

The Splattered Heart
Chapter 5

*Christmas at Holty Towers was an orgy of gluttony and
conspicuous consumption which Gina found ~~dangerously
tempting~~ absolutely disgusting. Mrs ~~Sinclair~~ Sinster gave Mr
~~Sinclair~~ Sinster a ~~yacht a private jet a Rolex watch a silver
hip flask~~ set of golf clubs, ~~although he already had four sets,
because he already~~ also had ~~everything else~~.*

Actually, let's face it, I have no idea what those sort of people
would give each other. Although the Sinclairs weren't the
super-rich Sinsters of *The Splattered Heart*, Ben and Stella were
their only grandchildren, and they did tend to go overboard
on the gifts at Christmas. Stella accepted everything with
effusive thanks and, when she was old enough, wheedled
the receipts out of the donors and took the items back to
exchange for the things she really wanted. Ben accepted
everything guiltily and donated the unwanted gifts to the
Animal Sanctuary, where he'd developed a special relationship with a rescued donkey called Dusty. Ben and Stella;
so dear, so different. I closed up my exercise book and lay
quietly in the dark, calling up their faces into my mind, missing them.

The day before New Year's Eve, the phone rang at about five
minutes to midnight. It hauled me up abruptly out of a deep
groggy sleep. I fumbled for the receiver and the bedside light,
and managed to knock my glass of water on to the floor.

'Hello?'

'It's me.' The voice sounded muffled and squeaky.

'Who's that?'

'It's me. Ben.'

'Ben! Whatever's the matter? D'you know what time it is?'

'Mum, will you be in tomorrow? I'm coming home. I forgot my key.'

His voice sounded unfamiliar – slightly croaky, with a touch of London that I hadn't noticed before.

'Of course. But I thought you were staying until after New Year.'

'I was. But now I'm coming back tomorrow. The train gets in at ten past three.'

There was just the hint of a tremor as he spoke. If I hadn't been his mother, I wouldn't have noticed it.

'Do you want me to meet you at Paddington?'

'No, it's okay. I'll get the bus.'

'Is everything all right?'

'Yeah. Fine.'

'But why . . .?'

'I'll tell you when I see you.'

Click.

After that, it was at least an hour before I could get back to sleep. Something must have happened, I thought. There must have been a row.

In fact it was about half past four by the time Ben got back next day. Either the train was late, or there'd been no bus. I found myself glancing at the clock, waiting with the same anxious eagerness as I'd once waited for Rip to come home after a business trip. Then the doorbell rang, and there he was, my boy, standing on the doorstep in the wintry dusk, with his bulging backpack and a carrier bag in each hand. My heart bounced with joy, even though it'd been only just over a week since we'd said goodbye.

'Hi, Mum.'

'Hi, Ben.'

He dumped his bags down in the hall and stood there, grinning stiffly with his arms by his sides while I hugged him, tolerating this embarrassing ritual, but not actively taking part. He looked both thinner and taller, as if he'd sprouted up an inch or two in the last week. There was a shadow of a moustache on his upper lip. His hair had grown, too, and he had it tied up in a little red kerchief knotted behind his ears, pirate-style. This was new.

He'd only taken the backpack when he went away, so the extra stuff in the carrier bags must have been presents. There was even a present for me from the Sinclairs – an enormous box of Belgian chocolates, a bit similar to the one that I'd sent up for them, but bigger and more expensive.

'How was your Christmas?' I asked.

'Fine.'

There was something scarily grown-up about the way that Ben had handled the separation between me and Rip; it filled me with admiration and awe. He never played us off against one another – he was fiercely loyal to both of us. But I was burning with spiteful not-grown-up curiosity to find out what had happened at Holtham at Christmas.

'So what made you come back early?' I said it very casually.

'Oh, I just got fed up.'

I might have believed him and just left it at that, but I remembered the phone call, his trembling voice at two minutes to midnight. That was more than just fed up.

'And Stella? Was she there?'

'Yeah. But then she left. I think she went to stay with her boyfriend.'

I'd sent a present for her, a hand-made silk shawl in different shades of rose – she would look lovely in it – it was her colour. I was hoping she'd ring, but all I'd got was a text message. *Thanx mum great prezzy happy xmas c u soon xxx.*

Although I'd left him a message before Christmas, it wasn't until the morning of New Year's Eve that Mark Diabello had phoned me back. I remembered I'd been trying to get to the bottom of Mrs Shapiro's turned-off water, and I was sure that either he or Nick Wolfe was responsible.

'Mrs Sinclair. What can I help you with? Did you see your aunty over Christmas?'

So, okay, I hadn't been quite truthful either.

'Look, Mr Diabello, I just want to know what's going on. You offer Mrs Shapiro half a million for her house. Then you up it to a million, just like that. Then your partner offers her two million.'

There was only a second of hesitation.

'With a unique property like this, Mrs Sinclair, it's difficult to arrive at an accurate evaluation, because there's nothing out there on the market to compare it with. At the end of the day, the market value is – how can I put it? – whatever the highest bidder will pay. That's why I suggest we float it on the market and see what offers come in. Does that make sense?'

Actually, it sounded pretty plausible.

'Then he goes round in the middle of the night and turns the stopcock off.'

'Nick did that?'

'I'm sure it was him. He'd been round there the same morning, plying Mrs Shapiro with sherry.'

A pause.

'I don't think you should jump to any conclusions, Mrs Sinclair. Do you mind if I call you Georgina?'

Did I mind? Didn't I mind? I couldn't hear myself think above the chatter of my hormones.

'I'll have a word with him if you like. Sometimes he . . . he does get a bit carried away. He falls for a property, and he forgets that it belongs to somebody else.' He hesitated. His voice changed. 'You know, this may surprise you, Georgina, but being an estate agent is a labour of love. You go into this game because you're passionate about property. The elegant terraces, the cosy cottages, the grand mansions and the stylish apartments – each property is a life to be lived – a dream come true for someone. Our job is to match the dream to the property.'

'So now you deal in dreams?' I was trying to sound hard-headed, but as he spoke, I was thinking, there's something exciting about black treacle – it's subtler, more complex than bland sugary golden syrup.

'We try to make dreams come true, Mrs Sinclair.' There was a breath like a sigh on the other end of the phone. 'But you spend most of your time flogging ex-council maisonettes to people who dreamed of something better, and converted buy-to-lets to amateur landlords who want to make a quick buck. Your passion goes cold; you just keep doing it for the money. Then once in a while something really special comes along, something you can lose your heart to. And your brains. Like Canaan House.'

As I said, I'm not a woman who automatically thinks of sex when she talks to a man, but Mr Wolfe seemed to have started a trend, and I found myself wondering what it would be like with Mr Diabello. And, mmm, I have to say, it was quite a lot nicer. But – I shushed my revving hormones – he *was* still an estate agent, and probably a crook.

'It's not a property – it's a home. It's not for sale,' I snapped.

It wasn't until he'd put the phone down that I realised the disjuncture in what the two of them had been saying. Mark Diabello had been talking about selling the house at its market value, whatever that was. But Nick Wolfe had wanted to buy it.

'What are you doing for New Year's Eve, Mum?'

Ben came and sat down on the arm of my chair, interrupting my thoughts.

'I don't know – I hadn't thought about it. It's tonight, isn't it?'

If Christmas is a time when families get together, New Year's Eve is a time for celebrating friendship – and most of my friends were up in Leeds.

'I haven't made any plans, Ben. We could cook something special, crack open a bottle of wine, watch the celebrations on TV. What would you like to do?'

He shuffled about on the arm of the chair.

'I was wondering about going out with some mates from school . . .'

'Yes, do that. I'll . . .' My heart leapt. I thought fast. '. . . I'll go and see Mrs Shapiro.'

'. . . but I'll stop in if you want. If you're going to be on your own.'

'No, no. Go for it. That's great.'

I didn't want him to guess that my heart was crowing. He had friends – he was part of a crowd – my poor broken-in-half boy – he'd spend New Year's Eve getting drunk and throwing up in the gutter, not sitting at home in front of the TV with his mum.

'Mrs Shapiro and me – we'll down a bottle of sherry and sing raucous songs. It'll be a ball.'

Actually, I was thinking, I'd be happy to have a break from

Mrs Shapiro and her smelly entourage, and spend the evening in on my own.

Then at about six o'clock the phone rang. My heart sank. I was sure it would be Mrs Shapiro. But it was Penny from *Adhesives*.

'Hiya, Georgie – have you got any plans for tonight?' she boomed. 'I'm having a bit of a bash round at my place. Some of the work gang'll be there. Just bring a bottle, and your dancing shoes.'

She told me the address, just off Seven Sisters Road. I hadn't realised she lived quite close by. I wondered briefly what to wear, then I remembered the green silk dress. I had intended to get it dry-cleaned, but what the hell.

21

The Adhesives party

I could hear the music as I turned the corner into the street. Penny greeted me at the door with a hug, helped me out of my coat and took the bottle of Rioja out of my hand. She was petite and curvaceous, in her mid-forties I would guess, wearing a short black skirt covered with swirls of sequins and a low-cut red top that plunged right down to her bra. Her short curly hair was dramatically bleached and fluffed up on top of her head, making her look like a buxom elf.

'Thanks for inviting me, Penny. It's great to meet you at last.'

I kissed her on each round warm cheek and followed her through into a room where the lights were turned off and a PA in the corner was pumping out such a volume that I had to put my hands up to my ears. The room was packed with people all swaying and shuffling and the air was thick with several types of smoke.

'They're all in here.' Penny was swaying her hips as she talked. 'Nathan's brought his dad.'

She gave me a little shove. I lurched forwards. I hadn't really been feeling in a party mood, but suddenly the atmosphere caught me, and shuffling in time to the beat I worked my way through the press of bodies further into the room.

'This is Sheila.' Penny introduced me to a girl of about Stella's age, wearing a little strip of red satin – the minimum amount of material that you could call a dress – and smooching with a young black guy, about six feet tall, slim and gorgeous. He was holding a wine glass in one hand and a cigarette in the other. There was a lot of hip-thrusting going on. Penny pushed past them and led me deeper into the room.

'Over there, that tall guy. That's Emery, one of the free-lancers on *Prefabrication*. I told you about his little operation?' she whispered.

'No, er, what . . .?'

I wondered what she'd told them about me.

'Here, meet Paul. Paul, this is Georgie. You know, from *Adhesives*.'

Paul was slightly built with a shy stoop and a yin-yang tattoo on his forearm.

He nodded in my direction and carried on dancing, mesmerised by the tiny dark girl spinning her torso in front of him. When I turned round again Sheila had disappeared, and the slim gorgeous guy was thrusting towards me. I felt my knees droop and my pelvis liquefy but somehow the rhythm got hold of my feet, and I found my hips doing unfamiliar gyrations. He moved in closer.

'Hi, beauty. I'm Penny's cousin,' he shouted above the boom of the music. 'Darryl Samson. I'm a doctor.'

Having a doctor like that would be enough to keep any-body in bed, I thought. A bit different to seedy Dr Polkinson at the Kippax surgery.

'I'm surprised any of your patients bother to get better.'

His laugh was deep and juicy.

'I'm Georgie. I'm a . . . writer.'

'No kiddin'!'

I could feel his hips – and not just his hips – pressing up close against me. Then Penny appeared at my side, grabbed me by the hand and pulled me away.

'Come on – you need a drink.' She threw Darryl a warning look, and he spread his palms with an apologetic smile.

'Take care with that one. He's my sister's brother-in-law. Don't believe anything he tells you.'

'Is he a doctor?'

'Ha!' She threw her head back. 'I've had a few complaints. He told Lucy he was a gynaecologist. And she believed him.'

When I looked back, he was moving across the floor with the same languid insolence as Wonder Boy, thrusting himself in between Paul and the girl with the spinning torso, and in no time they were grooving together, pelvis to pelvis. I stood in the drinks room clutching my glass of red wine and feeling mildly annoyed with Penny, when suddenly she dived into the crowd and pulled someone else towards me. 'Georgie, here's someone you gotta meet.'

I stared. This was incredible. Horn-rimmed glasses. Deep blue eyes. Dark hair swept back from brainy forehead. Yes, definitely hunkily intelligent – all he needed was a white coat. And maybe a few inches. Okay, he was a bit short – but did that matter? Was I so shallow that I couldn't fancy a man half an inch shorter than me? I was pondering on this when the small intelligent hunk stretched out his hand.

'Hi. I'm Nathan.'

'I'm Georgie.' I felt myself blush. 'Good to meet you at last.'

'The Chattahoochee Rose.'

'What?'

'Georgia. You know, on the Chattahoochee River.'

'Oh. Geography's not my strong point,' I mumbled. Already I'd revealed myself as an ignoramus. I noticed he was wearing a midnight-blue silk shirt that matched his eyes, and that the dark designer stubble that shadowed his chin and jaw was attractively flecked with silver.

'Awesome dress.'

'Thank you. It came from ...' There was a small vomit stain on one sleeve, but probably he hadn't noticed.

'I've been looking forward to meeting you, Georgia.' That low, confiding voice, with maybe just a touch of the mid-Atlantic about the vowels. I realised that our only topic of conversation over the years had been glue. Should I mention my thoughts about polymerisation?

'Me, too. I was thinking about what you said ...' I remembered his New Year's joke. Glue and a screw. No, that wasn't the right way to begin. 'I mean, after all these years. You know, talking about adhesives over the phone. I thought you must be ...' No, that wasn't right, either. I blushed.

'Mr Bond?'

'Something like that.'

Then an elderly man I hadn't noticed before, thin and wiry, with a bushy white beard and a glass of red wine in his hand, moved in beside me.

'Aren't you going to introduce me to your young lady, Nathan?'

I thought I saw a quick glimmer of annoyance flash through Nathan's eyes, but he just said, 'Tati, this is my colleague Georgia. Georgia, meet my father.'

'Georgia! Aha! State or republic?'

'Er ...' Was this another geography quiz? I hadn't done geography since I was fourteen. At Garforth Comp in those days you had to choose between history and geography. I felt myself turning pink under Nathan's curious gaze.

I was saved by the chimes of Big Ben. The lights came on. Corks popped and everyone held their glasses out. Nathan grabbed a bottle and topped us both up. I took a great gulp that went straight to my head. Putting his glass aside, the old man crossed his arms, took my left hand in his right one with a surprisingly firm grasp, and reached the other hand out to Nathan. Then he took a deep breath and started to sing. *Should auld acquaintance be forgot . . .* The room went still . . . *and never brought to mind . . .* His voice reverberated unexpectedly deep and mellow. What happened next was a bit like polymerisation – suddenly the individual people-molecules milling about in the room grabbed hands and formed a long covalent chain. Soon we were all holding crossed hands and swaying, everybody kissing everybody. I even got a quick snog with Darryl. That was nice. Then Sheila pulled him away and the old man pushed in and covered my face with his bristles. He started kissing me vigorously, a whiskery, spicy kiss – vindaloo. I struggled, but his grip was tight. Nathan came to my rescue.

'Happy New Year, Georgia,' he murmured, as though it was our special secret. For a moment, he held me in his arms. Our lips met. The room started to spin. But the old man squeezed in between us, coming in for another round, so I pulled myself away, grabbed my coat from the pile in the other room, and was out in the street in a flash.

It was incredibly cold. I started to run. The streets were full of revellers, and the sky was full of stars.

The house, when I got home, was quiet, dark, and warm. I didn't put the lights on. I flung off my coat and shoes, lay down on the bed, and almost immediately fell asleep. I woke up two hours later feeling cold, with a disgusting taste in my mouth. It was a mixture of rough wine and vindaloo. But it set me thinking how long it was since I'd been kissed. Actually, it had done me good. I should get out more often.

I had a wash, cleaned my teeth, put my nightie on, and went back to bed. I tried to call Ben, but his mobile was switched off. I suppose he didn't want his mum ringing to embarrass him. I drifted off to sleep wondering where he was, and thinking of New Year's Eve in Kippax in 1980, when I'd snogged Karl Curry, and wondering where *he* was now.

I woke up again just after dawn and wandered across the landing to see whether Ben was back. The curtains were drawn and the light was out. The air had a musty smell of sleep and old socks. But he wasn't in his bed. A red light was flashing on his computer – it was the screen saver whizzing about – a garish vertigo-inducing pattern of white-and-red swirls. I went to shut it down, and as I touched the mouse, the screen he'd been looking at came up.

I remembered it was the same red-on-black text as before. This time, the single word flashing in red on black in a circle of dancing flames was *Antichrist*. What was this rubbish he was looking at? Out of curiosity, I hit the 'back' button, and found myself in some sort of chat forum. There were only two names: Benbo and Spikey.

Spikey: hey benbo happy newyear this is the year of antichrists rein watchout

Benbo: who do you think is the antichrist putin or bush?

Spikey: putin is the king of the north who will join forces with the king of the south at the battle of armagedon daniel 11:40

Benbo: where is armagedon?

Spikey: its in the north of isreal

Benbo: phew quite a long way from highbury who is the king of the south?

Spikey: gadafi or sadam hassain or osama binladin take your pick

Benbo: do you think obl is still alive?

Spikey: check out *http://www.dramusic.com/endtime*

prophesies/obllives.html he has gout in his toes but is ok apart from that

Benbo: i think saddam is still alive did you notice something wird about those hanging photos the angle of the head is wrong and the eyes when someone is hanged their eyes bulge out from the pressure but saddams eyes look normal i think the head has been copied and pasted from a different photo

Spikey: your right if the pictures are fake mybe the execusion was fake too have you seen *http://www.saddamhussein lives.com*?

Benbo: i read somewhere that prince charles is the anitchrist because of the duchy of cornwall bar codes

Spikey: 666 is the mark of the beast check this link *Antichrist*

Benbo I supposed was Ben. How did he know so much about hanging? But who was Spikey? Whoever he was, I didn't think much of his spelling.

I clicked on the last link, which took me to the webpage of someone who called himself Isiah. He was a middle-aged man with a crew cut, drooping eyelids and a chunky wooden cross on a chain around his neck. Beneath the picture was a banner heading:

WHO IS THE ANTICHRIST?

Many Christians used to believe that Communism was the Antichrist, and *Armageddon* would be nuclear war between Russia and America. However, it seems that now the forces of Islam and Christianity are lining up for a definative battle before the third Temple is rebuilt in Jerusalem and Christ comes back to rule the earth in all His power and glory.

Infact all the signs are that the Antichrist, Satan the great Deceiver, is already stalking the earth. 'Take heed that no one deceives you. For many will come in My name, saying, "I am the Christ," and will deceive many.' (Matthew 24: 4–5)

In the Book of Revelation the *Mark of the Beast* is revealed as 666.

I rubbed my eyes. It was too early in the morning for this sort of stuff. But I was curious about how Ben spent his hours cloistered up here. There was a list of names, each underlined with a link and marked with a little flaming crest.

Osama Bin Laden
Saddam Hussein
Pope Benedict XVI aka Joseph Ratzinger
Vladimir Putin
Prince Charles of Wales

I opened the last link.

This English aristocrat is a surprise candidate – but look at the evidance. His full official name both in English and Hebrew adds up to *666* as described in the ancient Hebrew Gematria, and his heraldic symbols are based on the *beasts* of Daniel and Revelation. Also, he really is a prince, as predicted in Daniel 9. Rome is obviously the new Babylon, and the evil *European Union* is the new Holy Roman Empire. It's constitution is under discussion, and Prince Charles could one day be it's ruler. Infact the fact that he seems unlikely is the strongest argument in his favor, because as the Bible tells us in Revelation 12: 9 'The Devil and Satan deceives the whole world.' Check out *www.greaterthings.com/News/PrinceCharles/index.html*.

Up to this point I'd been reading with a kind of fascinated horror, but the bit about Prince Charles made me laugh out loud. Poor lad, I thought. And the grammar and spelling. How could anyone take seriously anything spelled infact, definative, evidance? I must definately (ha ha) pull Ben's leg about this. Out of curiosity, I clicked on the 666 link.

> The Mark of the Beast may already be in your home. Take a look at the bar code which is on every product you purchase. You may have bought goods marked with the Beast's sign 666 including products sold from Prince Charles's own sinister Duchy of Cornwall brand. Check out *www.av1611.org/666/barcode.html.*

Smiling to myself, I clicked on Start, Shutdown, then I went downstairs and put the kettle on. When I took my coffee through to the sitting room, I found Ben there, asleep on the sofa, clutching a large traffic cone to his chest, dead to the world. He stirred and opened his eyes.

'Happy New Year, Mum.'

'Happy New Year, Ben. What's with the traffic cone?'

He looked down at his chest, and shook his head in surprise.

'I've no idea, Mum.' He grinned sleepily. 'Absolutely no idea.'

Before I could ask him about the webpages, he'd drifted off to sleep again, his feet sticking over the end of the sofa, the traffic cone still cradled in his arms.

The light was flashing on my answering machine.

'Georgia. It's Nathan. Tati says sorry about last night. He gets a bit carried away when he's had a drink. Hope you got home all right. Happy New Year.'

I was going to ring him back, but I would probably end up

making a fool of myself. Quit while you're ahead, I thought. Instead, I phoned Penny and left a message on her answering machine.

'Great party. Thanks.'

That was it, then: Christmas and New Year, the festive season over. I'd survived.

22

Changing the locks

One of the hardest things I found, after Rip left, was sleeping by myself in that great empty bed. In the day I could keep myself busy, but at night the hours seemed to swell and expand, losing their definition. It wasn't just sex I missed, it was having someone warm to cuddle up to, a solid presence beside me on the cruel nightmare ride from dusk to daybreak. Sometimes I would wake to find myself snuggled up to the spare pillow, my arms and legs locked around it.

About three weeks into the New Year I came downstairs very early in the morning to make myself a cup of tea after a restless sleep. I'd woken up before dawn to find my pillow wet with tears. I could remember nothing about my dream except a faceless malevolent shadow dragging towards me. Somewhere in the still-dark streets a siren was wailing, a persistent, unsettling call like a sinister bird of the night. It was cold, the central heating hadn't come on yet. I shivered as I poured the tea, and was about to go back to bed when the phone rang. It was Mrs Shapiro.

'Georgine – please come quick. There is a burglary. Door is brokken.'

Feeling mildly irritated, I got dressed, put on my coat and went around straightaway. It had started to snow – not proper snowflakes, but miserable powdery stuff flaking down out of the sky like frozen dandruff. Mrs Shapiro answered the door wearing her pink dressing gown and *Lion King* slippers, her hair dishevelled, lipstick smeared on hastily. Violetta was hanging around, miaowing at her feet. She led me through to the kitchen. It was bitterly cold. One of the pretty Victorian blue glass panels on the back door had been smashed and an icy draught was whistling through. The key on the inside had been stolen. Nothing else seemed to be missing.

'Maybe it was your Peki. Maybe he is a teef.'

'Why would it be him?' I couldn't keep the irritation out of my voice. 'He didn't even charge you for coming out last time. He didn't steal anything, did he? You should be grateful, Mrs Shapiro, but all you do is moan.'

Okay, I know it wasn't a very nice thing to say, but I wasn't feeling very nice.

'Hm. But if not the Peki who can it be?' She gave poor Violetta a petulant little kick and shuffled across to put the kettle on.

'It could be anybody. A burglar or anybody.' I saw the look of terror flit across her face, and wished I'd held my tongue. I hadn't told her that Mr Ali had already changed the lock once – I hadn't wanted to alarm her. But now I was alarmed myself.

'But why they want to frighten me? Why they don't come into the house? Why they just tek the key?' She looked as if she was working herself up into a state.

'It might be someone who's planning to come back.' It was hard to imagine the sheer malevolence of someone who would terrorise a defenceless old lady in her own home. 'Listen, you'd better get the glass mended and the lock changed today. You should call Mr Ali. Unless you know of anybody better.'

She started poking around in her disgusting cupboards looking for the pond-water tea. Her back was turned towards me.

'He is a clever-knödel, this Peki,' she muttered.

Irritation and concern vied for dominance in my mind, and irritation was getting the upper hand. She poured the hot water into a jug and dangled a limp greyish tea bag in it by its string. After a moment, she looked up at me and said, 'But I think I will ask Mr Wolfe. My Nicky.'

Then she gave me a sly little grin as if to say, I may be eighty-one but I can still wind you up. And she succeeded.

'That's fine. Just the job. You and your Mr Wolfe can sort it out. I don't know why you bothered to call me at all.'

All of a sudden, my annoyance overwhelmed me. I stood up abruptly and made for the door. I'd had enough of her constant demands and her petty prejudices and her silly mysteries. I couldn't stand the stink in her house a moment longer, and I certainly didn't want to sit there in the cold, drinking her weak pondy tea when I'd left my own cup of tea to go cold in the kitchen. Let her sort herself out, I thought. I wanted to get back to my bed.

Once home, I heated the tea up in the microwave and climbed into my bed fully clothed. Outside the window, a feeble dawn was just breaking through a bruised purple sky, with long red streaks like bleeding cuts smearing the surface of the clouds. I pulled down the black knickers over my eyes to keep the light out, and tried to will myself back to sleep, but I was too wound up to drift off, and too tired to get up. That dream or nightmare that had woken me was still pushing at the edges of my consciousness – the malevolent figure with a blank eyeless face. I shuddered. For some reason I remembered the website Ben had been looking at – the Antichrist, the Deceiver, stalking the earth unrecognised, spreading evil and fear. It didn't seem quite so funny now.

Then the phone rang.

'Don't be engry mit me, Georgine. I am only jokking. I am

an old woman. Please, telephone to Mr Ali. I heff lost the number.'

'Okay, okay.'

She phoned me back a few hours later to tell me that Mr Ali had been and boarded up the back door and changed the lock. He had put a new mortise lock on the front, in addition to the Yale, and had fitted bolts to both doors.

'You will be as safe as prison,' he'd said.

'How much did he charge you?' I asked.

'I give him ten pound. Plus he mek me pay full price for locks and bolts.'

She said it with a grumble in her voice, as though she felt she'd been overcharged.

'You should be grateful,' I said, though she clearly wasn't.

'You are still engry mit me, Georgine, isn't it? Don't be engry. You are the only friend I heff.'

'No. I'm not angry, Mrs Shapiro.'

And it's true, I wasn't angry with her any more. I had other things on my mind.

Rip had returned from a business trip and had phoned around lunchtime to say he was coming to pick Ben up after work tomorrow. Even after all this time, his phone calls still agitated me. I needed time to get myself into the right frame of mind to face him on the doorstep. Upstairs I could hear the thud-thud of footsteps followed by the thud-thud of music – Ben's morning getting-up rituals, though it was well past midday. That boy could sleep for England. Something else – I still hadn't found out what had happened at Holtham at Christmas.

The doorbell rang a bit earlier than I'd expected on Monday afternoon. I went to answer it with my ready-for-anything smile fixed on my face. But it wasn't Rip on the doorstep, it was Mark Diabello. His black Jaguar was parked by the gate, and he was smiling a ready-for-anything smile, too.

'Hello, Mrs Sinclair. Georgina.' The deep creases in his rugged cheeks crinkled craggily. 'I hope you don't mind my dropping round like this. I've been following up on some of the concerns you raised in our last chat, and I wanted to bring you up to date.'

Maybe if I hadn't been expecting Rip to appear at any moment I wouldn't have asked him to come in. But it seemed too good an opportunity to miss.

'That's kind of you, Mr Diabello. Can I offer you a coffee?'

'Call me Mark, please.'

He followed me inside, looking around him as I led him through to the sitting room.

'I showed a client round this place when it was first on the market. You've done wonders to it, if I may say so. Added all your little feminine touches.'

'Thank you.'

As far as I was aware, I'd added no touches to it whatso-ever, apart from unloading my furniture and hanging some curtains up.

I positioned him on the sofa by the bay window, where he could be seen from the road. Then I put the kettle on and spooned some coffee into the cafetière.

'Milk? Sugar?'

'Black with four sugars.'

I laughed. 'It'll taste like black treacle.'

'Mm. That's how I like it.'

He must have noticed that I kept glancing towards the window because he said, 'I hope I'm not making you nervous, Georgina.' Black treacle with a hard mineral edge.

'No, not at all,' I blustered, feeling intensely nervous.

Then a car horn beeped outside – I recognised the distinctive note of Rip's Saab.

'Please excuse me.' I went to the bottom of the stairs and shouted, 'Ben! Rip's here!'

'Coming!'

A moment later Ben appeared, with his shoelaces still undone, his shirt hanging out, and his big backpack over his shoulder. God knows what he carted around in it because he always seemed to wear the same clothes. I went out to the car with him, my ready-for-anything smile fixed in position. But Rip just pulled the inside lever to open the boot and sat in his Saab, waiting for Ben to put his backpack in. He didn't even wind the window down. I couldn't even tell whether he'd noticed the black Jag or the man sitting in the window. I wanted to hammer on the window with my fists, I wanted to kick in the glossy, dark green door panels. But Ben was waving goodbye, so I blew him a kiss and went back inside, slamming the door.

My face must have been livid when I returned to the sitting room, for Mr Diabello gave me a sharp look and said, 'All going to plan?'

'Not exactly.'

His left eyebrow lifted a fraction, and his cheeks tightened, and I realised from that look that he had understood everything about my situation. I blushed as if he'd walked in on me naked in my bedroom. He was a man, I remembered with a shiver, who could read people's dreams.

'Want to talk about it?' His voice oozed sympathy. 'I can recommend a good solicitor.'

'No. No, it's not at that stage yet.' As I said the words I realised that probably it was at that stage, and probably I did need legal advice. But the thought of a friend of Mark

Diabello's crawling all over the intimacies of my life made me cringe. 'Just tell me what you came to tell me.'

'Yes – you were concerned that my partner, Nick Wolfe, might be behaving . . . how can I put it? . . . improperly.'

'Harassing an old lady in order to force her out and get possession of her house.'

My coffee had gone cold, but I sipped it anyway, to avoid looking at him. His gaze was making me feel uncomfortable and sweaty, like sitting under a spotlight. I could feel my cheeks going pink.

'I've had words with Nick. He admits he's fallen for the house, and has maybe been a bit too . . . er . . . enthusiastic in approaching Mrs Shapiro. But he denies absolutely having done anything improper.'

'But he admits to plying her with sherry. Hoping she'd sign a bit of paper that he just happened to have in his briefcase?'

However annoyed I got with Mrs Shapiro, I wasn't going to stand by and let these two shysters take her to the cleaners.

'I think the sherry was meant as a goodwill gesture. A gift. He didn't mean her to open it up and start drinking it straight-away. That was her idea. By all accounts, she was giving him the eye.'

'Oh, come off it! She's eighty-one. Anyway, why would he bring her a gift?'

'A token of appreciation for a valued client.'

'But she's not a client. He just turned up at her hospital bedside.'

'From what Nick says, she was a willing party. More than willing. Positively eager. He also told me, by the way, that she's not in fact your aunt.'

He looked up at me from lowered eyes, a small smile playing around his . . . how would you describe his lips? Not full and sensuous. No. But definitely . . . kissable.

'Okay, so I made that up. But it doesn't change anything.'

'It does raise the issue of what *your* interest is in the property.'

'I haven't any interest. I just don't want to see an old lady be ripped off. Someone must have told him about the house.' Then I realised. '*You* must have told him.'

Our eyes met. I noticed for the first time that his were not brown, as I'd previously thought, but dark sea-green, with sparks of gold and obsidian in their depths.

'I did mention our conversation to him. I didn't expect him to get quite so excited about it. He's a very passionate man, you know. It's our motto at Wolfe & Diabello. Passionate about property.'

'Passionate' – there was something about the way he lingered over the word.

'He thought Mrs Shapiro deserved a more focused view of his services?'

'Exactly so.'

'Like me?'

'That's up to you, Georgina.'

'Thank you. It's been nice talking to you.' I stood up abruptly, knocking my empty coffee cup over. He stood up, too, brushing past me as he made his way towards the door. I felt a shiver – or was it a shudder?

'The pleasure's all mine,' he said.

When I looked out of the window, I saw it was snowing again outside.

After he'd gone, I sat down on the sofa and breathed deeply. *In – two – three – four. Out – two – three – four.* For some reason, my heart started to thump. Yes, I knew, in my sensible core, that the last thing I needed was a man like Mark Diabello in my life – a treacle-voiced estate agent with black and gold in his eyes. But I was unhappy and furious and needy. And it was so long since someone had looked at me with desire. And a little voice in the back of my head was whispering – why not?

23
Stress fractures

It was still snowing that same powdery snow next day when I walked past the Islington branch of Wolfe & Diabello on my way to the bus stop. I'd been down to pick up a new laser cartridge, some more exercise books and a box of Choco-Puffs. (I think they're disgusting, but Ben likes them, and I'm in competition with whatever he gets in Islington.) I glanced in through the window and saw Nick Wolfe, bending over the desk of a young blonde woman who could have been a clone of Suzi Brentwood. On impulse, I pushed the door and went in. They both looked up as the door pinged.

'Mr Wolfe. I'm glad you're in. Have you a minute?'

The blond stubble on his scalp gleamed as he straightened up. He led me into an office at the back and pulled out two chairs.

'What can I do you for, Georgette?' He smiled wolfily.

I explained my concern about the mains water tap and the back-door keys, keeping my voice carefully neutral and avoiding any hint of accusation.

'You spoke to my colleague Mark Diabello about this, didn't you?'

His voice was slightly plummier than Mark's. I guessed he'd been to public school, whereas Mark had pulled himself up the hard way. Like me. He glanced pointedly at his watch. I ignored the hint.

'What I can't understand is what you and Mr Diabello are

up to.' I was smiling sweetly, looking him straight in the eye. 'He wants to sell it for half a million. Then he puts it up to a million. Then you go barging into the hospital with an offer of two million.' I spoke fast, conscious that his eyes were fixed on me in a not-very-friendly way. 'You must admit, it's a bit . . . worrying.'

'Look, Mrs . . . Georgette. To be frank, I don't really know what it's got to do with you. It's up to Mrs Shapiro what she does with her house, isn't it? I understand she's not even related to you.' He glanced at his watch again. 'I made Mrs Shapiro what I consider to be a very fair offer. More than fair. Generous. I don't know what Mark told you, but let's get one thing straight.' There was a bullying note in his voice that made me flinch. 'Just because it's floated on the market doesn't mean it reaches its market price. Nor that the person who makes the initial purchase is the ultimate buyer, if you see what I mean.'

What *did* he mean? In the close space of the office, I could smell his musky aftershave, and beneath it, a strong almost feral odour that reminded me of Wonder Boy.

'You mean Mark Diabello buys it for half a million, and sells it on to somebody else for two million, trousering the difference?'

'I did not say that, Georgette.' He emphasised every syllable forcefully. 'That is not what I said.' He looked at his watch again, and then stood up. 'If you'll excuse me, I have business to attend to.'

I stood outside on the pavement reeling. It had turned dark in the last half-hour, and a few stray snowflakes were spinning like scattered thoughts in the orange-tinged light. One or two of the shops had already closed up, but I noticed that Hendricks & Wilson was still open. Well, what did I have to lose?

Although the two shopfronts looked similar from the out-side, the interiors were startlingly different. Whereas Wolfe & Diabello had been all glass and chrome with laminate flooring and halogen lights, in the style of a city bistro, Hendricks & Wilson had red carpet and leather armchairs with brass wall-lights in the style of a gentlemen's club. I suppose it was meant to feel traditional and reassuring, but it just seemed ridiculously pompous in such a small space. A thin youth with spiky gelled hair was sitting at a computer, staring intently at the monitor. He looked up and smiled as I came in.

'I'm looking for Damian,' I said.

'That's me,' he beamed. His teeth were slightly crooked, and he looked reassuringly gormless. 'How can I help?'

I hadn't really prepared what I was going to say, so I tried the familiar line about my aunty selling a house in Totley Place. I watched his face carefully, but there was no sign of recognition. It seemed that whatever Mrs Goodney had been planning, she hadn't put it into action. Maybe I'd frightened her off.

'I think you need to speak to one of the partners about something like that. Would you like me to make an appoint-ment?' He reached for a large red-bound desk diary.

I hesitated. Did I really need any more estate agents in my life?

'Couldn't you give me just a rough idea?'

'Hm.' He chewed a fingernail. 'Tell you what – I'll drive past on my way home tonight and take a look.'

'Thanks. I'll give you a ring tomorrow. Thanks, Damian.'

'How did you know . . .?'

I quickly made for the door.

When I phoned Damian the next morning, I was even more convinced that he wasn't involved in the dirty tricks. He wouldn't give me a valuation, but he said, 'A big site like that in the heart of Highbury – it has development potential. You're talking millions. You'll have to speak to Mr Wilson.'

'I don't think my aunty would want it to be developed. But thank you for your help.'

I hung up quickly before he could ask me any questions.

If Damian wasn't involved, that meant it must be Wolfe & Diabello. Rage was burning in my head. I tried to calm myself down with Ms Baddiel's breathing exercises. *In – two – three – four. Out – two – three – four.* Wolfe & Diabello. What a pair of gobshites. I phoned their office – my hands were shaking so much I dialled a couple of wrong numbers before I finally got through. Neither of the partners was there. I left a message with Suzi Brentwood.

'Please can you get one of them to ring me back. No, I can't say what it's about. Just tell them I know what's going on. Tell them they're a couple of sleazy double-crossing crooks.'

It was Mark Diabello who phoned me back, within ten minutes.

'I got your message, Georgina. Strong language. What did we do to upset you?'

'It's not what you did, it's what I did. I got another valuation.'

'So you should, Georgina. And?'

'And he said it was a development site with potential. He said it could be worth several millions.'

'Who said that?'

'Somebody. Somebody from Hendricks's.'

'The office junior? They always make wild guesses.'

'No. Someone highly qualified. And reputable. Not a conman like you.'

'You're a very emotional woman, Georgina. I like that. But you've forgotten what I said.'

'What did you say?'

'I said I'd match any genuine valuation.'

Had he said that? It's true, I'd forgotten.

'But the other one – your sidekick – he offered her two million.'

'I can't speak for my partner. But I said I'd match their valuation. I think you owe me an apology, Georgina.'

'*I* owe *you* an apology?'

I put the phone down. I was shaking. Then I thought back over our previous conversations. Yes, maybe I'd been a bit hasty. Even a bit rude. I remembered now, he *had* said something about matching Hendricks & Wilson's valuation, but that had been in a different context. And it's true, Damian did seem to be the office junior. But what he'd said rang true. Actually, what all of them said rang true. That was the trouble. How was I to know who to believe?

'Stress fractures can occur in adhesive bonds when the materials have different coefficients of thermal expansion.'

I'd been staring at the sentence on my monitor for at least half an hour, as a cup of tea went cold on my desk, thinking maybe that's what had gone wrong between Rip and me. He's slow to get angry, but when he does, he stays hot much longer. I flare up quickly but quickly cool down again. My mind tripped back to that morning's conversation with Mark Diabello – yes, maybe I had flared up too quickly then. Maybe I should have given him the benefit of the doubt. What exactly *had* he said? I couldn't remember. The glue had got to my brain.

It was time to break for lunch. I wandered over to investigate the fridge. There were two eggs, a slice of bread and the remains of a supermarket bag of rocket salad. In the door was an opened bottle of Rioja. Should I? Shouldn't I?

I was whipping up some scrambled eggs, when the doorbell rang. Mark Diabello was standing on the doorstep with a bottle of champagne in his hand. It wasn't just any old supermarket champagne, either, it was Bollinger. Maybe it was just a trick of the light, but I could swear his eyes were smouldering. Deep sea-green, with flickers of obsidian and gold. Something in my heart did a funny little skip.

'A token of appreciation for a valued client,' he murmured.

'I'm not your client.'

'But you could be.'

'I don't think so. But come in.'

I went and fetched two wine glasses from the kitchen. I didn't have proper champagne flutes. We clinked.

'I like you, Georgina. You're different.'

The smile-creases in his cheeks deepened. My heart did that wayward skip again.

'Have you come to offer me a more focused view of your services?'

'Would you like that?'

I didn't say yes. But I didn't say no.

We ended up in my bedroom. He led the way. Of course, he was an estate agent, he knew where to go. It all happened astonishingly fast, with the well-oiled precision of a top-of-the-range Jaguar. He gave me just the right amount of champagne, kissed me in just the right way, holding me firmly but carefully under the chin. Then at exactly the right moment one hand moved down from my chin to my left breast. The other worked its way up between my legs. There was something reassuringly impersonal about it all. His hands found their way unerringly to the right places. His fingers were strong and supple. There was no fumbling with clothes – they just fell away. His body was hard and hairy. He produced a condom from his pocket. If I'd had time to think, I might have thought – what the hell am I doing? But I didn't think about anything. My brain was full of bubbles. My skin tingled like electricity. My body purred in his hands. I'd like to say I recoiled in disgust at the sheer efficiency of it. But actually, it was fantastic.

I can't remember what happened next – well, okay, I can, but I'm too embarrassed to write it down. Look, he was the only man apart from Rip I'd slept with in twenty years. It was as though I'd slipped out of my familiar skin and become a different person, someone whose body waved and fluttered like a piece of silk in a storm.

Afterwards we lay together watching the shadows lengthen in the garden and he pulled me into his arms and stroked my hair, murmuring sweet meaningless words. Then he reached into the breast pocket of his jacket, which was hanging on the back of the chair, and passed me a clean white handkerchief.

We didn't talk much. It wasn't about us as people. He left before Ben got back from school. I thought I might feel dirty, or used, or disgusted with myself, but I guess I realised deep down that having sex with someone else was part of a sticky repair process I had to go through. What was it Nathan had said? You get better bonding with glue and a screw. Maybe there's something in that. After he'd gone, all I felt was a great mass of melancholy like a rain cloud swelling over my heart. I didn't want him to see me cry, but as I heard his Jag pull away I let the tears come. I couldn't even have said why I was crying, or what it was that had stirred up such a storm in me. Maybe the sex had just loosened me up so there was no rigidity to hold back the tears.

★

About half an hour later, I heard the door-click of Ben letting himself in. I dried my eyes, pulled my clothes on, and went down to greet him.

'You okay, Mum?' He looked at me intently. 'You seem a bit sort of . . . weird.'

The scrambled eggs were still on the hob, yellow and congealed.

'Weird in what way?'

'Sort of hyper. Hyper-manic.'

'It must be all the coffee I've been drinking. I'm having a sticky patch with *Adhesives*. Ha ha. How about you? How's life in . . .' (I censored a number of sarcastic epithets.) '. . . Islington?'

'It's okay. Dad's a bit hyper, too.'

He poured the milk over the Choco-Puffs and sat down with his spoon.

'Oh, is he?'

I craved these snippets of information, but loyal Ben handed them out very sparingly.

'He says he's starting a new project?'

There was that rising inflection in his speech again. I found it troubling. It didn't sound like my Ben.

'Not the Progress Project?'

'He says it's progressing to a higher level?'

'Yes, he's always had high aspirations.'

A sarcastic note must have crept into my voice. Ben's look warned me that I was in danger of transgressing the subtle boundaries he'd drawn up between his two worlds.

That night, after Ben had gone to bed, I poured myself a glass of wine and reached for my exercise book. They were banqueting again at Holty Towers.

The Splattered Heart
Chapter 6

*Spurned by her errant husband, heartbroken Gina at last
found ~~love fulfilment~~ consolation in the arms of an itinerant
mandolin player with ~~obsidian cerulean sapphire amethyst
jade~~ lapis lazuli eyes. (Thanks, Mr Roget.) He brought her
beautiful gifts – hand-embroidered Spanish ~~underwear garters
hankies~~ mantillas.*

As I closed up my exercise book an hour later, I realised that
the wine bottle was empty, and I'd opened another one. This
was no good. Maybe Ben was right – I should go easy on the
Rioja. The house was full of silence. I listened. Faintly, I could
hear a car passing on the road and the tick-tick-tick of the
water in the radiators. That was all. Holty Towers, the ecstasy
and drama, the sumptuous meals and mandolin music, was a
world away.

24

Experimenting with Velcro

Mark Diabello came back again the following Wednesday, this time without the champagne, but with a bunch of flowers – red roses – and a small gift box, which I took to be chocolates. I was waiting for him, wearing a rather revealing top, which I'd bought the day before, and some lacy panties under a sleek clinging skirt, which I'd also bought the day before. I caught sight of myself in the hall mirror, my flushed cheeks and brilliant eyes, and didn't recognise myself. I could feel myself starting to melt as he kissed me. It took us about five minutes to get from the doorstep to the bedroom.

He was already undressing me as we fell on to the bed, his hands working with the same target-driven efficiency. When his shirt came off I could smell his body, soapy, sweaty, musky, and another smell, faintly chemical and disconcerting. What was it? I pressed my face to his skin. Sulphur? Chlorine. And in a flash I was sixteen years old, back in the locker room at the International Pool in Leeds, locked in a cubicle with Gavin Connolly, locked in his arms, lost in love.

'Have you been swimming?'

'How can you tell?'

'You smell of chlorine.'

'Don't you like it?'

'I do like it. A lot.'

'I'm a diver. High board.'

'That must be so terrifying!'

'It is. You just have to shut your eyes and plunge.'

I imagined him, hard and lean and straight as a pike, hurtling into the water. I shut my eyes and plunged.

'Aren't you going to open your present?' he murmured.

I reached for the little box that had slipped down at the side of the bed, and pulled the ribbon off. Something red and silky slipped out. I held it up. It was a tiny pair of panties, shiny red satin, trimmed with black lace. I stared. Blimey! Were they for me? I'd never owned anything like this before. I wasn't even sure I liked them.

'Aren't you going to put them on?'

I wriggled into them and felt them flutter like moth's wings against my thighs. There was something odd about them – the gusset – it was open. Surely that defeated the whole purpose . . .? What's the point of panties without a gusset?

She soon found out. Not me, not Georgie Sinclair, no, it was a different woman – someone sexy and shameless who frolicked around in red satin panties trimmed with black lace and an opening in the gusset, who smelled of sex, whose body melted like warm sugar in the arms of a dark handsome stranger who appeared on her doorstep and made love to her one afternoon.

The dark handsome stranger lay with the sexy woman, carrying his weight on one elbow. His other hand was exploring the opening in the gusset. She could smell the chlorine on his skin.

'Look, there's something else in the box,' he said.

The sexy woman fumbled shamelessly in the box and pulled out – what the hell were they? Two loops of red padded satin trimmed with black lace. Garters? No, there was a Velcro fastening.

'You naughty little slag,' he whispered. 'Let me . . .'

He leaned over her and fastened her wrists to the bedhead,

pressing down on her, pressing all the breath out of her till she had to cry out. She came almost at once, before he'd even entered her.

It was warm and steamy in the locker room, and we were wet and slippery, and then we towelled each other dry and got into our damp chlorine-sticky clothes. What had happened to Gavin Connolly? What had happened to Georgie Shutworth? I couldn't help myself – I started to cry. Mark Diabello dabbed my eyes with his hankie and kissed me lingeringly on my throat and neck.

'You're a very beautiful woman, Georgina. Has anyone ever told you that?'

I wanted to believe him. I almost believed him; but a cool whisper in my head reminded me that he probably slept with dozens of women, and said that to all of them. Then something from another age stirred in my mind, Rip's voice, husky against my cheek: 'If ever any beauty I did see, which I desired and got, 'twas but a dream of thee.' How long ago was that?

'You'd better go now. It's nearly four o'clock.'

'What happens at four o'clock? D'you turn into a pumpkin?'

'No, I turn into a mother.'

Just after four, the key turned in the latch, and I did turn into a mother.

'Hi, Mum.'

Ben flung his bag down and let me hug him, turning his head to one side. He looked tense and pale.

'Everything okay?'

'Fine. Cool.'

He wasn't looking at me. His eyes were fixed on the window.

'Do you want a sandwich? Some Choco-Puffs?'

'Nah. I'll just have water.'

He drank resting both elbows on the table, his brown curls falling across his eyes.

'I've been feeling a bit sort of . . . weird.'

I kicked Mr Diabello right out of my mind and sat down opposite him.

'How do you mean, weird?'

'I've been having these weird feelings.'

I could feel my pulse starting to pound, but I kept my voice soft and easy.

'What feelings, Ben?'

'Sort of . . . liminal.'

'Liminal?'

I had no idea what he was talking about. I waited, listening.

'Like we're living in liminal times. You can see it in the light, Mum – look – it's like it's seeping in from the edges of another world.'

He pointed at the window. I looked round. Between the houses, a low shaft of pinky sunlight was lighting up a bank of purple cumulus from below. The brick buildings and leafless trees were all backlit, cast in shadow, despite the vivid light. I could see what he meant – it did look unearthly.

'It's winter, Ben. The sun's always low in the sky at this time of year. Further north, in Scandinavia, they don't have any daytime at all.'

He looked up with a flicker of a smile.

'You're so literal-minded, Mum.'

The clouds rearranged themselves and the shaft of light disappeared, but still there was a fiery glow on the underbelly of the sky.

'I keep having these feelings, like the world's going to end soon.' He paused, gulping a mouthful of water. 'Like we're coming to the end of time?'

'Ben, you should have said . . .'

'So I Googled *End of Time*. And that's when I realised it wasn't just me?'

That's what they do, his generation, I thought. They don't talk to their parents or friends like we did – they look on the internet.

'There's like all these signs – predictions in the Bible about the end of time? Wars, earthquakes, floods, plagues and that – it's all starting to come true?' His voice was strained and crackly.

'But you don't believe all that stuff about prophecies, do you, Ben?'

'No, but . . . well, yes . . . I just think, like, if that many people believe it, there could be something in it?'

'But those things – wars, earthquakes, floods, plagues – they've been happening since the beginning of recorded history.'

'Yeah, I know, but it's all speeded up now. Floods and earthquakes – like, there's one every year. And AIDS, SARS, avian flu – all these new diseases. It's all started coming true. Like in the Bible, it's predicted the Jews'll return to Israel, and they did. You know, in 1948. After the Holocaust and that? That was the beginning of all the wars in the Middle East. The invasion of Lebanon. You can read it for yourself, Mum – it's all there in the Bible. And it's not just Jews and Christians? A lot of Muslims think their great prophet is coming? Like they call him the Last Imam?' The rising inflection in his voice seemed to challenge me to disagree.

How could I explain without sounding pompous that just because millions of people believe something doesn't make it true.

'Why didn't you tell me, Ben, that you were having these feelings? Or Rip?'

'I thought you'd think it was mad? You wouldn't listen? You and Dad – you never listen to anybody.' He dropped his voice to a mumble. 'Like, you're so sure you know everything already?'

He didn't say it as an accusation, but it stung like one. We were so preoccupied with our own lives and problems that we'd failed to hear our own son's cry for help.

'I'm sorry, Ben. You're right – we don't always listen. D'you want to talk about it now?'

'Nah, it's all right, Mum.' He grinned sheepishly, swallowing the rest of his water. 'I feel all right now. I think I'll have some Choco-Puffs.'

After he'd gone upstairs, I sat in the kitchen with a glass of wine wondering where we'd gone wrong. We'd brought him up to respect difference – diversity. To disrespect someone's faith would cause offence. At his primary school in Leeds, Rip and I, like good middle-class parents, had cheered enthusiastically as the children celebrated Christmas and Eid and Diwali. All belief was equally valid. Christianity, Islam, Hinduism, Judaism, astrology, astronomy, relativity, evolution, creationism, socialism, monetarism, global warming, damage to the ozone layer, crystal healing, Darwin, Hawking, Dawkins, Nostradamus, Mystic Meg, they were all out there vying with each other in the marketplace of ideas. How was anyone to know which was true and which wasn't?

25

The attraction between adhesives and adherends

Sometime in the night it started to snow. When I pulled back my curtains in the morning everything was white, and I felt a sudden burst of happiness, like I'd felt as a child waking up on a snowy day. No school; snowball fights with my brother; tobogganing on a tea tray down the slag heaps. In those days, before the advent of four-by-fours and working online, snow meant holiday, anarchy, delight.

In the garden, even the horrible yellow-spotted laurel bush was touched with magic, the leaves and branches bowing gracefully under their overcoat of snow. I noticed a move-ment – it seemed like three small black creatures hopping along, then I realised they were black feet attached to a white body. Wonder Boy prowled along the edge of the garden, tiptoed across the lawn, and took up his position under the laurel bush, staring up at the house. He was reminding me I should drop in on Mrs Shapiro today.

'Look, Ben,' I said, when he came down for breakfast. 'It's snowing. You could take the day off school.'

'It's okay, Mum. I feel better today. I've got to work on my technology project. The bus'll be running.'

How did he get to be so sensible? I hugged him.

'Take care.'

After he'd left, I sat down and tried to concentrate on an article for *Adhesives*. 'The attraction between surfaces in adhesive bonding.'

'*Powerful attractive forces develop between the adhesive and the adherend which may be adsorptive, electrostatic or diffusive.*'

There was something quite romantic, I was thinking, about those gluey time-enduring forces, bonds so strong that they could outlive the materials themselves.

Mmm. My mind started to drift. It was no good. *Adhesives* would have to wait – I wanted to get outside before the snow disappeared.

I phoned Mrs Shapiro, to see whether she needed anything from the shops. There was no reply, so I pulled on my wellies and my coat and went out anyway. The sun was low but brilliant, dusting every white surface with a sparkle of gold, but the snow had already started to melt and there were mini-avalanches all around as it slipped off roofs and branches. Wonder Boy followed me down the road. I lobbed a snowball at him, but he ducked out of the way.

When I got to Canaan House, I saw that the snow had pulled an end of the gutter down, and melting snow was dripping down the porch. Maybe I would have to get Mr Ali in again. There were footprints in the snow leading away from the house. I knocked on the door just in case but I wasn't surprised that there was no reply. She must have gone out already. Wonder Boy trotted up the path, sat down in the porch and started to yowl.

'What's the matter?'

I reached down to stroke him, but he hissed and went for me with his claws. I gave him a kick with my welly and went off to do my shopping.

In the afternoon I phoned Mrs Shapiro again. Still no reply. This was odd. I began to get worried. Why had she gone out so early in the snow? Then Ben came back from school and I got on with cooking supper. I'll ring later, I thought.

At about seven o'clock in the evening, the phone rang.

It was an old woman's voice, hoarse and throaty.

'She's in 'ere.'

'Sorry?'

'Yer pal. She's in 'ere. But she ent got 'er dressin' gahn wivver.'

'I'm sorry, I think you've got the wrong number.'

'Nah, I ent. She give it me. You're 'er what comes to 'ospital, in't yer? Wivve posh voice? She give me yer number. That lady wivve pink dressin' gahn. She says she wants 'er dressin' gahn agin. And 'er slippers.'

I realised in a flash that it must be the bonker lady.

'Oh, thank you for contacting me. I'll . . .'

'An' she says can yer bring some ciggies wiv yer when yer come.'

The telephone beeped a few times then went dead. She must have been calling from the hospital payphone.

I glanced at the clock. There was maybe half an hour of visiting time left. I'd given back the key to her house, so I bundled together my own slippers, a nightdress and Stella's dressing gown.

'I'll see you in a bit, Ben,' I called upstairs as I set off for the bus.

The snow had already melted and the air was surprisingly mild. I walked quickly, avoiding the slushy patches on the pavements. The newsagent by the bus stop was still open. Should I get some cigarettes? Or would it make me into a peddler of disease and death? Probably. But anyway, I did.

The bonker lady was hanging around in the foyer when I arrived. I saw her approach a departing visitor and cadge a cigarette off him. She was still wearing her fluffy blue mules, now more grey than blue, and her toes poking out into the cold air looked bluish-grey too, the yellow toenails crustier than ever. Feeling like a smuggler delivering contraband,

I handed her the cigarettes and she pocketed them swiftly. 'Fanks, sweet'eart. She's in Eyesores.'

It took me a while to track Mrs Shapiro down to Isis ward. I could see at once that she was in a bad way. Her cheek was bruised, one eye almost closed up, and she had a dramatic bandage around her head. She reached out and gripped my arm.

'Georgine. Thenk Gott you come.' Her voice was weak and croaky.

'What happened?'

'Fell down in the snow. Everything brokken.'

'I've brought the things you asked for.' I took the things out of the bag and put them in her bedside cabinet. 'Your friend phoned me.'

'She is not my friend. She is a bonker. All she wants is cigarettes.'

'But what happened? I telephoned earlier to see whether you needed anything.'

'Somebody telephoned to me in morning. Said my cat was in a tree stuck up in the park.'

'Who telephoned you? Was it somebody you know?'

'I don't know who. I thought it was Wonder Boy stuck. Poor Wonder Boy is not good up the trees.'

'Was he stuck?'

'Don't know. Never seen him. Somebody bumped me, I slipped and fallen. They put me back in the krankie house.'

Visiting time was over, and people were already making their way towards the door.

'Look out for the Wonder Boy. You will feed him again, will you, Georgine? Keys are in pocket, same like before. Thenk you, Georgine. You are my angel.'

I must say, I felt rather grumpy for an angel. Neighbour-liness is all very well, but there are limits. Still, I took the keys out of her astrakhan coat pocket again and joined the tide of visitors flowing towards the exit. Had it really been an accident? I wondered on the way home. Or had someone lured her out into the snow and pushed her over? What was it Mrs Goodney had said? 'Wouldn't want to be held responsible if she had another accident . . .?'

Ben was still up when I got back.

'Somebody phoned for you,' he said.

'Did they leave a message?'

'He said can you call him. Mr Diabello.'

'Oh, yes, the estate agent.' I kept my voice absolutely expressionless. 'I'm trying to get him to value Mrs Shapiro's house.'

'Funny name.'

'Yes, that's what I thought. It's a bit late. I'll call tomorrow.'

Should I or shouldn't I? I remembered with a shiver the brazen conduct of the Shameless Woman frolicking in scarlet panties, wriggling wantonly in the grip of Velcro – was that really me?

26

A gummy smile

On Saturday, after Ben had left with Rip, I changed into my old jeans, put a torch and a screwdriver into my bag just in case, and walked over to Canaan House. This was my chance to have another good poke around. I was determined to find out Mrs Shapiro's real age and to discover the identity of the mystery woman in the photo. There were two places I hadn't investigated yet – the sitting room with the boarded-up bay window and broken light, and the attic. I fed the cats and cleaned up the poo in the hall. Then I started to search systematically.

The catch on the sitting-room door was faulty and it hung slightly ajar. I pushed it open. The smell – feral, feline, fetid – was so overpowering I almost backed away, but I held my handkerchief over my nose and stepped inside, shining the torch around with my free hand. The beam fell on a high ornate ceiling with its defunct chandelier, a huge marble fireplace with a fall of soot spilling on to the hearth and, on the mantelpiece, an ornate gilt clock whose hands had stopped at just before twelve. There were two sofas and four armchairs, all draped in white sheets, a carved mahogany side-board with glasses and decanters – one decanter still with a few centimetres of brown viscous liquid that smelled like paint-stripper – and over by the window a grand piano, also under a sheet. I played the torchlight around the walls; they were hung with paintings – gloomy Victorian oils of Highland scenes, storms at sea, and dying animals – quite different to the intimate clutter of personal pictures and photos that covered the walls in the other rooms.

The bay window was covered by heavy fringed brocade curtains; an ugly box-shaped pelmet, covered in the same brocade, was sagging away from the wall, and when I looked up I could see why. A huge crack ran from the ceiling above the lintel right down to the floor, with a cold draught whistling through it. At the base, where it disappeared into the ground, it must have been several centimetres wide. It must be the roots of the monkey puzzle tree that had caused the damage, I thought. No wonder she wanted to cut it down.

Seating myself at the grand piano, I raised the dust sheet, uncovered the keyboard – it was a Bechstein – and struck a few keys. The melancholy out-of-tune twang reverberated in the silence of the room. There were books of music in the piano stool – Beethoven, Chopin, Delius, Grieg. Not the sort of stuff they listen to in Kippax. In the front of the Grieg piano concerto a name was handwritten in copperplate script, with old-fashioned curlicues on the capitals: Hannah Wechsler. In the front of the Delius lieder was another name: Ella Wechsler. I remembered the photograph of the Wechsler family seated around the piano. Who were they? As I leafed through the music a piece of paper fluttered to the floor. I picked it up and held the torchlight to it. It was a letter.

Kefar Daniyyel near Lydda 18th June 1950

My Dearest Artem,

Why you do not reply to my letters? Each day I am thinking of you, each night I am dreaming of you. All the time I am wondering if I was doing the right thing coming here and leaving you in London. But I cannot undo my decision. For this will be our place of safety, my love, the place where our people gathered out of every country where we have been exiles can be living finally at peace. Here in our Promised Land our scattered nation who have been swirling round the globe for many centuries like clouds of human dust are finally come to rest. If only you would be here, with us, Artem.

You cannot imagine, my love, the joyful spirit of working not for wages or profits but for building a community of shared belief. We will get old and die here, but we will build a future for our children. They will grow up fearless and free in this land we are making for them – a land without barbed wires, out of which no person ever again will drive us away.

At last we are moving from our temporary house in Lydda into our new moshav here at Kefar Daniyyel on a west-facing hillside overlooking the town. A few hectares of barren wasteland and a trickle of water, an empty abandoned place, but it will be our garden. In the east the sun is rising over the mountains of Judaea and in the west is setting above the coastal plain with its fields of wheat and citrus groves. At night we see the lights sparkling in the valley like Havdalah candles.

In the morning before the sun is too hot we are working outside clearing stones away from the hillside and preparing terraces for autumn planting. Yitzak has obtained some seed-stones for a new type of fruit-tree called avo-kado which he believes we can establish here once the irrigation problem is solved. The men are laying a water pipe that will bring life in this empty land that previously supported only a few dozen of people and their miserable livestocks.

My love I have some big news I hope will persuade you to come now even if you did not want to before, for our love will have a fruit. Arti you will be a father. I am with a child. Many evenings when the air is cool I am going up to the hilltop at Tel Hadid and watching the sun setting over the sea, and thinking of you living there beyond the sea and your baby growing here inside of me. My dear love please come and be with us if you can, or if you cannot come at this time please write me here at Kefar Daniyyel and I will understand.

With warm kisses,

Naomi

There was a smudge at the bottom of the page, which might have been a kiss, or a tear.

The letter was written in small neat handwriting on both sides of two sheets of thin paper folded together. Had it been hidden, or lost? I read it through again. Her English had been better then, I thought. I folded it back along the creases, and put it in my bag. I could picture the poor sad girl sitting out on the hillside carrying her baby inside her, watching the sun setting over the sea, and dreaming of her lover. But the story still refused to fall into place. Did he go to her in the end? Or was it Naomi who came back? Was he married to someone else? And what happened to the baby?

Curiously I rifled through the music books to see whether any more letters would fall out. The Delius songbook fell open at a page that had an English translation beneath the German original.

I have just seen two eyes so brown
In them my joy, my world I found

There was a time when Rip used to call me his brown-eyed girl, and I remembered how he would sing along to the Van Morrison tape when we were driving in the car to France, with Ben and Stella strapped in the back, and our bulky frame tent and Camping Gaz strapped to the roof rack. And I would squeeze his hand, and the kids would roll their eyes and snort in derision at this display of adult soppiness. What happens to love? Where does it go, when it's not there any more? Rip's love had all dribbled away into the Progress Project. Probably I was also to blame for letting it happen – for letting my eyes become less brown.

The light of the torch was beginning to flicker; the battery must be running low. I switched it off and climbed the stairs to the first-floor landing. The nine doors were all closed. I gathered together Mrs Shapiro's grey-white satin nightdress, pink candlewick dressing gown and *Lion King* slippers from her bedroom. Standing on tiptoe, I could just see that the Harlech Castle tin was still on top of the wardrobe where I'd left it. Then I closed the door behind me and opened the door that led up to the attic.

I'd not been up here before, and I'd sneered inwardly when Mark Diabello had talked about the penthouse suite, but as I climbed the steep dog-leg stair, light poured in from two high rounded gable-end windows and a vast light-well in the roof, revealing wide beamed eaves branching off into rooms with sloping ceilings and magnificent views over the treetops towards Highbury Fields.

The rooms, however, were full of junk – heaps and bundles and cardboard boxes, all piled dustily on top of each other. My heart sank. It would take ages to search through this lot. I opened one of the boxes at random – it was full of books. I pulled one out and flicked through the pages. *Saint Teresa of Avila: A Life of Devotion.* Not my sort of thing. Other boxes contained crockery, cutlery and some rather ghastly china ornaments. A cupboard that looked promising had nothing in it but rubber bands and jam-jar lids – dozens of them – and some pre-war recipe books and magazines. There were no documents or photos, or letters or a diary that would fill in the gaps in Mrs Shapiro's story.

On my left a narrow doorway opened on to a spiral staircase that led up into a small round room. This, I realised, was the fanciful little turret perched on the west side of the house. It was barely large enough to fit an armchair, and that's almost all that was in there, a wide armchair upholstered in faded blue velvet with claw feet and a scrolled back, and by it a little carved table in front of the window. As I sat down on the chair a cloud of dust rose up around me making me sneeze. I looked out over the jungly rain-washed garden, imagining how pleasant it would be to sit here on a quiet afternoon with a cup of tea, a Danish pastry and a good book; and then out of the blue I felt an intense sensation of presence – of someone else who had sat here looking out of the window just as I was. Whose chair had this been? Who else had sat here looking down into the garden? My restless hands had been stroking the velvet and now I felt something unexpectedly hard against my fingertips – a coin. It was one of those big old-fashioned pennies with a picture of Queen Victoria, pushed down the side of the chair. I carried on feeling with my fingers and pulled out a paper clip, a cigarette butt, and a small crumpled photograph. I smoothed it out. It was a picture of a baby, a beautiful brown-eyed baby. I couldn't tell whether it was a girl or a boy. Somebody's hands were holding it up under the arms as it grinned gummily into the camera.

'Yoo-hoo! Anybody there?'

I jumped. I'd left the front door open, I remembered. Guiltily, I shoved the coin and the photo back down the sides of the chair and made my way down the stairs. Mrs Goodney was standing in the hall with a smug smile on her face.

'I thought I'd find you here. Having a good snoop around, are we?'

She was wearing the same pointy cube-heel shoes and an ugly raincoat with a slightly scaly texture in almost the same shade of lizard green. I suppose someone had once told her the colour suited her.

'Mrs Shapiro asked me to feed her cats. She gave me the key.'

'Feeding them in the bedrooms? I don't think so.'

I blushed, more with fury than embarrassment, but I kept my mouth shut.

'Anyway, you can hand the keys over now, because we've established that you're not in fact the next of kin. She's got a son.'

I caught my breath – the baby! But there was something about the way Mrs Goodney looked at me that made me think she was bluffing. Or fishing for information. Well, that was a game two could play.

'But I don't think he'll be coming over from Israel to feed the cats.'

She blinked, a quick reptilian blink.

'We have our links with international agencies, you know. We'll be inviting him to help sort out his mother's business when the house goes up for sale.'

'You can't put it up for sale without her consent.' Or could she?

'Of course, he'll have an interest in the property, too – the son.' She watched me closely with her lizard eyes. 'In the meantime, she's in the care of Social Services. She said, by the way, that she doesn't want you to visit her any more.'

Her words sent a tremor through me. Had Mrs Shapiro

really said that? It was possible – she was cussed enough – but somehow I just didn't believe it.

'So,' Mrs Goodney held out her hand for the keys, 'I'll be taking over the care of the cats.'

Violetta appeared, as if on cue, purring and rubbing herself against Mrs Goodney's legs, and I noticed Mussorgsky creeping towards the bottom of the stairs, waiting for the right moment to sneak up to the bedroom. I realised Mrs Shapiro's bed was their love nest. I realised also from the way Mrs Goodney looked at them that her idea of care would be to call in the Council's pest control department.

'I'm not going to hand over the keys without her written permission.' I tried to make my voice sound snooty, but this just annoyed her more.

'I can always get a court order, you know,' she snapped back.

'Fine. Do that.'

Could she?

After she'd gone, I locked up the house carefully, putting the new key from the back door on to my key ring, grabbed the carrier bag I'd filled with Mrs Shapiro's stuff (of course that would have been the perfect reason for me to be looking around upstairs, but you never think of those things at the time, do you?) and headed straight for the hospital. I raced around the antiseptic maze of corridors looking for Isis ward. But when I got there, she'd gone. Someone else was in her bed. I looked up and down all the bays, but she was nowhere to be seen.

The nurse on duty was another teen-child, thin and harassed.

'Where's Mrs Shapiro? She was in that bed.' I pointed.

The teen-child looked vague.

'She's gone into a nursing home, I think.'

'Can you tell me where she's gone? I brought some things for her.'

'You'll have to ask in the social work department. It's in the same block as physio.'

She pointed vaguely in the wrong direction. Just the thought of the smug smile on Mrs Goodney's face if I went there to ask made my blood boil.

Maybe the bonker lady would know. I hadn't seen her in the lobby when I arrived, and when I went back to the ward where I'd first met her with Mrs Shapiro, I couldn't find her anywhere. I thought she might be down in the foyer cadging cigarettes, but she wasn't there either. I walked over to the porters' desk, but I realised I didn't even know her name. Then on my way out I spotted her hanging around outside the main entrance doors, by the No Smoking sign. She seemed to be involved in an argument with a couple of youths wearing baseball caps, one of whom had his leg in plaster. She grabbed me as I came out.

'They've tooken me cigs off of me.'

'Who? The nurse?' About time, I was thinking.

'No, them.' She pointed to the youths, who were both smoking hard, their heads bent over their hands, as though their lives depended on it.

I went up to them. 'Did you . . .?'

'She's bonkers,' said the one who had his leg in plaster. They ignored me and carried on smoking.

'You're better off without them,' I tried to console her. 'They're not good for you.'

She stared at me silently, a look that combined desolation and contempt.

'Okay, I'll get you some more. Do you know where my friend is? Mrs Shapiro? The lady in the pink dressing gown?'

'They've tooken 'er away. This mornin'. She give 'em some proper lip, too. You should've 'eard 'er carryin' on. Swearin' an' all. An' I thought she were a lady!'

She tutted disapproval.

'Do you know where she is?'

'Never 'eard naffink like it. Filfy tongue, she's got on 'er. They gonna put 'er in ar 'ome. Best place for 'er.'

'Do you know the name of the home? Where it is?'

'Nightmare 'ouse.'

'Nightmare?' That didn't sound good.

'It's where they all go. Bin there meself. Up Lea Bridge way. Not many comes aht alive.' She shook her head ominously and started to cough.

'Thanks. Thank you very much.'

I made to go, but she held on to my coat.

'Yer won't forget me ciggies, will yer?'

There was no Nightmare House in the telephone directory or on the internet. (Well, there was, but it turned out to be a video game.) I telephoned Ms Baddiel and left a message, but she didn't ring back. Eileen said mysteriously that she was 'on a case'. I was furious and frustrated. Should I go to the police and tell them my friend had been kidnapped by Social Services? I could just imagine their faces. Should I write to my MP? See a lawyer? It came to me that the only person who might be able to help us was Mark Diabello. He'd know what happened in situations like this; and he had a strong interest in making sure Mrs Shapiro's house wasn't sold from under her.

Ever since our last encounter, I'd been avoiding him and not returning his calls. It's not just that I'd decided he wasn't my type – I'd come to the conclusion that I wasn't his, either, and that I was only one of dozens of women he slept with in the line of business. I guessed he was probably much more interested in Canaan House than in me. Still, I swallowed my misgivings and dialled his number. It rang just once.

'Hello, Georgina.' (My number must be on his mobile.) 'Nice to hear from you.'

There was something in his voice that reminded me of ... Velcro. I felt a flush rise in my cheeks. If I got him to help me, would we end up in bed again? And was that what I really wanted? I pushed the awkward questions to the back of my mind.

'Mrs Shapiro's disappeared,' I blurted. 'She's in a nursing home, but I don't know where.'

He didn't seem surprised. 'Leave it with me, Georgina. When are we going to ...?'

'Thanks, Mark. Got to dash. Someone's at the door ...'

Before he could get back to me, though, Mrs Shapiro found a way of contacting me herself. One day when I went around to Canaan House, I found a letter on the mat inside the door; I almost didn't pick it out among the junk mail. It was a used envelope, originally addressed to a Mrs Lillian Brown at Northmere House, Lea Gardens Close. The address had been crossed out, and Mrs Shapiro's address written in. There was nothing inside the envelope except a scrap of paper torn off from the corner of a newspaper, with two words scrawled in what looked like black eyebrow pencil – *HELP ME*.

4

Adhesives Around the Home

27

The breeze-block fortress

Northmere House was not really a house at all, but a squat square two-storey institution, purpose-built out of plastered breeze block punctured at regular intervals by square windows that opened wide enough for ventilation but not for escape. The only access to the interior was via a sliding glass door operated by a button behind the reception desk, which was guarded by a fierce middle-aged woman in a corporate uniform.

'Can I help you?' she barked.

'I've come to see Mrs Shapiro.'

She tapped a few strokes on her keyboard and said, without raising her eyes from the screen, 'She's not allowed visitors.'

'What do you mean she's not allowed visitors? This isn't a prison, is it?'

My voice was a bit too shrill. Calm down, I told myself. *In – two – three – four . . .*

'That's what it says on her notes. No visitors.'

'Why not? Who made that decision?'

'It'll be up to matron.'

'Can I speak to her?'

She looked up at me finally, a cold, indifferent look.

'She's in a meeting.' She indicated a row of pink upholstered chairs along the wall. 'You can wait if you like.'

'And if I just go for a wander around while I'm waiting?'

I tried to sound cool, but my heart was pumping away, making my voice wobble.

'I'll have to call security.'

From a window in the lobby I could see through to a central courtyard with a square of trim corporate grass, surrounded by a concrete path which led nowhere, and four benches, one at each side. The access was by way of another pair of sliding glass doors on the far side of the courtyard, presumably also button operated. Through the glass, I had a glimpse of a corridor, with doors opening off it. In one of these breeze-block cubicles Mrs Shapiro would be sitting in her bed waiting for me to free her. Somehow I had to get a message through to reassure her that I was trying. She would still be bandaged up, I supposed, and hopefully receiving some kind of medical care in here.

I sat on a pink chair and waited for a while, wondering what to do. The place was eerily quiet, the sounds all muffled by the thick pink carpet and closed double doors, the air dead, with a synthetic smell that was sweetish and chemical. From time to time, a lift discharged someone into the lobby and the guard-dog lady pressed her button to let them exit the building. Some wore nurses' uniforms, some the same corporate skirt and jacket as the guard-dog lady, and there was a woman with a stethoscope who looked as though she might be a doctor. They all seemed busy and preoccupied. It dawned on me that the impassioned human-rights-violation speech I was composing in my head was going to cut absolutely no ice here.

On a low table next to the pink chairs was a bowl of polished waxy fruit, no doubt intended to reassure families that their incarcerated relatives would be getting a whole-some diet. I picked up a bright green apple – it was the same colour as Mrs Goodney's jacket – and bit into it, hard. The sound of my crunching filled the lobby. The guard-dog lady glared at me. When I'd finished it, I placed the apple core on the reception desk and left.

Walking to the bus stop, I racked my brains for ways of springing Mrs Shapiro. I imagined a video-game scenario with the two of us haring along the corridors dodging security guards and ampoule-armed matrons, violins playing wildly on the soundtrack as we burst out through the sliding glass doors down to the Lea Bridge Road and on to a passing bus.

There's something magical about sitting in the front seat up on top of a double-decker bus, wending among the tree-tops. I could feel the tension seeping out of my shoulders and neck as we swayed along high above the road, like riding an elephant. As we crossed the bridge I caught a glimpse of the slim glassy curves of the River Lea as it slipped into London. All around me the sky was full of scudding clouds that fleetingly turned to pink when they caught the sunlight – not the dead chemical pink of Northmere House, but a bright transient gleam of colour like an unexpected smile. I thought of the young woman pregnant with her baby, sitting on the stony hillside, watching the sunset redden over the western sea, waiting for her lover. Now she was locked up in that breeze-block fortress waiting for me to release her.

The bus jolted and turned as we came out from among the treetops at Millfield Park, and for a moment the whole skyscape opened up in front of me, turbulent, vivid, with apocalyptic shafts of light breaking through the clouds. Somewhere it was raining. A coloured arc glimmered briefly and disappeared. For some reason, tears came into my eyes. I remembered my strange conversation with Ben. Liminal. A time of transition. The threshold of a new world. Poor Ben – why did he take everything to heart so?

Mondays were my worst days for missing Ben – two days

still to go. They never warn you how much your children are going to hurt you; they never warn you about that needle-keen love-pain that gets in under your ribs and twists around just when you're trying to get on with your life. It was already four o'clock – home time. Would Ben be back at Rip's by now, eating Choco-Puffs and talking about his day at school? At the next bus stop, a load of schoolkids clambered on and joined me on the top deck, gabbling and laughing and throwing stuff at one another. Did they worry about Armageddon and liminal times? Actually, with kids, you can never tell.

As soon as I got home, I put the kettle on and while it was coming to the boil I listened to the messages on my answering machine. There was one from Mark Diabello asking me to ring when I had time, one from Nathan at *Adhesives in the Modern World*, reminding me of the new deadline, one from Pectoral Pete – no idea what that was about – and a bald peremptory three-word message from Rip, 'Ring me straight-away.' Like hell I would. I tried to delete the one from Rip and accidentally deleted them all. Now I'd have to remember to phone everyone back. Another time. I put a tea bag into the cup and looked in the fridge for milk. Drat. I'd run out. I was still fuming at Rip's message – at the tone of his voice. Once, not so long ago, he'd have left a message with love. What had happened to all that tenderness?

I hunted around for some powdered milk, and ended up pouring myself a glass of wine instead. Then another. The silence of the kitchen closed in on me. Two days still to go. Then the phone rang. It was Mark Diabello.

'Georgina, you're at home. I've been … er … making a few enquiries. Shall I come round?'

I should have made an excuse and put the phone down, but the wine had made me weepy, and the treacly sweetness in

his voice filled me with unexpected longing. No, not for sex –
I just wanted someone to be nice to me.

'Sorry I didn't ring you back. I've been feeling . . .'

I didn't get the end of the sentence out. A big sob rose up in
my throat and washed the words away. He was around
within ten minutes.

I suppose I'd been hoping for a little tenderness, but I could
see from the way Mark Diabello looked at me on the doorstep
that sex was what was on offer. He led me straight into the
bedroom, where he noted with a murmur of approval that
the satin and Velcro handcuffs were still in position from
last time. Then his shirt was off, and my top was off and his
trousers were off and my skirt was up and . . . what happened
next was far too disgusting to describe. He went through all
the stages like someone working through a car service manual, and I surrendered with all the abandon of a Ford Fiesta
having its eighty-thousand-mile service.

As the bedclothes cooled against my skin and my eyes
adjusted to the dimness in the room I noticed that his clothes
were folded up on the chair, while mine were all tangled in
the duvet. Circling me in his arms, he stroked the hair back
from my forehead.

'Georgina, you're a very sensitive woman. I like that.'

'I like you, too.'

I forced myself to say it, but the words felt wooden and
clunky in my mouth. I rested my cheek on his damp chest that
smelled of sweat and musky soap and chlorine.

He ran a finger down my cheek. 'You're special. I mean . . .
different. I'd like to see more of you, Georgina.'

'Mmm,' I murmured non-committally.

The touchy-feely talk was probably fake, I'd concluded, and
all he wanted from me was sex.

We hadn't spoken about Mrs Shapiro and Canaan House

last time, as if by tacit agreement, as if our relationship floated above the world and its sordid concerns in its own enclosed bubble. But there was something so *purposeful* about those neatly folded clothes.

'You know, Mark, I still wonder about that house . . .'

'What do you wonder, sweetheart?'

'. . . what you and your partner are up to.'

'I could ask you the same thing, you know, Georgina. Why did you come to me in the first place to have it valued? She's not your aunty. It's obvious she doesn't want to sell – so why the sudden interest on your part?' He propped himself up on one elbow, studying my face. 'I keep asking myself – what's in it for you? Why did you start this whole thing?'

I gasped. He thought . . . he thought *I* was like *him*. Mrs Goodney, I remembered, had made the same accusation.

'I didn't start it.' I had a sudden vivid recollection of the rusty-gate voice talking into the mobile phone. I remembered the phrase she'd used to describe Mrs Shapiro – an old biddy. 'It was the social worker who started it. She wanted to put Mrs Shapiro in a home and make her sell the house. She was going to have it valued by Damian at Hendricks & Wilson. I heard her say it.'

He sat up, his limbs suddenly taut.

'You should have told me that before. It's a well-known scam. All the estate agents have their contacts in Social Services. That's how we get to hear of properties with potential before they go on the market – old people going into homes, deceased estates, mortgage foreclosures. There might be a client in the wings, an investor or a developer, who'll pay a good price for the tip-off.'

My brain was struggling to keep up. The shameless red panties were crumpled under the bedclothes. Then I remembered something else.

'Actually, that social worker had a man with her the first time. He could have been a builder – I think she was showing him the house. She must have been talking to him on the phone. But surely . . . what if Mrs Shapiro has a family?'

'They do a deal with the family, Georgina – cash sale, no questions asked – the family get their hands on the money, and they get the house off their hands. There's always someone in every family that'll take that line. People – how can I put it? – in my line of business you tend to see them at their worst.'

'But I still don't understand why the family goes along with it.'

'If their old dad or aunty goes into a nursing home, the money from selling their house is supposed to pay the home fees, right? At five hundred quid a week or more, that can soon gobble up an entire estate that the family hoped they would inherit. But when the money runs out, the Council takes over the payment for the nursing home. So they get the valuer to put in a false low valuation. He gets his cut. They sell it cheap to an associate, based on the low valuation. The relatives pay the nursing-home fees until the money from the phoney sale's all gone, and the Council takes over the payments. After a few months, they can put the property back on the market at its true value, and they pocket the difference.'

I tried to follow what he said, but all I could see was a gyre of money and bricks swirling around in my head. I was wishing I'd kept my mouth shut.

'But that's just a rip-off.'

'You're very innocent, sweetheart. I like that.'

He kissed me on the forehead in a way that made me feel suddenly queasy.

'You'd better go now. Ben'll be back soon. Anyway, I don't think she has any family.'

He threw me a sharp look, as if he knew I was lying about Ben, and reached across for his underpants – sleek dark Lycra that perfectly defined his manly parts, as the shameless woman might have observed – but she'd gone off somewhere, and Georgie Sinclair was back home.

'So the social worker could just be flying solo,' he said.

'You mean, robbing solo?'

'That's one way of seeing it. But look at it from the social worker's point of view – they don't get paid much, do they?' He slipped his arms into his shirtsleeves. 'Not many perks. And it's a pretty thankless job. Then once in a lifetime an opportunity like this comes along. Who's she robbing? There's no family. The old lady doesn't need millions, she just needs a nice, safe, clean home. Why not help her and help yourself at the same time?'

I was shocked. 'Aren't social workers supposed to care for the elderly?'

He laughed, a cold laugh. 'Nobody cares for anybody in this world, Georgina.'

He was buttoning up his shirt now. The bleakness in his voice was like the mineral aftertaste of black treacle. I felt an unexpected pang of pity. Poor Mr Diabello with his sleek beautiful body and his sleek shiny Jaguar – condemned to live in a universe where nobody cares. I kissed his wrist where the black hairs curled out from under the starched white cuff of his shirt.

'I thought you cared for me.'

'That's different. *You're* different, Georgina.'

He bent down and kissed me so gently that I was just beginning to think he might mean it after all, and my undisciplined hormones started up their chatter. Then he raised his head and I saw the glint of his eyes darken from gold to

obsidian. 'So just out of interest – what did Hendricks &
Wilson value it at?'

'Seven million,' I hazarded.

'You're lying to me.'

'*You* might be lying to *me*.'

He laughed, tilting back his head to knot up his tie, so I
could see the attractive growth of five o'clock shadow dap-
pling the handsome cleft in his chin. The Velcro was chafing
against my wrists.

'Mark, you've forgotten . . .'

'Oh, yes.' He reached out and undid the fastenings. They
dangled limply from the headboard as he made his way out
into the dusk, and I retrieved my tangled clothes.

28

Ancient and inexplicable

It poured with rain next day, and I sat at my laptop trying to think about adhesives. Bonding. For some reason, my mind kept drifting to Velcro – fascinating stuff. All those sexy little hooks. After a while, I gave up trying to work, put my wellies on, and went round to feed Mrs Shapiro's cats. They were waiting for me as I approached Canaan House, circling disconsolately out in the rain. The porch where they usually waited was one huge puddle. I looked up and saw that water was now pouring down from the broken gutter I'd first noticed nearly a fortnight ago, and splashing straight into the porch. I fed the cats in the kitchen, and shooed them out through the back door. I noticed Violetta sneaking round the back towards the derelict outhouses, and a few minutes later Mussorgsky slunk off in the same direction. I watched to see whether Wonder Boy would follow, but he was still hanging around for the last scrapings out of the tin. I dished it out slowly, to give the lovers the best chance I could. Then I went home via the Turkish bakery and treated myself to a Danish pastry.

As soon as I got in I phoned Mr Ali. He was hesitant at first when I described the problem.

'I am a handyman not a builder. Big ladders needed for this job.'

But he agreed to take a look. Next, I rang Northmere House. I was annoyed but not surprised to discover that Mrs

Shapiro was barred from receiving phone calls as well as visitors. No doubt her mail would be censored, too.

Fortified by my cup of tea and Danish pastry, I returned to my desk. Adhesives. Bonding. Bondage. Mark Diabello. The trouble was, I caught myself thinking, as I stared at the screen of my laptop, that we didn't have anything at all in common. Once the initial excitement of sex wore off, I found him – I hadn't been able to admit this to myself before – a bit, well, boring. Maybe that was the trouble with *The Splattered Heart*. Those romantic hero types can be limited in their appeal. What I needed was someone I could talk to: someone intellectual; preferably someone hunkily intellectual.

I'd deleted Nathan's message without writing down the new deadline. Should I ring him to check? I hesitated. He already thought I was pretty stupid. I pictured him sweeping back his black hair in exasperation from his craggily intelligent brow – he was sitting down at his desk so you couldn't tell he was rather short. Anyway, size doesn't matter, does it? I dialled his number.

'Nathan, I'm sorry, I deleted your message by mistake. What's the new deadline?'

He sighed and tutted in a way that suggested he wasn't really cross.

'March twenty-fifth. D'you think you'll be able to have it ready in time, Georgie girl?'

'I think so. Actually, Nathan,' I lowered my voice, 'I keep on getting distracted.'

'Oh? Anything interesting?' he breathed. I wavered. No, better not mention Velcro.

'Nathan, have you ever heard of a place called Lydda?'

'You mean Lydda near Tel Aviv? Where the airport is? They call it Lod nowadays.'

'See? I remembered you were good on place names.'

'Are you thinking of going off on holiday? You'd better finish the April *Adhesives* before you go anywhere,' he added with mock sternness. 'The coast's nice down there. I've got some cousins who live at Jaffa.'

Somehow, it hadn't registered with me before that Nathan was probably Jewish, too. The thing is, in Kippax, everybody comes from Kippax. Mr Mazzarella who ran the chippie and his wife who ran the ice-cream van were the only exotic people in town.

'No, I've been visiting an elderly Jewish lady who lives near me. She's got an old photo in her hall of Lydda.' There was silence on the other end of the phone. 'I thought it was a person. I didn't realise it was a place,' I mumbled. 'That's all.'

'You thought it was a person? Like Georgia?'

'I told you geography's not my strong point.'

Somehow I'd managed to make a complete prat of myself again. But even as I said it, I was thinking – why does Mrs Shapiro have a photo of Lydda?

'There was a terrorist attack there in 1972. A bunch of Japanese terrorists gunned down a load of people at the airport. You might have read about it,' said Nathan.

I searched back through my memory. I would have been twelve years old at the time. Just finding my feet at Garforth Comp. It must have been one of those tragedies in a far-away place that flits across the television screen and vanishes in a day, wringing less grief than the death of Lionheart the school rabbit.

'What did they do that for?'

'They were avenging two Palestinian hijackers who'd been gunned down by the Israelis.'

My mind blanked over. Palestinians and Israelis killing each other – an enmity as ancient and inexplicable as Wonder Boy and Violetta. Somebody else's problem, not mine.

29

The Abomination

Next day I waited for a break in the rain to dash across to
Canaan House on my feline mercy mission. They were all
there, waiting for me, circling and purring. There's something
very nice about getting such a warm furry welcome, even
when you know it's really just the food they want – it isn't
love at all. Maybe the emotions don't matter – maybe if Rip
was just a bit more warm and furry when he talked to me,
I thought, I'd be able to cope with the lack of feeling.

I fed them in the kitchen, then just as I was about to lock
up and go home, the rain started again, big heavy drops,
presaging a downpour. I could have made a run for it, but
getting back to *Adhesives* just didn't seem that appealing. I
excused myself by thinking I should check the roof for leaks,
and made my way up into the attic. Despite the disrepair in
the rest of the house, the roof was surprisingly sound. There
was a place at the front, more or less above the bay window,
where a couple of slates were missing and water was dripping
in. I hunted among the junk for a container to catch the drips
and found a pretty Victorian chamber pot with a blue-iris
design, similar to the pattern in the bathroom.

In the turret room, the ceiling showed no damp patches.
I settled myself into the blue armchair to wait for the rain to
pass, and felt round the edges for the baby photo. It was still
there. I took it out and studied it. Mrs Sinclair had once said,
shortly after Stella was born, that in her opinion all babies

were alike. I'd been outraged at the time; but now, looking at this crumpled photo of a bald gummy baby, I thought she had a point. Only the lovely dark baby-wide eyes stood out. I gazed back at them, and something from long-ago 'O' level biology popped into my head: the brown-eye gene is dominant; the blue-eye gene is recessive. So this baby must have had at least one brown-eyed parent. Mrs Shapiro's eyes were blue. And so were Artem Shapiro's.

Now my curiosity was truly aroused. With my fingers, I explored the crevice around the edges of the armchair. There was a lot of fluff, cat hair and miscellaneous debris that stuck in my nails. At last, near the left armrest, I came across what felt like paper. It couldn't have fallen in by accident – it must have been pushed down deliberately – it must have been hidden. With one hand I held back the blue upholstery, and with the other I dug two fingers in deep enough to catch hold of one end and pull it out. It was a letter, concertinaed up, on the same flimsy notepaper as the one I'd found in the piano stool.

Kefar Daniyyel near Lydda 26th November 1950

My Dearest Artem,

I am writing with some wonderful news for you. Our baby was born on 12th November, a little boy. Every day I watch him grow a little more beautiful like his father. Truly he has your face, Arti, but he has my brown eyes. I am often talking to him about his daddy in London, and he smiles and lifts up his little hands in the air, as if he is understanding everything. I have called him Chaim after our great president Chaim Weizmann. One day your daddy will come here to us I promise to him. Why do you not come, Arti? Why do you not write? Have you forgotten about us?

We are so eagerly waiting for you, to wrap you up with our love. My dear one the air here is so good and clean after the horrible smogs of London I am sure that your health will be improved straightaway. My friend Rachel is expectant also. You cannot imagine how it is good after half a century of death to be surrounded with new life. You will be feeling like at home among these olim who have made aliyah from every corner of the world. Many here at Daniyyel are from Manchester and everyone speaks English, though the big thing now is to learn again our own ancient tongue.

There is so much of our people's history in this red earth and in these white stones that are lying across the landscape like the bones of our forebears, sometimes I imagine their spirits sitting beside us on the hillside in the evening to watch the sun going down and the first stars to rise in the east. Finally after so much suffering they are in peace. When the wind whispers over the hilltop it is like the voices of our dead singing their kaddish prayers. Six million souls who have come home. Dear one, I am still remembering our house in Highbury and our happy evenings by the piano, and then my eyes are full of tears. Why do you not write?

With all my love,

Naomi

I read and reread the letter as I sat waiting for the rain to ease off. Then I folded it up and pushed it back down the side of the chair with the photograph. Who *was* Naomi? She must have been the pretty brown-eyed woman – the mother of the baby. But then who was the old lady in Northmere House? How did the two Naomis fit together?

The rain showed no sign of easing off: the water streamed

down the windows as though someone was playing a hose on them. There was something almost apocalyptic about this never-ending downpour. Was it one of the prophetic signs of the End Times? Ben would probably know. I glanced at my watch. It was three o'clock, almost time for him to be back. In the end, I just resigned myself to getting soaked, and made a dash for home.

When I got in, I rubbed my hair dry with a towel, put on dry clothes, and guiltily sat down at my laptop. Okay. Concentrate. Glue. *Adhesive curing is the change from a liquid to a solid state.* Sometimes the science of stickiness can be boringly obvious. Maybe it was time to start another novel – a novel about an old lady who lives in a huge crumbling house with seven cats, and a secret. I pushed the dissident thought out of my mind and forced myself to focus. *Adhesives in the Modern World* was what paid the bills. Something else was niggling at the back of my brain. Ben seemed to be home later than usual.

When at last I heard his key in the latch, I folded up my laptop and went downstairs to greet him. As I came into the hall, I stopped and caught my breath. I saw a stranger standing there – a bald weirdo who'd broken into my house.

'Hi, Mum.' He grinned embarrassedly and hung up his wet coat. 'Don't stare like that.'

'What . . .?'

All his hair, his lovely brown curls, had gone. His skull, knobbly and pale, looked obscenely naked.

'It looks very . . .'

He met my eyes. 'Don't say it, Mum.'

I put my hand over my mouth. We both laughed.

'D'you want some Choco-Puffs?'

He shook his head.

'I don't know why you always get those for me. Dad gets them, too. I hate them.'

'I thought you liked them.'

'I used to. I've gone off them now. They taste funny. Sort of metallic?'

'So what would you like?'

'S'all right. I'll get it.'

He made himself some toast and spread it with peanut butter a centimetre thick, a layer of strawberry jam on top of that, then a sprinkling of cocoa powder. I'd expected him to take it up to his room, but he pulled out a chair and sat down at the kitchen table. Outside, the rain splashed and gurgled, overflowing the gutter. Surely such heavy rains in February were something new? I must remember to ask him. I poured myself a cup of tea. Ben, since our liminal conversation, had been drinking only water.

'So isn't it a bit . . . cold?'

He gave me a look of mild reproach. 'Yeah. But when you think our Lord was crucified, it sort of puts it in perspective?'

The rising inflection made him sound defensive. I felt a flutter of panic.

'Is it something you think about a lot, Ben?'

He opened his school bag, unzipped an inner pocket, and pulled out a book. With a shock of recognition I saw it was Rip's old school Bible – black, gilt-edged, with the crest of his public school inside the front cover. He leafed through to a page that was bookmarked with an old bus ticket.

'When ye therefore shall see the . . . Abomination of Desolation . . .' he stumbled on the clunky words, 'spoken of by Daniel the prophet, stand in the holy place, then let those who are in Judaea flee to the mountains. Let him which is on the housetop not come down to take anything out of his house. Neither let him which is in the field return back to take his clothes.' He read carefully, looking up from time to time to check I was still listening. 'And then shall they see the Son of Man coming in the clouds of heaven, with power and great glory.'

He paused to take a bite of toast. I had a sudden image of the skyscape I'd seen from the top of the bus. Those gleaming galloping clouds – they *were* like chariots of glory.

'And he shall send his angels with a great sound of a trumpet, and they shall gather together his elect from the four winds, from the uttermost part of the earth to the uttermost part of heaven.' When I didn't say anything, he added, 'Mark chapter thirteen? Verses fourteen to twen'y-seven?'

'Ben . . .'

In the silence between us, a sweet curly-haired child hovered on the edge of extinction. I wanted to hug him in my arms. I wanted him to be my little boy again, to tell him stories about rabbits and badgers, but he was somebody different.

'I'm not saying it's all rubbish, Ben. That language – it's very powerful. But don't you think it refers to things that happened a long time ago?'

'The Abomination that bringeth Desolation isn't a long time ago, Mum – it's in the future – soon. Some nutter'll drop a nuclear bomb on the Temple Mount at Jerusalem. The holy place. That stuff about fleeing into the hills, not going back for anything, not even picking up your coat. The mushroom cloud. It's all there.' He reached over for the cocoa powder and gave his toast another dusting, then he licked his finger and circled it round in the surplus cocoa on the edges of his plate.

'But . . .' How can you take this stuff seriously? I wanted to say. And yet I realised with a pang of apprehension that Ben was far from alone, and it was my own cosy secular world view that was in retreat before a sweeping global tide of belief.

'Daniel predicted it first. In the Old Testament? Then Matthew and Mark picked up on it? They didn't even know about nuclear weapons, but the way they describe it ... it's kind of uncannily accurate?' His voice, crackly and insistent, seemed alien.

'But isn't it just symbolic? You're not meant to take it literally, Ben.'

His eyes brightened with zeal. He licked his fingers again.

'Yeah, that's what it is. Symbolic. You've got to interpret the signs? They're happening all over the world, the signs of the End Times? If you know what to look out for?'

Without his crown of brown curls, the dark downy hair on his lip and chin seemed to stand out more against the pallor of his skin. He looked like a stranger – a stranger trying to impersonate someone I knew intimately.

'But they're nutcases, Ben, the people who run those websites.'

I shouldn't have let my exasperation show. His voice became whiny and defensive.

'Yeah, a'right, some may be a bit nutty. But the big guys that run the world – they all know it's going to happen? George Bush 'n' Tony Blair? Why d'you think they're always praying together? Why d'you think they're so, like, totally obsessed with the Middle East? Why are they getting so stressed about Iran going nuclear? *They* know it's the prophecy of the Second Coming that's working out in our time? Like, we're the last generation?'

He slapped two bits of toast together into a sandwich, and licked at the peanut butter that squeezed out around the crusts.

'Want to know why America supports Israel? Because in the Bible it says when the chosen people go back to their promised land, like they did in 1948, that's the start of the End

Times.' He bit into the sandwich with a crunch. 'It's sad cases like you and Dad that'll get left behind.'

'Left behind what?'

'The rapture? The Second Coming? When the elect get taken up to heaven, and all the sad gits with their *Guardians* and their anti-war placards'll be left behind to stew in the tribulations.' A spot of jam had oozed on to the edge of his plate. He licked it off. 'George Bush's pal Tim LaHaye wrote a book called *Left Behind*. It's all in there.'

'Just because George Bush believes it doesn't make it true.'

'Yeah, but maybe they know something you don't? Like, they've got their sources of information? The website's got five million subscribers?' He gave me a look that was both angry and pitying. 'Don't be so blind, Mum.'

Then he took a swig of water, got up abruptly taking his bag and his Bible, and stomped off to his room, his pale skull bobbing up and down as he climbed the stairs.

My stomach clenched into a knot. I finished drinking my tea and went upstairs to my bedroom. I sat on my bed with a pillow behind my back and opened up my laptop. In the rain-washed light from the window, the blue sky of my desktop image seemed absurdly optimistic. I typed *End of Time* into Google, just as Ben said he'd done. There were literally millions of entries. I started opening a few at random, following links, and all of a sudden I found I'd stepped over a threshold into an eerie parallel world I'd never even guessed existed. Ben was right – there were millions of people out there scouring their Bibles and actively trying to calculate the timetable for the end of the world from clues in the text.

At first I felt piqued. Why hadn't I read about any of this in the *Guardian*? Or heard about it on Radio Four? Why hadn't Rip told me? Then I started to feel scared. Some sites had bizarre names like *teotwawki* (The End of the World As We

Know It), *escapeallthesethings*, *raptureready*. Millions of people clearly *were* getting ready. The Old Testament prophecies of Daniel and Ezekiel, the four Gospels of the New Testament and the Book of Revelation were quoted again and again in rambling blogs by individuals offering their own personal interpretations of the prophecies, and in huge complex sites with links to dozens of organisations. There were even sites that marketed 'End Times Products'. One link led to a quotation from a speech by George Bush: 'We are living in a time set apart.' It was highlighted in red and animated with horrid little flames, sharp like razor teeth. Another linked mysteriously to a page called 'How to Fix Self-Tanning Mistakes'.

Alone in my dusky room, with only the fan of my laptop purring away intermittently, and these creepy fundamentalists as my guides, I could feel the boundaries of reason start to dissolve and notions from the irrational hinterland encroach into my consciousness. Was this what Ben had felt? I remembered my dream, the formless malevolent spirit, and despite myself I shuddered. Everything in this other world seemed illusive, like a nightmare in which everyday things like bar codes, seen through a prism of unreason, take on a sinister skew, while war, disease, terrorism, global warming – the scourges of our age – are seized on with glee as signals of the Second Coming. A man who called himself Jeremiah – his website showed him with a neat little goatee beard and a Scotch plaid cap similar to Mrs Shapiro's – explained that the parable of the fig tree – '*When his branch is yet tender, and putteth forth leaves, ye know that summer is nigh*' – referred to seasonal changes from global warming, which were a sign of imminent rapture. Power up the central heating and the air conditioning! Roll on, four-by-fours! Fly by jet! Consume! As the earth warms up and the fig trees blossom, those lucky ones, the elect, will be seized and whisked off into heaven! His smug little smile said it all.

How come I didn't know about any of this? I thought back to my religious knowledge lessons at Kippax Primary School, Mrs Rowbottom wearing her mauve bobble-knit jumper and a porcelain rose brooch; the smell of closely packed children, and Lionheart the school rabbit snoozing in his cage; the little bottles of pre-Thatcher milk waiting in the crates by the door. We'd learned about forgiveness and mercy. We'd learned about the wheat and the tares, and the Prodigal Son. I'd even got a gold star for my drawing of the Good Samaritan. Mum had proudly put it on the fridge in the kitchen, even though Dad was a subscriber to the opium-of-the-masses theory of religion.

When we were a bit older, we discussed motes and beams, and learned to recite the Beatitudes and Saint Paul's *faith, hope and charity* epistle off by heart. It had all seemed very uplifting and benign. I had no idea about all this other stuff. Had Mrs Rowbottom known? If so, she'd seemed unperturbed.

Jeremiah's website had a <u>*Promised Land*</u> link which took me to a whole page of links to both Christian and Jewish sites discussing God's promise to the Jews. When was that promise to be fulfilled? In God's time, in the prophesied future? Or now, in the present-day Middle East? Was the rebuilding of the third Temple in Jerusalem a metaphor for spiritual rebirth? Or was it about bricks and mortar? The cyber-arguments raged. Something else Ben had said came into my mind. When the chosen people go back into Israel, in 1948, that's the start of the End Times. My mind flashed to the letter in the piano stool. *Our Promised Land*. The date on the letter was 1950. When I'd read it first, it had seemed like a quaint voice from another age. Now past, present and future were in terrifying collision.

And it wasn't only Christians and Jews who were pre-occupied with the Second Coming. Ben had said something about a Last Imam. Google came up with more than a million links to websites anticipating the imminent return of the Imam al-Mahdi. It all seemed a long way from the Prince of Wales's bar codes.

As I surfed from one link to another, the light from my laptop screen threw an eerie coloured glow on the walls and ceiling. I was beginning to understand why Ben was so rattled. Compared with the vast inevitability of this Rapture machine, the world of our own little secular family seemed puny and insubstantial. Dusk dimmed into darkness outside the window, where flurries of rain still pattered on the glass. Yes, the rain. I forgot to ask him about the rain.

30

The broken gutter

By Saturday the rain had stopped but the pavements were still wet, and soft heavy drops dripped from the overhanging trees as I walked along to Canaan House, where I'd arranged to meet Mr Ali to take a look at the gutter. I'd set out a little early, hoping to catch him on his own. I wanted to ask him about Lydda; I wanted to find out about Islam and the Last Imam. But as I turned into Totley Place, I spotted a small battered red van parked in the lane that led to Canaan House, and then I heard men's voices in the garden, shouting. I quickened my step. The shouting got louder – I couldn't tell what they were shouting – it wasn't in English anyway. Violetta dashed out to greet me; she was running around in circles, mewing.

As I approached the gate, I glimpsed between the trees a terrifying sight – Mr Ali was dangling in the air, like a rather tubby Tarzan wearing a pink-and-mauve knitted hat. He was hanging on for grim death to a length of cast-iron gutter that had come away from the wall. I watched transfixed as he tried to reach with his toes for the window ledge, bawling something in a foreign language. All that was holding him up was a rusty iron bracket at one end, and a twine of ivy that had clambered over the roof and luckily got a grip on the chimneys. On the ground, floundering among the wet brambles, two young men in flowing white robes and Arabic headgear were grappling with an extendable aluminium ladder that had come apart.

They heaved it this way and that, their robes snagging in the brambles. The ladder definitely seemed to be winning. At last they slotted the three sections together and wielded it in Mr Ali's direction, trying to catch him as he hung with just one toe now resting precariously on the window ledge, and the other kicking at the air. But they swung the ladder too wide, then overcorrected and swung it too far the other way. Mr Ali let out a tirade of furious words. I could see the bracket straining under his weight and the ivy coming away from the bricks. If they didn't get their act together fast, he was going to plummet some thirty feet on to the stone terrace in front of the house. I held my breath, and a thought clicked in my head – these young men, they really are unbelievably useless.

In the end they managed to get the ladder under Mr Ali, but it was too short to reach the ground. So one of them held it up to Mr Ali's flailing foot, while the other one tried to extend it from below, jerking the catch-hooks down over the rungs, Mr Ali shrieking in terror at each jerk. Then he jerked too hard and the ladder fell apart again. Wonder Boy was sitting in the porch watching, flicking his tail with excitement, a beastly look on his face.

I stood on the path, petrified, thinking I should definitely keep out of this. I didn't want to distract the men's attention for a single second, for I could see that a momentary lapse might be fatal. But just as they'd almost reassembled the ladder, the one at the front lost concentration at exactly the moment that Wonder Boy decided to make a dash for it. Swerving to avoid the cat, his foot caught in a loop of bramble and he staggered forward, holding the ladder high and crashing the top section right through the bedroom window inches away from Mr Ali, completely smashing away the bottom frame. A shower of glass tinkled on to the flagstones.

Mr Ali was still balancing with one leg on the window sill and one thrashing the air, yelling his head off. Then he spotted me by the gate. Our eyes met. It was too late for me to back away. He called down to the two men in the garden, and they looked round, shouting and beckoning. So I ran over to help. I grabbed one end of the ladder, determined to show that although I was a woman, I was not utterly useless like them. But it was much heavier than I thought. As I swayed under its weight, the other end swung round, clonking one of them on the head. He staggered back into the bushes and lay there, motionless. I rushed to his aid. Oh, heck! Had I killed him? Mr Ali and the other young man had gone silent, too. Wonder Boy, who had come over to investigate, gazed up at me and I thought I glimpsed in his slitty yellow eyes a look of . . . was it respect?

After a few moments the young man pulled himself out of the bushes, no harm done, and between the three of us we managed to extend the ladder to its full length and get it up securely against the wall below Mr Ali's feet. He climbed down, bawling at the other two – he was literally spitting with rage. Then just as his feet touched the ground, all the fight seemed to go out of him, and he slumped down, his head resting on his knees, breathing deeply.

'This job is for a younger, fitter man. Not double excel gentleman my age.'

'But you *did* excel, Mr Ali. Keeping so calm,' I said, though calmness, to be honest, was not the first word that sprang to mind.

'No, size XXL, Mrs George.' He clasped his arms around his hamster tummy. 'My wife feeds me too much. No good for climbing up ladders.'

I laughed. 'Next time, you should get one of the other two to go up the ladder.'

He shook his head with a melancholy sigh, but said nothing.

The other two were perched uncomfortably on the triple edge of the ladder. They had got out a packet of cigarettes, and were lighting up. I wondered why they were wearing those bizarre outfits – they looked more like extras out of *Lawrence of Arabia* than any Palestinians I'd seen on TV. They were younger than Mr Ali, taller, and incredibly handsome in a dark-flashing-eyes white-flashing-teeth kind of way. (Tut. Isn't this an utterly incorrect stereotype? Get a grip, Georgie. They're young enough to be your sons.)

'Hello,' I smiled. 'I'm Georgie.'

They nodded their heads and flashed their teeth at me. It was clear they didn't speak a word of English. Mr Ali struggled to his feet.

'Allow me to make introductions. Mrs George, this is Ishmail, my nephew. He is completely useless. This is his friend Nabeel. He is also completely useless.'

The useless young men nodded and flashed their teeth. 'What a misfortune at my age to have two complete Uselesses for my assistants.'

Then he spoke in Arabic to them, and something about the way he looked at me suggested that he was saying I was pretty useless, too. They nodded politely at me and smiled some more.

When they'd finished their cigarettes and stubbed them out on the ground, they put the ladder up against the wall and Nabeel held the bottom of the ladder while Ishmail started to mount it, his feet tangling in his robe.

'No, no, no!' yelled Mr Ali, jumping up, then he yelled something in Arabic. It was obvious even to me that the ladder was too short and the angle too steep to be safe. 'We must get a bigger ladder. I told you this one is no good.'

The Uselesses heaved the no-good ladder on to the roof-rack of the van with a lot of puffing and shouting, then sat on the step of the porch and lit up again. They were grinning like a pair of naughty kids and batting each other with a folded newspaper printed in Arabic. Mr Ali reached across and confiscated it.

'This house – it needs too much work,' he sighed. There was a big damp patch on his trousers from sitting on the wet ground. 'I do not know if I can do it with these Uselesses.'

'I'm sure you can,' I said, making my voice especially calm, which I felt was called for in the situation. 'There's no hurry. I think Mrs Shapiro will be away for a while.'

'You think? Hm.'

He paused and gave me an oblique look. The Uselesses were still sitting in the porch, but now they'd started arguing in loud voices and shoving each other off the step. Then Mussorgsky appeared at the broken bedroom window (how had he got in there?) and began yowling with gusto, and Wonder Boy yowled back from the garden, a smug self-satisfied yowl.

'You know, Mrs George, I am thinking is a pity so big house must stand empty.'

Mr Ali stroked his neat beard and looked at me thought-fully again. 'This, my nephew Ishmail – he has no place to stay. Sleeping on floor in my apartment. Drive my wife mad. This other useless one, too, sometimes sleeping in there.'

I could see what he meant – they would drive me mad, too.

'Well . . . I don't know what Mrs Shapiro would think . . .' I started. Then it occurred to me that these two might be use-less at house repairs, but they could do a great job of keeping the likes of Mrs Goodney and Nick Wolfe at bay. And they could feed the cats. 'It would have to be on the strict under-standing that they move out when Mrs Shapiro comes back.'

'No problem. Even if they stay for short time it will make big difference for my wife. Give her chance to clean up.'

I wondered what Mrs Shapiro would say if I told her they were Palestinian.

'I am sorry they have no money for paying rent. But they will repair the house. Everything will be fixitup like new.' He saw the look on my face. 'I supervise, of course.'

I suppose I should have said no there and then, but there was something irresistibly cuddly about Mr Ali. And besides, I was on the scent of another story.

'Where did you learn all your building skills, Mr Ali? In Lydda?'

He shook his head.

'No. We were sent away from Lydda. Do you not know what happened there?'

'You mean the terrorist attack? I know about that,' I said, pleased with myself.

'Ha! All of the world knows this.' He seemed annoyed. 'Terrorists shooting on innocent Israelis. But you know why? You know what happened before?'

I shook my head. 'Tell me.'

In a clearing in the brambles Wonder Boy and Mussorgsky were now hissing and going for one another with their claws. Violetta was hovering close by, waving her tail and making little yelping noises of encouragement, though I couldn't work out which one she was encouraging. Mr Ali flicked the newspaper at them to chase them away.

'In 1948 all Palestinians were sent out from Lydda. Not only Lydda – many many towns and villages in our country were destroyed. To make way for Jews. People still are living in the refugee camps.'

He went suddenly quiet.

'But . . . but you learned to be a builder, yes?' I encouraged, wanting to reassure myself that something positive had come out of all that displacement, all that history clogged up with memories of unrighted wrongs.

'In Ramallah I trained for engineer.' (He pronounced it inzhineer.) 'Here in England I must make new examinations. But I am old and time has tipped his bucket on me. This useless one,' he pointed at his nephew, 'he will study for engineering, too. Aeronautical.'

'Aeronautical?'

That sounded quite brainy. I tried to imagine going up in an aeroplane engineered by Ishmail, and felt an uncomfortable tightening in my chest.

'He has a scholarship.' He had lowered his voice to a proud whisper. 'Other one, I don't know. Now they are both learning English. First-class English language course nearby to here – Metropolitan University, next door from Arsenal Stadium.'

The Uselesses, realising that they were being talked about, chipped in.

'Arsenal. Yes, please.'

Yes, it would need to be a first-class English course, I thought.

'So why did *you* come to England, Mr Ali? I mean, wasn't your family over there?'

'You are asking difficult questions, Mrs George.'

I could see he didn't really want to talk, but I was still filling in the gaps in the story.

'I'm sorry. It's a Yorkshire habit. Where I come from, everybody knows everybody's business.'

He hesitated, then continued. 'You know, after my youngest son died, I saw no hope. No possibility of end to this conflict. I wanted only to come away from this place. I have a good friend, Englishman, he was a teacher in Friends School in Ramallah. He helped me to come here.'

'Your son died . . .?'

Suddenly, my nosiness had led me into a darker avenue than I'd intended.

'He had a burst appendix.' He stared at the ground as though his son's face was pictured there. 'We were in Rantis, visiting wife's family. We wanted to take him to hospital in Tel Aviv but we were delayed at the checkpoint. My wife was weeping and pleading with the soldiers – one soldier – he was a boy of eighteen but he had a power of life or death over us. He was playing with his power. He said we must go back to Ramallah. When we got there it was too late.' His eyes glinted with a harder brightness. 'How can I forgive? My son was fourteen years old.'

On a corner of the newspaper, he started to draw a map.

'This was five years ago. Now with wall is worse. You can see. Green Line. Wall line.' He drew another snaking line. I stared at the map – the crazy curling line – and felt a flutter of panic. Maps. Not my thing. But why did it snake around so much. In fact, why was there a line at all?

'So you wanted to leave . . .?'

'Now my daughter is married with this Englishman. I have three grandchildren.' He smiled briefly. 'Drive my wife mad.'

I thought I'd like to meet his wife one day.

The Uselesses had finished their cigarettes, and gone off to sit in the van. They must have had a CD player in there, because I could hear strains of Arabic music, sweet and melancholy, drifting incongruously over the damp lawn and dripping brambles.

But maybe all places have their histories of sadness and displacement, I was thinking. People move in, others move on; new lives and new communities spring up among the

241

stones of the old. In school, we'd learned about the history of Kippax, how in the 1840s miners from Scotland and Wales had been recruited as scabs to break up the union in County Durham – desperate hungry men sucking the marrow out of the bones of other desperate hungry men. When the seam at Ledston Luck was opened up, their grandchildren and great-grandchildren were brought down from County Durham to Yorkshire and settled in Kippax. There are men who shape destiny, who draw lines on maps and shift populations about; and there are men like Dad and Mr Ali who live their lives in the interstices of the grand plans of others, labouring to provide food and shelter for their families.

'So, what you say, Mrs George?' Mr Ali interrupted my thoughts. 'They stay here and fixitup the house?'

'I don't know,' I said weakly. My heart ached for sad exiled Mr Ali and his charming useless assistants, but I owed a duty of care to Mrs Shapiro, and the scenario with the ladder had filled me with apprehension. 'Maybe if you fix the gutter first, it'll give me time to have a word with Mrs Shapiro.'

'Tomorrow,' he said, 'we come with the new gutter and big ladder. You will see.'

'And, er, the window. That needs fixing, too, now.'

31

The epoxy hardener

Sometimes when I try to understand what's going on in the world, I find myself thinking about glue. Every adhesive interacts with surfaces and with the environment in its own particular ways; some are cured by light, some by heat, some by the exchange of subatomic particles, some simply by the passage of time. The skill in achieving a good bond is to match the appropriate adhesive to the adherends to be bonded.

Acrylics, for example, are known to be fast curing, and they don't require as much surface preparation as epoxies, which have high cohesive strength but a slower cure rate. Epoxy adhesives have two components: the adhesive itself, and a hardening agent, which accelerates the process. On Friday, I was sitting at my laptop, pondering this profound philosophical duality, when a cunning thought slipped into my head. What I needed to re-bond with Mrs Shapiro was a hardening agent. And who could be harder than Mr Wolfe?

Flushed with inspiration, I rummaged in the desk drawer for a card and wrote a get-well-soon note to Mrs Shapiro, adding that I was doing my best to visit her and advising her under no circumstances to sign anything until we'd talked. I mentioned that I'd found some builders who might be staying at the house while they did some work there – I freely admit, I didn't go into much detail. I told her the cats were doing extremely well and that Wonder Boy was missing her (well, probably he was, in his own brutal and selfish way). I enclosed a stamped addressed envelope and a blank sheet of paper, put it all in an envelope with the card, and sealed it. Then I walked down to the office of Wolfe & Diabello. A quick reconnoitre in the car park round the back told me that Mark Diabello was out and Nick Wolfe was in.

In the small office, his physical presence was overwhelming; he seemed to fill the whole room, pushing me back against the wall. He greeted me with a bruising hand-grip and asked me what he could do me for. (Either he thought that old cliché was still amusing, or his unconscious was speaking.) I told him in my specially friendly voice that Mrs Shapiro had been asking after him. On a yellow Post-it note, I scribbled the address of Northmere House and, handing him my envelope, said that if he found the time to call round, would he drop off the card from me, too.

'Fine,' he said.

Then I went home and got on with *Adhesives in the Modern World*. The article I was editing was about the importance of good joint design in bonding. You see, however good the glue, a poorly designed joint can snooker you. End to end joints should be overlapped if possible, or tongued and grooved, or mortised and tenoned. Or you could go for a hybrid joint – I remembered Nathan's joke, glue and a screw. You should always prepare the surfaces to maximise the bonding area. *'Surface atraction is increased, by rouhgening or scraching the surfaces to be bonded.'*

The article had been written by a young man who knew his glues but seemed to have a total contempt for spelling and punctuation. What do they teach them in school these days? I tutted to myself. Ben was just as bad.

I found myself worrying about how he'd got on in school today. He'd struggled to settle into his new class when we'd moved down from Leeds; in fact the New Year's email chat with the strange semi-literate Spikey was the nearest I'd got to meeting any of his friends. I was anxious that his shaved head and religious leanings could make him a target for bullies, and while we were having tea that evening I tried to raise it with him.

'What did they say at school, then, when you turned up with your new hair-do – your no-hair-do?'

'Oh, nothing.'

Without his brown curls his face looked different. The brown hair was my genetic legacy, but those arched eyebrows, with their slightly haughty lift, and the intense blueness of the eyes – I could see more of Rip in him now.

'Didn't the kids take the mick?'

He shrugged. 'Yeah, a bit, but I don't care. Jesus suffered taunts an' that, din't he?'

Yes, and look what happened to him – I held back the thought, and loaded my voice with maternal concern. 'But wasn't it a bit . . . horrible? I mean, kids can be very cruel.'

'Nah,' he said. 'It's all earthly stuff. Don't bother me. Brings me closer to Our Lord.'

When he'd finished his meal, he laid down his knife and fork, put his hands together briefly and closed his eyes. Then he picked up his bag and disappeared upstairs. Maybe I should have been pleased that he wasn't stealing cars or taking drugs, but there was a scary intensity about him that was almost like an aura of martyrdom. I felt a stab of guilt. Was it our failure as parents that had led him to seek out a different kind of certainty? Sometimes I felt I wasn't grown-up enough myself to be a parent – I always seemed to be just a step ahead, making it up as I went along.

Rip didn't have any such uncertainties – he always knew what was right, and committed himself to making it happen. It was one of the things I'd loved about him – his commitment. Yes, perhaps I had been wrong not to take more of an interest in his work. But what exactly was it that he did? Something about global systems for iterating progress. Or iterating systematic progressive globalisation. Or globalising iterative progressive systems. I understood each word on its own, but together, they had the same effect on my brain as phenolic hydroxyls. I'd made some notes once, ages ago, on a bit of paper, while he was explaining it to me, thinking I'd get my head round it in my own time, that one day we would converse about progress, globalisation, systems and suchlike. It was in the desk drawer somewhere, jumbled up with the old rubber bands and the out-of-ink biros.

On impulse, I picked the phone up and dialled his number. A young woman answered – I nearly didn't recognise her voice.

'Stella?'

'Mum?'

The pain of missing her caught me off guard like a thump in the chest.

'Aren't you supposed to be at uni?' (Why was she visiting Rip and not me?)

'I ... It's reading week. I just came down to see ...' I guessed from her hesitation that it might be something to do with her complicated love life. 'Do you want to speak to Dad?'

Her voice – so sweet – still reedy like a child's, but with an adult's self-assurance. She'd always been a daddy's girl. Sometimes their closeness made me envious.

'Yes – no. Stella, can *we* talk? We always seem to communicate by messages and texts.'

'So?' A prickly tone. She didn't want me making her feel guilty.

'Listen, I'm worried about Ben. Have you noticed anything different about him?'

I realised she wouldn't have seen his haircut yet, but she and Ben were close – they'd fought and loved one another all through their childhoods, just as Keir and I had done.

'He's always been a bit mental, my little bro.'

She was always so confident in her judgements.

'But does he seem unhappy to you?'

'He's cool, Mum. He's got religion in a big way, that's all – like I had Leonardo DiCaprio when I was his age.'

'That's what I mean – religion – it doesn't seem quite normal for sixteen.'

'I don't know what's wrong with you, Mum. He could be shooting up or nicking cars, and you're stressing about him reading the Bible.'

Maybe she's right, maybe that's all it is, I thought, a schoolboy phase. But there was something terrifying about his intensity, the strained look on his face, the dilated eyes.

'He talks about the end of the world as though it's going to happen any minute now.'

'Yeah, Dad keeps on at him about it. They had a big row over Christmas. Then Grandpa got stuck in.'

'I wondered what that was about.'

'Ben started banging on about religion.'

'What did he say?'

'Something about miring the sanctity of Christmas with alcohol and consumerism. They all laughed. Ben got really upset and tried to shut them up.'

'Poor Ben.' I kept my voice even, but I could feel my rage boiling up in me.

'It was gross. Grandpa called him a pansy.'

'What did Ben say?'

'He said, I forgive you, Grandpa.' She giggled. I giggled, too. I tried to imagine my father-in-law's face.

'Good for him.'

Ben hadn't told me because he'd wanted to spare my feelings.

'Stella, it's lovely to talk to you. Have you finished your teaching practice?'

'Yeah. It was nearly enough to turn me into a mass child-murderer. I don't know if teaching's really me.' There was a slight whininess in her voice that I recognised, too. 'But anyway, I'll stick with it till the end of the course, then decide. Don't worry about Ben, Mum. He'll be fine.'

When I put the phone down I was filled with a wonderful sense of ease, as if a sack of rocks had just rolled from my shoulders; I wanted to run out into the street and hug everybody. Instead, I burst into Ben's room and hugged him.

'You all right, Mum?' He lifted his head from the computer.

'I've just been talking to Stella.'

'What did she say?'

'Oh . . . she said she wasn't sure about teaching – whether it was right for her.'

He gave me a long intense look.

'You need to calm down, Mum. You're getting hyper again.'

32

UPVC

On Saturday morning, after Ben had left for Rip's, I got a phone call from Mr Ali.

'You can come and see, Mrs George. House is all fixitup.'

They were waiting for me when I arrived – all three of them, plus the cats. The Uselesses were wearing jeans and baseball caps. I don't know what had happened to their Arabic gear. Mr Ali was grinning with pride.

'See?'

Upstairs, where the old Victorian window had been smashed, a brand new double-glazed white uPVC top-opening window unit had been fitted – it was a bit short for the opening, which had been bricked up with breeze blocks to make it fit. There was a new gutter running the length of the house, also in white uPVC. The brambles had been hacked back to make room for a white uPVC table and chair set, and a white uPVC birdbath sat in the centre of the lawn. Wonder Boy was sitting beside it, surrounded by feathers, licking his chops and looking very pleased with himself.

'It's ... er ... lovely ...' I put on a smile.

The useless ones beamed.

'You let them stay, they will fixitup everything for you,' said Mr Ali.

'Maybe ... maybe not too many repairs. Just essential things. Maybe the woodwork just needs rubbing down and a lick of paint.'

'Baint, yes,' he nodded enthusiastically, and said something in Arabic. The useless ones nodded enthusiastically, too.

'I'll give you a ring. I need to get a spare set of keys cut,' I said, playing for time, thinking maybe Mrs Shapiro would be back soon.

But on Wednesday morning there was a letter for me on the door mat. I recognised my own handwriting on the envelope. The letter inside was written with thick blue marker-pen – the sort Mum used for marking her Bingo cards.

Dearest Georgine

Thank you for your Card and for you sending my Nicky to comfort me in Prison. He is quite adorable! He was coming with Champagne and white Roses. A real Gentleman! We were talking for Hours about Poetry Music Philosophy the Time was passing too quick like flowing Water under a Bridge and I am always asking myself what matters it if there gives a Gulf in our Ages so long as there gives a Harmony inbetween our Souls. It was like so with Artem he was twenty years my older but we have found Joy together. I wonder if I would ever find such a Joy again with another Man to feel the arms of a Mans around me and the warmth of a good Body close beside mine better than Cats. He has said he will come again now every Hour is dragging too long I wait for him to come and you also my dear Georgine. How have I escaped Transportation and Inprisonment in all my Life only to face it now alone in my Older Age. They are wanting me to sign a Confession before I can return to my Home. They are saying I must give the Power of Returning but my Nicky also is saying I must not sign nothing so I am putting a brave Resistance. I must stop the Nurse comes soon with my Injection. Please help me.

Your dear Friend

Naomi Shapiro

I read it through a couple of times. Then I tried to read between the lines. Then I phoned Mr Wolfe.

'Thanks for taking my card round. How was she? She looked awful in hospital. I was surprised they let her out so quickly.'

'Bit of bruising. Gash to the head. Nothing too serious. We had a good laugh.'

'She seems to be very fond of you.' I was wheedling for information.

'Yes. And you know, in a funny way, I've grown quite fond of her, too.'

There was a glibness in his voice, as though it was something he'd been practising.

'Do you know anything about this confession she's been asked to sign?'

'Sorry?'

'Something about power of returning.'

'Ah. Yes. They're wanting her to sign a Power of Attorney.'

'What does that mean?' It sounded ominous.

'It means they – whoever she signed it over to – would have the power to sign legal documents on her behalf.'

'Like the sale of a house, for instance?'

'Got it in one.'

I felt my heart starting to race. Things seemed to be spiralling out of control again, but I kept my voice steady.

'What can we do to stop that?'

'I've been wondering that myself.'

Whatever he had in mind, he obviously wasn't going to share it. I needed to find out what he knew, without giving away too much myself. Then I thought of something that would put him on the back foot.

'Did she tell you about her son? Apparently he's coming over from Israel. That'll be a great help, won't it?'

I thought I heard a sharp intake of breath on the other end of the phone.

'Indeed.'

There was something else I needed to know.

'By the way, did you have any trouble getting in? They seem to have quite strict security.'

'Oh, yes, they told me she wasn't allowed any visitors.'

'So . . .?'

'I just told them not to be so bloody ridiculous.'

So that's how it's done, I thought.

An hour or so later the phone rang. It was Mark Diabello.

'Hi, Georgina. Glad I've caught you at home. Listen, I think I've got the answer to your dilemma.'

'What dilemma?' I tried to remember our last conversation. It was something unpleasant and incomprehensible about bricks and money.

'How to avoid Mrs Shapiro having to sell up if she goes into a home. Apparently the Council can just put a charge on her house. It's like a mortgage – the house is sold after the person dies, and that's when the Council calls in the debt. The residue, if any, goes to the estate.'

'You mean the debt to cover the nursing-home fees? Nobody told me about that.'

'Well, they wouldn't, would they?'

'But the thing is, Mark, she doesn't need to be in a nursing home at all. She's fine at home. She likes her independence.'

'You'd better get her back home as soon as you can, then. Or get someone else to live in the house till she gets back. These things've got a way of picking up their own momentum.'

'Tell me about it.'

The whole house saga had picked up far too much momentum, as far as I was concerned, and he'd been among those pushing it along.

'How about over dinner tonight, sweetheart?'

There was an earnest note in his voice that made me feel guilty; but I steeled myself.

'I can't. I'm meeting . . . somebody. And I've got a lot of work on at the moment – something I'm trying to write,' I added quickly.

'You're a very active woman. I like that.' A sigh or a crackle on the line. 'As it happens, I do a bit of writing myself. Poetry.'

'Really?' Despite myself, I was intrigued. The hero of the original *Splattered Heart* had been a poet, too. 'Will you show me?'

'I'd love to. When . . .?'

'I'll ring you.' I put the phone down.

I'd arranged to meet Mr Ali and the Uselesses in the afternoon, and I still hadn't got a set of keys cut, so I walked down to the cobbler's on the Balls Pond Road then back up to Totley Place. It had turned cold again, a spiteful, stabbing cold, with a mean wind shaking the naked branches of the trees against a washed-out sky and flinging swirls of litter and dead leaves against my legs. At least the rain had held off.

It was just after two when I arrived at Canaan House. The red van was already parked outside, and the three of them were hunched up in the front, the Uselesses puffing at cigarettes, Mr Ali reading a newspaper. The house looked startlingly different, the white plastic window with its breeze-block base seemed to wink at me like a diseased eye. As soon as they saw me they jumped down, talking excitedly in Arabic, and followed me up the path, carrying their stuff with them in dozens of carrier bags. They looked as though they were planning to move in for a while. There were sleeping bags, books, clothes, a CD player, and even an old PC. In one carrier bag I spotted what looked like the Arabic outfits – obviously they hadn't given up on them yet. I showed them upstairs.

While they were unpacking and sorting their stuff out, I walked around the house with Mr Ali, pointing out the things I thought needed fixing: the missing slates on the porch, the broken latch on the door to the sitting room and the faulty light, the peeling wallpaper in the dining room, the dripping taps in the bathroom and kitchen, the cracked toilet bowl, and the huge gaps around the edges of doors and window frames where the wind whistled in. Those were just the obvious things.

'Hm. Hm,' he said, writing it all down in a notebook. 'All will be fixitup good, Mrs George.'

He'd never seen inside the whole house before. As his bright hamster eyes explored the details of the rooms he made little murmurs of amazement. 'Hm. Hm.' When we went up into the attic, he gasped. 'In here we could make beautiful benthouse suite.'

'Let's just concentrate on the essentials to start with,' I said.

Down in the hall, he stopped once more in front of the picture of the church at Lydda, his arms folded in front of him. I tried to read the emotion in his face, but he was turned in profile, so all I could see was the shadow of a furrow in his brow.

'You know, exactly next door to this church was a mosque. Cross and crescent standing side by side in peace.'

'Tell me more about Lydda,' I said. 'Is your family still there?'

'Do you not know about Nakba?'

'Nakba? What's that?'

'Hm. You are completely ignorant.' He said it with a sigh, in the same way that he'd introduced the Uselesses. 'In my country we say that ignorance is the warm bath in which it is comfortable to sit but dangerous to lie down.'

'I'm sorry. I'll make some tea if you tell me.'

I put the kettle on, rinsed two of the less grotty cups as thoroughly as I could under the tap, and put a kräutertee tea bag into each of them. We sat on the wooden chairs at the kitchen table. Fortunately I'd cleared away the remnants of Mrs Shapiro's last unfinished meal. He drank his pond water with three heaped spoonfuls of sugar, so I put the same into mine – obviously this was the secret. We stirred and sipped.

'So you were going to tell me about your family,' I prompted.

'I will tell you how they left Lydda. But you know the history – about British Palestine Mandate?'

'Well, just a bit. Actually, not a lot.'

He sighed again.

'But you know about Jewish Holocaust?'

'Yes, I know about that.'

'Of course, everybody knows about sufferings of the Jews.' He sniffed irritably. 'Only suffering of Palestinian people nobody knows.'

'But I want to know, Mr Ali. If you'll tell me.'

This story – I could see by now that it was going to be much more complicated than a Ms Firestorm-type romance. But it had somehow got under my skin.

Mr Ali blew on his tea and took a sip, sucking the sweet liquid off the ends of his moustache.

'You know in the end of the war, after what they have done to the Jews, the whole world was looking for a Jewish homeland? And the cunning British say – look, we will give them this land in Palestine. Land without people, people without land. Typical British, they give away something which does not belong to them.' He looked up to make sure I was still paying attention. I nodded encouragingly. 'This land is not empty, Mrs George. Palestinian people have been living there, farming our land, for generations. Now they say we must give half of it up to the Jews. Did you not learn about it in school?'

'No.' I was embarrassed by my ignorance. Geography, okay I had an excuse. But I'd done history at 'O' level. 'In history lessons we learned about Kings and Queens of England. Henry the Eighth and his six wives.'

'Six wives? All at one time?'

'No. He killed two and he divorced two, and one died.'

'Typical British behaviour. Same with us. Some killed. Some sent away into exile. Some died.' Mr Ali shook his head crossly and took a gulp of tea, scalding his mouth and sucking in air to cool himself down.

'But that was a long time ago.'

'No. Nineteen forty-eight. Same like the Romans did to Jews, Jews did to Palestinians. Chased them out. We call it Nakba. It means disaster in your language.'

'No, I mean Henry the Eighth was a long time ago.'

'Before Romans?'

'No, after the Romans, but before ... Never mind.' I saw the bemused look on his face.

'It's all just history, isn't it?'

This seemed to make him even more annoyed.

'You have learned nothing in school. Apart from a man with six wives. History has no borders, Mrs George. Past rolls up into present rolls up into future.' He made agitated roly-poly movements with his hands. 'Young Israelis also are ignorant. In school, their teachers tell them Jews came into an empty land, but not how this land was made empty.'

I thought about the letter in the piano stool. Yes, that's what *she* wrote – a barren and empty land.

'So was it like . . . the Nazis and the Jews?'

'No, not like Nazis,' he tutted angrily. 'You must not exaggerate. Israelis do not plan to exterminate all Arab people, only to drive them out of the land.'

'But the Jewish people need a homeland, too. Don't they?'

He sighed. His mouth curled down.

'But why in Palestine? Palestinian people never made any harm to Jews. Pogrom, ghetto, concentration camp – Europeans made all this. So why they make their revenge on us?'

'It *was* their land, wasn't it? Before the Romans sent them away?'

'This land belongs to many peoples. All nomadic peoples wandering here and there, following their sheeps. Palestine, Lebanon, Syria, Jordan, Egypt, Arabia, Mesopotamia. Who knows where everybody was coming from?'

My mind blanked out. All those places – how on earth did they fit together? I would have to look it up on the internet.

'They will tell you Palestinians abandoned their farms and houses and ran away because their leaders told them. No, they ran away because of terror. Israeli state was made by terrorists. You think only crazy Arabs are terrorists?' Mr Ali was becoming intensely un-hamster-like.

'I'm sorry to be so ignorant. At school we just learned British history.'

'So you must know about Balfour Declaration?'

'A bit.' I couldn't admit how little that bit was. 'Wasn't it about partitioning the Middle East at the end of the First World War?'

I'd seen *Lawrence of Arabia* once, with Peter O'Toole. He was great. Those eyes. But I'd never understood who betrayed whom over what. I remembered the bit where he fell off the motorbike. That was sad.

'Balfour said to meet Jewish aspirations without pre-judicing rights of Palestinians.'

There was something about those words that reminded me vaguely of the Progress Project. He took a gulp of pond water, and continued.

'But Palestinian people still are sitting in refugee camps. They have lost their lands, fields, orchards. They have no work, no hope. So they sit in refugee camps and dream of revenge.' His eyes were glittering with unusual ferocity. 'They have no weapons, so they make their children into weapons.'

I put the kettle on again, wondering about Ben. How had he blundered into this thorny Biblical world?

'Isn't there a prophecy, Mr Ali? Don't the Jews have to rebuild the Temple in Jerusalem, where the Messiah will come back? The third Temple?'

'Their book says they must rebuild the Temple. But it is not possible at this time, because on this site now stands our mosque – al-Aqsa Mosque. Next to the Dome of the Rock. One of our most holy places.'

'But is it true that Muslims, too, are waiting for the Last Imam? The Imam al-Mahdi. Do you believe that, Mr Ali?'

He hadn't struck me as a man of extreme beliefs – beyond an extreme misplaced belief in white uPVC.

'I will answer your question. Mostly Shia believe in the

return of al-Mahdi. I am Sunni.' He gave me a curious look. 'You learned about this in school?'

'No. On the internet.'

I saw now that the hard glitter in his eyes was a trick of the light, and when he turned towards me his face was gentle and sad. I took a deep breath.

'Actually it was my son who told me. He found all this stuff on the internet. Weird sites about the end of time. The Antichrist. Armageddon. Great armies and battles. The Abomination, whatever that is. He's so preoccupied with it . . . I was worried, that's all. I wanted to understand what it was about.'

The kettle whistled, and I made us another round of kräutertee. Mr Ali spooned three more sugars into his cup and stirred, looking at me gravely.

'Mrs George, the young are ready to believe anything that will lead them into heaven. Even to die for it. And there are always some whisperers who will say to them that death is the gateway to life.'

'You mean . . .?'

I shivered as though a cold draught had touched my neck. I had a sudden image of Ben – my lovely curly-haired Ben – his eyes radiant with conversion, his boyish body strapped up to that deadly payload, attempting a little smile or a joke as he said goodbye. The thought made me feel sick.

Upstairs I could hear the young men – they'd managed to set up the CD player and bursts of wild jangling music were swirling downstairs. They were thudding about as though they were dancing, but probably they were just walking around. Ben, who's quite slim, always thuds like an elephant when he walks.

'Do not worry about your son, Mrs George. He will grow up before too long. Ishmail and Nabeel used to talk also about these things when they lived under occupation. Now they talk about football.'

The thudding upstairs turned into thundering on the stairs, and a few moments later the Uselesses appeared in the hall. They said something in Arabic to Mr Ali, and he translated for me.

'They want to say thank you. This is a very good place.'

His eyes were twinkling again.

'There's something else they have to do,' I said. 'They must feed the cats.'

I showed them the cupboard in the kitchen where the cat food was kept. They nodded enthusiastically.

'And they have to clear up the mess.'

I led them back into the hall and pointed out a small deposit the Phantom Pooer had left in the usual place. I'd spotted it earlier but not got around to cleaning it up. The taller one – I think he was Mr Ali's nephew, Ishmail – shuddered and put his hand over his nose and mouth. I shrugged and offered a sympathetic smile, but I was thinking, that's nothing – you wait till you find one of the big fresh ones. The other one, Nabeel, said something loud and urgent in Arabic. Mr Ali said something loud and urgent back. They argued like that, back and forth, for a few minutes. Then Ishmail went and got a piece of kitchen roll and started to wipe it up, but somehow just managed to spread it around even more. Mr Ali shook his head.

'Completely useless.'

Anyway, in the end, the cat poo was wiped up, and it was time for me to go, and I took the keys I'd had cut out of my pocket.

'If anyone comes to the house, anyone you don't know, you mustn't let them in.'

Mr Ali translated it into Arabic, and they nodded emphatically.

'No in. No in.'

They made waving 'keep out' gestures with their hands. I gave them the keys. And I must admit I felt a pang of extreme apprehension. The least bad thing that could happen would be that the repairs would be done less or more uselessly, and the house would be bedecked with white uPVC. The worst case didn't bear thinking about. Who were these young men? I didn't know anything about them. They could be illegal immigrants. They could be terrorists. Mr Ali could be the leader of a terrorist cell. A terrorist disguised as a hamster. He smiled.

'Don't worry, Mrs George. All will be fixitup good for you. I will subervise.'

33

Avocados and strawberries

The following Saturday afternoon I made my way down to Sainsbury's in Islington for my big weekly shop. Although there's a closer Sainsbury's in Dalston, this one is on a direct bus route. At the top of the end aisle, I spotted a crowd milling around – it was the sticker lady doing her reductions – and out of habit I made my way to join them. Without Mrs Shapiro there, it was all much more refined, just a bit of genteel basket-barging when something exciting turned up. One woman was helping the sticker lady by gathering up the sell-by-dates from the counters and passing them to her for re-stickering, standing over her to make sure she got first pick. What a cheek. Even Mum didn't do that. Still, I managed to get some good bargains on cheeses, and a plastic box with three avocados reduced to 79p, perfect apart from a dent in the lid. I remembered the letter I'd found in the piano stool at Canaan House – avo-kado she'd called them. They must have been newly discovered at the time. Mum called them advocados. Given her aversion to anything exotic, I'd been surprised to find she'd quite taken to them. She served them with defrosted prawns doused in salad cream. Even Dad ate them.

There were some bargains in the fresh-produce aisles, too. Bananas, slightly spotted – tastier that way – reduced to 29p; nets of oranges on buy-one-get-one-free; plastic-box strawberries flown in from somewhere or other, pretty but flavourless. I remembered the strawberries Dad used to grow on the allotment at Kippax – the fresh, intense flavour, the kiss of summer on your tongue, the occasional slug to keep you on your toes. Keir and I would go down after school and fill a bowl up for tea, then fight over them all the way home.

No, even at half price, these strawberries weren't worth it. Where can you get strawberries so early in March, I was wondering, as I made my way out of the store. A young woman was handing out leaflets near the entrance – I must have missed her on the way in. I took one from her hand absent-mindedly and was about to stick it in with my shopping when the words jumped off the page at me: BOYCOTT ISRAELI GOODS.

Seeing my interest, she pushed a sheet of paper towards me on a clipboard.

'Will you sign our petition?'

'What's it about?'

'We want the government to make a commitment to stop serving Israeli-sourced products in the Houses of Parliament. Until Israel accepts UN Resolution 242.'

'Isn't that a bit . . .?' I stopped myself. The word that had come into my mind was 'pointless'. She looked so solemn, her pale eyes fixed on me as she talked.

'It's all grown on stolen land. Watered with stolen water,' she said.

'I know, but . . .' But what? But I didn't want to think about it – I wanted to get home with my shopping. 'But, I mean, it all happened so long ago. It was terrible, I know. The Nabka.' (Or was it Nakba?) 'But isn't it just – what they had to do?'

'That's crap!' Then she checked herself. 'Sorry, I shouldn't get so worked up.' I realised she was very young – hardly older than Ben. Her hair was cut short and teased up into little spikes on top of her head. 'But it's not just something that happened long ago. It's still happening. Every day. They're stealing Palestinian land. Bulldozing Palestinian houses. Bringing in Jewish settlers. From Moscow and New York and Manchester.' She spoke very fast, gabbling as though frightened of losing my attention.

'That can't be true.' Surely if it was true, I thought, somebody would put a stop to it.

'It *is* true. The International Court of Justice says it's illegal. But America supports them. And Britain.'

'Why would anyone want to leave New York to go and live in the middle of a desert?'

'They believe God gave them the land. To make an Israeli state. The people who were there before, the Palestinians, they've cleared them off. Those that are left, they've walled them in. Given them a few poxy reservations. Like the American Indians. The Australian Aborigines. They think if they make life hard enough, they'll just vanish away. Inconvenient people. Who just happen to be in the way. Of somebody else's dream.'

'But you can't wind back the clock, can you?'

'Why not? You'd only need to go back to 1967. Before the Six Day War. You know, the Green Line. Gaza and the West Bank.'

This was all getting a bit too geographical for me. What Green Line? But there was something very disarming about her earnestness. I ran my eyes down the leaflet. On one side was a crude map, showing a thin straight line between Israel and Palestine, and another line, drawn in green, some way to the right, showing the Palestinian land that had been occupied after the Six Day War. There was a gap between the two lines. And there was a third line, hatched in grey, a contorted snaking line on the right-hand side of the green line. Right is east: left is west, I reminded myself. The key said:

Line of separation wall. I forced myself to study it, remembering the map Mr Ali had drawn and wondering why maps had
suddenly taken on such importance. The more I stared, the
less sense it seemed to make.

I turned the leaflet over. On the other side were pictures
of Israeli produce. Avocados. Lemons. Oranges. Strawberries.
Well, at least I hadn't bought the strawberries.

'But surely if they're on the sell-by date? If they're
reduced . . .?'

She fixed me with a solemn look. 'Have you any idea how
much water it takes to grow strawberries in the desert?
Where do you think it all comes from?'

Suddenly her head swivelled around, and following her
gaze I saw a police car draw up and two officers get out – a
man and a woman. They made their way towards us. They
looked very young, too.

'Would you mind moving on now?' said the man. 'You're
causing an obstruction.'

'No, we're not,' I said, though I could see he was really
addressing the girl. She was shuffling her leaflets and her
clipboard into a bag.

'We've had a complaint,' said the woman officer, almost
apologetically.

'We're just chatting,' I said. 'About avocados. Surely we're
allowed to stand on the pavement and chat?'

The policewoman smiled and said nothing. I looked round
to the girl, but she'd disappeared.

I was still wondering about the contents of my carrier bags
as I made my way back towards the bus stop at Islington
Green. After all, it was just the supermarket clearing excess
stock. It would be wasteful to throw it all away. Wouldn't
it? What would Mum have done? I remembered an incident

during the last miners' strike. It was the winter of 1984, bitterly cold. Firewood was in short supply. I'd brought home a bag of coal that I'd bought at a petrol station. Dad had refused to have it in the house.

'We're not burning no scab coal,' he'd said. 'I'd sooner freeze.'

He'd taken it outside, and tipped it into the dustbin. Next morning, though, when I went to put the rubbish out, it was gone. Mum didn't say anything, but I always wondered whether it was she who'd scooped it out of the bin in the night. Waste not want not.

There was quite a queue at the bus stop. The sun had gone, a cold wind had sprung up, and I was beginning to feel hungry. I hunted around in my shameful shopping bags and broke off a ripe banana – at least they were okay to eat – weren't they? I noticed a couple standing with their backs to me looking into a shop window. The man was tall, fair, solidly built; there was something oddly familiar about him. His head was slightly out of proportion to his body. I realised with a shock of recognition that it was Rip. I hadn't noticed before how big his head was. Gorgeous, but too big. Like Michelangelo's David. The woman was small, even in her high heels, with a sleek dark bob and scarlet lipstick. I stared. It was Ottoline Walker. What was going on? Where was Pectoral Pete? She was wearing a tightly buttoned coat that showed off her curves. I could see her reflection in the shop window. They were holding hands. She was laughing at something, looking up at him. The little bitch! He bent down and kissed her.

Something inside me snapped. A sound rose in my chest, swelled up and forced its way out – aaah! yaaah! – a high-pitched wail, rasping at my throat. They turned. Everybody turned. I lurched across the pavement. *Wait! In – two – three*

. . . Oh, sod that! The banana pitched forward and mushed into a soft slippery paste in her face. She struggled, but the banana in my hand – it just kept going round and round. It forced its way up into her nostrils. It smeared the slut-scarlet lipstick all around her mouth. It made soft feathery streaks in her eyebrows. Rip's mouth opened wide – that round trouty look – O! Then he grabbed my arm.

'Georgie! Stop! Have you gone mad?'

What a stupid question.

'Aaah! Yaaah!'

Next she turns on me, sputtering.

'What have I done to deserve this?'

That voice – her parents must have spent a fortune teaching her to talk like that. Spoiled brat. You can tell from her voice she's used to getting everything she wants.

'You just thought you could have him, didn't you? You didn't stop to think of me. Me and Ben and Stella. He belongs to us, not you.'

'What d'you mean?'

There's a bit of banana hanging down from her nose like a big creamy bogey. It makes me laugh.

'We were just inconvenient people, getting in the way of your lovely dream.'

I'm laughing like mad now, splitting my sides at the sheer symmetry of everything.

Then – this is good – the Scarlet-mouthed Slut scrapes the mush off her face with her hands and starts to smear it over Rip, over his clothes and his hair. And he says, 'Ottie! Stop! What's the matter with you?'

And she says, 'What's the matter with *you*? You told me it was okay. You told me she didn't mind. You lied to me.' She's wailing, too. 'You told me she'd gone off with another man! In a Jaguar!'

'She did. She is.' He backs away. 'You're both bloody mad. Both of you!' He backs away and breaks into a run. She runs after him, stumbling on her bitch-stilettos. And I run, too. I'm wearing my batty-woman trainers, so I can almost keep up. I run after him up the street, dodging through the startled pedestrians.

'Aaah! Yaaah!'

But he's fast, Rip, fast and fit, ducking and weaving through the Saturday crowd. He shakes us both off.

In the end, I have to give up. I've lost sight of him. I'm panting for breath, my chest heaving, my throat raw from screaming. My head is spinning. Everything's spinning. I stop and catch my breath, leaning forwards on to my knees. Then I straighten up and turn around. I've lost sight of her, too. She's disappeared somewhere, into her bitch-lair. Still panting, I make my way back down Upper Street towards The Green. About halfway down, on the pavement, I stumble across a discarded black suede stiletto shoe. I kick it into the road, and a Number 19 squashes it flat.

The crowd at the bus stop has thinned out. I look for my shopping bags where I left them on the pavement. But they've disappeared. Someone has picked them up and taken them. The settler avocados. The blood-soaked oranges. All gone.

Actually, it was worth it, I thought to myself, as I sat in the kitchen and poured a glass of wine. Okay, I'd made a fool of myself and I'd lost my week's shopping. But it was worth it just to see that creamy banana bogey hanging from her nostril. It was worth it to see his trout-mouth – O! To see him run.

I couldn't face going back into Islington, so I just went out and got a bit of shopping at Highbury Barn. When I got back I saw that the answering machine was blinking. There was a message from Ms Baddiel. She was sorry she hadn't been in touch before. She'd been on a course (not a case!). It seemed odd that she'd phoned on a Saturday, but maybe she'd left the message before and I just hadn't noticed. I rang her back straightaway but she wasn't there. The second message was from Nathan. He wanted to know if I'd like to go to the Adhesives Trade Fair in Peterborough tomorrow with him and his father. I pressed Delete. I know I'm sad, but I'm not *that* sad. I poured myself another glass of wine and settled down in front of the television. *Casualty* would be on soon.

As my euphoria wore off, I realised that there was only one more glass left in the bottle, and that if I finished it off then there would be nothing to stop me drinking a whole bottle again tomorrow night. And the night after. And then I'd be well on the road to becoming an Unfit Mother. *Casualty* was not satisfying – too much shouting and argy-bargy. What had happened to the heroic drama of life and death? What had happened to that dishy Kwame Kwei-Armah? I recalled my spree of shouting and bad behaviour earlier that afternoon with a prick of shame. Really, people don't want to watch that sort of thing. It's not gentile, as Mum would say.

Then the reality of three Ben-less days loomed, and I started to think that maybe a trade fair in Peterborough was what I needed after all. Maybe Nathan's father would be okay when sober. And the more I thought about it, the more I realised that short men can be incredibly sexy. I dialled Nathan's number. As he picked up the phone at the other end ('Nathan Stein speaking') I heard in the background the familiar theme as the trailer credits rolled away – he'd been watching *Casualty*, too.

34

The glue exhibition

Nathan picked me up next day at ten o'clock. I'd been trying to imagine what kind of car he would turn up in, but the last thing I'd expected was an open-top sports car, a Morgan, pale blue. He greeted me with a hug. I dropped my knees a bit so our cheeks were just at the same height.

'Sorry, my father couldn't make it.'

'So it's just you and me?' My heart skipped.

''Fraid so. Can you put up with me for a whole day?' (Could I just!) 'You'll need a warmer coat than that.' (I'd already put on my smart grey jacket over my revealing top.) 'And a scarf or something. Otherwise your hair'll blow away.'

I changed into my brown duffel coat, fastened it up to my chin, and tied a scarf down over my ears.

'Sit tight!' he said.

We whizzed up the Holloway Road and out on to the A1, the wind slapping my head, my eyes stinging, my ears ringing. Shops. Houses. Trees. Flats. Houses. Trees. Whoosh! We couldn't talk; I tried to open a conversation but my words just got blown away. All I could do was watch Nathan's hands on the wheel and gearstick – he was wearing fingerless leather driving gloves – and his hunky profile as he concentrated on the road. His silver-flecked designer-stubbly jaw was clenched in a daredevil look of defiance. My stomach was clenched in a knot. I was trying to decide whether it would be better to die instantly or to live out my life in a wheelchair.

Peterborough emerged suddenly out of a fenland mist, the elegant towers and arches of its cathedral swanning above the rooftops. I'd never been here before. The exhibition centre was on the outskirts, a low featureless hangar of a building. The car park was almost empty. Nathan pulled up near the entrance, switched the engine off, and turned to me with a dimply smile.

'Did you enjoy that, Georgia?'

I smiled weakly. I couldn't bring myself to say yes, even to him.

The exhibition itself was nowhere near as exciting as the journey. It was basically a display of tubes and phials with long technical explanations mounted on card, and samples of things glued together, mainly materials – laminates stuck to concrete, glass stuck to wood, steel stuck to steel. We seemed to be the only punters, apart from a man in a black-and-white shell suit who was walking round taking notes. Our footsteps click-clacked in the echoing space. Well, what did I expect? The most interesting thing was a car, an old Jaguar, glued to a metal plate on its roof which was bolted to a chain suspended from the ceiling, so it dangled there in mid-air, spinning slowly if you touched it, held up by the power of adhesion.

'Wow! That's amazing!'

'Yes, I'll have to remember that next time I want to hang my car up,' said Nathan.

I had a sudden thought.

'Nathan, do you think you could use glue to stick something like, say, a toothbrush holder on to bathroom tiles?'

'Absolutely. There are a number of purpose-made adhesives. Look for brands with "nails" in the name. No-nails. Goodbye-nails.'

'But you wouldn't use nails in a bathroom. It'd have to be rawplugs, wouldn't it?'

He gave me a sideways grin. 'You mean instead of cooked plugs?'

'What d'you mean?'

'They're called Rawlplugs, Georgie.'

'Rawlplugs?'

'But you're right about one thing – they're on their way to obsolescence. Adhesives can do many of the same things nowadays.'

My heart bounced up. Rawplugs were history!

Nathan was wandering around with a notebook, an intelligent frown furrowing his brow. I kept very close, hoping he would take my hand or slip an arm around my shoulder. Should I ask after his father? Should I mention *Casualty*? I cleared my throat.

'Did you enjoy . . .?'

'Hey, look at this, Georgia.'

He'd stopped to examine a photograph on display near the cyanoacrylates. It was a very distressing full-colour close-up of a bottom stuck to a blue plastic toilet seat. From the angle it had been taken, you couldn't tell whether it was a man's bottom or a woman's. It had obviously been shot in a hospital: there was somebody in the background wearing surgical gloves and a mask. Just imagine if that was you – it would be bad enough getting stuck on the toilet and having to call for help, and then having blokes with tools break down the door, unbolt the toilet seat and rush you to hospital, and people phoning up – they would phone an expert like Nathan in this situation – for advice about solvents. And all the time you'd be wondering who put the glue there; in fact you'd probably be able to guess. You'd be fuming. Fuming but helpless. Then you'd have to be photographed for medical records. Everyone would be solemn and respectful, but behind your back they'd be laughing their heads off.

The explanation card at the side of the picture simply read:

CYANOACRYLATE AXP-36C
A PRACTICAL JOKE

'Deary me,' said Nathan.

Actually, that's not a bad idea, I thought.

The next stand was a display about the history of glue. There were pictures of trees with gum or resin oozing out and dark-skinned men catching it in little cups. There was a picture which showed Aztec builders mixing blood into their mortar. The explanation card said the Aztec structures were so strong they would withstand an earthquake. It seems that blood is sticky stuff, too – stickier than water.

I tried another tack.

'You seem very close to your father . . .' I ventured.

'Ah, yes. Tati.' He paused. I waited for him to continue, but he just wandered on, looking at the exhibits.

'Have you always lived with him?'

'Not always.'

I followed him round the stand, casually brushing against him when he stopped at the corner of the display, but he didn't seem to notice.

'My parents live in Yorkshire,' I said. 'I miss them. But I couldn't live with them.'

'I don't know that I can live with Tati much longer.'

I brushed against him again, this time more determinedly. Surely my intentions must be totally obvious. He opened his notebook and scribbled something down.

'It might make a nice article for *Adhesives in the Modern*

World, Georgia,' he suggested. 'Something about the history of adhesion. Glue past and present. What d'you think?'

Maybe he just didn't fancy me. Maybe I wasn't intelligent enough for him. Maybe he was involved with someone else. The thought filled me with gloom.

'Mmm. Good idea.'

'Or even glue past, present and future.'

The designer stubble on his chin gleamed with dashes of silver as he spoke.

'I don't think I could do the future bit.'

I was thinking of Mrs Shapiro. When you see a good man you have to grebbit quick. Should I just grab him?

'You could just speculate. Glue made from recycled carrier bags. Glue made from liposuction by-products. Glue made from stray cats and dogs. Glue made from boiled-up illegal immigrants. Melted-down social undesirables.' He gave me a sideways grin. 'No?'

'Like you told me once the Nazis made glue out of Jews?'

'Very good glue it was, too. Now Jews are trying to make glue out of Palestinians. But with less success.' He dropped his voice to a whisper. 'They say God told them to.'

I stared at him. How could he joke about that? He saw the look in my eye.

'Sorry, it's only metaphorical glue. A sticky mess. And I mean the Israeli state, not the Jews. We have to distinguish.'

'Really?' What the hell was he talking about? 'I'm not sure I understand . . .'

'I'm what they call a self-hating Jew. A gay self-hating Jew.'

Ah! Gay! That explained everything! I smiled inwardly, grateful that he'd told me before I'd made an utter fool of myself. But why the self-hatred? Could it be because he was gay?

'Do you really hate yourself, Nathan?'

'As much as custard.'

'Custard's one of my favourite things,' I hurried to reassure him.

'Mine, too. Especially made with eggs and vanilla with a sprinkling of nutmeg.'

'So why . . .?' Maybe it was his height. 'You know . . .'

'Sorry, Georgia, I didn't mean to inflict my obsessions on you. Self-hating is just a label the neo-Zionists use for people who disagree with them; you're either an anti-Semite or a self-hating Jew.'

He gave me a hunkily intelligent grin, pushing back his horn-rimmed glasses that had slipped down his gorgeous nose. Gay. What a shame!

'We just got it out of a tin. Bird's.' I heard my voice prattling on, filling the silence. 'But they weren't anti-Semites, my parents. My dad's a socialist. He once thumped someone for calling the man in the fish and chip shop a wop. Mum's more . . . more of an anarchist, I suppose. She'd thump anybody for anything.'

Even as I said it, I was thinking about the banter of the men in the Miners' Welfare at Kippax. Poofs. Gays. Queers. Pansies. They were the casual everyday slights that were the currency of contempt down our way. Dad might not be an anti-Semite, but I'd never heard him threatening to thump someone for using those words. Mum on the other hand had once ticked Keir off for calling one of his teachers a poofter. 'He's very nice, your Mr Armstrong, even if he is hormo-sexual.'

'What about *your* father?' I asked.

'Yes, well, Tati moved in with me after Mother died, and Raoul moved out. It's sort of put paid to my love life.'

'Is he rude to your friends?'

'Oh, no. He just sings.'

I laughed. 'That sounds nice.'

'It is. But there are only so many lieder a person can take.' He murmured conspiratorially, 'I keep hoping a nice widow will take him off my hands.'

We'd stopped in front of another photo – it was a little girl whose hands were stuck together. She was crying, her mouth open, her eyes screwed up in pain.

'Oh, dear. As it says in the manual, one of the disadvantages of adhesive bonding is that disassembly is usually not possible without destruction of the component parts,' Nathan remarked drily.

It was one of the things about adhesives that had always secretly troubled me. I stared. There was something so hopeless about the mess the girl was in that my heart went out to her.

'I know what you mean by self-hating, Nathan. I hate myself sometimes.'

'Do you, Georgia?'

'Yes. I mean, I often feel stupid. Or hopeless. Or despicable. Or I just wish I was somebody else.' My voice was wobbling pathetically. 'I feel as though I've made a mess of my life.'

What would it have been like, I wondered, to grow up on custard made with eggs and vanilla and nutmeg, instead of on Bird's powder and oven chips? Would I have been a different kind of person, more articulate and witty? Would I have had a high-powered career, or a string of bestselling novels? Would my husband not have left me? The trouble is, I was bonded to Rip; cyanoacrylate: a permanent bond. He was the only man I'd really loved, and however much I raged against him I knew I would never love anyone in that way again. I felt tears brimming into my eyes. Nathan slipped his arm around me and gave me a friendly squeeze.

'Glue can be messy stuff.'

I rested my head on his shoulder, which was at just the right height if I bent my knees a bit, and let the tears roll down the sides of my nose, big and warm. Nathan didn't say anything. He just stood there and let me cry. After a while I pulled a crumpled ball of tissue out of my pocket and dabbed my eyes.

'Nathan, there's something I'd like to ask you.'

'Fire ahead.'

'Would you mind, on the way home, driving more slowly?'

35
Uses of superglue

I woke up next day feeling full of life. It was late – almost nine o'clock – and intermittent bursts of sunshine were pushing in beneath the elastic of the black knickers. The crying yesterday had refreshed me, like the rain in the night, and so much exposure to the possibilities of glue had fired me up with new enthusiasm for my work. Sitting up in bed I switched my laptop on. The article I was working on was about medical uses of adhesives. Cyanoacrylate (superglue) had been used effectively in emergency battlefield situations in Vietnam to hold wounds together until they could be sutured properly. Now a number of companies were trying to develop specialist adhesives to be used in place of suture. Human bonding.

There were two technical problems, it seemed, to be overcome. One, how to get the sides to hold together for long enough for bonding to take place. Two, how to achieve separation without tearing the flesh.

Then I remembered. Cyanoacrylate AXP-36C. I fumbled in the bedside drawer for a scrap of paper to write it down on before I forgot. I tried to picture Rip's face when he realised he was stuck. I tried to picture his bottom, the agony of tearing flesh as he tried to free himself. Who would rescue him? Who would call the ambulance? Ottoline Walker? Or would it be me? Would I laugh? Would I minister gently to his adhered behind? So many possibilities!

I put aside medical uses of adhesives, just for a moment, and opened my exercise book.

The Splattered Heart
Chapter 7

One evening, as the Sinster family ~~were was~~ were sitting down to their sumptuous ~~tea dinner~~ evening meal in the vast candle-lit dining hall surrounded by deer's antlers and other dead things, ~~they heard~~ the ~~plangent pungent poignant~~ melodious ~~twanging tinkling twinkling~~ (oh, sod this) sound of a mandolin ~~assaul~~tailled their eager ears and a moment later a tall dark handsome figure clad ~~only~~ (clad only – what was I thinking of!) in a swirling velvet cloak strode into the hall. After he had finished his performance Mrs Sinster threw him a few coins from her silk purse and said, 'Oh, Mr Mandolin Player, please come again. I am fascinated by your ~~large mandolin~~ charming folk culture.'

Poor Mrs Sinclair – was I being a bit unfair? When I'd first met the Sinclairs, their world had seemed so alien and intimidating – governed by unspoken rules and veiled assumptions – but she had really tried to make me feel at home, had inducted me kindly into the arcane mysteries of napkin rings and the *Daily Telegraph* crossword, and I suppose I must have seemed a sullen and ungracious daughter-in-law. At the time, it had irked me that they appeared to have no idea how privileged their lives were. It had irked me the way Mr Sinclair asked, in a hushed voice, whether I'd really met Arthur Scargill; I'm no great fan of the comb-over king, but the way the Sinclairs went on, you'd think he was the Antichrist himself.

It had taken me a long time to realise that the Sinclairs were probably as scared of me as I was of them. Okay, it can't have helped that on my third visit to Holtham I'd worn a large yellow badge with '*The enemy within*' in bold letters. They must have seen me as an outrider of a sinister army bent on destroying order, decency, *Horse and Hound*, and everything else they held dear. It wasn't long after the end of the miners' strike, and I thought they needed shaking up a bit – well, that's my excuse. Rip had tried to persuade me to take it off, but when I insisted, had stuck up for me valiantly and tried to explain to his bewildered parents what it was about.

'But if it's supposed to be a *secret* enemy, I can't understand why she's wearing a badge,' I overheard Mrs Sinclair whispering to Rip.

Yes, perhaps I was being a bit hard on Rip, too. But all's fair in love and fiction. I pressed on.

Surprised in a compromising position with the mandolin player, Gina is expelled from Holty Towers. She protests that it was only a response to Rick's philandering, and determines to seek revenge by glueing his bottom to a toilet seat. The secret is to match the right adhesive to the adherends. Hurray! That would mean another visit to B&Q (strictly for research, of course). The trouble is, I couldn't help feeling a touch of sympathy for Rick. After all, he was just a weak and deluded male – easily led by the cunning spotty Spanish maid – he couldn't really help it. And Gina should have known better than to get involved with that wayward mandolin player. Something else was bothering me. I tried to focus on the image of Rip's bottom in the toilet seat, but the other photo from the glue exhibition kept intruding: the little girl, her screwed-up eyes as she tried to pull her hands apart; her scream.

Hauling myself out of bed, I stood at the window and looked down over the garden, stretching my arms above my head and waggling my shoulders, which were still stiff from the cold and tension of yesterday's car journey. The ground was wet, and the leaves on the laurel bush were dazzling with captive raindrops, but the sun kept coming in and out behind the rain clouds, casting fleeting rainbows across the sky. At the far end of the garden, a haze of mauve crocuses had spread, almost overnight. Birds were hard at work, hopping about in pairs with bunches of grass in their beaks.

Then I spotted Wonder Boy slinking along the edge of the fence, making his stealthy way towards the blackbird couples. I banged on the window and they flew away. Wonder Boy looked up and gave me a long reproachful stare. I felt a pang of guilt. Okay, a visit to Mrs Shapiro was long overdue, I wanted to say to him, but it wasn't exactly easy, was it? The HELP ME note Mrs Shapiro had sent was on my bedside table – I'd just scribbled the glue code on the envelope. As I looked at it with its scrawled-out name and address, I had a brainwave.

36

The adhesion consultant

After lunch, I dressed myself up in a red jacket that had belonged to Stella – I had to leave the buttons undone – and a glittery Oxfam scarf, and pulled a woolly hat down low over my hair. I put on bright red lipstick and an old pair of sunglasses by way of disguise – and made my way to the bus stop on the Balls Pond Road. Though in fact when I arrived at Northmere House I saw that my disguise was redundant, for there was a different guard-dog lady at the reception desk.

'Can I help you?' she barked.

'I've come to see Mrs Lillian Brown.'

She consulted her list. 'Are you family?'

'A cousin. Once removed.' Well, I could have been.

'Would you sign in please? Room twenty-three.'

She pressed the button that opened the sliding door. And in I went – into the muted realm of the pink carpet, the sickly chemical air, the rows of closed doors from behind which, from time to time, a television blared eerily. On the other side of the corridor was the long plate-glass sliding door which gave on to the courtyard with its square of grass and four benches, now all damp with rain. A demented bleeper sounded constantly in the background, reminding the absent staff that behind one of these closed doors, someone desperately needed help.

I knocked on the door of number twenty-three. There was no reply so I pushed it open. The room was small and overheated, with a terrible deathly smell. A massive television set, volume on at full blast, dominated the room, so it took me a moment to notice the tiny figure lying motionless on the bed.

'Mrs Brown?'

There was no reply. I shouted louder, 'Mrs Brown? Lillian?'

I tiptoed over to the bed. She was lying there with her eyes closed. Her hand, I saw, was clutched around the bleeper on its cable. I couldn't tell whether she was breathing.

I backed out and let the door close behind me. My chest was thumping. A fat woman in a pink corporate uniform was coming down the corridor.

'In here,' I said.

'Are you Mrs Brown's niece?' She seemed to be unaware of the bleeping alarm.

'Actually, I'm . . .'

'I hope you're not smuggling cigarettes.' She scrutinised me fiercely.

'Oh, no. Nothing like that.'

'Because last home I worked at, someone give an old lady a fag and some matches, and it all went up in flames.'

'Oh, dear. Was anyone hurt?'

'We was saved by a dog.'

'Really?'

'A mongrel,' she snorted. 'And then they tried to smuggle in a gearbox.'

'A gearbox? What for?'

'Beats me. Anyhow, matron got rid of it. Said it weren't hygienic.' Her face softened for a moment. 'It were a shame really, poor old man. Still, 'e got 'is revenge.' She chortled. 'Anyhow, we don't allow that sort of thing in 'ere. We got rules.'

'Er . . . I think this lady needs some help . . .'

But she'd already vanished up the corridor. As I watched the door close behind her, I noticed there was now someone sitting out on one of the benches in the courtyard in the rain, a solitary hunched figure wearing a powder-blue dressing gown and matching peep-toe slippers, puffing away at a cigarette. It was the bonker lady.

I banged on the window and waved. She looked up and waved back. But when I slid open the door and went out to join her in the courtyard, she put on a sulky face.

'You never brought me cigs.'

'I did,' I lied. 'You weren't there.'

She sniffed as though she knew it wasn't true.

'Are yer lookin' for 'er? Yer pal?'

'Mrs Shapiro. Yes.'

'She's in solitary. She in't allaared visitors.'

'Why not?'

'Bin a naughty gel, ent she?'

'Why? What's she done?'

She stubbed out her cigarette on the path and threw the butt into the middle of the lawn, where there was already quite a scattering.

'It's what she ent done. She won't sign the Powah. Keeps refusin'. Bonkers, if yer ask me. They won't let 'er aht till she signs it.'

'Do you know which room she's in?'

The rain had almost stopped. She pulled a cigarette packet out of her dressing-gown pocket and looked inside. There were only two left.

'Yer won't forget me cigs next time, will yer?'

'No. I promise.'

She placed one of the cigarettes between her lips and let it rest there for a few moments, savouring the anticipation, before she took the box of matches from the other pocket.

'Twen'y-seven.'

'Thanks.'

'If she in't there, she'll be watchin' telly in twen'y-three. That's my room. They all watch telly in there.'

'Isn't there a day room?'

'Yeh, there is. But the telly's crap.'

Mrs Shapiro's room was just as small as the other one, and just as hot, but the smell was more sickly than deathly, and there was no television. She looked dreadful. She was lying on her bed, fully clothed, staring at the ceiling. Her hair was wild and matted, the silver line now a highway, her skin loose and baggy, folding in deep yellowy wrinkles around her mouth and chin.

'Mrs Shapiro?'

'Georgine?'

She struggled to her feet groggily and stared at me.

'How are you?' I hugged her. She seemed so frail, like a bird. All bones.

'Thenk Gott you come.'

'I'm sorry I didn't come before. I tried, but they wouldn't let me in.'

'Did you bring me cigarettes?'

'Sorry. I forgot.'

'Never mind. Good you heff come, Georgine. I do not want to die in here!'

She sat down on the edge of the bed and immediately started to cry, her skinny shoulders shaking. How small and bent she seemed. I sat beside her, stroking her back until the sobs turned to sniffles. Then I passed her a tissue.

'We've got to get you home. But I don't know how.'

'Too much guards in this place. Like in prison.' She blew her nose, then opened up the tissue to examine the snot. It had a horrible greenish colour. 'How are my dear cats?'

'They're fine. Waiting for you. I've got some young men staying there, looking after them. Fixing the house up.' I saw the look of alarm on her face. 'Don't worry. As soon as you're ready to come home, they'll leave.'

The smell in the room was making me feel faint. I stood up and opened a window. The soupy overheated air stirred, and we could hear the traffic on the Lea Bridge Road, and voices of children playing somewhere nearby. Mrs Shapiro took a deep breath, and her eyes seemed to brighten a bit.

'Thenk you, darlink.' She squeezed my hand, studying me with her wrinkled eyes. 'You looking better, Georgine. Nice lipstick. Nice scarf. You got a new husband yet?'

'Not yet.'

'Maybe soon I will heff a new husband.' She smiled archly to see the look of surprise cross my face. 'Nicky is saying he wants to marry mit me.'

'Mr Wolfe?'

I gasped. The scheming devil! I remembered how fluttery she'd been when he'd sat in her kitchen plying her with sherry.

'I was thinking he would be for you the perfect husband, Georgine. But you heff showed little interest. So maybe this is an opportunity for me.' Her smile now was coyly flirtatious. She had cheered up considerably. 'What you think? Should I marry my Nicky?'

'Does he know how old you are?'

'I tolt him I was sixty-one.' She caught my eye and giggled. 'I am too notty for you, Georgine, isn't it?'

'You are a bit naughty, Mrs Shapiro.'

'Why get ready for the grave? It will catch you soon enough anyway, isn't it? Why not to enjoy the moment as it flies.' She flapped her hands like birds' wings. 'You know Goethe?'

I shook my head. Then I thought of something.

'Maybe it's because . . .' I remembered his intake of breath on the phone. 'I told him you had a son.'

A son who would inherit her estate. Unless, of course, she remarried.

She looked at me sharply. 'How you know about this son?'

'The social worker told me. Mrs Goodney.'

She stopped. I pretended to be looking out of the window. Go on, go on! I was silently willing her, but she went quiet.

After a few moments, she said, 'Ach, this woman. All she thinks about is how to shvindel me. I told her I heff a son because she was wanting me to sign the Power of Returning. I said my son will be returning. He will heff the house.'

'But he's not your son, is he?' I said gently.

There was a pause. 'Not mine. No.'

'So who was his mother?'

She sighed. 'This whole *megillah* is too long for you. You will be falling asleep before I tell it.'

'But tell me anyway.'

'It was the other one. Naomi Shapiro.'

Little by little, I drew it out of her. Her real name was Ella Wechsler, she said, pronouncing it carefully, as though not quite sure it belonged to her. She was born in 1925 in Hamburg. I calculated that would make her eighty-one. Her family was Jewish, but of the pick and mix variety. Speck but no sausages. Sabbath and Sunday. Christmas as well as Hanukkah – not that all this made any difference to the Nazis, when the time came. Her father, Otto Wechsler, ran a successful printing business; her mother, Hannah, was a pianist; her two older sisters, Martina and Lisabet, were students. Their house, a solid four-storey villa in the Grindel Quarter, was a hanging-out place for musicians, artists, heartbroken lovers, dreamers, travellers arriving or departing, four cats, and a German maid called Dotty. There was always coffee *mit schlagsahne*, always music and conversation going on. She chuckled.

'We were better at being German than the Germans. I thought this life was normal. I did not know such happiness was not permitted to Jews, Georgine. I did not know what it means to be a Jew until Herr Hitler told me.'

But by 1938, Hitler's message was loud and clear – clear enough for the family to realise they had to get out of Germany before things got worse.

'You see in that time Hitler was thinking only how to clear out the Jewish people from Germany. The plan for exterminations came after.'

The Wechslers – Ella, Martina, Lisabet, and their parents – fled to London. Ella was nearly thirteen years old, Martina was seventeen, Lisabet twenty. In 1938 the Wechslers had been able to bribe their way out of Germany, but England did not hold out her arms in welcome. The 1905 Aliens Act meant that they could only come to Britain if they already had a job to come to.

'Even the English they did not want us. Too many Jews were running away from pogroms in Poland, Russia, Ukrainia. Everybody thought it was a big sport to chase the Jews, isn't it?'

Through a cousin on his mother's side, Otto Wechsler had managed to secure a job in a print shop on Whitechapel Road – it was a huge ancient Heidelberg press which he coaxed back into life. The owner, Mr Gribb, was a widower from Elizavetgrad who had changed his name from Gribovitch when his family fled the pogroms in 1881. Hannah Wechsler became his housekeeper. Lisabet worked in a bakery. Martina trained as a nurse. Ella went to the Jewish school in Stepney.

They lived in a poky two-roomed flat above the print shop ('Everything we touched was bleck from the ink') in the heart of the East End Jewish community, and they counted themselves blessed.

They received coded letters via Switzerland from their family describing the impact of the Nuremberg Laws, the enforced wearing of yellow stars, the terror of Kristallnacht, the expropriation of businesses, the expulsion from the professions (Cousin Berndt turned out of his surgery and made to sweep leaves in the park), the public humiliations, the increasingly ugly assaults in the streets (Uncle Frank's front teeth broken by a cheering, jeering gang of schoolboys). Actions that an individual would find morally repugnant became amusing when there was a crowd cheering you on. Then the mass transportations started, and the letters stopped.

I felt the tremor in Mrs Shapiro's shoulders, the long catch of her breath. We were still sitting side by side on the bed. The light had faded in the window, and the roar of traffic outside intensified with the onset of rush hour. But we were in a different world.

'Tell me about Artem. When did you meet him?'

'In 1944 he arrived in London. In the spring. Eyes crazy like a madman. Still asking if they had seen his sister.'

Skeletal, louse-ridden, hollow-eyed, he'd fetched up at the Newcastle docks on a British merchant ship that had snuck out from Gothenburg with a cargo of butter and ball bearings. The Seamen's Mission had taken him in and he was passed on, via Jewish relief organisations, to the flat in Whitechapel Road. He stayed with them for a year, helping to run the printing press and sleeping on a camp bed at the back of the workshop. He was clever with his hands. He didn't say much – he spoke Russian and only a few phrases of German and English – but his silence, brooding and mysterious, seemed to the girls to speak volumes. In his spare time, he started to make a violin. Lisabet, Martina and Ella watched him working with the fretsaw and the glue, his head bowed over the workbench, a thin self-rolled cigarette hanging from his lip, humming to himself. By then, Ella was eighteen, Martina was twenty-three and Lisabet twenty-six. All of them were a bit in love with him and a bit in awe of him.

'Did he finish the violin?'

'Yes. Gott knows where he got the strings. But in Petticoat Lane at that time you could buy all what you needed. When he was playing, it was like the angels in heaven. Sometimes I or *Mutti* accompanied mit the piano.'

I remembered the music in the piano stool. Delius. 'Two Brown Eyes'. Ella Wechsler. Her name was written in the front of the songbook, but the brown eyes had belonged to somebody else.

'Do you still play the piano, Mrs Shapiro? Ella?' Somehow, the new name didn't seem to fit the old lady I'd grown fond of.

'Look at my hends, darlink.'

She held them out in front of her, bony, with swollen joints and shrivelled brown-stained skin. I took them and warmed them in mine. They were so cold.

'And Naomi? Who was she?'

I had such a strong image from the photographs of the sweet heart-shaped face, the tumble of brown curls, the playful eyes. Mrs Shapiro didn't reply. She was gazing into a place beyond the dusky window. When at last she spoke, all she said was, 'Naomi Lowentahl. She was rather tall.'

Then she went quiet again. I didn't interrupt. I knew she'd tell me in her own time.

'Yes, nice looking. Always mit red lipstick, nice shmata. Who would heff thought she would be the type to go away digging in the ground in Israel?' Her mouth twitched. Another silence. She withdrew her hands from mine and started to fiddle with her rings. 'Some people said she was beautiful. Eyes always blazing like a fire. Yes, she was like a person on fire. She was in loff with Arti, of course.'

'And he . . .?'

She sniffed. 'Yes. And he.'

Artem Shapiro and Naomi Lowentahl were married in the synagogue at Whitechapel in October 1945, after the end of the war. Ella, Hannah and Otto Wechsler went to the wedding. Lisabet was away in Dorset on her own honeymoon with a Polish Jewish airman. Martina had been killed by a V2 rocket raid in July 1944, on her way home from the Chest Hospital in Bethnal Green – one of the last air raids of the war. But Mr Gribb put on a good spread for the couple. People came from all over Stepney just to get a bit of chicken.

A sharp rap on the door made us both jump. Then without waiting for an answer, the woman in the pink uniform, the same one I'd met earlier, barged into the room.

'Tea time, Mrs Shapiro.'

She caught sight of me.

'You'll have to leave,' she said. 'Mrs Shapiro in't allowed visitors.'

'I'm not a visitor. I'm a . . .' I thought fast. 'I'm an adhesion consultant.'

'Oh.' That stopped her in her tracks. She looked me up and down, trying to assess my status. 'I thought you was Mrs Brown's niece. You'll 'ave to make an appointment through matron.'

'Of course.' I stood up and put on a Mrs Sinclair-ish voice. 'If you could just leave us now. We've almost finished our consultation.'

'I'll have to report it to matron.' She shook her head. 'We can't just 'ave people wandering in off the streets.'

When we were alone again, Mrs Shapiro gripped my hands.

'You will keep my secret, Georgine?'

'Of course I will.'

'What should I do?'

'Don't sign anything. Don't marry Nicky.'

'But if I am married, they will heff to let me go home, isn't it?'

'I'll try to get you out.'

'If I will say no to him, he will stop coming. Is better if I say maybe yes and maybe no.' She winked.

'You're naughty, Mrs Shapiro,' I laughed. 'How does he manage to get in? Doesn't the matron stop him?'

'He told them he is my solicitor.'

'Ah. Clever. But . . .'

Actually, I thought, what she needs is a proper solicitor.

There was a sudden rush of footsteps and voices in the corridor. I kissed Mrs Shapiro on the cheeks and quickly said goodbye, just as they reached the door. The pink-overalled lady was in front, followed by a big green-cardied woman and a security guard. Their faces were flushed with purpose. But before they could say anything they were distracted by a ghastly scream from down the corridor outside number twenty-three. I ran out – we all ran out – to see the bonker lady waving her hands in the air and yelling, ''Elp! 'Elp! There's a dead body in 'ere!'

They forgot all about me in the ensuing chaos. I slipped out through the sliding door while someone else was rushing in, and kept my head down as I walked to the bus stop on the Lea Bridge Road. All the way home on the top deck of the bus, I was working out a plan to get Mrs Shapiro out.

37

A trip to B&Q

Next morning, I phoned Ms Baddiel. Amazingly, she answered on the first ring.

'Oh, thank goodness I've got hold of you. Something terrible's happened. Mrs Shapiro's been kidnapped,' I gabbled. I didn't want to complicate things by mentioning the body.

'Sssh. Ca-alm down, Mrs Sinclair. Now, take a deep breath for me. Hold. Two – three – four. Breathe out with a sigh. Two – three – four, and rela-ax.'

I did as she instructed. My stomach-knot eased and my fists turned back into hands.

'That's perfect. Now, you were saying . . .?'

I tried to explain that Mrs Shapiro had been kidnapped and held against her will until she agreed to sign away her house. I avoided directly accusing Mrs Goodney of theft, but Ms Baddiel was more concerned that Mrs Shapiro's lifestyle choices were being violated.

'There are a number of options open to her. If she is to live at home, the house needs to be made suitable. It's easy to move a bed downstairs and convert a living room into a bedroom. The problem is usually to create a downstairs bathroom. Alternatively, of course, she could install a lift. Even a stairlift.'

'Mm. Yes. Good idea. I've got some men in there at the moment, fixing it up. I could ask . . .'

'Perfect.'

I tried to picture Mr Ali and the Uselesses installing a stairlift. Mmm. No.

'There used to be grants available for that kind of work, but unfortunately now it usually has to be self-financed. Has she got any funds, do you know?'

I thought of the receipts from the secondhand traders I'd found in her bureau drawer.

'I'm not sure. I'll ask her.' Though I knew as sure as hell she wouldn't tell me. My heart sank. Then I imagined trying to persuade her to have a stairlift installed.

'And we could increase her care package. I take it that worked out all right?'

'Yes. Fine. Fantastic.'

We arranged to meet at the house on Friday. I wanted time to be sure that the Uselesses had made some progress, and to check that the place was at least habitable. Ms Baddiel undertook to visit Northmere House in the meantime, and to challenge the terms of Mrs Shapiro's incarceration.

'It's a violation of human rights,' she said confidently in her peachy voice.

On Wednesday afternoon I set out to visit Mrs Shapiro at Northmere House again. I walked down to the Balls Pond Road to get the Number 56, and I must have dozed off on the bus (or *sunk into a reverie*, as Ms Firestorm would put it) for when I looked out of the window we were already on the Lea Bridge Road, and I realised I'd missed my stop. I rang the bell hastily and raced down the stairs, and when the bus finally came to a halt I found myself standing near a familiar jolly orange-and-grey building. Another branch of B&Q! It must be destiny, I thought.

The B&Q store was tattier than the one at Tottenham and almost empty, silent with a hush of reverence – like a temple,

I thought, dedicated to some peculiar male cult. The high ceilings and echoing aisles, the air of solemn devotion, the acolytes walking with bowed heads, the obscure objects of veneration, the mysteries. Apart from me, there was only one other woman in the place, a stunningly pretty Asian girl with a sparkling nose stud, on one of the checkouts. With the air of a slightly bored priestess, she pointed me in the direction of the adhesives on aisle twenty-nine.

Cyanoacrylate AXP-36C. I had pulled the crumpled Mrs Brown envelope out of my pocket and started to look at the labels on the packaging. It was easy enough to distinguish between the PVAs, the epoxies and the acrylates, but there didn't seem to be one with that precise formulation. A number of them carried warnings about misuse. I browsed the packets, looking for the ones with the direst warnings.

After a while, a nice blokey type appeared and asked me if I needed any help. I showed him my paper. He studied it for a few moments with a puzzled frown, then asked, 'What's it for, sweetheart?'

I noticed that he had a Kent NUM tattoo on his forearm. How strange, I thought; if I had met him instead of Mr Ali when I was first looking for the lock, there would have been a different point of connection, and quite a different story.

'It's for ... er ... just, you know, general use.' I smiled mysteriously, picked up a few superglues, and put them in my shopping basket with a nonchalant air.

Another discovery I made, by the way, at the end of the adhesives aisle, is that duck tape has nothing at all to do with ducks. No quacking or waddling involved. In fact it's duct tape. What a disappointment.

Out of interest, I passed by to look at the toilet seats. Although they had exotic names – Chamonix, Valencia, Rossini – they weren't in fact very exciting. There were no musical ones or ones which lit up, as I'd seen advertised in the Sunday papers – seats designed to attract a curious bottom. I'd have to look on the internet. Ideally, I should get one that played a ridiculous but catchy tune like 'Jingle Bells' or 'The Birdie Song', that would keep going until the person got up – *if* they *ever* got up!

By the time I remembered I'd meant to call at Northmere House on the way back, I'd already overshot the stop again. That would have to wait for another day. I was filled with a pleasant feeling of satisfaction on my way home, sitting in my favourite seat, upstairs at the front, with my purchases in a bag on my knee, and enjoying the changing patterns of clouds and light as the bus lumbered down the Lea Bridge Road.

At Clapton a group of schoolboys got on, jostling and giggling. I didn't notice at first that they were wearing small skull caps. They crowded on to the top deck, and made a rush for the other front seat, all four of them, barging with their backpacks and trying to shove each other out of the way. Mrs Shapiro's story was still fresh in my mind, and I wanted to talk to them, to ask about their parents and grandparents – about the countries they'd left and the journeys they'd made. But why should they have to worry about any of that old painful stuff? These lads – they didn't have the air of exiles. They were gossiping about one of their teachers who, apparently, had been spotted at a Westlife concert wearing a dress that revealed too much. Let them be, I thought. Let them be happy. As we thundered along among the treetops, I closed my eyes and felt through my eyelids the brilliant spring light flicker over my face: dark-light-dark-light-dark-light. When I got off at Balls Pond Road, a few stops later, I could still hear their peals of laughter as the bus pulled away. Let them be happy while they can.

As I turned the corner into my road, I saw there was a car parked outside my house. A black car. A Jaguar. I stopped. How long had he been waiting for me? Since the debacle with Nathan, I'd been feeling a sort of blank emptiness inside me. Now I felt my heart quicken, a beat between panic and pleasure. Or maybe I was just inexorably drawn. I carried on walking, wondering what I should say. As I got closer, the driver's-side door opened, and he stepped out on to the pavement, all lean and hungry six-feet-something of him, with a bunch of flowers in his hand – blue irises. My heart did a skip.

'Doing a spot of DIY, are you, Georgina?' He was looking at my B&Q carrier bag with interest. 'Have you got time for a quick word? About Canaan House? There are some . . . er . . . developments you should know about.'

'Developments?'

I glanced at my watch. It was just turned three o'clock.

'It'll have to be quick. Ben'll be back soon.'

I noticed he had a fresh white handkerchief in his jacket pocket, and despite my resolution, a tremor like a Pavlovian response ran through me.

'I thought you should know . . . my colleague, Nick Wolfe. You were right. His intentions are not honourable. *Very* not honourable.'

'You'd better come in.'

He followed me into the house. I shoved the B&Q bag in the bottom of a cupboard in the mezzanine study on my way down into the kitchen, and put the kettle on. While it boiled, I arranged the irises in a vase. They reminded me of Mrs Shapiro's toilet bowl. He stood very close beside me, watching. I could sense the heat of his body through the centimetre of air between us, and that pleasant pelvic glow – it was the shameless woman, putting in a surprise guest (gusset) appearance.

'Tell me,' I said.

'Yes. Nick. He's – how can I put it? – he's got obsessed with Canaan House. He's commissioned an architect; had plans drawn up to turn it into a gated community. Luxury flats. Done out to the highest spec. Penthouse suite. Basement gym. Enclosed Japanese-style garden with pebble and stone water-feature. The full monty. Plus six mews studios.'

I took a deep breath. I could smell the expensive soap, and beneath it the chlorine.

'Okay. And so what's he planning to do with Mrs Shapiro?'

'He's planning to marry her.'

He delivered his punchline with a slight lift of the eyebrows. I pretended to be shocked, but inside I was smiling.

'Apparently they struck up quite a friendship, and one day he asked her age. She had him on that she was sixty-one. Well, that roused his suspicions, so he sneaked a look at her medical records in the nursing home. They gave her age as ninety-six.'

'No! Really?' I feigned surprise.

'He thought – well, at that age her life expectancy – how can I put it? – it left a lot to be desired. A couple of years, at most. He reckoned he was on to a good thing.'

'Did he tell you she has a son?'

'He mentioned something along those lines. That's why he's in a hurry to tie the knot. If she's married to him, he gets the lot when she pops her clogs. Unless she's made a will, of course.'

'The son's supposed to be coming all the way from Israel. He obviously thinks he's on to a good thing, too. But I don't know if he's really her son. Her husband was married before, you know.'

Before what? That's what I couldn't work out. If Ella Wechsler had married Artem Shapiro, her name would have become Ella Shapiro. But why had she changed her first name from Ella to Naomi? Why would someone change their whole name?

'If she wasn't married to him,' I was thinking aloud, 'if she was just living with him . . .'

'Mm. Good point. Would she still have a claim on the house?' I could see his mind working in the gold flickering of his eyes.

'Does it make any difference, who was married to who? Surely, if she's lived there all these years, the house is hers?'

'It depends on how the deeds were drawn up.' He was stirring the sugar into his coffee, tinkling the spoon against the china and looking at me with those vari-coloured eyes. I could feel myself melting inside. 'It'd be interesting to sneak a look, Georgina. Do you know where they're kept by any chance?'

They were probably among the sheaves of paper up in the attic. 'I haven't a clue,' I said, squeezing my tea bag sexily and fishing it out with a provocative little flick of the spoon.

'It might be possible to find out from the Land Registry,' he murmured.

He finished his coffee and stood up, leaning in the doorway, smiling darkly. 'Shall we . . .?'

He led, I followed.

'You said you were going to show me your poems,' I said, teasing, but to my surprise he produced a slim cream envelope from the pocket of his jacket – not the handkerchief one, the one inside the lining.

'I've written one specially for you, Georgina.'

The envelope was slightly warm and curved to the contours of his body. I opened it curiously as he undressed me. There was a poem, written out by hand, the letters squat and confident on the creamy paper.

I wandered through the city streets
My heart was burdened down with care,
And then I saw thee standing there
With raindrops sparkling on thy hair.

Sweet Saint Georgina, thou art
The dragon slayer of my heart.
Tell me thou love me, for I know
We'll never be apart.

I couldn't stop myself; I cringed; then I covered it up with an embarrassed kiss.

'Mmm. That's lovely,' I said.

'Glad you like it, sweetheart. Have you got the . . .?'

'The . . .?'

I fumbled in my bedside drawer for the shameless accessories, and slipped them on. He checked the gusset. He tightened the satin handcuffs. Thank heavens for IKEA slatted headboards. Where would we be without them? thought the Shameless Woman as she sighed and lay back on the pillows. But the poem – the ugly doggerel – jangled in my head. I tried to abandon myself to shamelessness but it was no use. 'Sweet Saint Georgina . . . Tell me thou love me . . .' And to think I had once dreamed of having an entourage of poet toy-boys! In the end I just had to fake it. Afterwards, when I was lying tense and sweaty in his arms, and he was stroking my hair and doing his hankie thing, I had a sudden memory of the first night Rip and I had spent together in his attic flat in Chapeltown. We'd lain together in the crumpled sheets looking at the candlelight flickering on the sloping ceiling, and he'd reached down a well-thumbed book from his shelf and read me John Donne's 'The Sunne Rising'. *'She is all states, and all princes I. Nothing else is.'*

What had happened to *that* Rip – not the always-in-a-hurry destiny-shaping Progress Project Rip, but the other Rip who was as bouncy as a puppy, curious, funny, eager, idealistic, who read Donne and Marvell when we made love, and brought me Marmite on toast in the morning? What had happened to *him*? A pain like the shock of bereavement hit me right in the heart, making me flinch. What was I doing here? Why was I in bed with this man?

'Why did you use those words, thee and thou?' I asked.

'Don't you like them?'

'I do, but . . . they're a bit old-fashioned.'

'You strike me as being – how can I put it? – quite an old-fashioned girl, Georgina.' He ran a finger down my cheek. 'I can change it if you don't like it, sweetheart.'

The trouble is, I realised, I only wanted him wicked and wolfy. I didn't want this touchy-feely gooey stuff. And I definitely didn't want the poetry.

'No, leave it. It's fine as it is. But . . . it should be thou lovest, not thou love.'

As soon as I said it, I wished I hadn't. I didn't mean it as a put-down – it was just my Eng Lit degree popping out in the wrong place.

'Lovest?' He sounded utterly crushed.

'But it's fine as it is. Romantic. Please! Don't change anything!'

But he was already sitting up and putting on his neatly folded clothes.

'Mark, you've forgotten . . .'

'Lovest!'

The door closed with a quiet click and he was gone.

I lay there for a while thinking about the poem. It wasn't just the archaisms that bothered me, it was the flaky metaphor of Saint George and the dragon, and that ugly foreshortened last line, like a broken tooth. You'd have thought he could have found a couple of spare syllables to patch it up with. A sudden vivid memory caught me off guard: it was the first time Rip and I went down to Holtham at Christmas. Rip slipped his hand between my thighs as I drove and read me Donne's poem 'Nocturnal upon St Lucy's Day' as we crossed the wintry Pennines, rough with browned-off heather beneath which new shoots were already pushing into the black oozing peat. *'I am every dead thing, In whom love wrought new alchemy.'* I was so overcome with passion that we had to stop in a lay-by. It's not easy to make love in the back of a Mini, but I remembered how our bodies closed together like two shells of a bivalve.

Riding in on the memory came an intense pang of longing for Rip – for his warm solid body, his alert clever mind. In spite of the Sinclair confidence that bordered on arrogance, in spite of the Progress Project and the destiny-shaping work, in spite of the dereliction of DIY duties and the irritating BlackBerry habits, in spite even of the Scarlet-mouthed Slut, he was still Ben and Stella's dad; yes, and he was still the man I loved. Maybe it was time to stop messing around with other men and start glueing together my marriage.

Just then, the front door slammed. It must be Ben letting himself in. I sat up and . . . no, I tried to sit up, but my wrists were still firmly strapped to the headboard. I tugged. Nothing happened. Irritated, I pulled harder, but the Velcro held fast.

'Mum?' Ben called from the kitchen.

'Hi, Ben. I'm just finishing something off. I'll be with you in a minute.'

For God's sake. It was only Velcro. But because of the way it was fastened on my wrists, when I tugged I was just pulling tighter on to the join. I tried to squeeze up my hands and slip them through the loops, but there was no slack. I could hear the crickle-crickle of the Velcro hooks under strain. Then the crickling stopped. My thumb joints were still in the way. My wrists were getting sore. My arms were aching. My heart was racing. *Don't panic. In – two – three – four. Out – two – three – four.*

'D'you want some tea, Mum?'

'Lovely, thanks. NO! No, it's all right. Just put the kettle on. I'll come down.'

Next I tried using my teeth. I found that if I strained and wriggled, I could get my mouth within an inch of my left wrist. Half an inch. But no more. I tried the other side. That was worse. My arms weren't long enough. Or maybe they were too long. I went back to the left side. I strained and strained. If I stuck my tongue out I could even touch the Velcro with the tip of it – I just couldn't get it with my teeth. When my shoulder felt as though it was going to break, I gave up. Exhausted, I lay back on the pillows and considered my options. Then I realised I had no options. Well, the only option was to call out to Ben for help. That wasn't really an option. I'd rather die. Then I became aware of another unpleasant sensation. I needed a pee.

'Kettle's boiled!'

'Right! Thanks!'

I could tell Ben it was an accident. Oh, yeah. I could pretend I'd been trying out an experiment. Playing a game. Practising for a pantomime. Like you do. Trouble was, the duvet was down around my knees, and I was still wearing the red panties. And nothing else. There was nothing for it but to go back to the crickling. Each little crickle-crickle was a hook opening, I told myself. Just take it slowly. Forget about the bladder. Concentrate on the wrists. Concentrate on one wrist at a time. I seemed to have more power in my right

303

wrist. I found that by moving the thumb joint and flexing my fingers up and down I could increase the crickling. Crickle-crickle-crickle. Crickle-crickle-crickle. The more gently I did it, the more it crickled. I could move my right thumb quite a bit now. I could fold it into my palm and ease it . . . ease it . . . yes, there it goes. My right hand was free. I reached across and freed my left hand. Then I grabbed my dressing gown and dashed to the toilet.

'Is everything all right, Mum?'

'Yes. Just get that kettle on.'

Two minutes later I strolled into the kitchen wearing my jeans and jumper and an insouciant smile on my face. I poured the hot water over the tea bag.

'Thanks, Ben. Just something I had to get finished by today.'

He studied me curiously. I slipped my hands behind my back so he wouldn't see the raw marks on my wrists.

'Are you all right, Mum? You look a bit . . . red.'

'Red?' I blushed.

'Have you been in a fight?'

'No. Not exactly. Why?'

'You seem – sort of – irregular.'

It wasn't until I had another pee at bedtime that I spotted the red lace-trimmed panties still crumpled up on the floor in the toilet. Had Ben noticed them when he went upstairs? Should I say anything? Should I pretend they were Stella's? (Shame on you, Georgie!) Or should I just keep quiet? That's what I did.

38

Without walls

Ben and I had taken to sometimes having our tea in front of the gas fire in the sitting room with the television on in the background – a comfy Kippax habit, which we'd adopted now there were just the two of us. So there we were on Thursday balancing our plates on our knees and watching the seven o'clock news – the usual gloom, doom and trivia. I was about to flick the remote when an item came up about the nuclear missile defence shield that the Americans were supposed to be stationing in Poland to stop missiles from Iran. I know my geography's a bit shaky, but wasn't that, like, the wrong continent? Then I noticed Ben had gone very still.

'I wouldn't worry,' I said. 'I'm sure it won't work, anyway.'

Ben was staring at the screen.

'It's the prophecy. Gog and Magog.' His voice was almost a whisper. 'They're getting ready for the missiles.'

'What missiles?'

Ben put his plate aside, slid off the sofa, and knelt in front of me.

'Mum, I'm begging you. Take Jesus into your heart.'

He stretched out his hands to me as if he was pleading or praying – my poor broken-in-half boy. I took his hands – they were shaking. I knew that nothing I said would be the right thing, so I kept quiet and just held his hands tight in mine. Then he closed his eyes, and started to speak – it was more like a chant – in that grating up-talk inflection.

305

'Ezekiel thirty-eight? Thus saith the Lord God? Behold, I am against thee, O Gog, Prince of Meshech and Tubal. I will turn thee back, and put hooks into thy jaws, all thine army, horses and horsemen? Persia, Ethiopia, and Libya with them? Gomer, and all his bands; the house of Togar-mah of the north quarters, and all his bands? All of them clothed in all manner of armour, shields and swords?'

It reminded me of the *Lord of the Rings* poster on his wall: the Orcs with their sub-prime dentistry, the vast exotic computer-enhanced armies marching into the field. I would have dismissed it as lads' fantasy, but for what came next.

'In the last days I will bring thee against my land? Thou shalt come into this land, that is brought back to peace from the sword, gathered out of many people to dwell amongst the mountains of Israel, which had been a wasteland before, but is brought forth out of the nations. And they shall dwell safely? All of them? Dwelling without walls, and having neither bars nor gates?'

His voice was wobbling.

'Oh, Ben . . .' I squeezed his hands. Phrases from Naomi's letter from Israel – the letter I'd found in the piano stool, which I'd reread so many times, flashed into my mind. *Our place of safety . . . of barren wasteland . . . our people gathered out of every country where we have been exiles . . . a land without barbed wires.* But Mr Ali had told me there were walls now, and checkpoints, and barbed wire.

'And I will rain upon him an overflowing rain, and great hailstones, fire, and brimstone.' Ben's eyes were still closed. Then he looked up at me. 'Take Jesus, Mum. Please? Before it's too late?'

'Okay, Ben. Okay.'

He was pale and trembling.

'But you don't believe it, do you?' He shook his shaved

head – covered now with fine dark stubble – in a gesture that could have been frustration or despair.

'Well . . .'

'You're just saying it to keep me happy, aren't you?' His eyes were liquid, backed up with tears. 'What's the point? What's the point in being saved, if everybody . . . like everybody you really love is going to be damned?'

The television was still burbling in the background, and I flicked the remote to turn it off – to cut off that terrifying stream of madness that kept leaching into our own little fireside world.

'Come here, you.' I pulled him up on to the sofa beside me, and put my arms round his shoulders, squeezing him tight. 'It's just talk and posturing. It'll all blow over.'

I said it with a confidence I didn't feel, putting on a brave face for Ben, for a part of me was scared, too. However much my rational mind dismissed the gibberish of prophets, there was a dark cave hidden away beneath my brain where the monsters slept, fears and nightmares chained up since childhood, but still with a residual power to instil dread. We sat together, holding hands and listening to the silence settling back into the room. It was raining again outside, a soft pit-pat, not a downpour. I could hear Ben's breathing getting slower. His hands were very cold.

Suddenly, outside in the street, we heard the sound of a car pulling up, tyres splashing in the rain, a diesel engine idling, footsteps on the path, a knock on the door. Ben and I stared at each other. There was another louder knock, then a man's voice – an unfamiliar voice – 'Anybody there?'

I got up and opened the door. I didn't recognise the man standing there, a bulky, dark-skinned man. But after a moment, I realised he was the driver of the taxi that had pulled up outside on the road. Then the door of the taxi opened, and out clambered Mrs Shapiro.

'Georgine!' she exclaimed. 'Please – help me! Do you heff some money for the taxi?'

'Of course,' I said. 'How much?'

'Fifty-four pound,' said the taxi driver. He wasn't smiling.

'Isn't that a bit . . .?'

'It should be more than that. We been going round in circles for hours.'

I went to look in my purse. I had forty pounds and some change.

'Ben, can you help?'

He was standing behind me, trying to work out what was going on.

'I'll have a look.'

He went upstairs. I remembered some loose coins in my duffel coat pocket. And there were some pounds I'd put in the Barnardo's envelope by the door. Ben came down with a fiver. Mrs Shapiro fished a pound coin out of the lining of her astra-khan coat. Between us we rustled together £52.73. The taxi driver took it crossly, mumbled something, and disappeared.

'Come in, come in,' I said to Mrs Shapiro.

'Thenk you,' she said. 'Some persons are living in my house. Will not let me in.'

As she crossed the threshold, Wonder Boy appeared out of the darkness and slunk in beside her.

She sat by the fire cradling a mug of tea in her hands, which Ben had brought on a tray, with some chocolate digestives.

'Thenk you, young man. Charming. I am Mrs Naomi Shapiro. Please – tek a biscuit.'

Wonder Boy stretched himself out in front of the fire and started rubbing himself up against the *Lion King* slippers, making a gruff rasping noise which was as close as he could get to purring. Through sips of tea and mouthfuls of biscuit crumbs, she told us the story of her escape.

After the discovery of the dead body, the bonker lady had become totally bonkers.

'Crezzy. Brain completely rotted away.'

Not content with hanging around in the corridor cadging cigarettes from visitors, she would embellish her patter with an invitation.

'I show you the dead body if you give me a ciggie.'

That upset the staff – they thought it was giving a bad impression of the home. From time to time, just to wind them up, she would rush down the corridor yelling ''Elp! 'Elp! There's a dead body in 'ere!' It came to a head when a party of relatives accompanying their aged mother on an inspection tour were accosted by the bonker lady, who somehow led them to believe (they were all smokers) that finding corpses was almost a daily occurrence. The staff member who was showing them round lost her rag and tried to push the bonker lady back into her room.

'But she was fighting them like a tiger. Clawving and skretching mit the hends!'

In the end the security guard had to be called. Then matron arrived in her green cardie with an ampoule of sedative and a needle, but the bonker lady kept struggling and yelling, ''Elp! 'Elp! They gonner kill me!'

The relatives, rattled by so much violence, tried to call the police on a mobile phone. By now all the residents – those of them who were upright – had crowded into the corridor and were cheering the bonker lady on. In all the kerfuffle Mrs Shapiro managed to slip unnoticed through the door into the lobby and out on to the Lea Bridge Road, where a passing taxi whisked her to safety.

'And here I am, darlinks!' she exclaimed, flushed with the excitement of her adventure. 'Only problem is some persons are living in my house. We must evict them now!'

She put her empty cup down and rose to her feet. I tried to persuade her to stay for a bite to eat, and even offered her a bed for the night, but she was desperate to get home. Wonder Boy had stopped purring and was thrashing his tail against the floor.

We set off down the road, Mrs Shapiro leading the way – it was surprising how fast she could move in those *Lion King* slippers – Ben and I lagging behind, and Wonder Boy bringing up the rear. It was quite dark and cold, the air still damp from the recent rain. As we turned into Totley Place a couple of the other cats appeared out of the bushes and tagged along, too. Violetta was waiting for us in the porch, ecstatic with pleasure at Mrs Shapiro's return. Wonder Boy hissed, batted her with his paws, and sent her packing.

There were lights in some of the windows, and this was surprising in itself, because I'd never before seen Canaan House lit up so brightly from the inside. I noticed that the front door had been painted yellow and the broken floor tiles in the porch replaced with what looked like modern bathroom tiles. While Mrs Shapiro was fumbling for her key, I rang on the doorbell.

It was Mr Ali's nephew, Ishmail, who answered the door. He recognised me at once, and beaming broadly gestured to us to come inside.

'Welcome! Welcome!'

He'd learned another word. The inside of the house had been painted, too, in white and yellow. It looked lighter and fresher, and smelled much better. I saw Mrs Shapiro looking around, and tried to judge the expression on her face. She seemed to be quite pleased.

'You've been busy,' I said to Ishmail. 'This is Mrs Shapiro. She's the owner of the house. She's come home now, so I'm afraid you'll have to leave. It's what we agreed. Remember?'

He smiled and nodded blankly. He obviously had no idea what I was on about. I tried again, talking more loudly, with accompanying gestures.

'This lady – live here – come back – you must go – go now.' I pointed at Mrs Shapiro and made shooing hand movements.

'Yes. Yes.' He smiled and nodded.

Then Nabeel appeared on the scene, and joined in the smiling and nodding, offering his three words of English.

'Hello. Please. Welcome. Hello. Please. Welcome.'

'Hello. Yes, please. Welcome,' said Ishmail.

I went through my pointing and shooing routine. They smiled and nodded.

'Hello. Yes. Please.'

We were getting nowhere.

Then Ishmail – you have to credit him with some intelligence – got his mobile phone out, keyed a number, and started talking in Arabic to the person at the other end. After a few moments he passed the phone to me. It was Mr Ali.

'You'll have to tell them to leave,' I said. 'Now that Mrs Shapiro's home. They can't stay. You promised – remember? I'm really sorry. I thought we'd have some warning, but . . .' I was getting a bit hysterical.

I passed the phone to Ishmail. He listened for a few moments, then uttered a stream of Arabic, then listened again, then passed the phone to me.

'Tonight too late. I have no van.' Mr Ali's voice sounded faint and crackly. 'Please let them to stay for tonight. Tomorrow I come with van.'

'Okay,' I said. 'Just tonight. I'll talk to Mrs Shapiro. Mr Ali, thank you for the work you've done – the painting – it looks wonderful.'

'You like this yellow colour?'

'Very much.'

'I knew you would like it.' He sounded pleased.

Mrs Shapiro had lost patience with our three-way conversation, and had disappeared somewhere. Ben and Nabeel had wandered off into the study, where a television had been rigged up with an internal aerial. They were watching football, sitting side by side grinning and cheering when a goal was scored. Nabeel pointed to himself and said, 'Hello! Please! Arsenal!' Ben pointed to himself and said, 'Hello, Leeds United!'

I found Mrs Shapiro in her bedroom. She was curled up in bed with Wonder Boy, Violetta, Mussorgsky and one of the pram babies. Wonder Boy had actually got under the covers with her. They were all purring, and Mrs Shapiro was snoring.

39

Home improvements

Next morning, I woke up with the feeling that I had something important to do, but I couldn't remember what it was. I'd left Mrs Shapiro sleeping at the house last night, and I thought maybe I should go back this morning and check up on her. Then the phone rang. It was Ms Baddiel, reminding me of our meeting. After I'd put the phone down, I had a bright idea. I picked it up again, and dialled Nathan's number.

'I wonder whether you could give us some advice. About the use of modern adhesives in home improvements. This morning. Eleven o'clock.' I gave him the address.

'Great. I'll bring the DIY demonstration kit.'

'Bring your father, too.'

I smiled as I put the phone down. Matchmaking is a game that two can play.

I went up there a bit earlier to make sure everything was shipshape for Ms Baddiel, and to supervise the departure of the Uselesses – I hoped they'd be all packed up and ready to go. When I rang on the bell at about half past ten, it was Ishmail who opened the door again and invited me in. The house was pleasantly warm, and smelled of woodsmoke, freshly brewed coffee and cigarettes. I followed him through to the study at the back of the house where a fire had been lit in the hearth. They were burning sheaves of papers and bits of old wood – including some of the boards that had been taken down from the windows. The television was on, and a sofa, still draped in a white dust sheet, had been dragged through from the sitting room. On the sofa sat Mrs Shapiro and Nabeel. They were smoking and drinking coffee from the silver pot and watching *The Hound of the Baskervilles* in black and white on the television. Mrs Shapiro was wearing her candlewick dressing gown and her *Lion King* slippers. Violetta was curled up on her lap, Mussorgsky was on Nabeel's lap and Wonder Boy was stretched out on the rug in front of the fire. It was a scene of cosy decadence.

'Georgine! Darlink!' She swivelled round and patted the empty space at the end of the sofa. 'Come and drink a coffee mit us.'

'Maybe later,' I said. 'We have to get ready. The social worker's coming.'

'What for I need the social work?' Mrs Shapiro sniffed. 'I heff my young men.'

'But they're going home now, Mrs Shapiro. They have to go.'

On the screen, the hound started roaring terrifyingly. Wonder Boy pricked up his ears and started swinging his tail. Mrs Shapiro gripped my hand.

'This dog is a monster. Same like the matron in the Nightmare House. Grrah! I will not go back to this place. Never.'

'No, definitely not. But *this* social worker is nice. She'll help you to stay at home. It's Ms Baddiel. You met her before. Remember?'

'I remember. Not Jewish. Too fet.'

She'd lost interest in our conversation, and was watching the fearsome hound racing over the darkening moors.

Ishmail thrust a cup of coffee into my hands. It was thick, black and bitter. He handed me the sugar bowl and though I don't usually take sugar I helped myself to a couple of heaped spoonfuls. I declined the cigarette he offered me, but Mrs Shapiro took it and lit it from the end of the one that was still smouldering in the ashtray at her feet.

'What is this brown boots?' she asked, coughing a little.

As I was trying to explain the significance of the black and brown boots in the plot, the doorbell rang.

The other three were completely gripped by the drama so I got up to answer it. Ms Baddiel was standing there. She was wearing a floaty silk aquamarine coat, and her honey-gold hair was twisted up in a loose braid. Behind her on the porch stood Nathan, with a large attaché case under his arm, and Nathan's Tati, looking very spruce in a collar and tie. They had obviously introduced themselves already.

'Nathan's come along to advise us about adhesives,' I said. 'In case there are any urgent repairs that need doing.'

'Perr-fect.' She followed me through to the study, sniffing the air and looking around her, taking in all the improvements. 'Lovely.'

Mrs Shapiro hardly looked up as we came into the room, her eyes were fixed on dashing Basil Rathbone on the screen, but Ishmail, with impeccable politeness, jumped up and offered Ms Baddiel his corner of the sofa.

'Hello, Mrs Shapiro.' She leaned forward towards the old lady. 'How are you doing? I understand you've had some adventures.'

'Ssh!' Mrs Shapiro held her finger to her lips. 'The hund is killing.'

Half an hour or so later, as the final credits rolled, she turned to us and said in a croaky voice, 'I heff seen this film once before. Mit Arti. When we were still in loff. Before the sickness snetched him away. So long ago. What has heppened to all the years?'

There were tears in the corners of her eyes. Ms Baddiel

leaned forward and hugged her in her plump arms. Then she reached in her bag for a vanilla-scented tissue.

'It's all right now. You can let it all out. Take a deep breath. Hold. Breathe out with a sigh. There. Perfect.'

Violetta stretched her paws and rubbed her head against Mrs Shapiro's thigh. Tati put a piece of wood – it looked worryingly like an antique chair leg – on the fire and reached down to stroke Wonder Boy, who rolled on his back, legs thrown apart abandonedly, and started to purr. Nathan and I exchanged smiles. Nabeel went and made another pot of coffee. Ishmail offered round a packet of Camel cigarettes.

'Are you her carer?' Ms Baddiel asked.

'Hello. Yes. Please.' He flashed his lovely teeth at her.

She took out her Labrador-puppy notebook and wrote something down. Then Nabeel came back from the kitchen with a steaming coffee pot and fresh cups.

'And you? You're a carer, too?'

'Hello. Yes. Welcome!'

'Well, you may be entitled to claim the Carer's Allowance,' she said. 'One of you. The Carer's Allowance is payable if you spend at least thirty-five hours a week looking after someone who is in receipt of Attendance Allowance. Are you claiming Attendance Allowance, Mrs Shapiro?'

'What for I need attendents?' said Mrs Shapiro. She was still sniffling a bit.

'Well, you know,' Ms Baddiel offered her another tissue, 'after what you've been through, Mrs Shapiro, I think you deserve a bit of help. Of course it's up to you, entirely.'

A skinny tabby cat jumped up into her lap. She ran her little chipolatas over its fur making it purr so much it started to dribble and she had to get another tissue out. Nathan's Tati was sitting watching all this with such a solemn look on his face I thought she'd have to hand him a tissue, too.

316

Then the doorbell rang again. Ishmail was already on his feet so he went to answer it. I heard him talking animatedly, and another quieter voice replying. A moment later, Mr Ali joined us in the study. He and Ishmail were still arguing in Arabic, and now Nabeel joined in. Mr Ali turned to Mrs Shapiro.

'They are saying they want to stay here. They are saying they can baint all house and fixitup and help you make it clean. I will supervise of course. You pay only for materials.'

I saw a quick flicker pass through Mrs Shapiro's eyes. She said nothing.

'You know in our culture we have great respect for old people,' Mr Ali pressed on. 'But I think mebbe you do not like to have young men into your house, Mrs Naomi?'

Everyone's gaze was now focused on Mrs Shapiro. She looked around cannily. Her eyes were still moist but her cheeks were flushed with excitement, or maybe with too much strong coffee, and I could see her mouth twitch as she weighed up her options.

'I donnow. I donnow.' She put one hand dramatically to her brow, and ran the other through Wonder Boy's shaggy belly-fur. 'Wonder Boy, what you think?' Wonder Boy purred ecstatically. 'Okay. We try it.'

There was a general exhalation of breath.

Mr Ali led us on a guided tour around the house to show us the improvements he'd made. The dingy hall looked much brighter under its coat of white paint, and the loose floor tiles had been fixed or replaced with shiny white bathroom tiles. I noticed with dismay as we climbed the stairs that the grand old mahogany banisters and handrail had been painted with yellow gloss to match the front door, but Mrs Shapiro didn't seem to mind.

However, the most spectacular change was in the bathroom. The original chipped and cracked white tiles had been retained, but beneath them an entire new bathroom suite had been installed. Well, it wasn't exactly new – it looked as if it dated back to the sixties and had been taken out of a house undergoing renovation – two houses, in fact. There was a wide rose-pink washbasin and matching lavatory complete with pink plastic seat cover, and under the window an avocado-green bath with curved chrome handrails. The rotten floorboards under the lavatory had been patched up, and a piece of lino in blue-and-white mosaic covered the whole floor. If you were colour-blind, it would have been lovely.

As my eyes scanned the room, they fell on a white porcelain toothbrush holder fixed on to the wall above the basin. I bent closer to take a surreptitious look while everyone was oohing and aahing over the bath. Yes, it was definitely the same one. There was a small chip on one side – must be from where I'd tossed it into the skip. It was quite stylish – clean lines, Scandinavian-style. But really, at the end of the day, it was just a toothbrush holder. To imagine I'd once got so worked up over it!

Then Mr Ali turned the taps on and off to demonstrate that they all worked. As he flushed the lavatory, steam rose. He stared into the toilet pan with a puzzled frown.

'Some small mistake. Maybe wrong beep. Soon fixitup.'

'But the hot water is much better!' cried Mrs Shapiro. 'You are a very clever-knödel, Mr Ali.'

He beamed at her. 'Colours you like?'

'The pink is nice colour,' she said. 'Better than the green.'

'Lovely,' I said.

'Lovely,' agreed Ms Baddiel, who had seen – and smelled – the original.

'They've developed a new kind of flexible non-crack tile

adhesive based on a thixotropic gel,' said Nathan, producing a tub of something from his demonstration pack. 'Should you be thinking of replacing the tiles.'

Nathan's Tati cleared his throat and sang a verse of the 'Toreador Song' from *Carmen* that resonated in the small space.

'Good acoustics!' he said. Everyone applauded, apart from Nathan.

The bedroom the Uselesses were sharing was the one with the white uPVC window. It had been replastered over the breeze block and actually, from inside, it didn't look so bad. The walls were freshly painted white, and the beds neatly made with the burgundy velour curtains for bedcovers. Their shoes, folded clothes and carrier bags were lined up tidily against one wall. I caught Nathan's eye.

'Admirably spic and span,' was all he said.

Mrs Shapiro's bedroom was untouched, the wallpaper a faded-out colourless fawn with small nondescript flowers picked out in muddy taupe.

'We will baint it up next. What colour you like it?' asked Mr Ali.

She pressed her fingers against her brow as she tried to envision a new room.

'What about the penthouse?' I whispered to Mr Ali. 'Have you started up there?'

'Not yet. Still clearing rubbish. Boys burning it. But slow.'

'They're burning all the papers?' I had an image of priceless historical records going up in smoke. 'Mrs Shapiro? Aren't some of your belongings up there?'

'Is all the rubbish belonging previous inhebitents,' she said dismissively. 'Was some type of religious persons living here before. Orsodox or Kessolik I don't know. They heff left behind all their rubbish and run away.'

'They ran away?'

'In the bombing. They ran and left it all behind. Yes, eau de nil.'

'But who . . .?'

'Eau de nil is the most charming colour for the bedroom, isn't it?'

'An admirable choice,' murmured Nathan's Tati sonorously into Mrs Shapiro's ear, brushing her cheek with the tips of his whiskers.

As we came back down the stairs, he held out his arm for Mrs Shapiro, and she rested her weight on it lightly. She seemed to be blushing more than usual under all the rouge. My plan was working!

The last room we went into was the large sitting room downstairs at the front – the one with the grand piano. The stench in there made us recoil as we stepped inside, and now it was obvious why the room had been out of use for so long. Mr Ali had removed the boards from the window, and in the daylight we could see the sagging ceiling and a great crack in the bay, so wide that you could see daylight on the other side and the green of the monkey puzzle tree. A trail of muddy paw prints led from the base of the crack across the carpet towards the door with its broken latch. So this explained the mystery of how the Phantom Pooer got in and out – even though I still didn't know which one was the culprit. In fact that was the least of our problems.

Nathan, Nathan's Tati and Mr Ali went over to examine the crack, rubbing their chins solemnly and pacing up and down with lowered eyes, the way men do in B&Q.

'There are new types of heavy-duty fast-setting foam fillers, called structural methacrylates, suitable for construction work . . .' Nathan began hesitantly.

'But this does not fixitup the problem,' Mr Ali scratched his head. 'First we must find out what causes. Maybe this tree . . .'

They were looking into the break in the floorboards below the ruptured skirting board. 'We could cut the tree down, dig the roots out, then pump the gap full of methacrylate foam,' suggested Nathan.

'Concrete may be better,' said Mr Ali. 'But pity to cut up such a fine tree.'

'Mind the gap,' Nathan's Tati murmured to Mrs Shapiro, who had come over to have a look, placing his hand on her shoulder and letting it linger there.

'What do you think, Mrs Shapiro? Should we cut the tree down?' asked Ms Baddiel.

Mrs Shapiro looked shifty. 'No. Yes. Maybe.'

I remembered her correspondence with the Council's tree department.

'It may have a preservation order on it,' I said. 'Shall I contact the Council and find out?'

Everyone seemed pleased with this suggestion. As we stood staring into the crack, a skinny feline head poked up between the floorboards and the Stinker eased himself into the drawing room. Crouching low, he looked around the semicircle of human legs, found a suitable gap, and made a dash for the door.

'Raus! Little pisske! Raus!' cried Mrs Shapiro, waving him on, but you could see she didn't mean it. A cheerful, almost skittish mood had come over her; she was revelling in the presence of so many visitors – or maybe of one visitor in particular. She moved over to the piano, lifted the cover and tinkled a few notes. Even those out-of-tune keys seemed to come alive under her touch. To my amazement, without any music to read, she started to play the 'Toreador Song', embellishing it with broken chords and little trills, and Nathan's Tati, standing behind her, gave us a full baritone rendition –

he was more in tune than the piano. Nathan joined in the choruses. At the end, Mrs Shapiro sat back, placing her gnarled ring-encrusted hands together with a sigh.

'Hends no good, isn't it?'

'Nonsense, Naomi,' said Tati, taking her hands and holding them in his.

Then we all made our way back towards the entrance hall to say our goodbyes. Nabeel had to intervene to halt a hissing and scratching match between Mussorgsky and Wonder Boy – despite his initial aversion to cat poo, he had turned out to be quite a cat lover. Mr Ali talked to his nephew softly in Arabic and embraced him in a hamstery hug. Mrs Shapiro sidled up to me and, nodding her head towards Nathan, whispered, 'He is your new boyfriend, Georgine?'

'Not my boyfriend. Just a friend.'

'Good thing,' she whispered. 'He is too petit for you. But quite intelligent. The father also is charming. Pity he is too old for me.'

After they'd all gone, Mrs Shapiro and her attendants went back to sit by the fire, leaving me alone in the hall for a moment, and that's when I noticed that the framed photograph of Lydda which used to hang above the hall table had disappeared. There was nothing but a nail sticking out of the wall to show it had been there. Who had moved it? I was still puzzling over it when suddenly I heard the distinct clack of the front gate. I thought it must be one of the others coming back for something they'd forgotten so I opened the door. Coming down the path towards the house was Mrs Goodney in her lizard-green quilted jacket and her pointy shoes, with an important-looking black briefcase under her arm. Behind her came a dark thickset man I'd never seen before, middle-aged, wearing a crumpled brown suit. Neither of them was smiling. There was something odd about the way the man was looking at me: his eyes seemed asymmetrical.

Mrs Goodney stopped in her tracks when she saw me standing in the doorway. She eyed me up for a few moments. Then she continued her advance. Now a third person, a tall spindly youth, appeared on the garden path and made his way towards us. It was Damian, the young man from Hendricks & Wilson, his hair sticking up with gel, his suit a bit too short in the legs. Blue socks. He was looking up and around, studying the house, avoiding my eyes.

'Feeding the cats again, are we?' said Mrs Goodney to me. I was so taken aback by her rudeness that I forgot to ask her what she was doing here. She turned to Damian and smiled toothily.

'Glad you could make it, Mr Lee. The gentleman just needs an initial estimate of value at this stage.'

The thickset man nodded. He was looking at the house in frank amazement, his misaligned eyes sliding around this way and that. Then I realised one of them was made of glass.

'Must be vort a bit, eh?' he said. 'Big house like this. Good part of London town. I am somewhat impressed.' His English was better than Mrs Shapiro's, if a bit pedantic, with just a slight guttural accent.

Damian took a dog-eared notebook out of his pocket and started to make notes with a stub of pencil. He was still avoiding my eyes.

'Unfortunately it's not worth as much as you think. It's in poor condition, as you can see.' Mrs Goodney was simpering at the glass-eye man. 'I've had a reputable builder to view it and he reports that it needs a substantial amount of money spending on it to bring it up to present-day standards. I'll show you his report if you like.' The glass-eye man sniffed discontentedly, but Mrs Goodney placed one plump red-nailed gold-ringed hand on his arm and the other on Damian's. 'Don't worry, Mr Lee'll quote you a good price. Won't you, Mr Lee?'

Damian nodded and chewed the end of his pencil.

'This is what you do for your five grand, is it, Damian?' I hissed. He ignored me and carried on chewing.

'Seems like she's already had some builders in. Cowboys, by the look of it.' Her eye had fallen on the uPVC window on the first floor.

'He's not a cowboy,' I blurted out. They all stared at me. 'He's . . .'

Then I noticed that their gaze had shifted away from me to a point somewhere beyond my left shoulder. I turned round. Mrs Shapiro was standing there, and behind her, Nabeel and Ishmail.

'Hello, Mrs Shapiro,' Mrs Goodney's rusty-gate voice squeaked with fake cheeriness. 'What are you doing here, sweetie? You're supposed to be . . .'

'I am come home. Finish mit Nightmare.'

'But you can't stay here on your own. This house isn't safe for you, poppet.'

'Poppet schmoppet.' She pulled herself up into her five-feet-tall, chin-out-fighting pose and looked the social worker in the eye. Her cheeks were still flushed from the excitement of the morning. 'I heff my Attendents. I will claim the Attendents Allowance.'

The young men standing behind her flashed their teeth and their eyes at everybody. Violetta, who seemed to have snuck up with Mussorgsky, was hovering around our feet rubbing herself against Mrs Shapiro's legs and purring. Unexpectedly, she arched her back and hissed at Mrs Goodney, who almost – you could see it in her face – hissed back.

Suddenly the man with the glass eye stepped forward and fixed Mrs Shapiro with his disconcerting gaze.

'Ella? You are Ella Wechsler?'

Mrs Shapiro drew back. I couldn't see her face, but I could hear her throaty intake of breath. 'You are mistooken. I am Naomi Shapiro.'

'You are not Naomi Shapiro.' His voice was gravelly. 'She was my mother.'

'I don't know what you talking about.' Mrs Shapiro elbowed past me, reached out, and slammed the door.

They didn't go away for about half an hour. Standing inside the freshly painted hall, the four of us listened to them ringing on the doorbell and rattling the letter box. Then we heard their voices as they walked round the outside of the house and started rapping on the kitchen door. Somewhere in the depths of the house, Wonder Boy started to yowl. Eventually they gave up.

I didn't leave until I was sure the coast was clear. I walked home slowly, trying to make sense of what had happened. He must be the real Naomi Shapiro's son – the child she wrote about in her letters, the gummy brown-eyed baby in the photo – this thickset, ugly middle-aged man who had embodied all the idealism and hopes of his beautiful mother. But who was she? And how had Mrs Goodney contacted him? Maybe this was why I'd found no documents or papers in the house – Mrs Goodney had got there first. Had got them and used them to summon up this genie from the past.

As soon as I got home I went up to my bedroom, and spread the photos out on the floor. Baby Artem; the wedding photo; the couple by the fountain; the woman in the archway; the two women at the Highbury house; the Wechsler family; the moshav near Lydda. At half past four, Ben wandered in to see what I was doing, and pointed out something so obvious I should have noticed it before.

'I wonder why he's carrying a gun.'

'Who?'

'The man who took the photo. Look.'

He pointed to a dark patch on the stony foreground in the landscape photograph. It was the shadow of the photographer – the sun was behind him, and you could see the outline of the head and shoulders, the arms raised to hold the camera to the eye, and something long and straight hanging down from one shoulder. Yes, it could be a gun.

He picked up the photograph of the woman standing in the stone archway and turned it over.

'Who's she?'

'I think she must be Naomi Shapiro.'

'The old lady down the road?'

'No, someone else.'

'It says Lydda.'

'That's a place. In Israel.'

'I know, Mum. It's in one of the prophecies. It's supposed to be where the Antichrist returns.' His voice had gone husky.

'Don't be daft, Ben,' I said. Then I saw the look in his eyes. 'Sorry – I didn't mean *you're* daft, I meant *it's* daft. All that Antichrist stuff. Putin and the Pope. The Prince of Wales and his evil bar codes.' I was trying to sound jokey, but Ben didn't smile.

'The Muslims call him Dajjal? He's got one eye? He gets killed by Jesus in this massive battle at the gates of Lydda?' There were beads of sweat on his forehead.

'Ben, it's all . . .' The word on my lips was 'rubbish', but I held back.

'I know you don't believe in it, Mum. I'm not gonna argue about it, all right? I'm not even sure I believe all of it myself. But I know there's something in it. I just know. Like, I can feel it coming?'

5
If Only It Came in Tubes

40

Heavy as watermelons

I walked round to Canaan House the next day, hoping to have a chance to speak to Mr Ali. I wanted to ask him about Lydda. After my unsettling talk with Ben last night, I'd logged on to the internet to look up information about the prophecies relating to Lydda. This story – I wasn't sure where it was leading me, but now, because of Ben, it had become my story, too, and I knew I had to follow it through.

The sun was shining for once, a hard clear brightness, with even a touch of warmth, and I could smell the trees and shrubs catching their silky breaths as if taken by surprise: this is it at last – a real spring day. Around the margins of the lawn, daffodils were poking their yellow heads up between the cut-back loops of bramble that had already started to regrow. Mr Ali was there, standing up on a ladder painting the outside of Mrs Shapiro's bedroom window, singing wordlessly to himself. Wonder Boy was supervising him, sitting on one of the white uPVC chairs in the garden with his tail wrapped round his legs.

'Hello, Mr Ali!' I called. 'Is everything okay?'

He came back down the ladder and wiped his hands on a piece of cloth from the pocket of his blue nylon overall.

'Hello, Mrs George. Nice day!'

Actually, I realised that Wonder Boy wasn't supervising Mr Ali at all; he was supervising a couple of thrushes which were hard at work building their nest among a thicket of ivy in one of the ash trees. I watched them come and go with their bits of moss and dry grass. Wonder Boy was watching too, flicking the tip of his tail.

'Tomorrow I borrow the van, we take Mrs Shapiro to choose a colour of paint for inside.'

'That's good.'

'How is your son?'

'He's okay, but ...' I hesitated. An image of Ben slipped into my mind, his waxy face, the fear in his eyes. He'd gone off to bed last night without eating anything. I'd knocked on the door of his room, but it was locked from the inside. I was beginning to doubt whether this was normal teenage behaviour, something he would grow out of.

'Mr Ali, that picture in the hall – of Lydda. Was it you who took it down?'

'Lydda.' He stuck his paintbrush in a pot of turpentine and swirled it around. 'In the old times this town was famous for its beautiful mosques. But do you know, Mrs George, that this town is a special place to you also? Is home town of your Christian Saint George. You are named from him, I think?'

I didn't want to admit that in fact I'd been named after George Lansbury. It was Dad's idea, and Mum hadn't been able to think of a suitably inspirational female socialist icon to suggest instead.

'Really? Saint George the dragon slayer came from Lydda?'

'You can see his picture carved above the door of the church.'

Sweet Saint Georgina. I recalled Mark Diabello's poem with a shudder. But Ben had also talked about a one-eyed devil.

'The picture of Lydda that was in the hallway, why did you take it down, Mr Ali?'

'Why you are always asking questions, Mrs George?' He

wasn't exactly being rude, but the easy friendliness of our previous conversation had gone. 'Everything is okay. Sun is shining. I am working. Everybody is happy. Now you start asking questions, and if I tell you the truth you will not be happy.'

'You were going to tell me about your family, remember? What happened in Lydda?'

He didn't say anything. He was concentrating on cleaning his brushes. Then he pulled up one of the white plastic chairs and sat down at the table. Wonder Boy had slunk off; I saw him sitting directly beneath the thrushes' tree, staring up into the branches. I shooed him away and sat myself down opposite Mr Ali. He put aside the brushes, poured some of the turpentine on to his hands, rubbed them together and wiped them on his piece of cloth.

'You want to know? Okay. I will tell you, Mrs George.' He put the cloth back in his pocket and folded his arms across his XXL tummy. 'I come from Lydda. I had one brother, born the same time.'

'A twin?'

'If you will please stop interruption, I will tell you.'

Mustafa al-Ali, the man I knew as Mr Ali, was born in Lydda in 1948 – this much he knew. He didn't know his mother's name, nor that of his twin brother, nor even his exact date of birth, but he reckons he was a few months old on 11th July 1948.

'Why, what happened then?'

'Have patience. I will tell you.'

Lydda was at that time a busy town of some 20,000 inhabitants that had grown up over centuries in the fertile coastal plain between the mountains of Judaea and the Mediterranean sea. But that summer, the summer of Nakba, the town was filled up with refugees from Jaffa and smaller towns and villages all up the coast. 'You can imagine how everybody was jittering, talking about expulsions and massacres.'

One late morning in July, when everything was hot and still, and even cats and sparrows had gone off to look for shade, there was a sudden roar of engines overhead. People who looked up saw a flight of planes swoop low out of the glimmering sky. Then the explosions started. One after the other after the other, as the planes began unloading their bombs on the sleepy little town. Houses, shops, mosques, market stalls. One after the other after the other. There was nowhere to flee to. No bomb shelters. No anti-aircraft guns. People just scurried around like frenzied ants. Some caught a blast and fell in the street. Some died when rubble collapsed on them. Some sat tight in a corner and covered their heads and prayed.

'But their purpose mainly was not to kill,' Mr Ali continued, fixing me with his eyes. 'They wanted to drive us out, with terror.'

Next day, as people were emerging from the rubble to inspect the damage and bury their dead, a battalion with mounted machine guns suddenly rolled into town at high speed. At first they thought it was the Jordanian army, come to defend them, but all at once the machine guns let rip, barrels blazing, bullets flying in all directions. Men, women and children were gunned down – some 200 fell and died in the streets. Others fled in fright.

'You can read it on your internet, Mrs George. How it was reported in American newspapers. Blitzkrieg. Ruthlessly brilliant. Corpses riddled with bullets by roadside. All this was done to create terror. This is how they emptied Lydda of its population.'

Some tried to take safety in the great Dahmash Mosque. But later that night, the people who lived nearby heard round after round of gunfire coming from the building. Next day 176 bodies were found inside.

As dawn broke, soldiers ran from house to house, banging on the doors with their rifle butts and ordering those inside to leave at once.

'"Go! Go to King Abdullah!" the soldiers shouted. What they mean is – get out of this country, and leave it for us! Go to Jordan! Flee to any Arab country that will take you! You never heard about this?'

I shook my head. 'Go on.'

The terrified population, expelled from their homes, grabbed what they could and fled. The al-Ali family – the women and children, for their father had disappeared – were dragged out of their house on to the street, given only a few minutes to grab their valuables. Soldiers were herding everyone out into the streets, shoving them with the barrels of their guns if they were too slow, shooting them if they resisted.

'Where are we going?' the mother had asked, grabbing her children to her in all the chaos.

Someone had said, 'They're taking us to Jordan,' and someone else had said, 'We're going to Ramallah.'

They were marched to the outskirts of the town, the soldiers firing shots in the air to make them run.

'Go! Run to Abdullah in Jordan!'

As they passed through a cordon, soldiers searched them, stripping them of their possessions. Ahead of them, one of their neighbours, recently married, who quibbled about sur-rendering his savings, was shot dead before the horrified eyes of his new bride. After that, no one protested. The al-Ali family were robbed of their money, their gold jewellery, their watches, even their silver coffee cups. All they were allowed to keep was a bundle of clothes, some bread and olives and a bag of oranges.

'Run! Run!' The soldiers fired volleys of shots above their heads. But the asphalt road was barred, and they were forced to make their way eastwards across the stubbly, newly harvested fields.

By now it was midday and the heat was intense, the sky so blue and hard it seemed to glimmer like lazurite. In the coastal plain, the temperatures in July can easily reach forty degrees. There was no shade at all – only a few prickly thorn bushes growing among the rocks. Beyond the plain stretched a long hill, and they could see a miserable procession of their fellow townspeople already stumbling towards the stony horizon.

Mr Ali paused. He sat back in his chair and stared at the sky, his eyes wrinkled up as though to keep out too much brightness.

'Each time I remember this story, my heart turns into stone.'

'Go on,' I said.

The al-Ali family joined the procession walking across the fields, stepping out briskly at first, buoyed up by their anger, and confident that this was just a temporary situation, that soon the Arab armies would drive out the intruders and they would be able to return to their home. After a couple of hours, as they mounted what they thought was the crest of a hill, only to find another steeper one stretching out ahead of them, their hearts sank. Sitting with their backs to the sun, the women with their scarves pulled over their heads for shade, they ate some of their bread and olives, and quenched their thirst on the oranges. They had brought so little water – who would think of carrying water instead of silver and gold? All around them, other families were sitting, too exhausted and dehydrated to move, while others abandoned the possessions they could no longer carry, and plodded on up the hill in the searing sun.

As the day waned, they came into the small village of Kirbatha. There was a well there – but no bucket. The women took off their scarves, tied them together, and lowered them down till they tipped the little black circle of water, then pulled them up and sucked the water from the damp cloth.

The third day of the march was the worst. The women's sandals were already falling apart, their feet were bleeding and swollen. Netish thorns and blue field-thistles snagged at their skirts and legs.

'Go,' said his mother to her older son, Tariq. 'Go on ahead and find us some water to drink. Maybe there is a village up there with a well.'

But there was no water. All along the way people were fainting from thirst and exhaustion. On a rocky scree the boy came across a woman staggering under the weight of a huge bundle. Two watermelons, it looked like; and he thought, if she drops them, I'll pick them up and take them back to my mother. But as he drew closer the woman sank to the ground and he saw that she was carrying two babies.

'Help me, brother,' she pleaded. 'My boys are too heavy for me. I cannot carry them.'

The boy hesitated. He was only fourteen years old, and he already had his mother and sisters to look after; but it was clear this woman was not going to make it.

'Take just one of them,' she said in a voice that was barely more than a whisper.

Tariq looked at the two babies. They looked terribly red and wrinkled, their eyes screwed shut against the light. How could he choose? Then one of them stirred and opened its dark bright eyes, which seemed to stare straight into his. The woman, seeing him waver, wrapped the baby in her shawl and thrust it into his arms.

'Go on ahead. Don't wait for me. Go. I'll meet you in Ramallah.'

Mr Ali went silent. I gazed at the green sunlit garden, the busy thrushes, the bursting daffodils, but I could feel a desert wind on my cheek, and all I could see was dry rocks and thorn bushes.

'That was you? The baby in the bundle?'

He nodded.

A door opened and from the interior of the house I heard the sweet jangle of Arabic music and the noisy patter of daytime television. Then Mrs Shapiro appeared on the doorstep wearing her dressing gown and her *Lion King* slippers.

'Will you take a coffee mit us?'

Mr Ali didn't reply. His eyes were fixed somewhere else.

'My name is Mustafa,' he said quietly. 'It means one who is chosen. My brother Tariq told me this story.'

I wanted to touch him, to take his hand or put my arm round his shoulder, but there was a reserve about him, a self-containedness, that made me hold back.

'Did he tell you what happened to the other baby?' I asked.

Mr Ali shook his head. 'He told me only that the soldier who shot the bridegroom had on his arm a tattoo – a number.'

Mr Ali's story had cast a shadow over me, and I found I couldn't join in with the cheerful gossip over coffee. I caught his eye once or twice, and I kept wanting to ask him what had happened to the al-Alis; whether they had all made it to Ramallah, and whether he, Mustafa, had ever found his mother and brother. But in my heart I knew the answer.

I was troubled, too, by the story of the soldier with the

338

number tattooed on his arm – what was in his mind when he shot the young bridegroom? How could a Jew who was himself a survivor of the death trails of Europe act with such casual cruelty against the hapless civilians of his promised land? What had happened in his heart? Then I started to wonder about Naomi herself – when she had let herself be photographed in the archway at Lydda, did she really not know what had taken place there two years before? Or did she know, and consider it a necessary price?

'What are you thinking about, Georgine?' Mrs Shapiro reached across and patted my hand. 'Is it your running-away husband, darlink? Don't worry, I heff a plan.'

'No. I'm thinking about . . . how hard it is to live in peace together.'

She threw me an oblique look. 'Ach, this is too serious.' She lit a cigarette for herself and one for Nabeel. 'Better to enjoy the happiness of today.'

After we'd finished our coffee I left to go home. The sun was still shining and Wonder Boy was still sitting patiently under the tree, gazing at the thrushes' nest. Mr Ali was back up his ladder. Inside the house, Nabeel was clattering pans and playing music, and Ishmail was vacuuming. A westerly breeze stirred the tips of the saplings and made the daffodils dance. But I kept thinking about the twin babies in the bundle, heavy as watermelons – the one who was chosen, and the one who was not.

If only I had Mrs Shapiro's gift for living in the present, I thought, as I walked home past the front gardens greening with new growth; trees, shrubs, weeds, grass – everything was coming to life. Near the corner of my street, a willow tree was sticking out its silvery buds through a railing. I thought-lessly snapped off a pussy-paws twig, and my mind flashed back to the bunches of pussy willows and catkins we used to bring in to decorate our classroom at Junior School in Kippax. Soon it would be Easter. I remembered Mrs Rowbottom's plonkety-plonk on the piano and our thin wobbly voices as we sang 'There is a green hill far away'. How that hymn had scared me as a child. It had seemed a harsh intrusion into the happy world of Easter bunnies and foil-wrapped eggs. I knew now, as I hadn't known at the time, that those hills were not green at all – they were rocky and barren. I'd been puzzled, then, by the absence of a city wall; now I realised that so many walls had been built and knocked down and rebuilt again over the centuries, that time itself had lost track of what belonged to whom.

'He hung and suffered there.' Yes, the history of that place was steeped in cruelty. Mrs Rowbottom had glossed over the details of what happened during the crucifixion and tried to convince us that 'without a city wall' meant 'outside'. But when I asked Dad he said, 'War and religion – they both 'ave an unquenchable thirst for human blood. They feed off each other like nuggins.'

Mum rolled her eyes to the ceiling.

''E's off again.'

'What's . . .?'

'Dennis, she's only nine.'

I never did find out what a nuggin was.

Mum always waited until closing time on Easter Saturday to buy chocolate eggs for us, when those that were left were reduced to half price.

'What d'you want them fancy eggs for, Jean?' Dad said. 'We're remembering an execution, not celebrating a birthday.'

But he ate them anyway. He had a real fondness for chocolate.

41

Cyanoacrylate AXP-36C

On Sunday I'd planned to make the most of the fine weather and do some gardening, to get some good dirt under my fingernails, have a go at the nasty spotted laurel bush and see off the fat brown slugs. But it felt like I spent the whole day on the phone, and each phone call left me feeling more upset.

The first call was at nine o'clock (on Sunday morning – would you believe it!) from Ottoline Walker, the Scarlet-mouthed Slut.

'Hello? Georgie Sinclair? Is that you?'

'Who's speaking?' I kind of recognised the voice already.

'It's me. Ottoline. We met. You remember?'

Like hell I remembered. Big banana bogey. Ha ha.

'Yes, I remember. Why are you ringing me?'

'It's about Rip . . .' (Well, it would be, wouldn't it?) '. . . I just wanted to tell you I had no idea you were still . . . sort of . . . involved.'

'Sort of married, actually.'

'He told me it was over between you two ages ago. He told me you didn't mind . . .'

'He told *me* he was advancing human progress.'

'Oh. I see.' There was a pause on the other end of the phone as she fumbled for a response. 'Look, I'm really sorry. It sort of changes things . . . I mean, when you're in love, you don't always do the right thing . . . you don't think about the consequences for other people.' She paused. I said nothing. 'I believe in commitment, you know.'

'Like you were committed to Pete. And now you're committed to Rip.'

'That's not what I mean. You make it sound terrible.'

'Actually . . .' I stopped myself. I didn't want her to have the satisfaction of knowing how much she'd hurt me.

'Ben doesn't know, if that's what you're wondering.'

'What about Pete? Does he know?' I almost called him Pectoral Pete.

'He found out. Poor Pete. It was awful. He was going to kill himself. Then he was going to kill Rip.'

She sounded as though she was sniffling on the phone, or maybe I imagined it. Anyway, for a moment I felt sorry for her.

'You'll not get much commitment from Rip. He's committed to the Progress Project.'

There was a silence. In the background, I could hear music on the radio – a woman singing blues.

'That's the other thing I wanted to ask you. This Progress Project. What is it, exactly?'

'Didn't Pete tell you?'

'He did, he talked about it endlessly. But he wasn't very good at explaining. I somehow couldn't get it.'

'It *is* quite complicated.'

'But then with Rip it was just the same. All those big words. I realised it must be me who's a bit thick.'

She gave a little self-deprecating giggle that was quite endearing.

'Er . . . hold on a minute. I've got written it down.' Where was that bit of paper? I rummaged in the desk drawer. 'Here it is.' I read aloud. 'The human race faces unprecedented challenges as we enter the millennium of globalisation. We

342

need to iterate new synergies if we are to make progress in meeting the aspirations of the developing world, while clearly understanding at the same time that nothing shall prejudice the economic achievements of the developed world.'

There was another pause. The woman blues singer let out a long throbbing moan.

'That's it?'

'Isn't it enough?'

'Well, sort of, I suppose. What does it mean exactly?'

'Why don't you ask *him*?'

She made that sound again on the end of the phone. It could have been a sniffle, or a giggle. I put the phone down.

Grabbing my secateurs, I pulled on my gardening gloves and stomped out into the garden. The sun was shining, but my head was full of dark clouds. Still fired up with thoughts of Rip and the Scarlet-mouthed Slut, I hacked away pitilessly at the ugly laurel bush – Wonder Boy's favourite haunt – grinding the fallen leaves into the mud. What gave her the right to ring me on a Sunday morning to cadge sympathy? Snip. Still sort of involved! Snip. I believe in commitment! Snip. Snip. I should have just put the phone down as soon as I heard her voice, instead of letting myself get drawn into conversation. Now I felt so wound up and angry that all thoughts of peace in the world had evaporated like water in the desert. And yet I had felt a frisson of fellow-feeling, and I was secretly glad to discover that despite her big scarlet mouth and her slut stilettos, it was the Progress Project that was his real mistress.

After an hour or so the phone rang once more. I carried on snipping and let it ring until the answering machine clicked on. Then a minute later it started ringing again. And again. This was some persistent bastard. I put the secateurs down and went to answer it.

'Hello, Georgina, I've been trying to get hold of you.'

That voice. I shivered as though a cool hand had touched my bare skin. It was the first time we'd spoken since the episode with the poem and the Velcro handcuffs. 'Have you got a minute? I just wanted to let you know that I've heard back from the Land Registry about Canaan House.'

I took a deep breath. Despite my resolution, I could feel that warm red-panties glow coming over me again. I mustn't let my hormones take over.

'And . . .?'

He explained that the house was unregistered, and that if Mrs Shapiro wanted to sell it she would need to register it, for which she would need the deeds. I had to force myself to concentrate on what he was saying.

'What about that son you mentioned, Georgina? The son in Israel? Maybe he knows where they are.' He was still angling for information.

'I met him the other day.'

I told him an edited version of our doorstep encounter. I didn't mention Mr Ali and the Attendents, but I told him about Damian.

'Damian Lee from Hendricks & Wilson. There he was, chewing on his pencil and pretending he was making a valuation.'

'Ah!' Mark Diabello caught his breath. 'That explains the BMW I saw parked round the back of their offices.'

'So Damian's job is . . .?'

'To persuade the son to let the social worker's friendly builder have the house for, say, a quarter of a million, then disappear back off to Israel with the cash in his pocket.'

'Just like you tried to persuade me?'

'That was different. I wasn't working for the buyer. Tsk. Naughty Damian.' His voice oozed disapproval. 'I told you they were crooks. And it's only a 1 Series two-door hatch.'

'You mean, just a starter model, really.'

I tried to picture Damian with his gelled-up hair sitting at the wheel of a secondhand BMW. The little shit!

At about five o'clock, just as I was trying to decide what to have for tea, Rip rang. I listened to his facing-unprecedented-challenges voice leaving a message on my answering machine, telling me to ring him immediately. Well, let him wait. He still thought he could boss me about. Typical. Probably he was ringing to tell me he wanted to take the kids up to Holtham at Easter with the Scarlet-mouthed Slut – 'He told me it was over between you two ages ago. He told me you didn't mind.' There was something about the tone of Rip's voice on the answering machine that reminded me of ... glue. Cyanoacrylate AXP-36C. I thought of the B&Q package stowed in the mezzanine study and smiled to myself. Peace in the world was all very well, but no way was it going to extend to Rip and me. No way. When someone hurts you like that, what you want is revenge, not peace.

I didn't ring back. I went upstairs to my room and got out my exercise book.

The Splattered Heart
Chapter 8
GINA'S REVENGE

Early next morning, heartbroken Gina made her tearful way to the Castleford branch of B&Q. The sight of the jolly orange-clad building made her ~~broken heart leap with~~ smile. Inside it was vast and creepily echoing like a church, and full of weird men prowling around the aisles, eyeing lovely curvaceous

Gina lustfully, and wiggling their saucy screwdrivers
suggestively. She made her way to the extensive adhesives
section. At last her eyes lit on a tube of glue that said in large
letters: DANGER! AVOID CONTACT WITH SKIN.

I stopped. The picture of the little girl at the glue exhibition stuck in my mind. Human bonding. Messy stuff.

The last phone call came just as I was getting ready for bed. I knew it was Mum – she usually rings about this time – but I was taken aback by the flatness in her voice.

'Your dad's been took poorly,' she said. 'He's got to have that operation on 'is prostrate. Doctor says it could make 'im imputent.'

I could just imagine poor Dad with that long-suffering look on his face and seedy Dr Polkinson telling him what did he expect at his age and we've all got to die of something. The operation date wasn't fixed, but it would be sometime soon after Easter. My mind went into overdrive at once, trying to work out the logistics of going up to Kippax, leaving Ben with Rip, and meeting my deadline for Nathan.

'D'you want me to come up to Kippax, Mum?'

'It's all right, duck. I know you're busy.'

'Mum . . .'

I was racking my brains for some cheerful or uplifting comment, when Mum chipped in.

'Did you hear about that friend of yours, Carole Ben-thorpe?'

'She wasn't my friend, Mum.' I shuddered as I remembered her watery reproachful eyes. 'Her dad was a scab.'

Carole Benthorpe *had* been my friend once, before the miners' strike – the short Heath strike of 1974, not the year-long Thatcher strike of 1984–5. 'Scabs take the gain without

346

the pain,' Dad had said. 'You never get a scab giving up his wage rise that were won on't backs o't strikers.'

There were only four scabs in Kippax, and Carole's father was one of them. After that she didn't have any friends.

'Dad always told me not to talk to scabs.'

'Aye, and he's right,' said Mum. 'But she weren't a scab, were she? She were only a little kid.' She sighed. All this had suddenly become too heavy. 'Anyroad, all I was going to say is, she won the Jackson's Saleswoman of the Year award. It were in t' *Express*. She got a weekend in Paris.'

'Oh, that's so brilliant! Good for her!'

I felt an unexpected burst of joy for Carole Benthorpe, not about Jackson's or the award, but because she'd survived what we did to her.

That cold winter in 1974 – the men hanging around in knots on the streets instead of disappearing underground as they were supposed to, the women pawning their rings and chuntering about how they would make do without a wage coming in. One day after school some of the kids waylaid Carole Benthorpe on her way home. They jostled and taunted her as she walked along, then things got a bit rough and a couple of lads pushed her into the icy tadpole ponds by the back lane. Everybody cheered and laughed as they watched her flounder. Me, too – I'd stood and laughed with the others. I recalled with a shock of remorse how great it had felt to be part of that cheering, jeering gang. Carole Benthorpe crawled out covered in slime and ran home, all wet and bawling. Next day in the school toilets she carved the word SCAB into her forearm with a Stanley knife.

'If you see her, Mum, give her my love.'

'Oh, I never see 'er. She lives up Pontefract way now.'

42

The right glue for the materials

I was half-heartedly trundling the vacuum cleaner around the house on Monday afternoon, worrying about Mum and Dad, when the phone rang. I thought it might be Mum with some more news of Dad's operation, but it was Mrs Shapiro.

'Come quick, please, Georgine. Chaim is mekking trouble.'

I realised I'd been half expecting it. Apparently Mrs Shapiro and Ishmail had gone off with Mr Ali in the red van to choose some paint at B&Q in Tottenham. Nabeel had stayed behind to start sanding down the woodwork and the kitchen door had been left unlocked. They got back at about four o'clock with their five litres of matt emulsion – 'Eau de nil – very charming colour – you will see it' – to find Nabeel and Chaim Shapiro wrestling on the carpet in the dining room.

'Fighting like the tigers. You must come, Georgine, and talk to them.'

'But what's that got to do with me?'

'Why you are always arguing, Georgine? Please come quick.'

By the time I got there, the wrestling, if it had ever really happened, was over and there was an uneasy truce around the dining-room table. Mr Ali was sitting on one side of the table, flanked by the Uselesses, and opposite them sat Chaim Shapiro, leaning back heavily, his arms and legs splayed out as

348

though the chair was too small for him, cracking his knuckles from time to time. Mrs Shapiro sat next to him, chain-smoking and fidgeting with her rings. Wonder Boy was sitting on a chair at the head of the table, looking very magisterial. I could hear their voices arguing as I came in through the front door, which had been left on the latch for me, but as I entered the dining room they went quiet. I sat down at the other end of the table, opposite Wonder Boy.

'Hello, everybody!' I said, looking round with a cheery smile. No one smiled back. The atmosphere was like curdled milk. Maybe we should start with Ms Baddiel's breathing exercises, I thought, just to calm us all down.

Mrs Shapiro poured me a glass of water from a jug and introduced the newcomer to me as Chaim Shapiro, adding, 'This is Georgine, my good neighbour.'

He pounced on me at once, demanding to know why I had invited these strangers into his house – I winced at the emphasis – '*my* house' – but before I could get a word out, Mrs Shapiro pounced back.

'Is not your house, Chaim. I been living here sixty year paying rets.'

'Shut up your mouth, Ella. You have no feet to stand on, letting Arabs come into your home.'

'You shut up the mouth,' Mrs Shapiro snapped. He ignored her.

'So, Miss Georgiana. Please, we are awaiting your explanation,' he rasped in a breathy voice not unlike Wonder Boy's purr. 'Speak up now or for ever hold your pieces.'

I started to explain that the house needed repair and renovation and that's why Mr Ali and his assistants had been called in. He gave a dubious sniff and rocked back in his chair. Then there was the issue of security, I told him, describing the stolen key and the turned-off water main and hinting at Mrs

Goodney's involvement. That made him sit up. The eyebrow above his glass eye started to twitch.

'That Goody with her young stick-up-the-hair-nik, they think I am made of short planks. They think I will sell them my house cheap so they can make some quick bucks out of me. But I have a different plan.'

'Is not your house, Chaim.'

'It is my father's house. Father likes son.'

'My house,' hissed Mrs Shapiro. 'When your father died, he give it me.'

'So what's your plan, Mr Shapiro?' I interrupted, to move the conversation on.

'My plan is to undertake some major renovations here in *my* house.' There were sharp intakes of breath all around. Wonder Boy's tail started to flick. 'In fact I am something of a do-it-myself enthusiast. I have already purchased a tool kit.' He looked around the table, but nobody met his eye. I glanced across at Mr Ali, but his face was impassive.

'Chaim, darlink, your mother would be eating her own kishkes to hear you speaking like this. She was giving up everything to build the new Israel. Beautiful homeland for the Jews. Why you are not staying there? Why you are coming back now and putting me on to the street?' There was a wheedling note in her voice.

'Nobody is putting you on to any street, Ella. You are putting yourself on to the street living with these Arabs.'

'These are my Attendents.'

'Ella, you have lost your screws. All Arabs are the same – they are only waiting for the opportunity to push Jews into the sea.'

Across the table, Mr Ali was whispering something to Ishmail. The Attendents' faces were sullen.

'Nobody is pushing me into the sea. The sea is a long way

350

from here, Chaim. Sea is at Dover. I heff been there mit Arti.' Her chin was sticking out defiantly.

'I know this Dover Beach. Where ignorant armies splash at night,' Chaim Shapiro tutted, taking little sips from his glass of water as if to cool himself down.

Mrs Shapiro stared at him. Then she leaned across and whispered to me, 'What is he talking about, Georgine?'

'It's a poem.'

'A poem? Is he med?'

'I am talking about terrorism, Ella. Look at my blinded eye. What I was doing? Nothing. Sitting minding my own businesses.' He was cracking his knuckles furiously as he talked, from nervousness or anger.

'We are in London now, Chaim. Not in Tel Aviv.'

'And you see they have commenced bombing here in London.'

Mr Ali translated for Ishmail, who leaned over and whispered to Nabeel. All three of them were scowling.

'We are already in the darkened plain.'

'Darlink Chaim, this is a house, not an aeroplane. Please, be a little calm. And these are my Attendents, not suicideniks. See, they are even animal lovers.'

Nabeel had reached across and was stroking Wonder Boy behind the ears, whose rhythmic purring was a soothing background to the fractious discussion. If only someone would stroke Chaim Shapiro behind the ears, I thought.

Now Mr Ali spoke, his voice splintering with anger. 'Arabs, Christians, Jews been living side by side for many generations. Making businesses together. No broblem. No bogrom. No concentration camp. Even we selled you some of our land. But this is not enough. You want whole bloody lot.'

Chaim Shapiro ignored him and turning towards me explained in a teachery tone, 'All Palestinians have the same

351

story. They come along with some old key, saying this is the key to my house. You must move out immediately! But when my mother came to Israel nobody was living there. It was empty as a desert. Abandoned. All the inhabitants had scarpered.'

'Driven out with gunpoint!' Mr Ali tried to shout, but his voice was shaking and it ended in a little squeak. The last time I'd seen him so mad was when he was sitting on the wet grass at the bottom of the ladder.

'If you want to live alongside us in our land, all you must do is to stop attacking us. Is that not fair enough?' Chaim smirked and spread his hands theatrically.

In – two – three – four. Out – two – three – four.

'Look, we're not going to solve all the world's problems today,' I said cheerily. 'But it's quite a big house. Especially if we convert the penthouse suite. Maybe everyone can live here together.'

They all turned towards me, and I could feel myself turning crimson under their collective gaze. In fact everybody had gone a bit beetrooty, even Mr Ali. Wonder Boy was snarling like a dog, swinging his fat tail from side to side.

'I do not want to share my house with three Arabs,' Chaim Shapiro grouched.

'Chaim,' said Mrs Shapiro appeasingly, 'the Peki is not living here. He is only a visitor.'

'You do not understand the Arab mentality, Ella. They will not let us in peace. Do you think Israel would exist today if half its population was Arab, and trying to destroy it from within?'

I felt a stab of anger, remembering the twin babies, heavy as watermelons, and the soldier with the number tattooed on his arm.

'But you can't expect people to give up their homes and land and not fight back!'

352

Mr Ali translated for the benefit of the Attendents, who nodded fervently in my direction. Chaim Shapiro's face was sweating, his good eye blinking rapidly.

'Ha! Then we have the right of self-defence! Every time you strike Israel we will strike back harder. You give us home-made rocket-launchers, we give you US-made helicopter gun-ships. Bam bam bam!' He aimed his hands like a gun across the table. Then, turning to me, he added, 'As your immortal bard William Shakespeare said, to do great right, we have to do a small wrong! It isn't pretty, but it is necessary, Miss Georgiana.'

When I said nothing, he lurched forward and slapped the table suddenly like a volley of gunfire. 'Bam bam bam! Bam bam bam!'

Wonder Boy, who was still sitting on the chair at the head of the table, flattened his ears at the noise and hissed, showing his horrible fangs. Then he leapt up on to the table in fighting pose, his back arched, his tail puffed out, and with a yowl he flew at Chaim Shapiro, going at his face with his claws. Chaim Shapiro fought back, trying to pull the big cat off, but Wonder Boy clung tight, his tail thrashing, his claws lashing. Mrs Shapiro shrieked frenziedly at both of them.

'Halt! Chaim! Stop this smecking! Wonder Boy! Raus!'

The cat hissed and fled, knocking over the jug of water that trickled down on to our legs. Chaim Shapiro pulled out a handkerchief and dabbed at his bleeding cheek. When he looked up, we saw that his glass eye had swivelled round grotesquely in its socket. Only the white was showing, staring out blankly like a hard-boiled egg.

Everyone went quiet, as if shocked at how quickly the confrontation had flared up, and a sudden thought lit up like a light bulb in my head: these people – they're all completely mad. In another part of the house, we could hear a menacing yowl – Wonder Boy sizing up his next victim (feline, I suppose, for Mrs Shapiro's slippers were on her feet). It was Mrs Shapiro who spoke first. I noticed an appraising look in her eyes as she leaned over to Chaim and patted his arm.

'Darlink Chaim, there is no need to fight. If you heff no home you can live here mit us. You can take any room what you like – except of mine, of course. You can make all your beautiful renovations, mit your tool kit. Build in kitchen units. Dishwashers. Meekrowaves. My Nicky has told me everything what is needed for the modern kitchen.' She took his hand and gave it a squeeze. 'We will make dinner parties mit cultured conversations. Concerts in the evenings. Even we will heff poetry recitals if that is what you like.' I could see his face softening as he pictured these delectable scenes. 'You are my Arti's son, Chaim. This is always your home whenever you want. But my Attendents also must stay here mit me.'

Her voice was so seductive that I might almost have applied for residency myself, even though I knew, as Chaim did not, about the Phantom Pooer. Chaim, I could tell, was already seduced.

'Ella, I can see you are quite a little home-pigeon, and I will gladly accept your invitation to take up my residence with you. And if the Arabs must stay, maybe we can divide the house between us. They keep to the top part of the house, and we stay in our part.' He beamed magnanimously across the table.

'Hm! Next you will build a wall,' said Mr Ali drily. 'Checkpoint on the stairs. Then you will steal some more rooms for settlements.'

Ishmail and Nabeel smiled confusedly.

'Have you got a sticking plaster, Mrs Shapiro?' I asked, to defuse the tension.

Chaim's cheek was bleeding badly – Wonder Boy had

354

taken quite a swipe. She scuttled off to find one. Mr Ali and the Attendants had convened a separate meeting in the kitchen. I could hear the clink of the coffee pot, and soon after the smell of freshly brewed coffee drifted into the room. So for a few minutes, Chaim Shapiro and I were alone together. He took off his jacket, hung it on the back of his chair, and undid the top button of his white shirt. He was sweating profusely under the arms. Without the jacket he seemed to shrink in size. His bulk, I realised, was mainly shoulder pads.

The eye that looked at me – his good eye – was dark and sad, but it reminded me of the blazing brown eyes of the young woman in the photographs, and his round pudgy face ended in a little pointed chin like a crude copy of hers. I was still thinking that someone should stroke him behind the ears, but instead, I leaned forward and said, 'You remind me of your mother.'

He turned towards me and his look changed entirely, lit up with a smile so sweet and childlike it seemed to have strayed on to the wrong face.

'You knew my mother?'

'I didn't know her,' I said. 'I've seen her photo. You look like her.'

'I wish you could have met her. Everybody who met her loved her.' He was smiling that same baby smile, his heavy cheeks dimpling with pleasure at the memory.

'And your father . . .'

'Yes, Artem Shapiro. The musician. She was always talking about him, like the legs of a donkey.'

'. . . why didn't he join her in Israel?' I found myself holding my breath.

'He was too sick. Lungs kaput. Ella was looking after him. Here in this house.'

The death certificate had said lung cancer.

'And your mother never went back to him?'

'She wanted to build a garden in the desert. Can you imagine – with her naked hands? She would never leave until it was finished.' A shadow settled over him and he seemed to shrivel up even more inside the white polyester shirt. 'Then she got sick. Blood sickness. She died when I was ten years old. A few months after my father.'

I remembered the date on the letter from Lydda. Chaim was born in 1950, so she must have died in 1960.

'I'm sorry. To lose your whole family ... And then your injury ...'

I wanted to ask how it had happened. I guessed he didn't know without looking in a mirror that the glass eye was turned the wrong way in its socket.

'But my family was the moshav – father, mother, sister, brother. After she died I stayed there with them. Everybody was family in our new nation.'

It must have been the same moshav she wrote about in the letter, the stony hillside where she'd cradled her newborn baby in her arms, looking out to the west and waiting for her husband. I still had her photo at home in my bedroom. I'd bring it for him next time.

'Was she from Byelorussia too?'

'No, she came from Denmark. But they met in Sweden. They were married in London. And I was born in Israel.' He smiled that chubby dimply smile. 'Naomi Shapiro. She was a person who knew how to dream.'

'She dreamed of a promised land?'

'Our homeland. Zion.' His cheeks dimpled again. 'Home sweet home.'

But something was niggling me. Why does everyone go on about homeland? Surely what really matters is the people we're attached to? Ben and Stella were my homeland – yes, and Rip. I tried to imagine what it would be like to love a country more than them. I thought about the woman in the photographs – those dark eyes blazing with conviction. She'd left her love behind to find the homeland of her dreams and someone else – another Naomi Shapiro – had stepped into her place.

'But isn't it your homeland, too, Chaim? More so, because you were born there? Haven't you got a family? Friends? Colleagues? I can't understand why you want to make your life here.'

At your age, I meant to add, but didn't want to seem rude.

'I was a teacher for thirty years. English language and literature.' He shuffled in his chair. 'Now I am retired. Not married. What woman wants to marry a one-eyed man?'

'Oh, I don't know . . .' Mrs Shapiro will soon sort you out, I was thinking.

She had reappeared with a rather grubby curling-at-the-corners sticking plaster, which she applied to his cheek with a little pat.

'Now your home is mit us, isn't it?'

I noticed that there were a couple of cat hairs adhering underneath.

'Thank you, Ella. My mother told me you were very solicitous to my father in his illness. And encouraging him to go to Israel upon his recovery. She showed me the letter you wrote.'

I glanced across at Mrs Shapiro.

'It was very long ago,' she said. Some inscrutable emotion flitted across her face and she gave a little shrug. 'Sometimes is better to let the past alone.'

'Yes, long ago.' He sat back heavily in his chair. 'You know, Ella, this country, this Israel, it is not the same country she dreamed of. It should have been a beautiful country –

prosperous, modern, democratic. Founded on justice and the rule of law. But *they* have spoiled it with their fanaticism.'

He gestured with his head towards the kitchen where Mr Ali and the Attendents were still chatting in Arabic. There was a clink of coffee being poured.

'You know, Miss Georgiana, no teacher wants to have blood of children on his hands. Not even of little stone-throwing Arab ratscallions.'

But I wasn't really listening, my mind had drifted back to what he was saying before Wonder Boy had lashed out with his claws. To do a great right, do a little wrong. That was Bassanio, in *The Merchant of Venice*. I'd done it for 'A' level. But what was it that Portia had said? Something about the quality of mercy. When mercy seasons justice. That was it.

'So what do you think is the solution?' I asked.

'There is no solution. I can see no possibility of peace in my lifetime.' He sank lower in his chair, resting his chin on his hands. 'So long as they continue with their attacks, we will continue our defences. We are trapped in tits for tats. It is impossible for someone so sensitive like myself to live life this way.'

'But . . . it's never too late, is it? For peace? I mean, if only the will is there . . .'

I was thinking even as I spoke that the words sounded good, but they were probably tosh. The will for peace – Rip and I had still not managed to work it out, had we?

'Too late for me, Miss Georgiana.' He sighed. 'For at my back I always hear time's horse-drawn chariot galloping near.'

'Wingèd.' I couldn't stop myself, but he was lost in his thoughts and didn't hear. Maybe I should introduce him to Mark Diabello. They would have the same taste in poetry.

*

I noticed, as I walked home in the early evening, that the silver buds of the pussy willow had opened out, and flaunted golden flecks of pollen in their fur. The air was soft and moist. A fine spring rain dampened my face and settled like mist on my hair; it glistened on the leaves and fell in slow heavy drops from the overhanging branches. Everything was cool and green. It was a different world to that of Chaim Shapiro and Mustafa Ali – but it was the same world. We all had to learn to live here somehow.

I'd felt so full of pity when Mr Ali had told me his story, if I'd had a gun, I would have gone out myself to seek revenge for his lost home and violated family. Now I was beginning to feel sorry for this sad crumpled man, this one-eyed orphan of his mother's broken dreams. My parents had taught me always to look out for the underdog, but even underdogs can snap and snarl. How could I know who'd started it? Whose fault it really was? Maybe that was the wrong question to ask in the first place. If you could just get the human bonding right, maybe the other details – laws, boundaries, constitution – would all fall into place. It was just a case of finding the right adhesive for the adherends. Mercy. Forgiveness. If only it came in tubes.

It wasn't until I was almost at home that I remembered I'd never asked Chaim how he had lost his eye. Had he been caught up in the revenge attack at Lydda airport? I recalled my conversation with Ben a few days ago – the ancient prophecy of the battle between Jesus and the Antichrist at the gates of Lydda which was supposed to precede the end of the world. An airport *is* a kind of a gate to a city – isn't it? But surely the terrorists wouldn't have known the words of the prophets. I felt a small quake of dread in my guts. How could the present reach back into the past? What mysterious tendrils of causation could have brought about this connection? No wonder Ben was so rattled. And Dajjal, the devil with one eye? But Chaim Shapiro was no devil; he was a casualty, too – a stray soul who had lost his mother too young. Without his shoulder pads, he was just a sweaty middle-aged man in a polyester shirt. Still, I felt a shudder as if an ancient hand had tapped my shoulder and a voice from another world had whispered, *'Armageddon.'*

43

Unpromising adherends

As I approached my house, the daylight was already fading and I could see through Ben's window that his computer monitor was on, the screen saver flickering white, red and black. That was strange. Ben was supposed to be with Rip. Maybe he'd forgotten to turn it off before he left. Or maybe he'd come back early.

'Hi, Ben!' I shouted up the stairs as I came in through the door. There was no reply. I put the kettle on, then I went up and tapped on the door of his room. No answer. So I pushed it open.

There was that musty smell of socks and trainers, and there was the screen saver whizzing around in the dusk, hurling its dizzying pattern against the walls. White! Red! Black! White! Red! Black! Whoosh! Whoosh! Whoosh! The walls lit up, burst into flames, blackened to char. My ears were filled with a terrifying sound that I thought at first was the computer until I recognised the roar of blood beating in my own head. From across the room, a lumbering monster with hideous teeth lurched towards me – Ben's Orc poster, fleetingly illuminated by the flare of the screen. Then I saw Ben. He was lying on the floor between the bed and the desk, crumpled like a bundle of rags among his scattered clothes.

'Ben!' I screamed. But as if in a nightmare the word came out of my mouth as a voiceless croak.

Then I realised it wasn't just the jerky light; Ben was

moving, twitching. Head thrown back, eyes open and rolled back in their sockets like Chaim Shapiro's glass eye, flecks of foam or vomit dribbling from the corners of his mouth. I stumbled towards him, and as I did so, I knocked the chair which was snagged around the cable of the mouse, and the screen he'd been viewing came up – the same fiery red on black screen with dancing flames and one flashing word: *Armageddon.*

I screwed up my eyes and reached across to pull the plug out of the socket. The room went dark. I switched the light on. Ben moaned and flailed with his arms and legs. A sickly sour smell was coming from him. A trickle of moisture darkened his trousers and puddled on the floor. I lay down beside him and folded him in my arms, stroking his cheeks and his forehead, whispering his name. I wasn't sure whether it was the right thing to do, but I held him tight until he lay still and his breathing slowed down. Then I phoned for an ambulance.

The next stage all happened very fast, in a whirl of panic and brisk paramedics and blue flashing lights. I tried ringing Rip from the ambulance but there was no reply so I sent him a text. After a few minutes Ben came round. He lifted his head from the stretcher, looking around him with a dazed expression.

'Where am I?'

'You're on your way to hospital.'

'Oh.' He seemed disappointed.

'I'm your mum.'

'I know that.'

I held his hand, whispering little mother-words as we ripped through the evening streets, siren howling.

★

The ward they admitted him to was the same one Mrs Shapiro had been in that first time. The sister – I didn't recognise her – came and drew the curtain around us. It was frightening to be on the inside of that drawn curtain. I remembered the gurglings that had come from the next bed as the lady of the pink dressing gown passed away. The doctor who came round to see us seemed hardly older than Ben – in fact he had the same gelled-up hairstyle as Damian.

'It seems like he's had a fit,' he said. His voice had a nasal Liverpool twang.

'What – epilepsy?'

'Could be. Could just be a one-off.'

'But why?'

'Too early to tell. We'll have a better idea when we've done the MRI scan.'

'When will that be?'

'Tomorrow. He'll see the neurologist. Let him sleep it off tonight. We'll keep an eye on him, don't worry. It's not that uncommon, you know, in young people his age.'

He smiled awkwardly, fiddling with the stethoscope that hung round his neck. He was trying to be kind, but he was too young to be convincing.

Then the curtain parted and Rip and Stella came in. Rip ignored me, and I think I might have done a runner if Stella hadn't come straight up and hugged me.

'What's up with Ben, Mum?'

How pretty she was, but so thin – too thin. She smelled of apple shampoo and neroli. I held her and stroked her hair which sheafed down her back like dark silk. I wanted to burst into tears, but I forced a cheerful grin on to my face.

'Something happened – he had a fit, or something. I think he's going to be okay.'

Stella squeezed her brother's hand. 'Yer daft little beggar.'

She was putting on a thick Leeds voice, the voice of their shared childhood banter.

He opened his eyes and looked around with a beatific smile on his face.

'Hey, everybody!' Then he drifted off again.

Rip stood framed by the curtain, trying to hector the doctor into conversation, demanding explanations and clarifications which the young man was clearly unable to give, and all the time carefully avoiding meeting my eyes. When the doctor left Rip came and sat on the other side of the bed, still ignoring me, and took Ben's other hand, leaning over and talking in a sickly cooey-cooey voice. I got up and walked out.

I went as far as the swing doors, then I stopped. I knew I was being ridiculous. I turned round and went and sat in the day room to calm down, clenching and unclenching my hands – *in – two – three – four; out – two – three – four* – breathing in the heavy medical air that was thick with all the anxiety and grief that had been exuded in this room. I remembered the drip lady, and the wild cackling. It seemed an age ago.

A minute later, the door swung open and Stella came in. Her face was red and blotchy. At first I thought she was upset; then I realised she was furious.

'Mum, you're mental – you and Dad – you've got to stop acting like kids. We're sick of it, me and Ben. We want you to ... I dunno ... like, grow up.'

She was chewing at a strand of hair that had straggled across her face, just like she'd done as a child. I stared at her. She was twenty years old, as skinny as a twig, and she was wearing a skirt that showed her knickers when she bent over; and I'd carried her in my belly and fed her at my breast, and here she was telling *me* to grow up.

'Yes, but what about *him*?' I whined.

'Him, too. I've told him, too. Both of you. You've got to stop it.'

She sounded just like Mrs Rowbottom reprimanding Gavin Connolly for flicking pellets.

'But he started it.'

'Doesn't matter who started it. We're fed up of it. *And* it's not doing Ben any good.'

She brushed back the hair from her face and tried to look stern.

'Okay. Well, I will if he will. But I'm not . . .'

'So just go back in there, and smile at him, and . . . I dunno . . . just be *normal*, Mum.'

So I did. I smiled at Rip, and he smiled at me, a bit awkwardly, and he explained that he'd had to move out of Pete's place, and he'd tried to ring me to tell me that Ben was coming home earlier than expected, but I'd not rung him back. When an accusing note slid into his voice, Stella threw him a warning look.

'Dad!'

She would make a great teacher, this girl.

When I think of the turning point, the point from which it all started to get better again, I think of that Monday in March, that scene in the curtained cubicle at the hospital, Ben sitting up and trying to remember what had happened, Stella perched on the edge of the bed tickling Ben's toes through the bedclothes and making him laugh. It reminded me of the glue exhibition, with me and Rip sitting awkwardly on each side of the bed like lumpy unpromising adherends, and Ben and Stella in the middle holding us together like two blobs of glue.

We sat together like that in the neurologist's office next day, Rip, Ben and I, with Ben in the middle. The neurologist took us through a series of questions, and asked us about the circumstances of Ben's fit. When I described the whirling screen saver and the flashing flames of the Armageddon website, he told us about a cluster of 685 cases of epilepsy in 1997 in Japan that had apparently been triggered by a single Pokémon episode on television.

'It's possible for photosensitivity to trigger an epileptic seizure,' he said, peering at us through his small rimless glasses. 'What we can't tell at this stage is whether it will happen again.' He turned to Ben. He had a surprisingly mischievous smile for a neurologist. 'Try and be more selective about which sites you visit, young man. It's wild out there in cyberspace.'

'Right,' Ben nodded. He was embarrassed by all the attention.

But there must be more to it than that, I thought. I remembered our liminal conversation, the haunted look in his eyes.

'I can understand the computer flashing could set something off,' I said. 'But what about ...?' I cast my mind back. 'Sometimes you said you were feeling strange when you got back from school, before you'd even turned the computer on. Don't you remember, Ben?'

He blinked and frowned.

'Yeah. It was when I was on the bus. We passed these trees. I could see the sun through the branches.' He described a long road where low winter sunlight flickered through branches of an avenue of trees as he sat on the upper deck of the bus. 'That's when I started having, like, *feelings*.'

'But when you've stayed with me in Islington you've been perfectly all right.' There was an edge of accusation in Rip's voice, as though I'd caused the problem.

'I got a different bus.'

The neurologist nodded. 'If you find yourself in that situation another time, young man, just try closing one eye.'

So that's all there was to it – the generations of prophets, the reign of the Antichrist, the tribulations, the Abomination of Desolation, Armageddon, the fearsome battle of all the armies of the world, the rebuilding of the Temple at Jerusalem, the end of time with trumpet clarions and fiery chariots, the return of the Messiah, the rapture of the elect – it was all down to a frequency of flashing lights, a temporary short circuit in the wiring of the brain. All you had to do was close one eye.

I felt both relief and disappointment. For there was a part of me that yearned to believe – to surrender to the irrational, to be swept away by the rapture.

'So all that religious stuff is just nonsense?' Rip's voice was irritatingly smug. I wanted to kick him, to shut him up, but I saw Ben wasn't listening. He was studying a chart of the brain pinned on the wall at the side of the neurologist's desk.

'It's now believed that some prophets and mystics were in fact epileptics,' the neurologist said. 'There's thought to be a physiological explanation behind much religious experience.'

Rip misread the look on my face, and leaned across to squeeze my hand.

'Why didn't you tell me Ben was having these problems? You should have told me, Georgie.'

'I . . .' *In – two – three – four. Out – two – three – four.* 'You're right – I should have.'

I squeezed his hand back.

As we left the hospital, Rip asked me rather sheepishly whether it would be okay if he moved back in temporarily, and I replied rather grumpily that it made no difference to me but I was sure Ben would appreciate it. Yes, I was pleased, on the whole; things were going in the right direction. But I was surprised to find that my feelings were ambivalent. I'd got a life of my own now, and I wasn't ready to give it up. When Rip was around, he had a way of taking over. While he'd been away, I'd been remembering all the things I missed about him, but being with him again reminded me of all the things that irritated me. It occurred to me that maybe he felt the same way about me. So there was still a lot that needed to be resolved between us. He brought his stuff over from Islington in his Saab later that afternoon, and set himself up on a camp bed in the little mezzanine study. We tiptoed around each other, being excessively polite and considerate.

Him: Would you like a cup of tea, darling?
　Me: That would be lovely, darling.

That kind of tosh.
　I had to clear out the spare room to make space for Stella, who'd be coming home soon for Easter. Buried at the bottom of one of the drawers I found an envelope of photos. Rip and me on our wedding day: Rip was wearing a top hat and tails. His hair curled down on his collar and he had curly side-burns. I was wearing a cartwheel hat and a fitted dress with big shoulders and slut-style high heels. My pregnant bulge was clearly visible. We looked ridiculous – and ridiculously happy. Then a picture of Rip and me and baby Stella in a buggy walking round Roundhay Lake. Then Rip and me and five-year-old Stella and baby Ben on the beach at Les Sables d'Olonne. Rip and me and Ben and Stella and Mum, taken one Christmas at Kippax. Rip and I were wearing Santa hats; Mum was wearing reindeer antlers; Ben was wearing his new *Lion King* slippers and a gawky smile – what a funny little kid

he'd been; Stella – she must have been thirteen – was pouting red lipstick at the camera, wearing a figure-hugging red top with a tinsel wreath draped around her shoulders. Dad wasn't in the picture – he must have been behind the camera. The Christmas tree wearing millennium-themed baubles was clearly visible in the background. I pored over the photos, then slid the envelope under my mattress. It seemed like a good omen.

At the end of term Stella came home, and from being empty, the house suddenly became full. It was Stella who told me, over a quiet cup of tea, that Ottoline had thrown Rip out. He'd spent the night before coming to the hospital in a hotel. That's why Ben had come home unexpectedly that Monday.

'Ben says he overheard them having a row. Apparently she told him he had a poor attitude to commitment,' she murmured in a grave voice, lowering her head, so if I hadn't been looking I wouldn't have seen the flicker of a grin at the corners of her mouth.

Stella made the most of her holiday, sleeping in late and taking long showers, sometimes twice a day, clogging up the plughole with her long hair and filling the house with the smell of apple shampoo. Ben filled the house with techno music and thumped around cheerfully, no longer glued to the computer. Rip went off to work every morning, just as he had before, and in the evenings he sat at his desk and filled the house with brainwaves. We took turns to cook – we had two teams: Rip and Stella, who cooked mainly Thai curries, and Ben and I who cooked mainly Italian. Then Ben announced one day that he'd become a vegetarian, and we spent ages adapting and devising recipes for him. I once caught him sitting at the table and poring over a book with that same intense concentration that he had once read the Bible, but it turned out to be a cookery book: *One Hundred Recipes to Save the Planet*. The knobbly skull had disappeared under a growth of new brown curls, which he wore tied back with a red bandana.

The neurologist had suggested Ben change the screen saver, and warned him off websites with animation. He advised him to get a flat-screen monitor, which apparently runs at a different frequency, and not to sit too close to the television. We watched anxiously, to see whether he could handle his condition without medication or whether he would need to take anti-epileptic drugs.

Rip and I fell into a pattern of sharing the same space while keeping out of each other's way. We didn't actually divide the house but we learned each other's habits and avoided unnecessary contact. It wasn't positively amicable, but it wasn't hostile, either. Sometimes, on Stella's insistence, we all watched TV together.

'Just try to be *normal*, okay?' she coached us.

Rip and I sat on armchairs on opposite sides of the fireplace, with resolutely normal expressions on our faces, while Ben and Stella sprawled on the sofa, their arms and legs casually intertwined. From time to time one of them would try to shove the other off.

At Easter, we didn't go to Kippax or to Holtham. We stayed at home, and Rip and I made a tentative stab at collaboration, hiding a trail of miniature Easter eggs around the house for Ben and Stella. They whooped around, pretending to be surprised. The radio was on in the background, and at one point I heard a church congregation with miserable whiny voices singing that hymn. *There is a green hill far away . . . He hung and suffered there.* I switched it off quickly. Why let that morbid long-ago stuff spoil a nice family holiday?

44

Water creases

On the Tuesday after Easter I nipped into the local Turkish supermarket and bought a large Easter egg, reduced to half price. It was a hideous-looking thing covered in mauve foil with Space Invaders figures wielding ray guns all over the packaging. Someone somewhere must have thought this was an appropriate Easter gift for a little boy – in fact maybe it *was* surreally appropriate to the new reality of the Holy Land – but at least it had been left on the shelf by discerning parents, for it was the only egg they had. I carefully peeled off the REDUCED sticker, wrapped the egg in tissue, and set off for Canaan House.

It was a fresh, cold day, with splashes of sunlight spilling through raggy clouds. Small bright buds were bursting on the ash-tree saplings in the garden at Canaan House – it seemed as though they'd appeared overnight – and the white plastic garden furniture gleamed invitingly.

Nobody answered the doorbell when I rang. I crouched down and peered in through the letter box. There were no signs of human life, though a couple of felines were dozing in the pram which was parked under the stairs. I thought I caught a glimpse of movement at the end of the corridor, and then I noticed something very alarming – water seemed to be dripping down from a crack in the ceiling and collecting in a pool on the hall floor. A moment later, Chaim Shapiro appeared in his shirtsleeves. I rang the doorbell again to get his attention, but he just looked up at the leaking ceiling, shouted something into the back of the house, then vanished up the stairs. The drip of water had intensified into a trickle. Suddenly Nabeel and Mr Ali materialised, legs first, running down the stairs and shouting at each other. I rang the bell again, and Mr Ali came and opened the door. I thought he'd opened it for me, but he raced right past me, out through the door and round to the back of the house. I followed him, and watched as he started frantically pulling away at the grass and weeds near the kitchen door to reveal a small metal hatch cover, which he removed. Still shouting at Nabeel, who was behind us, he rolled up his sleeve and reached into the hole in the ground.

'What's happening?' I asked Nabeel.

Nabeel flashed his beautiful eyes, pointed a finger upwards, and shouted back to Mr Ali. Then he raced back to the front of the house. I followed behind. The two tabbies in the pram in the hall were awake by now. They roused themselves, stretched mardily, and slunk out into the garden, their ears flat with irritation at being disturbed. Then Mrs Shapiro turned up, tottering on her high heels, waving a cigarette in her hand.

'Ah! Georgine! Thenk Gott you come!' She flung her arms around me.

'What's going on?'

'Votter creases! I was telephoning to you!'

'Water creases?'

'They are trying to mek votter pipe diversion into the penthouse suite. Chaim! Chaim!' she yelled up the stairs. 'What you doing? Heffn't we got enough votter pissing down already?'

The trickle of water had become a steady stream; I noticed that the water was pleasantly warm. The hall was filling up with steam like a bathroom. Above us, the plaster ceiling was beginning to bow, while Mrs Shapiro was mopping determinedly but hopelessly at the puddle with a silk blouse she'd pulled out of the pram, kneeling down on all fours and holding her cigarette between her lips. Now Mr Ali appeared in the doorway. He shook his head with a philosophical air and sighed as he gazed at the stream of water, which was fast becoming a torrent.

'It comes out of the tank. Not men's water,' he explained to Mrs Shapiro. Then he shouted something at Nabeel, who bowed his head and slouched off upstairs. Mr Ali shrugged apologetically. 'Completely useless.'

I was still puzzling over the gender status of the hot water when Ishmail and Chaim Shapiro came running down the stairs, almost colliding with Nabeel on the way up. Chaim pointed at the water coming through the ceiling, and shouted, rather unnecessarily, 'Water water everywhere!'

'Men's now off, but water still coming out,' Mr Ali shouted back.

Ishmail shouted at Nabeel. Mrs Shapiro shouted at Chaim, who shouted back at her. I shouted at him to shut up. Soon everybody was shouting at everybody else. Somewhere in the house, Wonder Boy started to yowl. Mrs Shapiro had given up trying to mop the floor with the silk blouse, and started flicking it at her stepson.

'Is all your fault. You wanted to make votter separation. Jewish votter, Arab votter. So! Now we have pissing votter.'

'Not my fault, Ella. Useless Arabs cut the wrong pipe.'

Then the doorbell rang.

We all fell silent and looked at the door. Through the frosted glass I could see a tall dark figure looming. Nobody moved. The bell rang again. I opened the door. It was Mark Diabello.

'Hello . . .' He stared at the scene in the hall, taking in the flushed faces peering through the clouds of steam, the wet floor and the pouring water. 'Georgina, I just wanted to . . .'

'Come in. We're having a bit of a water crisis . . .'

'Who is this?' asked Mrs Shapiro, pulling herself up straight and smiling at the handsome stranger. 'Are you another Attendent?'

'Let me introduce Mr Wolfe's partner,' I said. 'Mark Diabello.'

'My Nicky's partner? How charming!' She fluttered her eyelids.

He stepped forward, proffering his hand, his chin-dimple winking, his smile-creases crinkling, his green-gold-black eyes flickering non-stop.

'Delighted, Mrs Shapiro. If I could just trouble you for a second – the house deeds . . .'

At that moment, there was a horrible wrenching sound above our heads. Everyone looked up. One of the ornate Doric-style plaster corbels supporting the Romanesque arch where the water had come through had started to crack away. Even as we watched, the crack widened. The corbel slipped sideways and slid. Mr Diabello seemed to stagger as he took a step back. His knees sagged. His mouth opened, but no sound came out. Then he fell to the ground with a thud. He had been stunned by a stunning period feature.

Poor Mr Diabello. By the time the ambulance arrived he was sitting up on the wet floor, propped against the wall beneath the grey mark where the picture of Lydda had hung – it was the cat-poo spot, though any lingering cat poo would have long since been washed away – pressing a clean white handkerchief to a gash in his head.

Yet after his accident, a strange exhausted peace fell on

the house. The water finally stopped running when the hot-water tank that held the immersion heater had emptied out. Ishmail got a broom and started sweeping the water out of the hall through the front door – there must have been several gallons. The cats danced around the eddies of water, excited by all the action but not wanting to get their paws wet. Mrs Shapiro danced around, too, making encouraging noises. Nabeel went into the kitchen to make a pot of coffee. As the door swung open, I overheard a snippet of conversation.

Mr Ali: Where you get your tool kit, Chaim?
    Chaim Shapiro: B&Q. You want to see it?

I sat with Mr Diabello until the ambulance arrived.

'I thought you might be here. I came to see you, Georgina,' he murmured. 'I didn't realise your hubby was back.'

'Yes. I should have told you. I'm sorry. You and me – it's over between us, Mark.' I squeezed his hand as they led him away to the ambulance. 'But it was fun.'

'Mrs Shapiro,' I said, keeping my voice casual, 'do you happen to know where the deeds for this house are kept?'

Mr Ali and Chaim Shapiro had gone off to B&Q together in manly silence and we were having a companionable cup of coffee by the fire in the study, with Prokofiev's piano sonatas tinkling on the record player and the soggy *Lion King* slippers steaming away on the fender.

'What for I need deeds?' She looked at me through narrowed eyes.

'Apparently the house isn't registered with the Land Registry.'

'On this house I been paying rets sixty years no problem.'

'Mr Diabello said it would be better to register in case you want to sell up at any time.'

'I am not selling nothing.'

'Of course there's no reason why you should sell.' There was no point in arguing with her. 'But it would be better for you if the house was registered in your name, Mrs Shapiro. Then no one could take it away from you.'

She reached in her bag for a cigarette and stuck it between her lips.

'You think Chaim wants to take it away from me?'

'Everybody wants it. Chaim. Mrs Goodney. Even Mr Wolfe and Mr Diabello. It's a desirable property.'

'And what about you, Georgine?'

She said it casually, fumbling in her bag for the matches, not looking at me. I wondered whether it was an accusation.

'It's a really lovely house,' I said, 'but I already have a house of my own.'

'When I am dead, Georgine, darlink, you can heff it.'

I laughed. 'It's kind of you, but it's too big for me. Too many problems.'

'You can heff it, so long as you will liff in it and pay the rets.'

She gripped my hand and pulled me towards her. Suddenly she was intensely serious.

'This house – it belongs to no one. Artem found it empty. Abandoned. Inhebitents ran away.'

'But why . . .?'

'You know, Artem was just new married. He was needing somewhere to live.'

'With Naomi?'

She avoided my eyes. 'It was the wartime. German bombings. People running everywhere.'

Above our heads there was a clang of copper pipes and

a tirade of words. Chaim and Mr Ali must have got back from B&Q. There was suddenly a lot of running up and down stairs and clattering and shouting going on in the background.

'So they moved in?'

'Such a beautiful house, isn't it? Even a piano. Bechstein. Sometimes *Mutti* and I came to play on it. He played on the violin, we accompanied mit the piano.'

'Two brown eyes.'

'You know, Georgine, I was only a young girl. I didn't know anything – I knew only that I was in loff.' She pursed her lips and puffed a couple of smoke rings; they drifted towards the fire on the warm draught, and vanished in the flames. 'When you are in loff, when you heff an idea in your head, you are not always thinking about the consequence.'

My mind tripped back to my conversation with the Scarlet-mouthed Slut, her tentative apology that I'd accepted with such bad grace.

'You thought being in love made it okay?'

'I thought only that I could not live without him. And she was no good for him, that one. Always she was nagging him to go to Israel. A poor man like this with ruined lungs. What use he will be in Israel?'

'So she went on her own?'

'She was blazing like a person on fire. She could not sit still. Always talking of Zion – of making a homeland for all the Jews of the world. But he wanted only to die in peace.' A bit of wood shifted on the fire and clouds of ash drifted on to the fender. 'Already he was dust.'

'Didn't you feel . . .?'

She shrugged and tossed her head in a vague gesture. 'I was looking after him. He could not be on his own. He was saying he will go there when he is better.'

What I really wanted to ask was – did she feel guilty? For stealing Naomi's husband, and Chaim's father.

'She wrote to him from Israel, didn't she?'

She nodded. 'Yes. Those letters. I burned them all.'

Her face was turned away towards the fire, so I could not read her expression.

'Not all of them.'

45

The dance of the polymers

It wasn't until I got home that evening that I realised I still had the Space Invaders Easter egg in my bag. I unwrapped it and put it at the back of the cupboard. It was so vile that I couldn't bring myself to give it to Stella or Ben.

'Who was that man?' Stella asked as we were clearing up together after a Thai curry dinner. We were alone together in the basement kitchen. Rip and Ben were watching football upstairs.

'What man?'

'That smooth creepy guy in the Jag who came round this afternoon while you were out?' Her lip curled with disapproval.

'Oh, he must have been the estate agent. He wants to buy a house from an old lady I know who lives at Totley Place. Why?'

'Daddy answered the door. They both seemed a bit surprised to see each other.' She gave me a hard look. 'He had a bunch of flowers. White roses.'

'Really? They were probably for someone else.'

'No, he left them. They're in my room. I told Daddy they were for me.'

'Thanks, Stella. You can keep them. I don't want them.'

She grinned, a quick glimmer of a grin.

Next day Rip gave me a peck on the cheek before he left for work, and maybe that's what made it difficult to write about

Gina's revenge. Although I had some glue stuff to catch up on, I was determined to finish Chapter 8, so I set my laptop aside and opened up my exercise book.

The Splattered Heart
Chapter 8
GINA'S REVENGE (continued)

Disguised as an ~~itinerant window-cleaner rag-and-bone woman~~ Avon lady she made her way to Holty Towers and in the dead of night, she tiptoed through to the luxurious ~~ensuit onsite ensued~~ (bloody Microsoft! – I was using the spellchecker on my laptop because my dictionary was still propping up a shelf in the mezzanine study) *bathroom and got the deadly ~~tube vial~~ phial out of her Avon box and squeezed a thin layer of extra-strong adhesive on to the seat of the ~~toilet~~ lavatory. Then she turned the cold tap on in the basin so that it ran in a steady stream. Tinkle tinkle tinkle. A smile suffused her rosy lips.*

But something wasn't right. I was starting to feel a bit sorry for Rick. Okay, so he had his flaky moments, but there was something endearing about him, wasn't there? Those blond tumbled curls. The vulnerability of the sleeping man. And Gina – wasn't she a bit off the rails too, falling for that dodgy mandolin player? What a pair of idiots Rick and Gina were. Why couldn't they just sort their differences out and stick together? I realised that something inside me had shifted – I was no longer very interested in revenge. I was ready to move on.

I closed my exercise book and clicked open the *Adhesives* document I was meant to be working on. 'The Chemistry of Adhesive Bonding.' On New Year's Eve, when we'd joined hands, like molecules grabbing hold of each other, and sung 'Auld Lang Syne', I'd had a flash of insight into polymerisation. Now I had discovered something even better – polymerisation depends on sharing. An atom which is short of an electron looks out for another atom that's got the right sort of electron (it's called covalency, for the chemically inclined), then the atom grabs the electron it needs. But no theft or nastiness is involved. The two atoms end up sharing the electron, and that's what holds all the atoms together in one beautiful long endlessly repeating dance – the beauty of glue!

Canaan House was still on my mind, and I started thinking about the two Naomis, each trying to grab Artem. Had there been sharing and dancing? Or was it a case of theft and nastiness? Would Artem have made a different choice if he'd read Naomi's letters? Would Ella's heart have been broken instead? Burning the letters seemed such a monstrously wicked thing to do; yet I couldn't think of her as a wicked woman. It's as though love gives you a special licence to do anything you like. In the end death, the ultimate fracture line, split Ella and Artem apart. And Canaan House itself had been part of the dance, too, shared by one couple, then another. But whom did it really belong to? There were still some parts of the story that weren't clear. There must be a way of finding out.

After lunch – four radishes and half a bagel with a bit of crusty cheese was all I could muster from the fridge – I nipped up to use the loo, and that's when I realised the other thing that was wrong with 'Gina's Revenge'. Men and women – we're different. Men stand up to pee.

In the afternoon the rain stopped long enough for me to pull on my Bat Woman coat and wing off down to the library on

Fielding Street, just off Holloway Road. The reference library was up on the top floor, a hushed high-ceilinged room susurrating with the nasal snifflings of damp people and the dry rustle of pages being turned. The wet weather had brought in all the homeless folk, whose moist unwashed smell mingled with the musty odour of books and the municipal aroma of wax and disinfectant. Silent hunched figures eyed each other furtively above the pages. Ms Firestorm would have a field day in here.

'I'm trying to find out the history of a house near where I live. It's called Canaan House. In Totley Place.'

The woman at the counter raised her eyes from her computer.

'That's an interesting name. There was quite a fashion in Victorian times, you know, to give places Biblical names. There's no end of Bethels and Zions. And there's a Jordan Close in Richmond. Different Jordan, of course,' she giggled mousily.

'Are there some old maps or anything like that?'

'They've moved the local history archive to the Finsbury Library. We've just got a small local history section over there on the right.'

Of the twenty or so volumes, the only specifically local book was one called *Walter Sickert's Highbury*. I flicked through the chapter headings and illustrations. On page 79 was a lithograph of a large house with a tree in front of it – the more I stared, the more sure I was that it was the same house with the same monkey puzzle tree, but much smaller. The caption read: 'The Monkey Puzzle House, home of Miss Lydia Hughes, whose portrait Sickert painted in 1929 when he was living in nearby Highbury Place.' Perhaps the name of the house had been changed. I looked in the index and browsed through the chapters, but there was no more information.

Then my eye fell on a slim booklet in a yellow card cover: *A History of Christian Witness in Highbury*. It was obviously self-published. I took it through to the reading room and sat down at one of the desks. The booklet was mainly a rather dull list of Anglican and Catholic churches with scratchy line drawings, but the last chapter was devoted to what the author called the 'sects': Methodists, Baptists, Congregationalists, Quakers, Unitarians, Presbyterians, Seventh Day Adventists, Jehovah's Witnesses, Pentecostals, Sandemanians, Christadelphians, Swedenborgians, Latter Day Saints, Plymouth Brethren. So many different faiths all waiting, as Ben was, for the Day of Judgement that would bring about a new Heaven and a new Earth – not just over there in that dry, thorny, tortured land, but here in damp, leafy Highbury. Still waiting. Well, let them wait, I thought.

Towards the end of the chapter was a short entry that read: 'A Teresian community was established in the late 1930s in a house in Totley Place. It was evacuated following an air raid in 1941 and the community dispersed.' I felt a rush of excitement – this could be it! But there was no more. The author was a Miss Sylvia Harvey. The book was published in 1977, thirty years ago. I scribbled the details on a piece of paper. The room was so quiet that you could hear the squeak of my pen as I wrote. There was no other sound apart from the snuffling and rustling and an occasional intermittent gurgle of the water cooler, like a dyspeptic gut. It reminded me that Dad's operation had been due today. I wondered how he'd got on.

Over in the far corner by the magazines and newspapers, a tall heavily built man was wrestling with the *Financial Times*. He was sitting with his back towards me. He had curly grey hair – no, it was blond, streaked with grey. I stared. At first I thought my eyes were deceiving me, but there was no mistaking him. It was Rip. Beside him on the floor were his briefcase and our large blue Thermos flask. I wanted to rush up to him and put my hands over his eyes to surprise him, but something held me back – something about the way he was sitting – that sagging posture, staring straight ahead, his big shoulders hunched. He looked defeated. He wasn't even reading the newspaper, I realised, he was just passing the time. He was passing the time in the library because he didn't want us to know he wasn't at work.

I took the booklet across to the desk.

'How can I trace this author?' I asked in a low voice.

The woman smiled vaguely. 'You could try the telephone directory. Or the internet. Would you like me to have a look?'

'No, it's all right. Thanks for your help.'

I gathered my things together as quietly as I could and tiptoed out through the door.

46

Smoke circles

I'd already started cooking dinner when Rip came in just before six o'clock. It was something elaborate involving tofu and lemon grass. Stella was out and Ben was stretched out on the sofa with a book. Since his seizure, he'd been avoiding the computer, and only watched television occasionally.

'D'you want a hand, Mum?' he'd shouted down to me. His voice sounded deeper, less croaky, than a couple of weeks ago. How quickly he'd changed.

'It's okay,' I'd shouted back.

I liked to see him with his nose stuck in a book, as I'd been at his age, though when he came down to eat later on, I saw that the book was *Revenge of the Busty Biker Chicks*.

'Hi, Ben! Hi, Georgie!' Rip called as he came in, then he went straight up into the mezzanine study. I could hear him pottering around in there, playing music. Half an hour later, I stuck my head round the door.

'Dinner's ready.'

'What's all this, Georgie?'

He was standing in the middle of the room holding a B&Q carrier bag in his hand.

'Where did you find that?' Then I remembered. I'd shoved it in the cupboard when Mark Diabello came round.

'Are you planning a bit of DIY?' He was looking at me intently, curiously. I could feel myself turning red.

'No, not DIY. Collage.'

'Collage?'

I smiled inwardly at the incredulity in his voice.

'You know – sticking things. It's a form of art.'

Our eyes met. He grinned. I grinned. We stood grinning at each other across a bridge of lies. I would never tell him that I'd seen him in the library, that I'd glimpsed his vulnerability. I reached out my arms and took a tentative step forward. There was a faint crackle and a smell of scorching, and Ben called from the kitchen, 'Come on, you two! The rice's burning!'

Dad always used to say, 'I like a bit of burned,' which was just as well, because Mum often obliged. Sometimes she went too far, like the first Sunday lunch Rip had with us at Kippax, when she placed a charred and shrivelled chicken in front of Dad for him to carve.

'Poor little bugger looks like 'e's been cremated,' said Dad.

'Nowt wrong wi' cremation,' said Mum. 'Keeps you regular.'

I hadn't told Mum yet that Rip had moved back in – I didn't want to tempt fate – but I rang her after dinner to find out how Dad's operation had gone. She was in an ebullient mood.

'They did a biopic. Doctor says it in't cancer.'

'Oh, that's good. How's he feeling?'

'Full of chips. Food were lovely in 'ospital. Got into a blazing argument with the bloke in the next bed about Iraq. Keir's coming home, by the way. Did I tell you?'

'No, you didn't. That's good news, too.'

It would be good to see Keir again. Since he'd joined the army, our worlds had drifted apart; nowadays all we had in common was our shared childhood, but Mum resolutely held us together like the family glue.

'She sent us some lovely flowers, by the way, your Mrs Sinclair. And a card. Best wishes for your recovery.'

'I didn't know she knew about Dad.'

'Oh, we keep in touch. She rings up from time to time. Or I ring her.'

'Really?'

This was complete news to me. I tried to imagine what Mum and Mrs Sinclair would talk about. Then I realised they probably talked about us.

I poured another glass of wine and put my feet up on the sofa while Rip and Ben put the rice pan to soak and cleared up in the kitchen. Then the phone rang.

'Georgine, come quick! We heff an invitation!'

Mrs Shapiro's breathy voice shrilled down the telephone, but I was going nowhere.

'What've we been invited to?'

'Wait! Let me see – aha, here it is! We are invited to a funeral!'

My heart lurched. The last thing I needed was bad news.

'Oh, dear. Who is it?'

'Wait! It is here! What is this? I cannot read this name. Looks like Mrs Lily and Brown, ninety-one years old, passes peacefully in the sleep at the Nightmare House.'

So she never did break free, poor thing.

'Who is this Brown Lily?'

'She's the old lady you made friends with in the hospital. And at Northmere House. You know – who was always asking for cigarettes?'

'This one who got the dead woman slippers? She is not my friend – she is a bonker.'

'But it's nice that you've been invited to her funeral. Her family must have remembered you.'

'What is so nice about a funeral?'

'Don't you want to go?'

'Certainly we must go!'

The crematorium was in Golders Green, miles away beyond Hampstead Heath. I mentioned this to Nathan, and suggested he might like to come along with his Tati.

'He'll enjoy it,' I said. 'There's sure to be plenty of singing.'

Somehow, the four of us fitted into Nathan's Morgan, even though it was really a glorified two-seater. Nathan and Mrs Shapiro sat in front. She was wearing a long black coat that smelled pleasantly of mothballs and Chanel No. 5 – better than the stinky astrakhan – and a chic little black beret with a veil and a feather. Nathan's Tati squeezed into the back with me. He was wearing a raincoat and a Bogart-style trilby. I was wearing my smart grey jacket and a black scarf. The car struggled under the weight of us all as we crawled up the Finchley Road. It was a Saturday morning in April, the air warm and sparkling in the slanting sunlight. In the residential streets the front gardens were already frothy with cherry blossom.

Nathan's Tati took Mrs Shapiro's hand to guide her up the step to the crematorium, and she acknowledged the gesture with a gracious nod. There were only two other people in the chapel when we arrived: a grey wispy-looking woman who introduced herself as Mrs Brown's niece, Lucille Watkins, and her father, Mrs Brown's brother. He was tall and lean, with rosy cheeks and a twinkle in his eye – one of those wiry sprightly ninety-somethings who go on for ever.

'Charlie Watkins,' he introduced himself, lingering over Mrs Shapiro's chipped-varnish fingers which she extended graciously to him. 'I think we met at the 'ospital once. Did you know our Lily well?'

Out of the corner of my eye, I saw Nathan's Tati watch him, bristling with annoyance.

'Not well,' Mrs Shapiro replied, fluttering her eyelids. 'Only from smoking. And from slippers. She got the dead-woman slippers.'

'Smokin' like a kipper!' he chuckled, nodding towards the flower-covered coffin in front of us. 'That sounds like our Lily.'

I wasn't particularly surprised when Ms Baddiel turned up, too, just as the service was about to start.

'It's always so-o sad when a client passes away,' she murmured, searching in her oversize bag for a packet of tissues.

There was music playing in the chapel, spooky-sounding organ music that made you feel as though you were already halfway into the next world. The coffin with its large wreath of lilies rested on an ornate catafalque to the left of the altar. A plaque on the wall solemnly reminded us *Mors janua vitae*. Death is the gateway to life. Where had I heard that before? Tall leaded windows filtered and chilled the sunshine leaking in from outside, turning it into a cool greenish fluid. It reminded me of the bivalves, clinging on under the sea.

We spread out around the pews, trying to make ourselves look like more than seven. Mrs Shapiro sat in the front row, and Nathan's Tati took up his position beside her. Nathan and Ms Baddiel sat in front on the other side. The niece and her father spread out in the middle, and I sat at the back. How sad, I was thinking, to have just seven people at your funeral, two of whom had never even met you. A thin man in a black suit droned through a short liturgy and disappeared. We all looked around, wondering whether this was all. Then suddenly there was a rustling behind us; the organ music stopped mid-note and gave way to a jolly lilting big-band number. Ba-doop-a-doop-a! Ba-doop-a-doop-a!

You could hear everybody gasp. Charlie Watkins rose to

his feet and did a little hip-swing in the pew, then he squeezed out past his daughter and bopped up to the lectern. As the music faded away, he cleared his throat and began.

'Ladies and gen'lemen, we're 'ere to celebrate the life of a great lady, and a great dancer, Lily Brown, my sister, who was born Lillian Ellen Watkins in 1916 in Bow. She was the youngest of three sisters and two brothers (he was reading from a sheet of paper he'd fished out of his jacket pocket, modulating his voice like an actor). Now I'm the only one what's left, and all that past life, the 'appiness and sorrow, the triumphs and disappoin'ments, is all washed away on the tides of time.' He fumbled in his pocket for a handkerchief. There was a general shuffling in the pews. This wasn't at all what we'd expected. He blew his nose and continued. 'Even when she was a young gel, our Lily danced like an angel.'

The Watkinses were a Music Hall family. Charlie described how Lily enrolled for dance classes at the City Lit, got pregnant, ran off to Southend, then came back to London a year later, without the baby and without the boyfriend. Her breakthrough came when she got a place in the chorus line at Daly's. He paused, snuffling into his hankie – it wasn't for effect, the emotion was genuine – then he leaned forward, departing from his script.

'I seen 'er up there on the stage, kickin' like she could kick the bollocks off a giraffe.'

In the front pew, I could see Ms Baddiel quiver like a soft jelly, dabbing at her eyes with a tissue while Nathan slipped a solicitous arm around her shoulder. There was something about that gesture that sent a pang of longing through me – not longing for Nathan – that was in the past – but for the warmth of human comfort.

Lily settled in Golders Green, married and lost a soldier.

'That's when she took to smokin',' said Charlie, 'puffin' away like she wanted to be up in 'eaven.'

He blew his nose again and raised his eyes. 'Ladies and gen'lemen, I ask you to pray for the soul of Lillian Brown. May she dance with the angels.'

The band music started up again, Ba-doop-a-doop-a! Ba-doop-a-doop-a! Then with a clatter of rollers, the coffin disappeared through the wooden doors. I thought of the old woman I'd known as the bonker lady, trying to keep her image in my mind's eye as the coffin rattled away, and despite the cheerful music, tears welled up in my eyes. What cruel tricks time plays on us! Before the cigarettes and the crusty toenails, before the deep-grooved wrinkles and the crumpled mind, there'd been another Mrs Brown – a young woman who danced in one of the most beautiful chorus lines in London, who lived life to the full, who could kick the bollocks off a giraffe.

Ba-doop-a-doop-a! Ba-doop-a-doop-a! Ms Baddiel and Nathan and Nathan's Tati were swaying in time to the music and fluttering the tissues which Ms Baddiel had handed out. The niece and Charlie Watkins were sobbing and bopping, and I found my feet, too, were pulled by the irresistible rhythm. Only Mrs Shapiro was standing stock-still – her back was to me, so I couldn't see the look on her face. Suddenly a current of air caught the folding door behind which the coffin had disappeared, making it swing forward, and, I swear I'm not making this up, as it gusted towards us a puff of grey smoke eddied out into the chapel, circling and wreathing around us before it drifted away.

The sunlight stung our eyes as we shuffled outside into the Garden of Rest and walked in a sad tight knot between the flower beds. Mrs Shapiro lit a cigarette and sat on a bench puffing away, as if in honour of her fractious former smoking companion. I wandered along looking at the names on the memorial plaques on the walls – there were so many. Some names I recognised – Enid Blyton, Peter Sellers, Anna Pavlova, Bernard Bresslaw (Mum's favourite actor), H. G. Wells (one of Dad's gurus), Marc Bolan (died so young!) and alongside them all the hundreds of anonymous dead, jostling together for a bit of memory space. Soon enough we'll all be anonymous except to the few people who knew us, I was thinking, until they in their turn become anonymous, too.

That's the thing about funerals – even if you hardly know the person who died, the closeness of death itself makes you melancholy. I recalled the people whose mysterious lives had brushed against mine – beautiful Lily Brown, before she became the bonker lady; Mustafa al-Ali, the chosen one, and his anonymous twin who died on the hillside; Artem Shapiro who had trekked across the Arctic; Naomi Shapiro of the blazing eyes; and the old lady I thought of as Naomi Shapiro, but who was really someone else. Were they exceptional people, or was it the time they lived through that made them seem exceptional? Had our safe post-war world stripped all the glamour and heroism out of life (sob) leaving us with the husks (sob) – consumer goods wrapped up in stylish packaging (sob, sob)? By now the tissue Ms Baddiel had given me was completely soggy. Blinded with tears, I stumbled on a step, stubbed my toe on a stone plinth and almost fell into the pond.

Charlie Watkins was clutching his daughter's arm, his tall thin frame shaking with each breath. I wanted to ask him what had happened to the baby – had she aborted it or given it up for adoption? I wanted to know about Mr Brown – was he the one who brought her here to Golders Green? Had he loved her? Did he stay with her to the end? But Charlie'd crumpled the bit of paper back into his pocket, and his eyes were full of tears. He pointed up at the chimney, where a faint wisp of smoke curled into a perfect circle, wavered in the wind, and was gone.

'There she flies! Our angel!'

Wheeee! A high-pitched whining sound carried on the air, like the distant whirr of angel wings. We all stopped and looked around. It was an eerie sound, as if her spirit was amongst us, trying to speak from another world.

Charlie's daughter leaned over and whispered in his ear, 'Dad, you're whistling!'

'Sorry. Sorry.'

He reached up and adjusted his hearing aid.

That gesture broke the tension. Everybody laughed, brushed their tears away, and started to move purposefully towards the car park. It's all very well thinking about the passing of time and the presence of death, but there's work to be done, dinners to be cooked, life to be lived. I put the soggy tissue away, and that's when my fingers touched something hard and long at the bottom of the jacket pocket. It was a key. I fished it out. Where had that come from? When was the last time I'd worn this jacket? Then I remembered. It was when I first met Mrs Goodney over at Canaan House.

It wasn't until we got to the car park that we realised Mrs Shapiro was missing. With a mutter of irritation, we split up to scour the gardens. Everybody was ready for home by now. A cool wind had sprung up, and all the emotion had made us hungry and tired. It was Nathan's Tati who found her. She'd strayed right out of the crematorium and across Hoop Lane into the Jewish cemetery. He'd come across her wandering among the graves and led her back solicitously, supporting her on his arm.

'She keeps going on about some artist,' he whispered to me. 'Poor old thing.'

47

The penthouse party

It was Mrs Shapiro's idea to hold a house-warming party for the penthouse suite. We drew up the guest list together one morning over a cup of coffee in the kitchen. The sun had come out, and a mild blossom-scented breeze wafted in through the open back door. Mrs Shapiro was in an effervescent mood. Her hair was pinned up and she was wearing a crumpled not-very-white cotton blouse with her smart brown slacks and the *Lion King* slippers. She saw me looking at them, and gave a little shrug.

'They are quite ugly, isn't it? But Wonder Boy adores them.'

'Mm,' I said.

'We can invite the charming old man from the crematorium. He is good at singing. Pity he is so old. And his petit son.'

'Good idea. Who else?'

It seemed incredible that Mr Ali and the Uselesses had managed to install a functioning shower and toilet and three Velux windows in the attic rooms, without further mishap – but it was true. They'd moved their stuff up there, and all the junk – what was left of it – was piled up in a side room whose ceiling was too low to make a useful living space.

'It will be a musical soirée. Or maybe it will be a garden party. What you think?'

'I think we should be flexible. You can never tell what the weather's going to do.'

'You are very wise, Georgine,' she nodded, as though I'd offered some great insight into the human condition.

Upstairs we could hear thudding and hammering as Chaim and the Uselesses put the finishing touches to the floorboards. They'd hired a sander for the day without realising the amount of preparation that was needed. Mr Ali had gone off on some mysterious errand to B&Q. I noted how tidy everything was in the kitchen, a stack of washing-up still covered in soapsuds draining at the side of the sink.

'Maybe when they've finished the penthouse suite we can discuss some kitchen improvements with Chaim and Mr Ali.'

'What for I need improvement?'

'Remember what you said – dishwasher, microwave?'

She looked at me in astonishment. Obviously her previous plans had vanished from her head, and something else was preoccupying her.

'Now, Georgine, this party will be a good opportunity for you to find a new husband.'

'Oh, really?' You had to give her credit for persistence.

'We will invite my Nicky and the other one also, the hendsome one. Maybe more hendsome even than Nicky, isn't it?'

'Yes, very handsome, but . . .'

I hadn't yet told her that I was not looking for a new husband, I just wanted to recondition the one I'd already got.

'You must make more effort, Georgine, if you want to catch a man. You are a nice-looking woman, but you heff let yourself go. You must wear something nice. I heff a nice dress, red spotted mit white collar. Will look nice on you. And lipstick. You must wear a nice lipstick in metching colour. I heff one you can borrow. Will go good mit this dress.'

I smiled non-committally, remembering the grotty decomposing make-up in her bedroom drawer.

After a while the banging from upstairs stopped and Chaim put his head round the door. He was wearing jeans and a T-shirt, and there were bits of sawdust in his hair and eyebrows.

'What shall we do with all the junk, Ella? The belongings from the previous inhabitants?'

'The ones that ran away?' I teased.

'This is no laughable matter. All over Europe Jews are coming and demanding their property back.'

'Like the Palestinians with their keys?' I smiled smugly. He looked cross.

'You – you are not a Jew, Miss Georgiana. You cannot understand what it means.'

'It's a Yorkshire thing – calling a spade a spade.'

'A spade is like a spade?'

'But they were not Jews living here, Chaim,' Mrs Shapiro intervened soothingly. 'Why you are always mekking problems? Leave the junk where it is. Sit down and drink a coffee mit us.'

Chaim pulled out a chair rather nervously. Wonder Boy had sidled in with his ears pricked back and was lurking under the table, his tail quivering.

'Raus, Wonder Boy! Go and make your little wish elsewhere!' Mrs Shapiro shooed him away.

Suddenly a horrible juddering whine shook the whole house. It was the sander springing into life. Wonder Boy set off a competing yowl of protest. Chaim Shapiro jumped to his feet.

'You know, I better give those boys my hand. They are completely useless.' He grinned at me. 'A spade is like a spade.'

When we were alone again, Mrs Shapiro leaned across and whispered to me, 'He is crezzy, isn't it? He was hit in the eye

396

mit a piece of glass, you know. Some boys were throwing stones at the bus. I think also a piece went in his brain.'

After we'd drawn up the party list, we divided the duties. Mrs Shapiro said she would ring Wolfe & Diabello, and reluctantly agreed to invite Ms Baddiel, too. I was delegated to call Nathan and his Tati. I picked up the phone as soon as I got home.

'Your father's made a conquest, Nathan.'

'Wonderful! I knew from the moment you met that you were made for each other. You'll be a fine stepmother, Georgia.'

The thought tickled me. 'Yeah, I'll lock you up and feed you on poisoned apples. Don't you want to know who it really is?'

'I think I can guess. It's your old lady, Mrs Shapiro?'

'Has he said anything?'

'He says it's a pity she's so old.'

'That's what *she* says about *him*. Anyway, you're both invited to a party.'

I told him the day – it was a Saturday, about four o'clock.

'Put it in your diary. It might be a musical soirée or a garden party.'

'So hard to know what to wear,' he murmured cheesily.

'If it's any help, I shall be wearing a red dress with white polka dots and a white collar.'

I would have rung off then, but my conversation with Chaim was still on my mind and I suddenly remembered the glue exhibition.

'Nathan, you know what you said about being called a self-hating Jew?'

'Did I say that?'

'You did. I thought it was because you were gay. Or sm . . .' I stopped myself. '. . . or something.'

'Look, Georgia, some people get excited about what sets them apart. I get excited about what bonds people together. That's all.'

'But . . . isn't it something about not believing in a Jewish homeland?'

'That place you come from – Kippers – is that your homeland?'

There was an edge of irritation in his voice.

'Kippax, not kippers. It should really be called Oven Chippax.' Even as I said it, I felt a pang of shame at my disloyalty. 'It's just that people go on about their homeland as if it was the biggest thing in their lives. It seems strange to me . . .' I could hear Nathan's prickly silence on the other end of the phone. But when he spoke, his voice was sad, not prickly.

'That was Tati's generation. Zion was their big dream. It was a good dream, too. But they found you can't build dreams with guns. Just nightmares. Does that answer your question?'

I paused. It did and it didn't.

'I expected the Jews would be . . . you know, after all that suffering . . . more compassionate.'

'Why would suffering make anyone compassionate? It doesn't work like that, Georgia. Abused children often grow up to become abusers themselves. It's what they learn.'

'Mmm. But . . .'

'And if you've convinced yourself that you're really the victim, or even just potentially the victim – well, it gives you a free rein, doesn't it? You can kill as many people as you like.'

But we didn't bully Carole Benthorpe because we'd been abused, I wanted to say. We did it because we truly believed that something – something higher than us – gave us the right.

'It's like glueing a joint, Georgia. That article you edited. Surface attraction is increased by roughing up the surfaces to be bonded. Like an abusive relationship. It's the mutual damage that holds the two sides together.'

I'd never heard such passion in his voice. Gay. What a shame!

Our conversation stayed in my head after I'd put the phone down. But we didn't have a wall in Kippax, I was thinking. When the strike ended the community was split, and the bitterness of betrayal and defeat was on everyone's mind. People badmouthed their neighbours. Taunts and bricks were thrown, cars were scratched, drunks and kids picked fights. But still life went on. You had to go to the same schools, shop in the same shops, dig in the same allotments, sit eyeball to eyeball in the doctor's surgery – and after a while the habit of living together slowly turned into peace. Eventually a generation comes along that doesn't remember what the conflict was ever about. Maybe forgiveness isn't such a big deal, after all. Maybe it's just a matter of habit.

Later that day, as I settled down with a cup of tea and a Danish pastry, I remembered the other thing I'd meant to ask Nathan: Danish. *She* was Danish. I knew nothing at all about Denmark except the pastries. And Hamlet, of course. Why had she left Denmark? What had happened there during the war? I'd have to ask him next time.

In the end, the party was neither a musical soirée nor a garden party – it was a barbecue. That was Ishmail and Nabeel's idea, and they got so excited about it that no one had the heart to argue with them, though personally I thought the combination of scorched half-raw meat, bugs from Mrs Shapiro's kitchen and barbecue lighter fuel was potentially lethal. Anyway, they built an improvised barbecue in front of the house out of spare bricks and some metal racks they got out of an old oven which Mrs Shapiro had spotted on a skip. They got a job lot of cheap Halal lamb chops and chicken wings from a butcher on Dalston Lane and Mrs Shapiro produced some discoloured burgers of unknown provenance from the depths of her fridge. I made a mental note to avoid those.

I'd suggested that Mr Ali invite his wife, but apparently when she heard that Ishmail and Nabeel were involved she declined.

'Give her headache,' Mr Ali explained.

However, she sent along a huge bowl of hummus laced with olive oil and sprinkled with fresh coriander leaves.

'What is this thing?' Mrs Shapiro poked her finger in and licked it, wrinkling her nose, then I saw a smile of pleasure spread across her face.

Have you ever noticed the similarity between BBQ and B&Q? My theory is that that's why men feel the urge to take over the cooking on these occasions. It's what Rip would call synergy. At one point all four of them – Chaim, Mr Ali, Ishmail and Nabeel – were crowded round the smoking barbecue, puffing and flapping to try and get it lit. Ishmail and Nabeel took turns splashing squirts of lighter fuel on to the smouldering charcoal, then jumping back howling with laughter as the flames flared up. In fact they managed to splash a fair bit of lighter fuel on themselves, too. Probably Mrs Ali was wise to stay away. I watched them from the window of Mrs Shapiro's bedroom, where I was trying on the red-and-white spotted dress, while Mrs Shapiro fussed around for the right shade of lipstick.

We were blessed with the weather. The sun had come out after lunch, and stayed out all afternoon. The thrush was up in his tree, his chest puffed out, singing his war song, and all seven of Mrs Shapiro's cats, plus a few feline guests from the neighbourhood, were circling, attracted by the smell of the cooking meat. Mrs Shapiro and I chopped up salads and split pitta breads and set out plates and glasses on the white uPVC table. A spare table from the study and some dining chairs had been carried out on to the grass, too.

Nathan and his Tati were the first to arrive. Nathan had brought two bottles of Blind River Pinot Noir, and his Tati had brought a bunch of blue irises for Mrs Shapiro.

'Thenk you so much!' Her bright blue eyelids fluttered ecstatically. That was a good start. 'Will you heff a drink?'

She was wearing the same brown slacks and striped jersey in which she'd first entertained Mr Wolfe, with her high-heeled slingbacks that kept sticking into the grass as she tottered about. Her hair was freshly dyed and elaborately pinned up with three tortoiseshell combs. In fact she looked quite elegant. I was wearing the little red-and-white number. Nathan looked me up and down.

'Nice dress.'

'Thanks. I like your trousers. We match.'

He was wearing red trousers with what looked like a white waiter's jacket.

Ms Baddiel, when she arrived, was wearing a flowing muslin garment which might have been a coat or a dress or a skirt and top – it was impossible to say how it all fitted together – tie-dyed in swirling shades of amber, bronze and gold. It fluttered lightly in the breeze, making her look delicate and ethereal, despite her size. I saw Mark Diabello eyeing her with interest as he came up the path, and felt a small stab of annoyance. Okay, so I'd given him the push, but he was supposed to be eyeing *me*, not her. He was wearing the same dark suit as always, the white handkerchief winking invitingly in his jacket pocket. The Shameless Woman poked her head up briefly, and thought an utterly shameless thought: I bet they don't do the red open-gusset panties in *her* size.

'Nice dress, Georgina. Suits you.' He pecked me on the cheek and handed me a packet of Marks & Spencer's sausages and a bottle of champagne.

'Oh, lovely. Mrs Shapiro'll like those.'

'Is your hubby coming?'

'Yes, later,' I lied. Actually I hadn't invited him. It wasn't because of Mark. It was because he'd have come out of a sense of duty and then complained that he was missing the football. Besides – I don't know – I just wanted to keep Canaan House and its eccentric inhabitants to myself.

'Nick's coming later, too. He had some . . . er . . . work to catch up on.'

'Mark, there's something I think you should know. Something you and Nick should know. Only . . . I don't know whether I should tell you.'

He raised a quizzical eyebrow.

'You're being very mysterious, Georgina.'

If I hadn't already had a couple of glasses of wine I might have kept quiet, but I blurted out, 'The deeds to the house . . . there aren't any. Her husband just moved in. It was abandoned. After a bombing raid. Actually, I don't think he was even her husband.'

A strange look came over him. His eyes flickered through many changes of colour, and the smile-creases in his cheeks twitched furiously. He looked as though he was about to explode. Then I realised he was trying to stop himself from laughing.

'No title! Wait till I tell Nick!'

'But can't she . . . I don't know . . . what about squatter's rights?'

He burst into a chuckle. 'No title! Ha ha! No, maybe on second thoughts I won't tell him! Where's the old lady?'

Mrs Shapiro and Tati had disappeared into the house. They'd opened the window in the study and moved the old gramophone up to it, so we could hear the music in the garden. Now they were poring through Mrs Shapiro's collection, trying to decide what to play. You could see them through the window, talking and laughing together. They chose an orchestral piece that sounded vaguely familiar. It might have been one of Rip's old vinyls. What will she say, I wondered with a pang of conscience, when I ask to have them back?

'Penny sends her apologies.' Nathan sidled up to me. 'Her cousin Darryl's getting married.'

'That's nice.' I felt a small prick of regret.

'Who's the guy in the brown suit?'

Over by the barbecue, Mr Ali and Chaim Shapiro were cooking and arguing. Seeing them together like that, I was struck by how alike they were. Chaim was stabbing at the chicken wings to see whether they were done. Mr Ali shoved a mouthful of lamb chop into his mouth and beamed as he caught my eye, patting his tummy.

'XXL.'

'Trouble with you Arabs,' Chaim was saying, 'is you always pick bad leaders.'

'You Jews put all the good ones in prison.'

Mr Ali speared another lamb chop on a skewer and brandished it in the air. The chicken wings were beginning to smoke. Chaim flipped them over.

'We put only terrorists in prison.'

'You not heard of Nelson Mandela? You want peace you free Marwan Barghouti,' said Mr Ali, emphasising his point with the skewered lamb chop.

'This Barghouti – is he Hamas or Fatah?' Chaim picked up a smoking chicken wing with his fingers – ouch! hot! – and bit into it with a crunch, sucking cool air into his mouth.

'Hamas, Fatah – all listen to Barghouti!' The lamb chop flew off Mr Ali's skewer and whizzed over our heads. It landed on the ground and he speared it up, covered with bits of grass, and started flashing it about again. 'He only can bring peace.'

'Mr Ali, Chaim, this is my colleague Nathan Stein,' I butted in. They stopped in mid-sentence, and turned towards us.

'Come! Eat something!' Chaim waved a chicken wing at him.

'We are discussing politics,' said Mr Ali. When he looked round at us, I could see he had a grin on his face and bits of barbecue sauce in his beard. They both looked as though they were enjoying themselves. On the barbecue, things were sizzling away.

'Discussion is the better part of valour!' added Chaim.

In the middle of the grass, Mussorgsky and the Stinker were fighting over a chicken bone. The neighbourhood guest cats, the ones with proper homes to go to, were looking on askance at this display of bad behaviour.

'Very tasty.' Nathan took a bite of the chicken wing.

'Better than a poke in the eye with a sharp piece of glass, eh?' said Chaim, and bellowed with laughter at his own joke.

Denmark, I reminded myself. Mustn't forget to ask him about Denmark.

Ishmail had rigged up an ingenious rotating spit, but the chops and wings were too bony to spear, and the sausages just split. Brainy but useless. It's often the way. Now he and Nabeel were racing about with plates of charred meat as it came off the barbecue, flashing their smiles as they offered it around. They were in a skittish mood, and kept on barging into each other and dropping bits on the floor. Wonder Boy was in the bushes attempting to rape one of the visiting guest cats (little did he know that it was to be his last fling!), Mrs Shapiro was sitting on one of the white chairs with her feet up on another, smoking a cigarette and discreetly feeding the uncooked M&S sausages to the cats, who were snatching and snarling. Tati was sitting at the table beside her, slugging back red wine and eating a burger – it must be one of the ones from the back of her fridge – I hoped he had a strong constitution. Mark Diabello was topping up the glasses. Ms Baddiel was keeping everyone supplied with tissues.

'I work mainly with old people,' I overheard her explaining peachily to Mark Diabello. 'Sorting out their housing needs to enable them to live independently.'

'Fascinating,' he murmured. 'I'm in housing myself.'

The music poured out into the garden, wheeling and soaring above it all.

Everything that happened next happened very quickly, so I may have got the order of events slightly wrong, but it was something like this. The thrush started it. From his perch in the ash tree he'd spotted a piece of pitta bread that had fallen on to the ground. Wonder Boy, having satisfied his lust, was lurking in the bushes watching the bird. As the thrush swooped down Wonder Boy flattened his nose to the ground and wriggled into pouncing position, his tail twitching. The bird went for the bread. The cat went for the bird. I grabbed the first thing that came to hand – it was a lamb chop – and lobbed it at Wonder Boy. It arced through the air spinning like a boomerang. Normally I'm hopeless at throwing, but this time I scored a direct hit. Wonder Boy let out a yowl and leapt sideways right under the feet of Nabeel who was carrying a plate of chicken wings up the garden. Nabeel barged into Ishmail, who lurched and stumbled against the barbecue, which collapsed scattering hot coals everywhere, setting fire to the barbecue lighter fuel that hadn't been screwed up properly and had spilled on the ground right under the open study window, where a curtain was flapping in the breeze. The cats fell on the scattered chicken wings in a frenzy. Wonder Boy grabbed the biggest one and raced off down the path. The wind gusted; the curtain caught and blazed. Mark Diabello sprayed champagne over the flames, but it was too little too late. Outside on the lane there was a screech of brakes and a thud. The flames leapt through the window. Nick Wolfe appeared at the gate, holding up Wonder Boy's limp lifeless body gingerly by one leg. Mrs Shapiro jumped up, screamed and fainted. Tati tried to give Mrs Shapiro mouth-to-mouth resuscitation. The fire spread from the curtains to some loose papers on the bookshelf under the window. The music slurred and stopped. Mr Ali phoned the fire brigade on his mobile phone but failed to make himself understood. The fire roared through the study and into the hall. Nathan phoned the fire brigade on his mobile phone, and did manage to get through. I just stood there watching, clenching my hands into fists, wishing I could recall the flying lamb chop, and feeling terribly terribly terribly guilty.

Hours later, after the fire brigade had been and gone, and Mrs Shapiro had been carted off into temporary accommodation accompanied by Ms Baddiel, and Ishmail and Nabeel had gone home to Mrs Ali, and Chaim had gone home with Nathan and his Tati, and Wolfe and Diabello had finished off the booze and slunk off back to their lair, I walked home through the balmy dusk. *In – two – three – four. Out – two – three – four.* I breathed deeply, noticing that the air, despite its taint of London traffic, carried the sweetness of rising sap and fresh growth. I noticed peonies in the front gardens, and the greenness of leaves newly uncurled. I noticed that my hands were clenched into fists, and that my palms carried deep imprints of my fingernails. I uncurled them and let them relax. They hung like new leaves. When I got to my front door I noticed that Violetta was there beside me.

Ben and Rip were home already. They'd been out to the football, and now they were drinking a beer and watching the television – a round-up of the week's news.

'Good party?' asked Rip, without looking up.

'Great.' I came and slumped on the sofa. Violetta jumped up on to my lap, purring.

'Look at this,' said Rip, pointing at the screen. 'Who would have believed it?' Two men were being interviewed, grinning in front of a bank of cameras and microphones. One of them looked a bit like the Reverend Ian Paisley. I had no idea who the other one was. 'Those two old bastards!'

'Who are they?'

'Ian Paisley and Martin McGuinness,' said Ben, who'd been watching the item from the beginning. 'They've done a deal.'

'Really? You mean, in Northern Ireland?'

I tried to think back to a time when that conflict hadn't been in the news. How had this peace thing happened? How come I hadn't noticed? I remembered something about a woman whose hair fell out. She'd died while Rip and I were still living in Leeds, hadn't she?

'Who'd have thought it was possible? Peace has broken out!' Rip turned to face me. He was smiling, then the smile broadened into a lop-sided grin. 'What the fuck are you wearing, Georgie?'

'Oh, I thought I'd dress up for the party.'

My jeans and jumper and Bat Woman coat had been swallowed up by the blaze – or even if they were still there, the firemen had barred access to them.

'You . . . You've changed, Georgie. You're different.'

He was still staring at me, as though he hadn't seen me before.

'Less . . .?'

'More . . .'

'I've been experimenting . . .' I hesitated. How could I explain that in the last six months I'd been Georgine, Georgina, Georgette, Mrs George and Miss Georgiana? Not to mention Ms Firestorm and the Shameless Woman. '. . . with different ways of being myself.'

'It suits you, Mum,' said Ben. 'Sort of retro.'

Later that night, after the football highlights on TV had ended, and the thud-thud of Ben's music was quiet, and Violetta had wolfed down a tin of tuna and curled up on the sofa, I lay in bed, reflecting on what had happened at Canaan House that day, and tuning in to the silence around me. And that's when I heard a faint crackling sound – so faint that if I consciously tried to listen, it disappeared – it was the crackle of brainwaves coming from the mezzanine study. I put on my slippers and dressing gown and went to investigate. There was a sliver of light under the door. I tapped softly.

'Come in.'

Rip was sitting at the computer in his boxer shorts, a cold cup of coffee at his elbow, staring at the screen.

'You're working late.'

'Got a report to finish,' he said, without looking round.

'Progress Project?'

'No. I'm done with the Progress Project.'

I glanced over his shoulder and I could see quite clearly on

408

the monitor that he was working not on a report but on his CV. He didn't even try to close or minimise the window.

'Is it . . . are you okay, Rip?'

'What do you think?'

I slipped an arm around his shoulder – it was a habit of physical affection that bypassed the picky brain and the un-reliable emotions. How warm his skin was, how big his shoulders; yet there was something about the way he was leaning forward in his chair, sagging almost, that struck a sudden chime of pity in me. I stroked his hair.

'You're tired. You should go to bed.'

'I need to get this done. It has to be in tomorrow.'

'What's it for?'

'Something called the Synergy Foundation.'

I can't explain why, but my heart sank. Synergy Founda-tion. What the hell was that? It sounded like something you put on your face. *In – two – three – four . . .*

'That sounds interesting. Shall I make you another coffee?'

'That'd be nice.'

I went down to the kitchen and made two cups of coffee. Then I remembered the Space Invaders Easter egg lurking at the back of the cupboard.

'D'you fancy a bit of chocolate?'

I smashed up the egg inside its foil wrapper, and we polished off the sickly chocolate between us. An hour later, when he crawled into the low canvas camp bed, I crept in beside him.

48

A lot of bargains

Canaan House is now a building site. The destruction from the fire wasn't extensive, but after the fire brigade had gone the surveyors checking the damage found an unexploded bomb left over from the war, buried deep in the roots of the monkey puzzle tree. The whole street had to be evacuated while the bomb squad carried out a controlled explosion. We all stood behind red-and-white barrier tape and watched. It was a bright windy day and dust blew everywhere – that's all that was left in the end, dust. Mrs Shapiro was weeping quietly, and when I put my arm around her to comfort her I suddenly started sobbing, too. In fact I think I cried more than she did.

'You know, dear Georgine, you were right,' she said, patting her eyes with the disgusting hankie from the pocket of the astrakhan coat. 'This house was too big for me. Too many problems. Too many memories. Like caught in a trap. Now is the time for moving on.'

Fortunately, Mark Diabello had managed to get the title registered in Mrs Shapiro's name, using the evidence of her sixty years as a ratepayer to justify her claim, so she was able to sell the site to a developer for a substantial sum. Only Mark knows how substantial, and he is sworn to secrecy.

She has bought herself a lovely apartment in a sheltered housing development in Golders Green – sadly no pets allowed – and she has set up Chaim and Mussorgsky in a flat in Islington. Violetta has stayed with me. We keep each other company, and in a quiet moment when everybody is out we sit on the sofa together and share our smelly memories. I sometimes ask myself whether she misses Wonder Boy, but somehow I don't think she does. The remainder of the money from Canaan House went, with the remaining feline residents, to the Cats Protection League. Mrs Shapiro won't tell anyone how much, but I'm sure it was more than enough to keep any number of lean and hungry moggies in pet food for the rest of their stinky little lives.

I never got a chance at the party to ask Chaim about Denmark, but we meet up one Saturday in September at a café on Islington Green, near where he has his flat. It's raining again – it seems to have been raining most of the year – but he's found a cosy corner near the window and is flicking through a travel brochure. I almost don't recognise him at first, he looks so completely different to the man in the brown suit. He's wearing black jeans and a blue open-necked shirt, and stylish rimless glasses. Unless you knew, you wouldn't even notice that he has a glass eye. I shake out my umbrella and we hug, my wet cheek against his bristly one, and order our coffees. He tells me about his new job at a travel agent's specialising in Holy Land tours, but I'm not in the mood for small talk. I want to put the last piece of my Canaan House puzzle into place.

I pull the photo out of my bag – the one of the young woman standing in the stone archway – and push it across the table to him.

'This is for you, Chaim. Tell me about her.'

He picks up the photo and studies it, and that sweet dimply baby smile creeps over his face.

'Yes, this is her. Smiling like a Monalissa.'

'You said she came from Denmark.'

'Do you know the story of the Danish Jews? It was like no other Jews in Europe.'

'Tell me.'

He has taken off his glasses and is sitting back in his chair. The photo is still in his hand, but it's as though he's gazing right through it into another time and place.

'Naomi Lowentahl was her name. She was born in 1911 in Copenhagen. Wonderful wonderful Copenhagen! You been there?'

'No.' I shake my head.

'Nor me. Maybe I will make a trip next year. They lived in the Jewish quarter. My grandparents are buried there, in the Jewish cemetery. She was the youngest of three children. Their mother died when she was ten. Like me.' A cloud drifts over his face. 'But she still had her father and two older brothers. She was spoiled like a rotter, I think, having all those men running around after her.'

Naomi's father, Chaim's grandfather, was a mathematician at the university, and Naomi herself taught maths in a high school. Her brothers were active in the Zionist movement in the 1930s, which had taken root in the Jewish communities of Europe, seeded by anti-Semitism and persecution.

'And Naomi?'

'Naomi was sometimes with her brothers, sometimes with her father. My grandfather was one of those who believed that Jews could be assimilated as equal citizens into the countries where they lived. He believed the storm clouds gathering over Europe would simply be blown away by winds of progress and enlightenment.' He pauses, fiddling with his glasses. 'But alas, eventualities were to prove him tragically wrong.'

When the Germans invaded Denmark in 1940, those

arguments took on a new urgency. The Danish Government had come to an agreement with the occupiers – Danish butter and bacon in exchange for self-government. Nor would they hand over their Jews. 'Jews and Christians, we are all Danes,' they said.

Despite the agreement, there was little active support for the Nazis, and by 1943 the agreement with Germany started to break down. The Nazis began to make secret preparations to round up and exterminate all 7,000 of the Jews in Denmark. Chaim smiled. 'They thought their "final solution" would be not so final when these insolent Danish Jews are strutting around Scots free.'

In fact it was a German attaché who foiled the Nazi deportation plan by leaking the details to a Danish politician. What was to have been a swift and secret operation was thwarted when the Danish people simply said no. Not here in Denmark. Not to *our* Jews.

Spontaneously, haphazardly, as word got around, friends, neighbours and colleagues offered help, money, transport, and places to hide. They would have no truck with the horrors that defiled the rest of Europe. It was Naomi's head of department, a Lutheran, who called at her apartment late on the night of 29th September and warned her that there were two passenger boats moored at the docks with orders to take 5,000 Danish Jews away – they were due to sail on 1st October. He advised her to go to the Bispebjerg Hospital, where a shelter had been set up.

She and her elderly father stuffed what they could into a suitcase and made their way to the hospital. They found a quiet corner in the psychiatric unit and watched with apprehension as more and more of the city's Jewish population arrived, alone or in groups, bewildered, anxious, carrying their most precious possessions in cardboard suitcases. In the end some 2,000 people were crammed into the psychiatric wards, the nurses' accommodation, and anywhere else they could be fitted in. Secrecy was impossible, and there was no need for it – everyone in the hospital from the director to the porters was involved. The staff looked after them and fed them from the hospital kitchens, and as word spread, gifts of food and money poured in from local people. Day and night, ambulances drove them to secret hiding places on the coast.

Other Jews, including her brothers, were hidden in churches, schools, libraries, and many in private houses by their neighbours. In holiday villages all along the northern coast, support groups sprang up to shelter the fleeing Jews while they waited for a boat and the right weather conditions to cross to neutral Sweden. Even the coastguards were in on it.

Squashed up in the stinking hull of a fishing boat with twelve others, Naomi and her father made the short crossing to Sweden on 3rd October 1943. They were stopped by a German patrol, but the fisherman sucked obtusely on his pipe and offered them a pair of herrings, while under the hatch beneath his feet the passengers held their breath. The fisherman thought it was a great adventure and posed with his beaming human cargo in the Swedish port before setting off home to pick up another load.

'I have the picture,' says Chaim. 'I will show you.'

Sweden was teeming with refugees, and seething with talk of resistance, of freedom, of an international union of Jews, of safety, of Zion. In the refugee centre in Gothenburg she was reunited with her brothers. Although they were Zionists, they had struck up a friendship with a young socialist Bundist from Byelorussia. His name was Artem Shapiro.

'Did they fall in love on sight?'

Chaim grins. He has a little frothy moustache on his upper lip from the cappuccino.

'I haven't a foggy. Remember, I was not born yet.'

Of more than 7,000 Jews in Denmark, the Nazis got fewer than 500, and even most of those survived in Theresienstadt, for the Danish authorities sent medicines and food over for them. Those Jews who returned to Denmark at the end of the war found their homes intact and looked after, their gardens watered, even their dogs and cats sleek and well fed.

I don't know why it's the thought of those plump Copenhagen moggies that finally makes me choke up and reach for a tissue as Chaim gets to the end of his story. I've seen the pictures of the stick-like walking dead of Belsen, the heaps of corpses, the terrible piles of children's shoes. I know all that happened, but I want to believe that something else is possible.

'Thank you, Chaim. You told me what I wanted to know.'

It's still drizzling as I make my way across Islington Green towards Sainsbury's. I've arranged for Rip to pick me up in the car park at one o'clock, so I have a couple of hours to do my shopping. He's gone off to a meeting with the team at the Finsbury Park Law Centre, where he's starting his new job next week. The Synergy Foundation turned him down.

It seems that if you hang around for long enough in Sainsbury's on a Saturday morning, the whole world passes by – or maybe my imagination has filled in the gaps. I see the same *Big Issue* seller, lurking under the canopy by the entrance, and there goes the Robin Reliant man crossing the road with his stick. The Boycott Israeli Goods girl is there, brandishing her clipboard, though her hair has grown a bit and she's now collecting signatures on a petition to save the whales. Ben is there with her – he often comes down here on a Saturday morning – and his hair is longer, too, twisted into incipient dreadlocks and tied behind his neck with the red pirate-style scarf.

'Hey, Mum!'

I stop to sign their petition, though I've already signed it several times. The girl looks a bit sheepish, maybe thinking I despise her defection, but I just smile, because I understand now that everything – whales and dolphins, Palestinians and Jews, stray cats, rainforests, mansions and mining villages – they're all interconnected, held together by some mysterious force – call it glue, if you like.

While I'm picking up some beer for Rip, I spot Mark Diabello and Cindy Baddiel lingering hand in hand in the wine department. He's wearing a check shirt and beige trousers, and I notice that a small bulge is developing above the waistband, and his hair has grey streaks at the temples, but as he turns towards me I feel that pleasant pelvic glow – yes, he's still the hero of *The Splattered Heart*.

'Hello, Georgina!' He greets me with a kiss on each cheek, and Ms Baddiel hugs me in her roly-poly arms. She looks exactly the same. I check discreetly for signs of Velcro burns on her wrists – shame on you, Georgie! – but they are plump and wholesome.

'Thanks for everything you did with getting the house registered,' I say to Mark. 'How's it going?'

A couple of months ago, Wolfe & Diabello mysteriously disappeared from the high street to be replaced by Wolfe & Lee. Mark tells me he is now running a housing association for ex-offenders.

'It's – how can I put it? – more satisfying.'

The mineral edge in his voice makes me shiver.

'I'm glad it all worked out.'

'Take care,' they say.

Here's someone I don't want to see. It's Mrs Goodney pushing her trolley towards me. I'd duck out of her way and avoid her if I could, but the aisle is narrow, and there's nowhere else to go, so I just stand still and smile.

'Hello,' she says. 'I didn't expect to see you here.'

'No. Nor me.' I'm still trying to decide whether to be friendly. 'How are things up at the hospital?'

'Oh, I gave all that up. Too much hassle. No one thanks you for anything.' She sighs. 'It was for her own good, you know. Do-gooders like you, you have this romantic idea that old people want to stay in their crumbly grotty houses until they die. But they don't. They want somewhere small that's easy to keep warm and clean, with all mod cons. Making the move is always a wrench. They may need a bit of help. But once they've done it, they never want to go back. Anyway, I'm running a little nail bar now, up Stoke Newington Church Street.' She glances down at my hands. 'Drop in one day.'

At the deli counter I bump into Nathan and Raoul, gravely discussing the comparative merits of olive and avocado oils. Nathan has his arm round Raoul's shoulder in that casual gesture with which he once comforted me, though Raoul is several inches taller than he is, and only half as handsome. They greet me with warm hugs, and bring me news of Mr Ali, who has just installed a new jacuzzi at their flat in Hoxton. Ishmail is still living with the al-Alis out Tottenham way, and is due to start his engineering course later in the month, but Nabeel has gone back to Palestine. His older brother was killed during an Israeli air strike on Gaza only a week after our barbecue – a bystander casualty – and now Nabeel is the head of the family. Gentle animal-loving coffee-making Arsenal-supporting Attendent Nabeel – my heart aches – it's hard to imagine him as head of anything.

'Come and have dinner with us one day,' says Nathan.

'I'd love to. Will you make French-style egg custard with vanilla?'

'We need to get some vanilla,' says Raoul seriously. 'We used it all up on that bavarois, remember?'

'Look out for Tati and Ella,' says Nathan. 'They're around here somewhere.'

Sure enough, there they are, pushing the high-sprung pram down one of the aisles, leaning together like a pair of newly-weds. I watch her lift her face up as he bends to give her a whiskery kiss and whisper something in her ear. She laughs, and rests her head against him. The way they're gazing into the pram, you'd think there was a baby in there, but when I peep inside, all I see is a lot of bargains.

Acknowledgements

Many people have contributed to the making of this book. Thanks to Ewen Kellar for first getting me interested in adhesives, to Cathy Dean for DIY discussions, to Mikey Rosato for giving me the low-down on estate agents, and thanks to all those who have shared tales of bad lovers, bad pets, bad plumbing and other bad things – you know who you are, and I won't embarrass you by naming and shaming. Thanks to those who have helped me to appreciate the many-layered complexity of the Middle East – Raja Shehadeh, Donald Sassoon, Saleh Abdel Jawad, Naomi Ogus, Eitan Bronstein, Graham Birkin – I have learned such a lot from talking with you. Thanks to Merilyn Feickert for Biblical references, and to Val Binney and Steve Blomfield for helping me to understand epilepsy.

Writing can be a lonely business, and I'm very grateful to the many people who gave me hospitality and nurture while I was writing, especially the Widgers, the Pierces, Anne MacLeod and family, Mina Hosseinipour, Janine Edge, Theo and Viv at Bushy Park and the Sisters of Compassion at Whanganui River Road. Thanks to the Tyldesleys for looking after me and to Dave and Sonia for putting up with me.

Finally, a big thank you to my agent Bill Hamilton and my editor and publisher Juliet (Ms Whiplash) Annan, for being so horribly tough and for not letting me get away with anything. And thanks to the wonderful team at Penguin for everything else.